"Like a good recipe, the ne... ...s a little bit of everything that makes a sati... ...aylor pairs the past with the present to please history ... ...s those who like tales of family secrets, reinvention, and renew.... . . . Taylor, who lives in Virginia, conveys the essence of the community, of regular shop patrons, and history, literally around every corner in centuries-old buildings . . . Taylor serves up a great mix of vivid setting, history, drama, and everyday life in *The Union Street Bakery*. Here's hoping she writes more like it." —*The Herald-Sun*

"Interesting and intriguing . . . [A] fast-paced story of sisters, family, what really matters, betrayal, faith, healing, and life in general. If you enjoy historical facts, heritage, adoption, family, and love, you will enjoy *Union Street Bakery*. Modern-day story mixed with historical facts, a ghost, mystery, and romance brings this story and characters to life. Oh, at the back of the book are some Union Street Bakery recipes. Wonderful story!"
—*My Book Addiction Reviews*

"An excellent job of showing how important a family can be and who your real family is. Ms. Taylor . . . makes you care not only about Daisy but about all the family and friends involved . . . I enjoyed reading this book and walking along with Daisy as she grows . . . Get a copy and settle in a comfortable chair with a cup of tea or coffee . . . You might also want a pastry."
—*Long and Short Reviews*

"Readers will love Daisy and the McCrae family and be engrossed in both the historical and the present puzzles Daisy and her family must solve. Taylor never takes the simple plot path or gives in to melodrama. The story feels real. Ultimately, the book is about what we think we need versus what really matters and what it really means to be a family. It is highly recommended for anyone who loves family stories with intelligence and heart." —*Blogcritics*

"I found myself so caught up in this family's lives and turning the pages late into the night. You will not be able to put this book down until you turn the very last page. As a bonus, Mary Ellen has included some of the recipes from the bakery. I can't wait to read more by Ms. Taylor." —*Fresh Fiction*

Berkley Books by Mary Ellen Taylor

THE UNION STREET BAKERY

SWEET EXPECTATIONS

SWEET EXPECTATIONS

Mary Ellen Taylor

BERKLEY BOOKS, NEW YORK

THE BERKLEY PUBLISHING GROUP
Published by the Penguin Group
Penguin Group (USA) LLC
375 Hudson Street, New York, New York 10014

USA • Canada • UK • Ireland • Australia • New Zealand • India • South Africa • China

penguin.com

A Penguin Random House Company

SWEET EXPECTATIONS

This book is an original publication of The Berkley Publishing Group.

Berkley trade paperback ISBN: 978-0-425-25970-2

An application to register this book for cataloging has been submitted to the Library of Congress.

PUBLISHING HISTORY
Berkley trade paperback edition / November 2013

PRINTED IN THE UNITED STATES OF AMERICA

10 9 8 7 6 5 4 3 2 1

Cover art by Alan Ayers.
Cover design by Diana Kolsky.

To my favorite bakers Michael and Nancy,
Coordinators2inc's Birth Parent and Adoptee Support Group,
and, as always, for Julia

Chapter One

Saturday, 4:00 A.M.
14 days, 4 hours until grand reopening
Income Lost: $0

S ome disasters meander or stroll into our lives at an easy pace. A leaky dam, a slow-moving storm, or a crack in a foundation all creep up nice and easy. If we're paying attention, we see the trouble coming and can dodge, bob and weave, or duck to avoid calamity.

I've never known that kind of catastrophe. No sir, my kind of trouble never ambles or strolls. Nor does it saunter, promenade, simmer, or fester. My trouble steams into my life like a runaway freight train, a Cat 5 summer twister, or a sweeping avalanche. It strikes like a snake, hits hard, and takes no prisoners.

Boom. Fast. Just like that. Disaster hits.

Consequently, I'm now good at rolling with the punches, picking myself up, and moving forward. I don't dwell on the past too much anymore. Eyes forward is my new motto.

But as I clutched the little white pregnancy stick and stared at the test strip, willing a minus sign, I wasn't sure how I'd handle this jam. A baby wasn't like an expensive pair of shoes that needed returning, a bounced check, or a really bad hair perm. A baby was forever.

And ever.

Threading fingers through my dark hair, I fought back the nausea and allowed a groan to rumble in my chest as I thought about my boyfriend, Gordon. We'd broken up last year. It had been a bitter, sad breakup, leaving me far more wounded than I could have imagined. I'd tried to move on with life, but regrets over Gordon always lingered. In the last month, we'd both landed back in Alexandria, trying to rebuild broken careers, and somehow we'd found our way back to each other. There were days when our rekindled love touched on miraculous.

However, in a bid to be mature and thoughtful about our newfound love, we'd not reestablished relations, if you know what I mean. No nookie. No sex. We were going slow. Didn't want to upset the apple cart. Friends-before-lovers kind of situation, because the first time we'd been together, the sexual attraction had been hot and furious. Couldn't-keep-our-hands-off-each-other kind of sex. We were intimate by the second date and had moved in together after a month. Gordon had asked me to marry him by week six, and by week nine, I'd freaked out over the looming commitment and pushed the self-destruct button on us.

So this time the theme was slow and easy.

Don't get me wrong, since our reunion, sex had been on both our minds, big, *big* time. Old sparks still flickered bright and hot.

However, Gordon was the one staying strong, suggesting we nurture a friendship before we jumped into bed. I didn't like it, but I understood. Gordon wanted me to be sure about him enough as a friend as well as a lover.

A simple concept except for the fact I'd just peed on a pregnancy stick.

Gordon and I had officially broken up last year and officially gotten back together four weeks ago. A muddled middle filled the months we'd been apart, and halfway through our separation—exactly four months ago—I'd made a less-than-wise choice I thought was forgotten forever.

I stared at the still white window of the stick. If it went nuclear pink, it meant I was four months pregnant. I didn't need a calendar or any fancy guesswork to know the day. March 21. It was my last night in my Washington, D.C., apartment. The financial management company I'd worked for had gone under overnight, a casualty of the mortgage market. The job prospects were slim, so I'd yielded to pressure from my mother and agreed to come home for a few months and manage the family bakery. My newly widowed sister struggled with the job and in Mom's mind it could be a win-win for everyone. I was not thrilled about the move. I loved my family, but the bakery held bitter memories of a birth mother who had abandoned me at the shop when I was three years old.

Needless to say my last night in Washington wasn't happy. Self-pity brimmed as I pined for the past and dreaded the future.

So, to cheer myself up, I'd invited friends over for a final good-bye. The six of us had gathered to mourn the demise of our beloved company and to toast my bright, albeit underemployed future. Bonded by grief and loss, we clung to ties doomed to fray even as we swore we'd lunch, text, and talk all the time. We were more than friends, we'd said after I'd opened the sixth bottle of wine. We were *family*.

Yada, yada, yada.

One key friend, now to my great regret, lingered longer than the rest. Roger Traymore. We'd both been tipsy as we'd argued the roots of our company's demise. We'd both fought hard to save the company. Worked crushing hours. Endured difficult meetings with clients and watched others buy us out and cut us loose.

In those hazy, drunken moments, we both understood each other. We were kindred spirits. And our momentary bond had translated into sex. Not super-great sex, but in the big picture the sex didn't matter. What mattered was the condom had broken. I'd been too drunk to worry, but when the sun rose, we'd sobered enough to realize the gravity of it all. Instead of acknowledging what had happened, I'd been as anxious for him to leave as he was to go. And on the heels of more empty promises of friendship, we'd scattered like two rats from a sinking ship.

He took a job teaching in China, and I moved home across the Potomac River to Alexandria, Virginia, to my parents' bakery, which also teetered on financial oblivion.

Out of the frying pan and into the fire.

Long story short, if the white stick turned pink, I was not only starting my fourth month as the Union Street Bakery manager, but I was entering my second trimester.

Pregnancy. Knocked up. Bun in the oven.

Damn it.

Clutching the stick, I walked across my attic apartment located atop the bakery and set it on my nightstand. Sitting on my squeaky bed, I buried my face in my hands. *Don't borrow trouble. Don't borrow trouble.*

Glancing up, I surveyed my tiny attic apartment. My parents had converted the third-floor space into a room when I was a kid. They'd cleared out the junk, finished the walls and added a bathroom. Not hugely spacious but okay for me now. Since my return I'd whitewashed the walls, added a desk for papers and a chest of drawers to stow clothes. There wasn't a lot of storage space, but I didn't need much now. I'd saved one all-purpose black dress but had sold my other D.C. clothes weeks ago for quick cash to pay the bakery's electric bill.

There was a small television in the corner. It wasn't attached to cable, but I'd bought a digital converter and on a good day it broadcast four channels. My red bike hung above my desk on twin hooks, a rag rug warmed the floor, and blue thrift store curtains covered the two dormer windows. In the corner, I'd also squeezed in another twin bed that doubled as a couch. No kitchen, but the bakery in the basement had all the cooking power I needed. My attic was not huge, but it worked for me.

For me.

Not me and *a baby*!

I sat on my sofa bed, unmindful of the squeaky spring poking my backside, and switched on my nightstand light so I could stare at the strip under the bulb's glare. The white had turned a very faint pink tint, but it wasn't exactly dark pink. And I was pretty certain it was supposed to be a dark pink. The back of the box said a pink plus sign indicated positive results. It didn't say faint pink or a little bit pink. No such circumstance as a little bit pregnant.

"How pink is pink enough?"

Damn. With a groan I curled up on the side of the bed and stared at the stick, willing it to fade to white.

It hadn't occurred to me until yesterday to buy a pregnancy test. I'd been walking by the Potomac River on the trail, trying to settle my stomach and doing my best to figure out when I'd had my last menstrual cycle. I'd missed last month and the month before, but with the job loss and the transition, I chalked the delay up to stress. Unlike my sisters' cycles, mine weren't totally regular, so I didn't get too worked up. I'd considered talking to Mom, but she was like my sisters. Like clockwork. Her biology wasn't mine.

The fact was, no matter how much we loved each other, I was the daughter she'd adopted and not birthed.

When I was three, my birth mother had abandoned me in the bakery's outdoor patio. It had been Easter time, and the place had been a crush of tourists and regulars enjoying our very decadent hot cross buns. Sheila McCrae, the hippie bakery shop owner, had spotted me sitting alone. She'd stopped her frenetic collection of dishes and trash and waited to make sure my mom was close. After several minutes, she'd realized my mother wasn't hovering close or standing nearby with a watchful eye on me. I was alone. My birth mother had vanished, leaving no traces or clues. There'd been a police investigation but my birth mother had gone. So Sheila had folded me into her family as effortlessly as she folded whipped egg whites into a batter, and life had gone on for both of us as mother and daughter.

Though Mom loved me like her biological daughters, we did not share genetics. The only person to ask would have been my birth mother, whom I'd met for the first time months ago. Our recent reunion wasn't exactly storybook. She'd been clear she didn't want a relationship. She'd rebuilt her life with a husband and two young sons, and there was no room in it for me. She'd given me some biological information and had said she'd answer questions.

But her sudden arrival into my life had left me stunned and had silenced the millions of questions I'd had as a kid. Now as I stared at the light-but-not-dark-pink stick, the questions flickered to life. What was it like when she was pregnant with my two half brothers and me? Did she have morning sickness? Did her feet swell? How much weight did she gain? How was the delivery? Genetic time bombs in the family tree, maybe?

Damn.

Stupid stick. It had stirred up more questions for my birth mother, Terry, and more of my own unresolved emotions. Even if the stick stayed a light, light pink, today's stirring had disturbed the cauldron.

So why exactly did she leave me? I'd never really gotten the question answered, other than she'd been young and troubled. *Why do you love your sons but don't want to see me again?* I imagined them to be special young boys who gave her no trouble at all.

I shook the stick, held it upside down, and then studied it again. No change.

Me. Daisy Sheila McCrae. With a kid.

The image simply did not compute. I'd never pictured myself with children. My sister Rachel had two of the cutest girls in the world, and I'd give my life for them. My older sister, Margaret, always talked about marriage and having a family one day, and I could picture her sitting cross-legged on the floor, finger-painting with a half-dozen red-headed children. Both my sisters grew up assuming motherhood would be a part of their lives. But for me babies hadn't been in the master plan.

Logically, I understood my abandonment was a big part of the no-kid policy. What if I made a baby and couldn't raise it? My mom always assured me I'd be a great parent, but the fear that I'd hurt my child never left.

Some people say young children forget trauma, but they're wrong. We might not have words or vivid minute-by-minute memories, but we remember on a cellular level.

And with no genetic background to review, making a baby was akin to Russian roulette. I know, I know, we all play a form of the game when making a baby, but my genetics had been such an unknown for so long, a baby hadn't made sense.

Since my reunion with Terry, I've gained a good bit of medical history and could trace back her family—my family—for several generations. I had more answers now than I ever did. But the extra knowledge wasn't enough to prepare me for motherhood.

I glared at the stick. Was it a little more pink? Was it pink enough? "One simple direct answer is all I want. Yes or no?"

Footsteps sounded on the stairs leading to my room, and I glanced at the stick as if I feared it would somehow shout, *Daisy might be pregnant!*

I hustled into the bathroom, took one last look at the sorta pinkish center, and tossed the stick in the trash. Smoothing hands through my hair, I glanced at myself in the mirror and smiled.

"If you were pregnant," I whispered, "then it would be bright pink. The box promised it would be pink within a minute and it's been five minutes. Don't borrow trouble. There's no baby and Gordon and I will be fine."

"Daisy?" My sister Rachel's voice echoed from outside my door.

"Be right there, Rachel." I combed fingers through my hair, pulled the rubber band from my wrist, and twisted and secured my hair in a topknot.

A strained smile plastered on my face, I opened the door.

Rachel was eight inches shorter than me, had strawberry blond hair, and her skin was five shades lighter than mine. Hers was a peaches-and-cream complexion that easily burned in the sun whereas my olive complexion soaked up the rays.

She was our bakery's pastry chef and was considered a talent in the restaurant circles though she'd never been formally trained. She'd wanted to attend an upscale cooking academy in Maryland, but financially my parents couldn't swing it. So what she didn't learn from our father she'd taught herself with books and videos.

Beyond her baking skills, Rachel also had an annoying knack for reading me like one of her recipes. Her smile faded. "What's wrong?"

I cleared my throat and shrugged my shoulders. "Nothing's wrong, other than it's four o'clock in the morning."

Blue eyes narrowed. "You're used to the hours."

"I don't complain like I did in the beginning, but I refuse to become *accustomed* to a baker's life. Every sane person in this city is asleep now."

She shoved out a relieved breath. "Irritated. A little bitchy. My Daisy. The smile was unexpected and it scared me."

As I stepped into the hallway, I pulled my apartment door closed. "I'll try to remember smiling is bad."

"Not bad, but out of character for you."

"Duly noted." We descended the narrow staircase.

The Union Street Bakery had been in business for over one hundred and fifty years. The original building had been located on Alexandria's shoreline along the large wharfs, but had burned in a fire in the 1880s. Our great-great-grandfather, Shaun McCrae, and his wife, Sally, had rebuilt the business and moved it to the current location on Union Street. They raised five children here, and there'd been a McCrae in this locale ever since.

Whereas fifty years ago a bakery had been a daily stop for most, that wasn't the case anymore. Most folks these days did their shopping at grocery stores and rarely made a side trip to a mom-and-pop operation like the Union Street Bakery. We had our steady customers, and in the last couple of months had supplemented our income with several catering jobs. But the retail business had not really grown. People loved us, but they just didn't want to go out of their way for us.

I'd come to realize that if we were going to survive, we had to reach out to some of the smaller grocery stores and get them to carry our goods. But to accomplish this we had to correct logistical problems at the bakery first. The kitchen was located in the basement. A manageable obstacle if you had a strong guy like my late brother-in-law or my dad in his prime to carry the hundred-pound sacks up and down the stairs. When Rachel had run the place alone, she'd gotten around the heavy-lifting problem by ordering small bags of flour and sugar, but small translated into expensive. If we were going to show a higher profit, we needed to move the kitchen to the main level. We also needed a freezer. Until now we made all our dough the day of or the night before. Fine for daily customers but if we planned to expand, we needed a freezer to stockpile dough and cake.

All this meant we needed a serious renovation, requiring that we close the shop for two weeks. It was a painful financial proposition, but necessary if we wanted to take the business to the next step.

"You're looking a little rough this morning," Rachel said.

"How do you look remotely human this time of day?" And she did. Rachel had a way of springing out of bed looking, well, perfect. Strawberry-blond hair in place, makeup on and wearing T-shirts I'm pretty sure she ironed. "You make the rest of us look bad."

She grinned. "I've made coffee."

"Great." The idea of my favorite brew had my stomach flip-flopping as I moistened my dry lips.

What I really craved was one of the ginger ales I'd hidden in the refrigerator downstairs. If I was lucky, I'd be able to stomach the ginger ale and a handful of saltines.

I'd not been sick until just a couple of weeks ago. And the more I thought about my upset stomach, the more convinced I became it wasn't morning sickness but the flu. The good thing about my sickness was that it lasted all day and I was fairly certain nausea associated with pregnancy was restricted not only to the mornings but also the first trimester mornings.

"Demo starts today," I said.

Rachel somehow summoned a smile. "I bet it goes real smoothly."

I held my index finger to my lips. "Shh. Don't speak so positively. You'll jinx us."

She gently elbowed me. "You've got to learn to think positively."

"Right."

I shoved out a breath, already dreading the construction. To make room for the kitchen equipment in the basement we needed to knock out my office wall. My office would move to my apartment and the reclaimed square footage would hold the freezer and the basement ovens.

One of the selling points of the Union Street Bakery was our brick oven. Located in the basement, it gave our breads a fine crust a conventional oven couldn't duplicate. This old oven would remain in the basement, because as much as I wanted to move it up to the main floor, the oven was grandfathered in by the city, and if we moved one brick we'd have to demo it totally. And instead of building a new oven, we would patch the cracks in the side and hope it lasted a few more years.

Our new head baker, Jean Paul Martin, had arrived on our doorstep four weeks ago. He had proven himself to be a talented baker, but when he'd assured us he could tackle the renovation, I'd been skeptical. He'd fixed and built several brick ovens in his native France. He'd also framed several kitchens. Our project should take ten to fourteen days, he had promised. We'd lose one selling Saturday and would be back in operation by the second Saturday.

"Ne t'inquiète pas. Tout est en ordre." Don't worry. Everything is under control.

I remained skeptical when he told me his fees, which were dirt cheap. He'd barely make a dime off the job. But a dime was all I had to spare. So I'd agreed.

The bakery's accounts had tipped barely into the black and this downtime would land us back in the red. But ten to fourteen days was a survivable delay. We could do two weeks. But not a day more.

"He needs us to haul away all the pots and pans this afternoon, and then we remove the brick wall separating my office from the work space. The plan is to save the old bricks and then sell them. Jean Paul says people pay for old brick."

It was a simple and straightforward plan.

Simple. I hate it when someone makes a *simple* plan. In my book, it's the equivalent of thumbing your nose at the Fates.

"Tell me what to do, and I'll do it," Rachel said.

"First we sell today, business as usual. Then we tackle the rest."

We moved down the back staircase toward the kitchen. The building stood three stories tall, not including the basement where the baking was done. The shop took up the first floor, Rachel and her two daughters lived on the second floor, and the attic was all mine. There were times when the girls were running and playing on the stairs so that the noise grew annoying, but I reminded myself this was how people lived one hundred years ago—several generations under one roof.

My dad had bought the building next door thirty years ago when the city had fallen by the wayside and land was cheap. His friends thought he was crazy. They had been encouraging him to leave Alexandria and he'd invested in more property. But Dad wasn't a quitter and about that time he and a handful of folks pushed for a new plan for Alexandria. It didn't happen overnight but these days the city enjoyed a steady stream of tourism. More For Sale signs had popped up on some of the retail shops and last week there'd been a bankruptcy sale, but the city seemed to be holding its own. And if the bakery could get back up and running, we'd do the same.

The sound of Jean Paul's hammer striking brick reverberated up from the basement.

Rachel cringed. "He said he'd wait until we closed at noon."

Hammer hit brick. I winced. "Maybe he's testing the wall. Preliminary whacks."

Her lips flattening, she shook her head. "He drives me crazy."

My stomach tightened. "The man is a master. He could bake wonderful bread out of the flour he sweeps up off the floor."

"But he doesn't stick to bread. He is telling me what pastries I should bake."

Rachel had had issues with him last week over the menu. She'd wanted to keep several items her late husband had put in place, and Jean Paul wanted them gone. I agreed with Jean Paul but had yet to tackle the menu with Rachel. The renovation had bought me some time, but the battle would tee up again when we reopened.

We found Jean Paul, a tall wiry man with slicked-back dark hair, cigarette dangling from his mouth, poised over the basement brick oven. He had a chisel and hammer in hand, and he seemed to be studying the best angle of attack.

"Jean Paul, the city inspector will not let us alter the oven. If we do, then he will make us remove it."

Jean Paul's gaze remained on the oven. "I am taking out a brick or two."

"The deal was no bricks."

"That is why I started early. I have never known an inspector to rise early, and by the time ours does, the repairs will be made and no one will be the wiser."

The smell of cigarette smoke and the coffee sent my stomach into somersaults, forcing me to brace. "Jean Paul, no cigarettes in the kitchen."

He raised his gaze, one eye squinting as the smoke trailed past. "It's not a kitchen today."

"It's still a kitchen for a few more hours. Put it out!" My stomach tumbled as I moved to the large stainless steel refrigerator and pulled an ice-cold ginger ale from the back. I popped the top and sipped carefully. The cool liquid soothed my throat and for the moment my stomach handled it. Yesterday, I'd drunk the soda too fast, and it had come up within a matter of minutes. My stomach didn't love the first tentative sips but had also not rejected them.

Maybe my stomach's acceptance of the ginger ale was a sign. Maybe this was indeed the flu and my panicked trip to the drugstore last night was all for nothing.

Please, oh, please, oh, please.

Rachel poured herself a cup of coffee and eyed me over the rim. "So what is going on with you? You have too much to drink last night?"

I pressed the cold can to my head. "Yeah, too much to drink. I'll be fine."

She sipped, studied, and looked ready to comment, when Jean Paul struck his hammer into the motor. The strike was hard and loud and made us both jump.

"How many more bricks?" I shouted.

"Six, maybe ten, no more than twenty."

"Twenty bricks." I pressed the cold can to my cheek. "That will ruin the oven."

He shook his head. "This is for me to worry about. You two must get ready for the day."

A heavy weight pressed on me and for a moment unbearable worry tightened around me. The old oven had served this bakery so well for sixty years, and he was dismantling it bit by bit. "Don't screw up my oven."

He grunted, raised his hammer to a stone and then seemed to think better of it before moving to another section.

Since the spring, I'd had a lifetime worth of change. This might not be my dream life, but it was *my* life. I wanted this renovation done as fast as possible so that everything would settle. I wanted the bakery to keep growing and improving. I wanted numbers once red to stay black, and pink to remain white. Gordon to keep on loving me.

I didn't want more change.

Want.

Wanting could be as bad as planning. Both invited trouble.

Chapter Two

Saturday, 7:45 A.M.
14 days until grand reopening
Income Lost: $0

F our hours later the sun had risen, and the store was set to open in minutes. We'd baked extra yesterday, knowing Saturday would be our last sales day for a couple of weeks. We'd carefully carried all the baked goods upstairs and kept them in covered bins for freshness. We'd intentionally finished the breads and dozens of cookies this morning so the bakery smelled sweet and inviting.

Jean Paul finished removing his bricks and had spent the next hours mixing mortar and replacing bricks. While visions of surprise inspections had plagued me all morning, he'd not been the least bit worried. And as it turned out, I'd worried over nothing. By seven, Jean Paul had completed the job. His smile had been smug and self-assured, and I'd wondered what other rules would get bent or broken over the next week and a half.

My stomach had settled by the time we opened, and I was really feeling sure I had just gotten hold of a bug. Give it a day or two and I'd be my old self. The pregnancy test could be chalked up to a moment of hysteria.

As Rachel arranged chocolate-chip cookies on a tray, I hefted a tray of pies destined for the front display case. We were putting out six today, though we normally did ten.

"Is Margaret here yet?" I asked. Our third sister, Margaret, was the oldest. She worked part-time at the bakery.

On cue, I heard the front door bells jangle and the door close. I glanced at the clock. Ten minutes to eight. Early. Margaret was never early. "Margaret?"

"That would be me," she called back.

Rachel met my surprised gaze. "Sounded like her."

"How can it be her? She's early."

Rachel shook her head. "You were smiling this morning and she's early. This is all so wrong."

I pushed through the double saloon doors separating the work area from the sales area and found Margaret putting her purse away.

"Everything all right?" I asked as I raised the back of the display case and slid the pies inside.

Margaret, like Rachel, had reddish hair, though hers was curly and wild and had to be tamed daily with a rubber band and bobby pins. "Life is great!"

I paused and glanced up at Margaret. Life was never good with my oldest sister. The glass always tipped at the half-empty mark.

Red ringlets framed Margaret's round face. Freckles peppered skin looking flushed with excitement. She wore a loose, pale blue peasant top and a full black skirt that skimmed her calves. Birkenstocks.

Margaret had a PhD in history and a master's in forensics. If there was one industry that was tougher than the bakery business it was forensic anthropology. Last year she'd had an opportunity to take a job out west, but she had refused it so she could stay close to Rachel. Family loyalty had her helping in the bakery, but she didn't love it. The customers never saw her frustration. She reserved those gems for me.

"What's wrong?" I said.

She actually laughed. "Why does anything have to be wrong, Daisy? Do you have to be such a downer?"

My stomach tightened, and for a moment I mentally traced the steps to the bathroom. "I'm a happy person."

She laughed again. "Right."

"I *am* happy." Carefully I rearranged the pies in the case. I was happy. I had a lot to be thankful for.

Bracelets jangled on her wrists. "You are as bad as I am. We are soul sisters when it comes to our innate unhappiness."

I'd always known I had a bitter edge but wasn't comfortable with having a reputation as perpetually sour. Suddenly, unsettling images of me as an old, wizened bakery woman flashed. "So why are you in such a good mood today?"

She flicked away a lock of hair away from her eyes. "It's summer. The air is warm, not hot."

I rose, stretching the tight muscles in my back. "If you say the birds are singing, I'll hit you."

"But they are!"

"Rachel," I shouted. "Come here quick!"

Rachel quickly appeared above the saloon doors, a look of alarm on her face. "What's wrong?"

I jabbed my thumb toward Margaret. "Margaret has been kidnapped. I don't know who this is, but it's not Margaret. She says the birds are freaking singing."

Rachel's confused gaze danced between Margaret's smiling face and mine. "She looks like Margaret."

I shook my head. "Look closer. There's a twinkle in her eye, and there's a grin on her face."

Rachel's brow knotted. "You were smiling when I first saw you this morning."

I shook my head. "Mine was fake. Hers is real."

Rachel studied Margaret's face and when our sister grinned, retreated a step. "Should I call the cops?"

Margaret laughed and shook her head. "You two. You act like I'm never happy."

"You aren't," Rachel said.

"I can't argue," I said. "We match each other foul mood for foul mood." I folded my arms over my chest. "What gives? You meet a guy? This some kind of sexual euphoria?"

"No," Margaret said. She didn't laugh again, but her eyes still danced.

"Really, Margaret," Rachel said, all humor gone. "What gives?" Rachel, our cheerleader, could find a rainbow in a room full of manure. But since Jean Paul's arrival, her temper had shortened, and her smile had grown a tad brittle.

Margaret reached for her green Union Street Bakery apron and carefully pulled it over her head. We both watched and waited as she crisscrossed the apron strings in the back and tied them in a bow in the front. "I've kinda been offered a dream job."

My heart slowed a beat. With the three of us, the bakery had run well. Rachel baked. I managed the money and Margaret handled customers. *We* were a three-legged stool.

I summoned a smile, swearing I'd not let my mind go to the disaster place it liked to scurry when change occurred. "So where is the job?"

Her eyes brightened. "It's an archeology dig up on the Chesapeake Bay in St. Mary's County, Maryland."

"That's about an hour north of here." I calculated the miles, the traffic, and the lost hours behind the counter.

An hour away wasn't the end of the earth, and I was thinking this gig like many of the other history jobs would be part-time. Good history positions were so rare. Basically, someone had to die for a slot to open.

"So what would you do?" Rachel asked.

Margaret rubbed nervous hands over her apron. "An old pre–Revolutionary War community has been discovered. The dig has already started, but they need extra hands."

"So is this a volunteer job?" I said.

"Not exactly. The gal heading it up has to take a leave. She's pregnant and has to go on bed rest." She shook her head. "Who in their right mind would get pregnant during the dig season? God, contraception anyone?"

I folded my arms over my chest. "So you'd be there for the dig season."

"Or maybe longer."

I knew enough about archeology digs to know the season had started in March and would extend to early December. "So you would leave when?"

"Today would be my last day."

A rush of air escaped from Rachel's lips.

"I know this is very short notice." Doubt mingled with Margaret's euphoria. "I know I'm leaving you in the lurch. I *know* that. But I swear this is the best job ever."

I shoved back a pang of jealousy. I'd had a great job until the financial company I'd worked for had blown up. I'd made great money. Wore designer suits. People sat a little straighter when I entered a room. Now I worked eighty-hour weeks either in hot kitchens covered in flour and icing, ringing a register, or balancing a lopsided budget.

Sarcastic comments danced in my head, but I refused to unleash them. As much as I wanted to bust Margaret for her lack of notice, I didn't. Couldn't. This was a dream for her. "So can we at least throw you a going-away party tomorrow?"

Relief rushed past Margaret's lips in a rush. "I have to be on-site Monday morning."

"Then it will be tomorrow afternoon." I faced Rachel. "We can do a little something tomorrow afternoon, right?"

Unshed tears glistened in Rachel's eyes. Her bottom lip quivered, but still she nodded and smiled. "Great."

Margaret pursed her lips. "I wouldn't have taken this, Rachel, if Daisy wasn't here. I know the two of you can manage."

Rachel cleared her throat. "Of course." She turned and vanished into the kitchen.

Margaret moved to follow.

I blocked her path. "It's okay. Let her go. She's been wound tight lately."

Worry erased her happiness. "What's going on with her?"

"Jean Paul is insisting on changes, and it's upsetting her. And the renovation is not helping."

Silver bracelets jangled from Margaret's wrist as she tugged at a key-shaped earring. "She's the boss. If she doesn't like it then she should tell him so."

"That's not her style."

"Maybe it should be."

"I know. You know. But this is about more than changing menu items. The latest menu was Mike's."

Margaret rolled her eyes. "Doesn't mean it was great. I mean Mike could bake, but he wasn't the expert. I didn't like all his choices."

Mike had been a talented baker and seemed to be the perfect fit for Rachel. He liked to make decisions, and she was happy to let him. Their relationship wouldn't have worked for me or for Margaret, but it worked for them. Since his death, Rachel had been hurled out of her comfort zone and forced to make tougher choices. So far, she'd not done so well.

"Don't worry about it. I'm here, and Rachel and I will figure this all out."

"I'm leaving you in a terrible spot."

"Not really. You've done a lot to keep the bakery going, carried the load when I didn't. Let me worry about it for a while."

Margaret tugged at the apron strings. "I didn't think I'd feel this guilty about leaving."

"The place has a way of sucking you in."

"So what are you gonna do? This isn't your forever kind of place. I figured sooner or later you'd job hunt in New York or on the West Coast."

"I'm going to give the bakery a full year, see it through the renovation and the wholesale transition."

"When did you decide this?"

I glanced around the shop at the cookies in the display, the cupcake clock on the wall, the blue trim needing fresh paint. "When we committed to the renovation."

"So you're going to stop looking for another job?" Surprise and doubt wrapped each word.

My defenses rose. "A year isn't forever, Margaret. And if the right job came along I'd sure look at it."

"You mean like opportunity knocking on the door?"

"Something like that."

"Kinda Zen and kinda passive for you." A frown furrowed her brow. "I remember Dad saying when he was a teen he'd never work in the bakery. That he wanted to be a pilot. And then his dad died and life locked him into this place."

The comparison didn't sit well. I didn't resemble the McCrae clan but temperament-wise I was a lot like Dad. We thought alike. Mom said we both had type A personalities. "I don't think he has a lot of regrets."

"He does, too. He never says, but those regrets are there. I don't want you to end up with regrets, Daisy."

Dad said he was happy with his choices. Had he simply fooled himself like I was trying to now?

My stomach gurgled. Right now I could not think that far ahead. "Let me get through the next two weeks, and then I'll worry about the rest of my life. You take this job. In fact, consider yourself fired as of noon today."

Margaret laughed. "Fired?"

"That's right. We want you out." I wagged my finger at the front door. "Don't ever darken our doorstep again."

Margaret tapped a ringed finger against her thigh. "And if it doesn't work out or last?"

"It will." Better she think of this as a one-way ticket. Trap doors, outs, and nets had a way of making us not try as hard. "Now would you flip the sign to Open? Customers should be here soon."

She moved toward the door and spun the sign around. "I thought I was fired."

"Like I said, you are fired at noon."

Margaret stopped and stared at me for a long moment.

"What?" I grumbled.

"Thanks."

This time my smile was real. "You're welcome."

I'd barely slipped on my apron before the first throng of customers arrived. Saturday was our busiest retail day. Folks who'd denied themselves sweets all week arrived ready to sin and enjoy. Some planned ahead for Sunday after-church meals and others were the random tourists who'd found us. Weeks ago, Rachel and I had visited all the area hotels within walking distance and handed out samples and offered a 10 percent discount to hotel guests. The ploy seemed to be working, which made me all the more frustrated by this much-needed closing. I'd planned to renovate and move the kitchen in September or October but when the wholesalers agreed to give us a try, I knew I needed to have the new operation in full swing by fall. Again, plans and me, we didn't fare so well.

As Margaret welcomed a customer, I turned toward the saloon doors leading to the back. As I took a step, an odd wave of energy passed over me. Cold. Frigid. It took my breath away and for a moment I froze, not sure what was happening. Maybe more flulike symptoms but this didn't feel so physical. The sensation was dread mixed with a jolt of energy. As my head spun, I imagined the floor under me shifting. The sounds of Margaret and the customer faded and the loneliness enveloped me. Instinctively, my hand slid to my unsteady belly. I was going to be sick.

Stumbling forward, I pushed through the saloon doors and hurried up the back staircase to my room. I made it to my bathroom seconds before I threw up. After the nausea had passed, I sat on the bathroom floor, my eyes watering and my head aching. I leaned my head back against the tiled wall. "This is such bullshit. Such bullshit."

Whatever was going on with me needed to stop. I did not have time to be sick. And I sure as hell did not have time to be pregnant.

I'm not sure what drew my gaze to the trash can, but there it went, catching the edge of the pregnancy test strip. Absently, I reached for it so I could stare at the light-pinkish window, which had refused to confirm a pregnancy this morning.

When I looked at the strip, the color was no longer a light pink. It was dark pink plus sign. A really dark pink plus sign.

I blinked, shook the test strip as if a hard jolt would dilute the color, and then looked at it again. The plus remained as bright and pink as before. Weren't these tests no longer valid after twenty or thirty minutes?

I fished out the box and read the back instructions thinking maybe, just maybe, the plus meant something other than pregnant.

Quickly I scanned the tiny type. I found in bolded letters *Results*. A negative sign meant no pregnancy. A plus indicated pregnancy.

The instructions had the good sense to remain neutral and oddly calm, though it could have said, *Daisy, you dumbass. You are thirty-four years old, and you are by no stretch a virgin. So how the hell did you get pregnant? You know better!*

Clutching the strip in my hand, I leaned back against the wall and closed my eyes. Tests like this weren't perfect. There was at least a 10 percent margin of error, I was fairly certain. The definitive test, according to Rachel, was a blood test.

Clutching the strip, I swore. "Why couldn't you have given me a straight answer in the time listed on the back of the box? Then I'd have a real answer. Not a maybe *yes*, maybe this is a bad test *yes*."

Shit.

I thought about another drugstore test but I couldn't imagine doing this all over again tomorrow morning. No more dime-store tests, which could have been left in the rain, heat, or cold by a hapless delivery truck driver.

Yeah, the test was faulty. Yeah. Faulty.

The blood test would prove once and for all that I was not pregnant.

Rachel's smile was as brittle and fragile as spun sugar, which was as easily admired as shattered. As she boxed up assorted cookies for a mother with two toddlers screaming to be let out of their double stroller, she tried to imagine herself at a beach. Soft sand. Cool breeze. The sun on her skin.

But as hard as she tried to summon the image, she could not. She'd not been to the beach since high school, and when she'd been there it had been with Mike. They had barely started dating. She'd been a cheerleader. He'd been on the football team. They'd not had much money, but there'd been no worries for either of them in those days. Their biggest concerns were getting a base tan before prom, which was weeks away. She'd been so worried her pale skin would all but glow in her new black dress.

The lost, long-ago beach day had been magical. They'd had a beer or two. Soaked up the sun. Laughed with friends. No worries.

Perfect had ended during the car ride home when she'd broken out in chills. She'd sunburned. Badly. When they'd arrived home her skin simmered with heat. Mike had laughed and reminded her he'd told her so. Her mother had coated her skin with aloe vera.

"Could you throw in another dozen sugar cookies?"

Rachel glanced up toward the voice that sounded as if it were a million miles away. The woman wore her dark hair pulled back in a ponytail, sunglasses on her head and gold earrings dangling. She looked annoyed.

"Another dozen cookies?" Rachel said. "Sure."

"Sugar cookies," she repeated as Rachel reached for the lemon bars.

"Right. Sure." She carefully stacked the dozen in the box before sealing it with a gold Union Street Bakery sticker. "That'll be twenty-one dollars."

The woman handed her a credit card. "I saw the sign out front. So how long are you going to be closed?"

If the woman had seen and *read* the sign she'd know. But Rachel summoned a smile as she swiped the card. "Two weeks."

A manicured finger smoothed over a sleek eyebrow. "My son's birthday is August 12. I'd like to order a cake."

Rachel handed her back her card and receipt. "I can take it now."

"You are sure you'll be open on time? I've never known construction to go as planned."

"We will be fine. We've built in extra days of cushion."

"It's been my experience when there's a remodel days turn into weeks."

"We'll be fine." And they would. This was about knocking out one wall and moving kitchen equipment, not rebuilding the entire place. "Would you like me to take the order?"

She opened the cookie box and handed one to each child. "It needs to look like a ninja. A red ninja. Chocolate. Must feed twenty children."

"A ninja?"

"You can do that can't you?"

"I don't see why not."

"And he has to be red. Billy likes the red ninja. He has a red ninja doll and is obsessed with it."

"I can do a ninja. And red. Vanilla icing. Chocolate cake."

"Yes. But not buttercream. I like the icing made from Crisco. I know it's not the fancy kind, but I like the taste better. Tastes like the canned icing. I know we shouldn't like it, but we do. So do the kids."

As Rachel wrote up the order, she pressed so hard with the tip of her pencil it broke and she had to fish another out of her apron. Ninja. Crisco. What else? Food coloring in the batter? "Sounds good. You'll pick it up on the eleventh?"

"Yes."

She recorded the woman's information and watched as she left. "Why don't you go to a chain store at get your ninja cake? Why bother to come here?"

Margaret glanced up from the register. "What are you mumbling about?"

"People who come to a specialty bakery wanting their cake to taste like the ones in the grocery store."

Margaret looked unworried. "Money is money. Does it matter as long as they pay?"

Rachel glared at Margaret. "I feel like a cake whore who mixes up whatever to keep the customer happy."

"Cake whore?" Margaret cocked her head. "That doesn't sound like you."

Rachel could see the surprise in her sister's gaze but didn't really care. "What am I supposed to sound like?"

"I don't know. Happy, I suppose. Daisy and I are the bitter, grumbly ones, remember? You are supposed to be the happy one."

"Maybe I don't feel like happy. Maybe I'm a little bit annoyed in general today." The bells rang on the front door as several more customers wandered in. Rachel watched as they absently searched the menu above for ideas, and she realized if she had to answer one more question about the difference between white chocolate and chocolate, she'd scream. Without a word, she left Margaret to deal.

She considered escaping to the kitchen and baking to burn off stress, but remembered the ovens had been unplugged and Jean Paul was downstairs dismantling them for the move.

She smoothed her hands over her hips and rolled her head from side to side, trying to work the kinks out of her neck. Margaret was right. She was the happy one. She didn't get pissed and didn't do bitter well. And yet here she stood, annoyed and angry living in skin tightening by the moment.

Daisy reappeared red-eyed and pale.

"Where have you been?"

The sharp edges on her words had Daisy raising a brow. "Bathroom."

"Are you hungover or something? Gordon's been gone since Thursday night on his bike trip, and you're not the type to sit in your room and drink alone."

Daisy moistened her lips. "It's less like a hangover and more like *something*. A bit of a bug, I think."

Immediately contrite, Rachel struggled with her anger as if she didn't have the right to express negative emotion with anyone, especially

Daisy, who had damn near ridden to her rescue months ago. "You need to hang back when we pack and move equipment."

"No. I'm good. I already feel like I'm on the mend." Daisy glanced at the clock on the wall. "T-minus fifteen minutes."

"And the bakery closes for fourteen days."

"Margaret out front?"

"Figured I'd leave it to her since she's abandoning us." Bitterness melted into her voice.

"That's not exactly fair. She's hung in there with you."

"Yeah, she has. And Mom and Dad helped her with grad school and last I checked the bakery pays her for her time." She rubbed her hands over her arms, craving a beer. She'd had a couple since Mike died, always denying herself a second, fearing if she gave in to the grief she'd never stop drinking.

"You on the rag?" Daisy challenged.

Rachel shook her head. "Can't I be annoyed without being on my cycle?"

"You are only edgy during your period."

"Well, today, I'm annoyed, and I'm not on the rag."

Daisy's gaze narrowed as she studied Rachel. "How was the girls' sleepover with Mom and Dad?"

She huffed out a breath. "No one called so all systems must be go."

Mom and Dad had offered to take the girls on a beach vacation when Daisy had proposed the renovation. It had made sense to all, so her parents rented a cottage on the Outer Banks of North Carolina. The Sunday-to-Sunday rental began tomorrow, but Rachel had been worried about her aging parents chasing after very busy twin five-year-olds. She'd suggested sleepovers as practice. So far, they'd gone well. The girls had been happy and Mom and Dad hadn't died from exhaustion.

"The acid test will be the beach vacation. Ellie and Anna are going to kick their asses."

Rachel loved her girls more than life but she needed this break. Needed a little time to reacquaint herself with Rachel.

"They raised us," Daisy offered.

"You lose the stamina real quick. If I had to go back to the infant stage now, I think I'd die. All those sleepless nights. I thought I'd go insane."

Daisy's gaze sharpened. "Mike helped, didn't he?"

"When he could. But he had to be up at three to bake, so for the most part I took care of the babies."

"Yeah, but you had two."

"True. But all it takes is one with colic and life as you know it is over. Gone. Dead in the water."

Daisy untied her apron and carefully hung it on the wall. "Good to know."

"What do you have to worry about? You're on the no-kid plan."

"Right."

The front door bells jangled, Margaret wished the last customer good day, and then she pushed through the saloon doors. "Mission accomplished. We are now officially closed."

"So we pack up equipment now, right?" Rachel said.

"Sure," Margaret agreed. "I'm about all packed on the home front, so you have me all afternoon."

Daisy's smile made her pale features look a little ghoulish. "Great."

Seeing the finish line brought with it a kind of euphoria and Margaret could see hers. Rachel had been robbing Peter to pay Paul time-wise for so long, she'd forgotten what it felt like to be excited. Her finish line was so far off in the distance, she wondered if it existed.

Chapter Three

Saturday, 2:00 P.M.
13 days, 22 hours until grand reopening
Income Lost: $0

The three of us worked for several hours. While I cleaned out my office, Margaret and Rachel packed all the cooking supplies, pots, pans, and spoons. Jean Paul finished his repairs to the brick oven.

By four we'd cleared out the space, and we were ready to demo the wall of my office. The wall had been in place for as long as I could remember and was made of brick. Jean Paul had gone to the basement, studied the floor joists, determined the office wall was not load bearing and we were safe to remove it.

"Don't worry," he said.

Hammer and chisel in hand, I stared at the wall. "You are sure about the wall?"

He shrugged and brushed back a lock of hair with his long fingers. "Of course."

"If the bakery collapses, Jean Paul, I'm coming after you."

He grunted, took the hammer and chisel from me and cut into a chunk of mortar. The first bricks were slow going, but after about the fifth or sixth removal the demolition went faster. Soon, my sisters and I were carrying bricks to the back alley behind the bakery and stacking them in neat piles.

Since Jean Paul's arrival I'd noticed whatever he did, he did very well. However, he could only do one task at a time, and he could not be rushed. So when we had no bricks to move, I swept mortar from the floor, Margaret texted friends, and Rachel paced.

It wasn't an efficient system, but like I said, Jean Paul wasn't charging more than his baker's salary, and I didn't have the money to hire a real builder. And so we moved slowly and carefully.

In a couple of hours, about 40 percent of the wall had been dismantled. We'd created a neat hole into the space that had been my domain for the last couple of months.

"I'm gonna miss this space." Closing the office door had been a treat in itself. The space had been small, but it was a sanctuary of sorts. And soon it would be gone for good.

Rachel shook her head. "Not me. I always tensed up in the space. Balancing the budget made me want to cry."

Margaret texted. "Maybe you can make an office in the basement. Other than the bread oven, space is now open, right?"

"Twelve hundred square feet." We could use it as storage but the basement square footage needed to work for us to survive. I didn't know what we'd do with it yet, but we needed ideas.

An unlit cigarette dangled from Jean Paul's mouth as he studied his work. Hands rested casually on his lean hips. "Make it a wine cellar."

"Wine. We are bakers," I said

"Bread and wine are natural pairings," Margaret said. "A loaf of bread, a bit of cheese, and a bottle of wine. Perfect for a day by the river."

"I don't know anything about wine. I know what I like, but I wouldn't know how to sell it."

Jean Paul shrugged as if this were a simple problem. "I might know a guy."

"A guy?"

"He is selling his restaurant. He has wine to sell."

"How much?"

Jean Paul straightened, as lazy as a cat on a hot day. "I will ask."

With no further explanation we returned to work. As the day went on, the heat outside rose and the temperatures in the kitchen grew hotter. We had the back door propped open to allow a breeze because Jean Paul had shut off the AC so the intake didn't suck up the dust.

"This is BS," Margaret said. Her good humor of the morning had faded. "I can't believe we are doing this ourselves. Why don't you hire someone, Daisy?"

I swiped sweat from my brow. "Can't afford a someone. We are it."

"We are bakers, not construction workers," she said as she accepted a brick.

Rachel had been silent through the afternoon, but it was clear she didn't like this any better than Margaret or me. Normally she found positive topics to talk about, but not today. Something chipped at her good humor as Jean Paul chipped at the mortar.

He set his chisel against a chunk of mortar and hit hard. The mortar fell free and he wrestled another brick loose. This was a maddening process. My head pounded and I considered calling it quits for the day when Jean Paul said, "That is unusual."

No surprises, please. "What?"

"There is a hole where the side wall meets the main wall." He took a small, dented, silver flashlight, clicked it on, and peered into the crevice left by the missing bricks.

"Do you see anything?" Margaret said.

"Always the archeologist," I said.

She shrugged. "Be nice to land a big discovery during this adventure. Makes the chipped nails and sore back muscles worth it."

"Maybe it's buried treasure," I teased.

Margaret's eyes brightened. "Now that would be totally cool."

"I hope whatever it is," Rachel said, "it's worth a ton of money. Then we can hire someone else to do this and we can go on vacation with Mom, Dad, and the girls."

"Poverty is a drag," I said.

When I'd first rejoined the bakery, I'd seen the income issues as an exciting challenge. I was sure I could come up with a scheme to turn this place around and make real money. I'd slashed costs and turned a very marginal profit, which was enough to pay the quarterly taxes and cushion us for fourteen days of downtime. Hardly setting the world on fire.

When I'd been in finance the money was been great. And I'd spent it freely, enjoying all the fruits of my labors. I'd assumed the job would always be there and the money would keep rolling into my bank account. I cringe now when I think about how much I'd spent on shoes and eating out and trips. If I'd saved 20 percent I'd have no worries now. But I'd pissed it all away on crap. And now the job had vanished and I was here, schlepping bricks in the heat.

Jean Paul ignored us as he always did, peering inside the hole. Finally he grunted, pushed up his sleeve and put his arm in the opening.

"Is that such a good idea?" I said as his arm vanished into the opening. "You don't know what's in there."

He grunted and leaned deeper into the hole. And then without warning he screamed as if in agony. He thrashed. Screamed more. We all squealed. Rachel jumped up and down as I raced toward Jean Paul. *Please don't let his arm get bitten off.* The thought of blood made my stomach flip-flop.

"I'll call 9-1-1!" Margaret shouted as she reached for her cell.

I reached Jean Paul ready to do . . . I don't know what, but I was there ready to attempt a rescue. And then the anguished expression on his face vanished and he smiled. He pulled his arm effortlessly out of the hole. Clutched in his non-bloody fingers was a rusted metal box.

My heart racing, I stared at him through narrowed eyes as he laughed. "Women. So easy to scare."

I took a step back and glanced at my sisters. The anger burning in their gazes mirrored mine. "Should we kill him fast or slow, ladies?"

"Definitely slow," Rachel said. Her cheeks remained flushed and her eyes were wide with lingering worry.

"Super slow." Margaret tucked her phone back in her rear pocket.

Chuckling, Jean Paul handed me the box and then glanced up at the clock on the wall. "It's five. Time to stop."

Thank God! I can now crawl into bed and focus on not throwing up. However, despite my first reaction, I said, "What do you mean stop? We have hours of daylight."

One of his thick brows arched. "It's a beautiful day. And I've plans with friends."

"Friends. You moved here a month ago." I'd lived here my whole life and had, well, no friends other than my sisters and Gordon. I wasn't sure if my current circumstance was my fault or the bakery's.

Another casual shrug lifted his shoulders. "It is not so hard to make friends."

Instead of summoning a rebuttal, I glanced at the box. "What is it?"

"A box," Jean Paul said.

"Thanks. I did figure that much out."

He reached in his pocket for his rumpled pack of cigarettes and headed toward the back door. "Until tomorrow."

As he vanished out the door, Margaret peered over my shoulder. "Open it."

Rachel pushed her hand through her hair. "If we're knocking off I'm headed upstairs. I want to make sure Mom packed everything the girls need."

"Don't you want to see what's in the box?" Margaret said.

Rachel waved a tired hand. "Pass."

"Suit yourself," she said.

As I went to the refrigerator, peeled back the plastic now covering it, and pulled out a ginger ale, she opened the box. Rusted hinges squeaked and groaned. I popped the top and savored several small sips. "What's inside?"

"Looks like recipes."

"Recipes?" As the liquid hit my stomach, it lurched. I refused to get sick again today. "No gold?"

She shook her head. "No gold, silver, or precious gems. Old recipes. And . . ." She fished her fingers into the box. "A set of dog tags."

"Dog tags? For who?"

Margaret squinted and studied the embossed lettering. "For a Walter F. Jacob."

"Who would put a box of recipes in a wall with a set of dog tags?"

"This wall must have been installed in the early nineteen forties. So this must have been put in as it was being built."

"Yeah, but why?"

"A mystery." Margaret handed the box to me. "Which I do not have time to consider. I've friends to meet for drinks at seven, and it would be nice to take a shower before I meet up with them."

I traced my fingers over the dust coating the top of the box. "Sure, fine. Leave me alone."

Margaret arched a brow. "Is self-pity lingering under those words? Really, Daisy, that's beneath you."

Wallowing wasn't my usual way, which meant I should be entitled to it once in a while. "What if it is?"

Margaret rolled her eyes. "Whining does not become you, Daisy. You love solitude."

"Not always."

"Where's Gordon?"

I traced my finger through the dust on the box. "On a hundred-mile bike ride in the Shenandoah Valley with a group of tourists from Japan."

"One hundred miles?"

"I know. Crazy. But he loves to ride, and his adventure/extreme tours are becoming popular."

Margaret scrunched up her face as if she'd bitten into a lemon. "Popular with who? Masochists? That's not exercise. It's torture."

"You're preaching to the choir."

She shrugged off her apron and hung it on a peg by the door. "So are you two getting kind of serious?"

My smile masked my panic. "We're trying to be friends. A new and different approach for us."

"I mean, I have guy friends, and I know you've had one or two, but you were going to marry Gordon at one point."

"Yeah. But the engagement was rushed. We moved too fast." Gordon had never considered our pace fast. The speed had been my complaint.

"He is cute."

I smiled as I sipped more ginger ale. "Yes, he is."

"Better grab Gordon, Daisy. He strikes me as a keeper."

"Yeah." I thought about the dark pink plus sign on the pregnancy test buried deep in my bathroom trash can. How would I explain this to him? How could I tell a guy I really loved I was pregnant with another man's baby. "He is."

"When will he be back?"

"Monday." When he'd left a couple of days ago I'd been sorry to see him go. Now I was glad for the break. I had to find a doctor and get a blood test so by the time he returned I knew one way or the other about the pregnancy. I tried to think good thoughts about flu and food poisoning.

"Well, if you two decide to take your relationship up a notch and tie the knot, call me. You getting hitched is an event I'd like to see."

I imagined us standing by the Potomac saying our vows. "No one is getting hitched anytime soon."

"Never know." She gave me a quick salute. "So are we doing the going-away party tomorrow?"

"We are. Mom and Dad shove off with the girls in the morning so let's shoot for five. You, me, and Rachel."

"We'll walk to a pub and drink like we did when we were teenagers."

I offered a thumbs-up, already knowing if I drank a drop of wine I'd throw up. "Right."

"See ya."

Alone in the dusty kitchen I stared at the hole and thought about the wall that had stood guard here all my life and provided a refuge office for my grandfather, my dad, and me. And now it was gone.

The front door bells of the bakery chimed and I cursed Margaret for not locking the door. One fact I'd discovered about retail was that no matter what time of day or year, if the front door was unlocked someone assumed we were open.

I pushed through the saloon doors to find an attractive man dressed in dark, pleated pants, an ironed monogramed white shirt, and expensive tasseled loafers. I recognized him from my financial days and the five or six custom orders he'd placed with the bakery. Chocolate espresso cake. Simon Davenport. He was on the verge of launching a new development near the river, and the Union Street Bakery had done some catering for him in the last weeks. Nothing large yet, but the stream of business had been steady. And best of all he paid on time and his checks always cleared.

Reaching for a towel behind the counter, I wiped my hands. "Simon, what brings you to our neck of the woods today?"

He adjusted horn-rimmed glasses. "I hoped to place an order. But I see you are closing for a couple of weeks. The party is week after next."

My dad's heart for business beat strong in my chest, and I couldn't let potential income pass without at least asking. "We're making minor renovations. What kind of party?"

"Launch of the Waterside Project. We're inviting key investors to walk the site. Always nice to have good food on hand when you're trying to make a sale."

"Fat and sugar do make the world go round." The last job we'd done for him had netted us a grand. One thousand dollars would sure take the sting out of being closed for the next thirteen days. "We might be able to help you. I'm always willing to work with a good customer. How many people at the party"

"Forty."

A good number. Not so huge but big enough for a decent payout. "And you'd need this when?"

"Nine days." I ticked through a mental calendar. It was a Monday. "What would you like?"

"I hoped Rachel would have suggestions. She has a knack for knowing what people like."

"Let me get her. Wait right here."

"Great."

I found Rachel upstairs in her apartment, standing in front of a pile of clean but unfolded children's laundry. She stared at the pile. "Packing for the girls?"

"Attempting." She reached for a pair of little red shorts. "They're going to need so much, and I don't know where to start."

Recognizing she obsessed over details when she worried, I kept my tone light. "They're going to the beach. They need a bathing suit, one change of clothes and flip-flops."

She plucked the matching set of red pants from the pile and studied the two together. "I always rotate their outfits."

"Why?"

"Because."

Stress deepened normally nonexistent lines on her forehead. I was stressed about closing the bakery and so was Rachel. Love it or hate it, the bakery was the glue in her life. "Don't worry about the clothes. Keep it simple. You know Mom. The girls will likely wear the same clothes the whole time. Like when we were kids, she'd wash our clothes at night and have them ready for us in the morning."

A grim smile tugged the edge of her mouth. "We looked like urchins half the time."

"We're well fed, and the clothes, though they might not have matched, were clean. And we survived, like the girls will survive a less-than-perfect fashionable week." I jabbed my thumb toward the door. "Simon is downstairs, and he wants to place an order."

"We are closed."

"Not for a good client. He wants to talk to you."

She clutched the red pants close to her chest. "Where will I bake?"

"Find out what he wants and we'll take it from there. We can always bake in your apartment or mom's kitchen."

"That's not right."

"Rachel. He's waiting. Let's go now." She looked up at me, her expression so glum it took me aback. "Hey, I thought you were Ms. Positive."

"I'm out of positive vibes right now."

I raised my hand in a mock cheer pose hoping to coax a smile. "You can do it. Let's go see Simon."

Without smiling she nodded. "I can do it."

"I didn't hear you?"

"I can do it."

Pitiful. I lowered my arms, wondering how the hell I ended up with the cheerleader job. "He's out front. He wants your ideas."

That bit of news had her lifting her gaze. "Out front now."

"In the front of the store as we speak."

She tucked a stray curl behind her ear. A warm blush colored her cheeks.

For a very split second I considered teasing her about her reaction. She acted as if she liked the guy. But if I hinted about a sexual attraction, she'd retreat. Rachel had been a near saint since Mike's death, and the idea she might harbor an attraction for another male, in her mind, would be akin to a betrayal.

"You need to talk cookies with the man. Now. Before he thinks we ran off or died."

"Okay. Sure." She tossed the pants aside and followed me down the stairs.

When she pushed through the saloon doors, he nodded when he saw her and then adjusted his glasses. "Rachel. Good to see you."

She offered a shy smile. "Simon. It's good to see you. I hope those éclairs worked out for your last gathering."

"They were perfect. I told your sister you seem to know what people like."

I puttered behind the counter, pretending to straighten as they talked cookies, pies, and cream puffs. After fifteen minutes, they came up with a menu of assorted cookies.

Simon, his gaze still on Rachel, said, "Daisy, you'll work up a price."

"I'll have it on your desk in the morning."

"And the construction won't be a problem?"

"Piece of cake."

As I headed in the back my phone chirped, and I glanced at the text.

MISS YOU! It was from Gordon.

My fingers teetered over the keys. I missed him. My hand slid to my stomach. I prayed I'd not screwed it all up.

Chapter Four

Sunday, 7:35 A.M.
13 days until grand reopening
Income Lost: $0

Five-year-old twins Ellie and Anna, dressed in matching pink polka-dotted bikini bathing suits, squealed as they ran around Rachel's apartment. Anna was the fair-skinned child with a full blond ponytail and peaches and cream complexion, whereas Ellie had olive skin, and her ponytail was a deep rich brown. Both wore blue sunglasses and flip-flops. Rachel's artist's eye allowed her to coordinate the colors of a cake as easily as her girls' swim apparel.

As I leaned against the doorjamb of their apartment, cradling another ginger ale, I watched the girls chanting, "Going to the beach," as they ran around the overstuffed sofa.

Rachel's second-floor place was bigger than mine, though by most apartment standards it was small. However, she made the best of the space. The sofa was also a pullout bed. Storage chests doubled as coffee and end tables. Shelves lined the entire north wall and exhibited a neatly organized collection of books, pictures, and knickknacks. The dining table was round and sat four but there were leaves somewhere, which extended the eating space.

Off to the side was a small L-shaped kitchen outfitted with a full pot rack, butcher-block island, and narrow granite countertops. Her stove was electric and small, nothing special, but she'd baked delicacies in the oven. Dishes filled the sinks and a glance into hers and the girls' bedrooms revealed unmade beds.

Any available wall space showcased pictures of the twins. It seemed every moment from birth until now had been documented. And of course there were pictures of Mike. In one shot he hugged Rachel and her very pregnant belly. In another he looked bleary-eyed and tired as he cuddled his infant daughters. In another, he stood behind the counter of the bakery, grinning broadly.

Rachel and Mike had met in high school. His home life had not been the best. I knew his parents were divorced, and his dad had moved away by the time he'd met Rachel. He'd fallen in love with her and also with the entire McCrae clan, who offered a sense of security he'd never enjoyed.

He and I had never gotten along. We could be polite, but he enjoyed making me the butt of jokes that weren't really funny. The jokes all had to do with my not being a real McCrae. I can look back now and recognize he was jealous of my spot in the family. He wanted to nudge me out and take the lone spot for the non-McCrae McCrae. But I've always said never cross swords with an adoptee, especially if they have abandonment issues. We are tenacious fighters, and my grip on this family would have to be pried out of my cold dead hands. Needless to say, we bickered a lot.

"I get to go in the ocean first," Ellie announced.

"No, I get to go in the ocean first," Anna countered.

The girls volleyed words and declarations back and forth. Soon a headache pounded behind my eyes as Rachel calmly packed the final items for the girls.

"How do you do it?" I asked.

She didn't look up from the suitcase as she counted, for the second time, sets of socks. "Do what?"

"The kids. I think I'd run screaming into the street."

A faint smile lifted the edges of her mouth. "There are days when I am tempted."

As if realizing they were the center of conversation, the girls stopped and stared at their mother and then me. Anna, the more aggressive of the twins, looked at me with a clear direct gaze. "How come you and Mom aren't coming to the beach?"

"Got a kitchen to renovate, kid," I said. "Can't knock out walls from the beach."

"But Jean Paul is building the kitchen," Ellie said.

"Someone has to be there to answer questions."

"Like what kind of questions?" Anna asked.

I pressed the cool can of ginger ale to the side of my head. "I don't know."

"How come you don't know?" Ellie said.

"I just don't."

Anna studied me. "But how come?"

"I don't know Jean Paul's question until he asks it. And only when he asks it can I figure out an answer."

"What if he doesn't have any questions?" Anna said.

"He will."

"How do you know?" Ellie said.

I glanced at Rachel, who grinned. "You do this all the time?"

"All the time."

I sipped my ginger ale. There was a doc-in-the-box medical center opening at eight, and I planned to be first in line for a blood test. I'd never prayed so hard for the flu.

Anna ran up to me and showed me her hair bow. "Do you like pink?"

"Pink." I scrunched up my face as if thinking. "On you, it's very pretty. But it's not my first choice."

"What color do you like?"

"Right now?" I sipped my soda. "Plain white."

Heavy footsteps sounded outside Rachel's apartment, and we all turned to see Mom and Dad dressed in shorts and matching Hawaiian shirts. The shirts had to have been Mom's idea. Back in the day, Dad would never have been caught dead in such a getup. But then he'd never been going on vacation. He'd worked seven days a week for fifty-plus years and not once had he closed the bakery outside of the few weeks after the holidays. Since he'd retired two years ago, they'd driven to a dozen different cities. I'd never figured my folks for the wandering traveler kind, but then fifty years was a long time to work on a bucket list.

The girls squealed louder as they ran up to Mom and Dad. Both my parents laughed and hugged the girls close. No denying Ellie and Anna were getting the fun vacation energy my parents had never been able to lavish on their own children.

Rachel zipped up the suitcase and hauled it off the couch.

"So," Dad said, giving me a hug. "How goes the renovation?"

"I'm surprised you haven't had a look."

"Nope, you girls are running the show." His cheery tone had me wondering if he believed the words or practiced them so many times so he could sound convincing. "I'm a bystander."

Mom laughed. "I threatened to break his feet if he looked."

Dad shrugged. "I wasn't going to look."

"Yes, you were," Mom said.

I'd been careful since taking over the bakery to minimize how much I told Dad about business problems. He'd carried the load of working and raising a family for a long time, and those old work habits, so deeply ingrained, could make tugging him back into the fray easy. After all he'd done for us, it would break my heart to see him working again. He and Mom really did deserve to savor their golden years.

"It's good. We packed up all the equipment yesterday and demoed the office wall. A little slow going because we want to reuse the brick."

His gaze grew wistful. "Spent many an hour in that office. Like an old friend as far as I am concerned."

"Yeah, I'll miss her, too, but she had to take one for the team. We need the space for the freezer. But no worries, we've talked about building a new office in the basement."

Old Spice aftershave wafted around as he gave me a hug and kissed me on the cheek. "That's my girl. And you have Rachel and Margaret to help."

"I'll have Rachel," I said. "Margaret has a great job up in St. Mary's County. A big dig."

He frowned. "She didn't tell me."

Thanks, Margaret, you coward. "She's excited and rushed. And with the shop closed there really isn't much for her to do."

He nodded. "When she's not busy, she grumbles and complains."

"You've noticed?"

He chuckled. "I have."

"Frank," Mom said, "if we don't get on the road now we are going to hit traffic. It'll take us every bit of six hours to get to Nags Head, and I don't want to waste a minute of beach time."

The girls squealed. Dad clapped his hands together and laughed. "Then let's get this show on the road."

The six of us proceeded down the stairs and out the back alley where Dad had parked his white Buick. The girls scrambled into car seats Rachel had installed this morning, and as Dad crammed the girls' bag in the trunk, Mom gave me a hug.

"You look tired." She spoke softly so Dad couldn't hear. "You feeling all right, honey?"

"Never better, Mom. Please go and take your vacation."

"Are you sure?" Her blue eyes darkened with mother's guilt and worry. "I can always stay and take care of you."

A part of me wanted to pull her aside and ask, *What does pregnant feel like?* But that question would have sent both my parents into a hysterical tailspin. They'd cancel their vacation and spend the week hovering over me.

No, this very explosive question—if I were lucky—would never, ever have to be asked.

Rachel kissed her girls, Dad slid behind the wheel, and Mom hugged us both again. Finally, after a great deal of fanfare, my parents and nieces set off on the grand beach vacation.

As the car turned the corner and vanished out of sight, Rachel and I stood there savoring the silence.

"Amazing how much noise two well-behaved little girls can make," I said.

Rachel shook her head. "They weren't trying to be loud."

"I can't imagine."

"Any bets on how soon it'll take for the girls to break Mom and Dad?"

I sipped my soda. "Three or four days."

Rachel shook her head. "This time tomorrow they'll be wondering what truck hit them."

"Mom swears this is going to be so much fun."

"*Too* much fun."

I laughed. "Two days. They'll cut it short in two days."

"Three days," Rachel said extending her hand.

"And the winner gets what?"

"A free round of drinks at O'Malley's. You can name your poison."

Drinks. If this pink-plus problem didn't clear up, my poison was going to be milk.

Making a lame excuse to Rachel about a drugstore run for peanut candy bars and a Diet Coke, I left the bakery for the doctor's office. Weekend office hours began at eight and by the time I drove the five miles and parked, it was eight twenty. Already, the waiting room was full.

I signed in and spoke to the receptionist through the little glass partition. "What's the wait look like?"

A young girl not more than twenty with bleached blond hair and darkly lined eyes didn't spare a glance away from her computer screen. "Thirty or forty minutes."

Somewhere behind me a kid hacked and coughed. "So where did all these people come from?"

"It's Sunday. The line was five deep when I opened the doors."

"Next time I'll be sure to come early." I'd hoped to make a personal connection with the girl, believing it might get me bumped up in line. But she hadn't spared me a single look.

Reception girl pressed a computer key over and over. "I'll call you when I need to take your insurance card."

I sat in a corner as far away from everyone resembling sick and hugged my purse close to my chest. The magazines on the small table ranged from *Good Housekeeping* to *Parenting* to *Time*. I picked up *Time*. The issue was six weeks old and the pages fairly beaten up.

I flipped through the pages, glancing at headlines and the occasional picture but found concentration in short supply.

"Ms. McCrae."

Grateful to have my name called, I tossed the magazine aside and hurried to the little cubicle room where another young girl asked for my insurance card and a picture ID. Thanks to the buyout at my old company, my insurance would remain intact for another six months, which, if I really was pregnant, was right around the due date. I had visions of watching the insurance clock tick away as the baby stubbornly refused birthing. How much did it cost to have a baby? Ellie and Anna had been six weeks early and had cost a fortune, but I'd never gotten hard numbers. I wasn't sure if two babies earned a discount on each unit.

I slid my card and ID across the desk.

"Have you ever been here before?"

"No."

"And why are we here today?" This gal was dressed in light blue scrubs as if she were in the medical field, but I suspected the scrubs were for show.

I leaned forward, trying to make light of what could be a disaster. "We are here for a pregnancy test."

My use of *we* earned me a raised eyebrow before the woman typed my info into the computer. After more moments of silent typing, she slid my cards back to me and rang a bell. Another nurse appeared and escorted me to a curtained room.

The nurse snapped the curtain closed behind her and moved to a station equipped with a computer. I climbed up on the table lined with white paper.

"You are here for a pregnancy test, correct?"

Her deep voice carried and I envisioned a customer or God forbid a family member standing outside the curtain. Wishing for a door, I shifted my weight, causing the paper under my rear to crinkle. "That is correct."

"Do you have any idea of how far along you might be?"

"Sixteen weeks, one day."

She glanced back at me, her gaze direct. "You're sure?"

I folded my arms over my chest grateful to give voice to the thoughts dogging me. "March 21 at about 1 A.M."

The nurse frowned. "Did you take a home pregnancy test?"

I wished she'd stop saying the P-word. "I did. The pink plus didn't show up right away. Took a couple of hours. I have it in my purse in a ziplock if you'd like to see it." I'd considered throwing it away but had visions of Rachel finding it. My plan was to save it, then deposit it in a trash can far, far away from the bakery.

"That's not necessary."

I leaned forward. "These home tests, they are kind of bogus, right? They aren't really good."

"They're pretty accurate."

"But what do you mean by accurate? I mean, I would think a real positive would show up right away and not take its sweet time."

She faced me with a needle and syringe. "Let's get some blood."

I rolled up my sleeve and looked away. After a small pinch, seconds passed and she stuck a Band-Aid on my arm. "Test results will be in this time tomorrow."

"You can't tell me now? The home test promises fast results, so it seems like you could match or best that time. You are a medical facility."

She laid a hand on my shoulder. "You want accurate or fast?"

"Both."

Her gaze softened. "Sorry, hon, but either way you'll have your answer this time tomorrow."

"You do understand right now time has stopped for me and in my world twenty-four hours is equal to an entire decade?"

She patted me on the shoulder. "Keep busy. Don't think about it."

"Really?"

She typed into a computer screen and printed out a receipt for me. "You feeling sick in the mornings?"

"More like morning, noon, and night. Though I seem to get about an hour's break a half hour before bedtime."

"Ginger ale and crackers. Have 'em both on your nightstand and have both before your feet hit the ground in the morning."

"Right. Thanks."

As she turned to leave, my phone buzzed. I fished it out of my purse and glanced at it. The text was from Gordon. HEY, BABE. EVERY-THING ALL RIGHT? DIDN'T SEE A TEXT BACK FROM YOU LAST NIGHT. SEE YOU TOMORROW. G.

I stared at the text for long, tense seconds. I should tell him it was all good. But it wasn't all good. I slid the phone back into my purse and left the doctor's office wishing like hell the next twenty-four hours would pass fast.

Rachel, Jean Paul, and I spent the day clearing out the remainder of the wall. The next step was for Jean Paul to install the electrical work, and once done we could call the city inspector, get the all-clear, and then put it all back together.

By five I stopped working to take a hot shower. A grateful sigh escaped my lips as I stood under the hot spray while it washed away the sweat and grime clinging to my body. If only problems could wash away as easily as dirt, I'd be set.

As I toweled off, I glanced toward the desk in my room and caught sight of the recipe box. I'd all but forgotten about it. Crossing the room,

I carefully thumbed through the cards. I glanced at the neatly written cards and for a moment was tempted to sit and look at each one. But I had barely ten minutes to dress before Rachel and I met Margaret.

Rachel and I arrived at O'Malley's after six.

I wanted a stiff drink but knew I'd be settling for soda. My phone buzzed again and I glanced at it. Gordon. Another text. DAISY. CALL. Shorter and more terse. He was officially annoyed. I could have brushed off yesterday with the excuse of the demo, but today I had officially crossed over into rude.

"Why don't you call him?" Rachel and I walked along Union Street. The gentle breeze wafting off the Potomac warmed my skin. Smiling tourists filled the paths.

"I'll catch up with him later."

"Is he having fun on his big bike ride?"

"Gordon loves his bikes. He should have taken up this career after college."

"Why didn't he?"

"Too smart. His parents did not want to see an Ivy League education go to waste. And he is very good with numbers." I'd not known him back in college. In fact, I'd not known his story until weeks ago when he'd told me. We'd both dropped the walls. And now I was putting one back up.

"You don't talk much about the time you two were engaged."

"Both of us weren't ready to be a couple. The sex was great. So great. And for a time, it was enough. But I feared we were building a life on shaky ground."

She nibbled her bottom lip, a question burning in her gaze. She dropped her voice to a near whisper. "So is the sex as good as it used to be?"

My mature assessment of my relationship buzzed right over her head. She'd been blinded by the mention of sex. "Rachel. I'm shocked. Since when did you ask questions like that?"

She shrugged, still chewing on her lip. "I might as well live vicariously through you. One of the McCrae sisters has to be getting it."

Laughter rumbled in my chest. "You never talk about sex."

"Yeah, well, I've changed. Death, kids, and a bakery will do that." She shoved her hands in her pockets. "Motherhood changes you. We moms still like sex but other things get in the way. My heart is now controlled by two little girls in bathing suits at the beach with parents who haven't had young kids underfoot in thirty years."

I reached for the brass door of O'Malley's. "You worried about Mom and Dad taking care of the girls?"

Music and laughter washed out from the bar. "I worry about everything. It's my specialty."

"Have you called Mom?"

"Twice. She forgot to turn her phone on again."

"You know Mom loves her landlines. She'll call once they're settled."

"I know."

Deeper inside the bar, music mingled with the buzz of conversation and the smell of beer on tap. For a Sunday night the place hummed with activity. The bar served a light dinner, and weeks ago I'd called on the owner to see if they'd like to order rolls for their dinner service. I'd gotten a big maybe. Would be real nice to have more restaurant orders to supplement the grocery store order.

I scanned the crowd for Margaret and spotted her in a corner booth. She saw me, raised her hands, and we wove our way toward her.

Rachel slid into the booth next to Margaret, and I sat on the other side. As we settled, a waitress appeared with three beers and set them on our table.

"I went ahead and ordered," Margaret said. "Figured you could use a cold one after your day."

A grateful Rachel picked up her cold glass and took a long, liberal sip. She closed her eyes as she drank.

Margaret looked at me, amusement dancing in her gaze. "Little sis, you looking to tie one on."

Rachel nodded. "Yes. It's been years since I had a full beer without worrying about the girls. I figure I've a day or two maximum before the girls break Mom and Dad, and they all come rushing home. I need to make hay while the sun shines."

Margaret chuckled as she raised her glass. "Well, drinks are on me, babe, so as long as you can slam 'em down I'll buy 'em."

I raised my glass. "A toast to Margaret. Super history sleuth who loves to dig in the dirt and play with old bones."

Margaret nodded. "Amen."

Rachel swiped the back of her hand over her mouth as if she were a sailor fresh in port. "I hope you have lots of fun digging in the dirt."

As I pretended to sip, Margaret took a long drink. "I am going to make a huge discovery. I can feel it in my bones. I am going to be an archeological rock star."

Grinning, I couldn't help but enjoy her enthusiasm. "And we will say we knew you when."

Rachel finished her beer.

As I swapped out my beer for her empty glass, the bandage from this morning's blood sample rubbed against my skin under my shirt. "Still a bit of that bug. Take mine, and I'll get a soda."

"Must be serious," Margaret said. "You never get sick."

I caught the waitress's attention and ordered a soda. "Bound to happen with all the customers we deal with. I'll be fine in a day or two." Eighteen years at the outside.

"So you demoed the wall today?"

"We did. Monday is wiring and new studs."

Rachel smiled. "To studs."

Margaret burst out laughing.

"Our little girl is growing up," I said. "She's been asking about S-E-X."

"Really?"

Rachel shrugged as she finished another half beer. "It's been a long, long dry spell. I mean you try being married to a guy who's stressing about a business while you are chasing twin girls. Not much been going on in Rachel's love life for a very, very long time."

"There's time for love," I said.

"Yeah, like when? I will be thirty-five in two months. I've slept with exactly one guy in my life." She held up her index finger as if we needed visual aids. "I want to know what it feels like to have a man touch me again before I die."

Margaret sat back in her booth. "Okay, I take back what I said about buying you all the beer you want. I figured I was in for one, maybe two beers, but I can see you could drink me out of my life savings tonight."

The waitress delivered my soda and I took a long sip. My stomach lurched but didn't buck. I'd arrived at the sweet spot in the evening when I wasn't exhausted or sick. Most nights I turned in by nine but tonight, with no store to open tomorrow, I could actually enjoy an adult bedtime.

"Did you two go over the recipe box?" Margaret asked.

"Honestly, demolishing the wall didn't give us any time."

"I wish I had a little time to go through it," Margaret said. "Like a mini–time capsule."

I glanced around the bar, hoping to spot the waitress who could bring me bread to soothe my stomach. As I did, I spotted Simon Davenport by the bar. Dressed in jeans, a V-neck sweater, and expensive loafers, he appeared to be alone.

"Rachel," I said. "Don't look now but Simon is at the bar."

"Who?"

"Simon Davenport. Remember, he's the dude who hates sweets but who has placed five big orders in the last couple of months. The dude who must have a little crush on you."

Rachel moistened her lips. Beer had left her cheeks flushed. "Do you really think he likes me?"

Margaret glanced in his direction, studying him as if he were an artifact found at a dig. "Totally."

Alone we were articulate woman in our thirties. Together we reverted to middle school and might as well have been standing by the hall lockers with our arms full of textbooks as we ogled the football quarterback.

"You should go over and talk to him," Margaret said.

"Yeah," I prodded. "I mean you do want another beer, and it would be so much easier to get it from the bar."

Rachel nodded. "I could get a beer from the bar."

Margaret handed her a ten-dollar bill. "Go get a beer and say hi to the nice man."

Rachel ran her fingers through her blond hair. "Do you really think he likes me?"

"Yes."

A frown furrowed her brow. "How can you tell?"

"Rachel, go," I said. "Worst-case scenario you get a beer, say hi, and come back here."

She nibbled her lip. "That's not such a bad scenario."

"No, it is not."

Rachel rose, swayed a little, and walked stiffly toward the bar.

"She's not had a date since high school," Margaret said.

"I know. But she might as well practice, or she'll spend the rest of her life in the bakery."

Rachel stood at the bar, her ten-dollar bill clutched in her hand. Simon leaned a fraction closer as he spoke to her. To Rachel's credit she looked up at him with what looked like genuine surprise.

"Our little girl is a player," I said.

"I'm so proud." Margaret leaned forward, staring with open interest as Simon, head slightly tilted, spoke to Rachel. She tucked her hair behind her ear, rested her hand on her hip, and then slid it in her pocket as if she didn't know what to do with it. She was a fluttering butterfly whereas he stood tall and strong like a hundred-year-old oak. Rachel needed a guy who could be fun and make her laugh. Simon's fun-meter didn't look like it registered high. But he was nice, and this wasn't a marriage or a date. It was a little practice flirtation.

Rachel took her beer from the bartender and gave him the ten. He put five back on the bar as change but she didn't seem to notice.

"She's not brothering to pick up the change." Margaret slid to the edge of the seat as if to rise. "I should get five bucks back."

"Don't you dare."

"Five bucks is a lot of money." But Margaret halted, clutching the edge of the booth as if ready to sprint to get her five.

Rachel tucked her hair behind her ear and laughed. He leaned a little closer to her. It looked good. Real good.

And then a tall brunette approached Simon and slid her arm in his. He didn't pull away. Didn't blink. The woman was tall, slim, and wore a short silk dress skimming tanned, very well-toned thighs. Tall metallic high heels matched gold bracelets and hoop earrings.

Rachel's smile froze on her face. She raised her beer to her lips but didn't take a sip.

"Shit. A She Devil has staked her claim," I said.

Simon at least had the decency to stand a little straighter. He looked like he'd been caught with his hand in the cookie jar.

Margaret's eyes narrowed. "We can't leave her hanging. Cover me. I'm going in."

"What do you mean?"

She pushed to her feet and crossed toward Rachel, Simon, and the She Devil.

"Well, hey," Margaret said as she moved to the bar beside Rachel and picked up her five. "Never seen you here before."

Groaning, I slid out of the booth and came up behind Margaret in time to catch Rachel's shocked expression. "Hi, Mr. Davenport."

"Simon. Please call me Simon."

"Right. Sure." I looked at She Devil. "Hi, I'm Daisy McCrae. My sisters Margaret and Rachel."

She Devil's smile didn't reach her eyes. She'd sunk her talons into Simon, and she was not going to let go. "Elizabeth Wentworth. Nice to meet you. But I know Rachel. We cheered together in high school."

Rachel's smile turned brittle as she smoothed her hands over worn jeans and surveyed Elizabeth's watered-silk dress. "Elizabeth. You look great."

Rachel and I were the same year as Elizabeth in school but I hung with the drama kids and the nerds. Rachel and Elizabeth were strictly with cheerleaders and football players.

I'd never formally met Elizabeth but had heard stories. Passive-aggressive. Lots of lip gloss and hair spray. Dated the backup quarter-back. "And you look, well, like you've been working hard."

Simon's gaze sparked with interest. "You two went to high school together?" he asked.

Elizabeth laughed. "Hard to believe, right? Rachel, you still work in your parents' bakery? Gosh, she used to make the cutest cupcakes for the team. Of course, we were all on diets and couldn't eat a bite."

"Rachel and I both own the bakery now," I said.

"They've done some catering for my company," Simon offered.

Rachel drew in a breath. I kept waiting for the perky smile guaranteed to make everyone feel as if it would be okay. Her lips flickered at the edges but the hundred-watt smile would not fire.

"So what brings you all here tonight?" Elizabeth said as she glanced beyond us to see who else was here.

"My sisters are giving me a going-away party," Margaret said. "I've a job working on an archeological dig.

Elizabeth looked bored. "Awesome."

Simon to his credit raised a brow. "Where?"

"St. Mary's Church up in Maryland. On the bay. Leaving tomorrow." Her grin broadened. "Old bones rock my world."

"Sounds like a great challenge," Simon said.

"I'm working for Simon's company," Elizabeth offered. She smoothed a manicured hand over perfect hair. "Vice president of sales. So far breaking all quotas."

"Super." Margaret glanced at Rachel. We'd made fun of Elizabeth when we were in high school. If one of us were having a petulant moment, we were pulling an *Elizabeth*.

Rachel seemed to have forgotten. Whatever had fired when she'd first spoken to Simon was extinguished, and now she had a hurtpuppy vibe.

As I scrambled for reasons to drag Rachel away, Margaret turned and wobbled, and her beer sloshed wildly in her hands. The beer splashed up all over her, Simon, and She Devil.

She Devil arched back as if she'd been splashed with acid, but Simon remained calm. He reached for a napkin, She Devil squawked, and Margaret apologized.

"I can be such a klutz," Margaret said. "Gosh, I'm sorry."

Gosh, I'm sorry. Margaret hadn't said *gosh* or *sorry* in a sentence . . .

well, ever. She'd basically told Rachel and I in secret sister code, *I wish I'd drenched She Devil.*

"Hey, good seeing you two." I hooked my arms into Rachel's and Margaret's. Another minute and Margaret would douse Elizabeth, and I might be tempted to help. I pulled my sisters toward our table and we sat. Margaret and Rachel drank heavily, and I was grateful my stomach was settled.

"What's it like to be Elizabeth's kind of successful?" Rachel said to me. "When you were in D.C. you had her kind of vibe."

"It was great. To know you were in a groove. Yeah, great."

"And life sucks for you now?" Rachel said.

"Not exactly sucks. It's different."

Margaret studied me. "Would you go back if you could?"

In a heartbeat. "I don't know."

Margaret's gaze narrowed. "Of course you know. You aren't saying."

"I'd go back in a snap," Rachel said. "I wasn't Elizabeth, but I was in a great place. Hard work and crazy hours, but I really did love my life when Mike was alive."

Margaret sipped her beer. "I've lots of education and dozens of part-time jobs to look back on, but there's no great accomplishment. I'm thirty-six and can finally hold my head up when someone asks me what I do for a living."

I understood. I held my head high, but it was a lot of bravado these days. "I'm glad you have the job in St. Mary's. It was made for you."

"Enjoy it," Rachel said. "Savor every moment."

Margaret frowned. "You make it sound like it's not going to last."

I wished I could have said otherwise but having a company shot out from under me had changed my worldview. "I hope it lasts forever."

Margaret held up her half-full beer mug. "A statement loaded with enthusiasm."

Rachel shook her head. "The fact is, Margaret, it doesn't matter how hard you love your work, sometimes life dumps on you. You can fight, scream, scrap, or beg, but life doesn't give a shit and it takes what it wants."

Jobs came and went and some really were terrific . . . really terrific, but losing family was a game changer.

Adding family also changed the game. What had Mom always said in high school? *For God's sake, whatever you do, don't get pregnant.* Damn.

"I don't want you to leave. Crap, Margaret, we were getting into a groove," Rachel mumbled. "I know you have to go, but I'm not going to like it."

Margaret was silent, and I could see leaving wasn't going to be easy. When I'd left the bakery at eighteen, I'd been full of steam and had no intentions of looking back. But Margaret had stayed in Alexandria and had tried to help when she could. Yeah, she could be bitchy and grumpy but she was loyal to the bone.

"I swear on Mom and Dad's lives if you stay, I will kill you," I said.

Rachel finished her beer. "Ditto."

Chapter Five

Sunday, 9:00 P.M.
12 days, 10 hours until grand reopening
Income Lost: $0

By the time I climbed the stairs to my room, my limbs drooped as if each weighed thousands of pounds. My stomach was settled, but my head pounded.

It had always seemed if you were carrying life inside of you, you'd feel good and full of energy. It never occurred to me you'd feel as if a truck had slammed into you. Mom and Rachel both had had great pregnancies. Tons of energy and no morning sickness. But I didn't share their genetics. I shared my birth mother Terry's DNA.

Terry and I had reunited a couple of months ago. It had not been a greeting-card moment but rather a tense and very trying meeting. She'd been more nervous than me, and she'd also feared I'd tell her husband and sons I existed. Hard learning you were someone's dirty little secret.

While we'd sat in the upscale Alexandria hotel lobby, she'd tried to explain the reasons behind my abandonment. I had been a good kid, she'd said. It wasn't my fault. She'd been a young mother, she'd explained. It wasn't personal.

Intellectually, I understood what she was saying. But my brain and emotions didn't always communicate so well. If I'd been such a great kid, then why not tell the world about me? Why did I need to be a secret?

I pushed through my bedroom door, flipped on a light and sat on my bed. The springs groaned and squeaked as I pulled off my shoes.

My phone rang, and I glanced at it. Gordon. Drawing in a breath I hit Send. "Hey."

"Hey, yourself." He sounded surprised to hear my voice. "Did you get my texts?"

"Yeah, and I'm sorry." I pinched the bridge of my nose with my fingertips. "Demoing the wall was a mess and then Margaret said she's quitting."

"Why's Margaret leaving?" The tangible reasons seemed to ease the edge from his voice.

"She's gotten a great job. Long story. I'll tell you when you get back."

"You doing okay? You sound tired."

Morning memories of my doctor's visit flashed. I wanted so much to tell Gordon. He was my friend. I wanted him to be my lover again. I wanted a life with him.

But the words wouldn't come. Instead, sudden tears filled my eyes, and as I glanced toward the ceiling they trickled down my face. "I am tired. It's been a long day." Clearing my throat, I said, "How did the bike ride go? You didn't lose anyone, did you?"

"Nearly lost one or two, but we had a head count of twelve when we reached the inn."

"Same twelve?"

He chuckled. "More or less."

"When do you get back?"

"Tomorrow afternoon."

"Well, I'll be here protecting the home front as Jean Paul rewires electrical outlets."

"I'll come by."

I'd have the results by ten tomorrow. "I'll come by your place. It's insane here."

"I love you."

I drew in a deep breath. "I love you, too."

When I ended the call, I held the phone to my chest. Tears dampened my cheeks. I had been nudging my life back to a new sense of normal, and now it teetered on the edge.

Setting the phone down, I rose and moved toward a small desk in the corner. I wanted to call Mom. I wanted her to take me in her arms and tell me I would be okay. But she was somewhere on a beach in North Carolina likely exhausted after chasing two five-year-olds around all day.

And right now, what did I have to tell her? I was afraid. I might have messed up.

I slipped the phone on the charger and stripped off my clothes, letting them remain where they hit the ground. The air cooled my skin as I grabbed an extra-extra-large T-shirt hanging on the back of the door and slipped it on. I pulled my hair from a ponytail and ran my fingers over my scalp, letting my gaze land on the recipe box.

I flipped open the lid and glanced at the browning, brittle cards. Gently I thumbed through the cards.

Moving back to my bed, I sat, pressed my back to the wall, and cradled the box in my lap. I chose a card from the center because it appeared more worn and tattered than the others. It was a recipe for pumpkin bread. Judging by the subtle stains and the frayed edges, it had been a favorite. The handwriting was delicate and precise. Clearly whoever had copied the recipe had taken great care. Sixty years ago there had been cookbooks of course but many relied on recipes passed from generation to generation.

I raised the card to my nose, expecting the musty scent of time but instead inhaled the scents of cinnamon and nutmeg. Closing my eyes, I tried to imagine the bakery seventy years ago. America would have been at war with Germany and Japan. There'd have been rations. Alexandria, a port city so close to Washington, D.C., would have been awash in soldiers. The art center on the waterfront, now called the Torpedo Factory, was really a torpedo factory. No Internet. No cell phones or laptops.

The idea of traveling back seventy years did not appeal. And yet people then had lived their lives as we do today. They'd loved, married, and had children—every emotion lived before by another. The cadence of life had been slower before technology but the experiences were the same.

"So why did you hide this box in the wall? What was so precious in this box?"

Flipping through the cards, I saw more entries written as neatly and carefully as the first. Pies, cakes, and cookies. All had been used but not so worn as the pumpkin bread.

Behind all the cards was a small photo featuring three people. A twentysomething young woman dressed in a white bakery uniform stood in the center of two men, both dressed in military uniforms. The woman pinned her dark hair back in a bun and though she wore no makeup, her vibrant smile made her beautiful. The men appeared to be a bit older. The one on the left was shorter and broader and wore his cap cocked to the left. The other man was tall and lean with fair hair, had set his cap straight, and though he also smiled, he seemed a bit more serious. Each wrapped their arms around the woman, but she leaned a little closer to the man on her right. The trio stood in front of a sandwich board reading, UNION STREET BAKERY.

Smiling, I leaned in and studied the building behind her. I recognized the bakery's front door. I knew the door had been changed out several times but the style remained the same. I flipped over the picture and saw written on the back, *Jenna, 1944.*

So who were you, Jenna? I fished the dog tags out of the box and ran my fingers over Sergeant Walter Franklin Jacob's name.

"I'm guessing the tall, serious one is Walter." But I could have been wrong.

Dad had said once he'd stowed the bakery archives in his attic. In 1944, Dad would have been two, so if he had crossed paths with Jenna he wouldn't have remembered.

I studied Jenna's profile and looked closer. Her smile, her brightness, and her zest captured my imagination. Gently I traced her profile. I'd never thought much about the archives but now I was curious about Jenna. She'd been young. She was clearly close to two different men and she'd taken the time to hide a recipe collection in the walls of the bakery with Walter's dog tags.

I searched the box for any other photos but found none. I closed the lid and then my eyes. Worries quickly crowded out Jenna's questions.

"In the morning the doctor is going to tell me I have no worries. Gordon is going to come home. I am going to tell him how much I love him, and this will all be forgotten."

Chapter Six

Monday, 7:55 A.M.
12 days until grand reopening
Income Lost: $300

The morning weatherman had rambled about temperatures reaching the upper nineties, but I wasn't feeling the heat. The clinic was scheduled to open at eight and I'd arrived ten minutes early, hoping to be first in line and avoiding any kind of wait. I'd hoped the receptionist would look through the glass doors, take pity on me and let me in early. But the lady at reception did a fine job of avoiding eye contact with me.

A car pulled up behind me and a coughing woman got out. I nudged a little closer to the door, not wanting to lose my first place slot or to catch her cold.

She came to stand behind me and sneezed. "Jeez, you'd think they could open. It's one minute to eight."

I folded my arms over my chest. The minute didn't mean much to the folks inside the building, but it was a lifetime to me. "Yeah."

The woman sneezed again. "I got a cold."

"Rough."

"What's going on with you?"

"Flu."

"You look like you're holding up well."

I stared through the glass doors at the receptionist, willing her to rise and unlock the door. "It's a front. I'm a mess."

At exactly eight o'clock the receptionist did stand, cross to the door and unlock it. She wasn't smiling and her slumped shoulders suggested this was the last place she wanted to be. Back at you, sister.

Managing a smile, I moved toward the front desk sign-in sheet. Carefully I signed *Daisy McCrae* and took a seat, not bothering with a magazine. Tapping my foot I folded my arms over my chest. Don't borrow trouble. Mom had said it to me a million times. I was the kid always ready with a detailed worst-case scenario in no time flat. Once Mom was driving Rachel and me to a classmate's six-year-old birthday party. She'd been running late because of work at the bakery and so she'd been driving fast. Long story short, she'd gotten a speeding ticket.

Rachel had been devilishly curious and calm when the officer had walked off with Mom's driver's license, because in Rachel's young world life always worked out. I, however, did not know that. I'd been abandoned at age three, and I understood on a cellular level the world could indeed crumble.

"Momma, if you go to jail," I asked, "who will take care of me?"

Mom glanced in the rearview mirror, her eyes sparking with annoyance. "I'm not going to jail, Daisy."

My fingers drew into tight fists. "Yeah, but what if you do? Who is going to take care of me?"

She'd squeezed her fingers on the steering wheel and studied the officer in her side mirror. "Dad would take care of you."

I'd clung to the strap of my seatbelt. "What if Dad can't come?"

Mom huffed out a breath as she watched the officer. "Dad will come."

"But what if he can't." One backup had not been enough.

"Then I'll call Mrs. G. from next door or I will call your grandmother. There will be someone."

My churning stomach had eased, and I'd settled back, accepting that the bench of potential rescuers was indeed deep enough to keep me safe.

"Daisy McCrae."

I glanced up to find a gray-haired woman dressed in scrubs looking to the woman with the cough. I rose. "I'm Daisy."

"Come on back."

I followed her to a curtained room where I sat on the gurney as the nurse read my chart.

"Can you tell me if it's a yes or a no?" I said.

The nurse punched keys on the exam room computer and pulled up my name. "The doctor will be right in to see you."

I lowered my voice. "Blink once for yes and twice for no."

She smiled. "He'll be right in."

Doomed to more waiting and wondering, I shifted on the gurney, crossed and uncrossed my feet, stretched and then shoved out a sigh. Finally the curtain snapped back to reveal a tall, slim man of Indian descent. His rich dark hair was neatly combed back and his white starched jacket covered khakis, white button-down, and tie.

"Mrs. McCrae?" he said.

I didn't quibble with the mistake. Sitting straighter, I fisted handfuls of the gurney paper sheet in my hands. "Hey."

"Mrs. McCrae." He glanced at my chart as if to double check. "You are indeed pregnant."

For a moment, time stopped. The sounds of the nurses and patients outside my room faded. The air around me grew thick and heavy and my heart slowed. I could feel myself shrinking into the gurney and resisting the urge to pull the paper sheet over my head.

I cleared my throat. "Are you sure?"

He didn't make eye contact as he nodded. "We ran a blood test. And they are very accurate."

"Very. Is your kind of very like a one hundred percent kind of very or a ninety percent very?"

He lifted his gaze to mine so there'd be no confusion. "One hundred percent."

"Really?"

"Really."

I shoved out a breath and then more to myself said, "Now what?"

The doctor frowned. "You were not expecting this?"

Threading my fingers together and resting them on my lap, I nodded. "An understatement."

"There are options available to you." His voice sounded distant and far-off.

Options. The word sounded so neat, clean, and nonthreatening, as if we were talking about removing tonsils or an appendectomy. I'd known women who'd exercised their options, but I'd never been faced with this choice before because I'd always been so careful. I'd never wanted to make a baby I didn't want, because I'd been that baby.

"Mrs. McCrae?"

I glanced up. "It's *Miss* and I know the options." I hopped off the table. "Thanks. That option is not for me." I had no idea what the hell I was going to do, but I was certain what I wouldn't do.

"Do you have an obstetrician?"

"What? No, not yet. My sister likes hers. I'll get on with her." I was saying the right words, but I was so not feeling them. An obstetrician for me. Shit! "Thanks, I'll take it from here."

As I reached for the curtain, he said, "Are you going to be okay?"

A ten-ton weight had settled on my shoulders and he was asking me if I was going to be fine. I had no idea. "Yeah, sure. I always find a way to bounce back."

As I gave the receptionist my credit card and waited for her to process the payment, I fought a tremendous sense of loneliness.

My support bench, the one Mom had relied on all those years ago when she'd gotten her speeding ticket, had thinned. Mrs. G. and Grandma were dead. Mom and Dad were on vacation. Margaret had left. Rachel was struggling. And Gordon, well, there was the minor detail that the baby was not his.

There wasn't much I could do to help Jean Paul with the electrical work, so Rachel and I focused on the front of the store, which needed a new coat of paint. My life was out of control, and I was so grateful for any basic task able to fill my day and occupy my mind. And so instead of thinking about the kid, Gordon, and the next eighteen years of my life, I fixated on paint samples.

Rachel, hidden behind dark sunglasses, climbed into the passenger seat as I slid behind the wheel of the bakery's delivery truck. Balancing my can of ginger ale, I clicked my seatbelt.

My sister's hair was pulled back into a ponytail but the style wasn't smooth. In fact, it looked like she'd simply combed her fingers through her hair and tied it back. In the rush of getting the girls and our parents out of town yesterday, I'd not noticed how rough she looked.

"You feeling all right?" My stomach flip-flopped as I turned on the car and waited for the chug-chug of the engine to warm and settle. I unrolled my window, breathed in fresh air, and sipped my soda.

She also unrolled her window. "Great."

A sideways glance in her direction didn't jive with the adjective. "You look a little upset. You can't be missing the girls already."

She straightened and brushed a lock of blond hair off her forehead with the back of her hand. "I'm not missing them yet."

"You look rough."

She tossed me a glare. "You don't look so hot yourself."

Thinking about not feeling well made me sicker. I put the gear in reverse and backed out of the alley. "Did you get drunk last night?"

She reached for my ginger ale, which I reluctantly surrendered, and sipped carefully. "And then some. I had a couple of bottles of champagne I found in the cabinet in my apartment. They were leftover from a New Year's Eve party Mike and I had a couple of years ago. I polished them both off."

"Warm champagne?"

"I added ice."

"You're kidding?"

She shook her head, wincing as if it hurt, and handed the soda can back to me. "I wish. Note to self: Ice and champagne are okay, but consuming two bottles of iced anything is begging for trouble."

"Duly noted."

She moistened her lips as if the memory of the champagne was too much to tolerate. "So what was your poison?"

A broken condom four months ago. "Just under the weather."

Rachel shook her head. "You never get sick."

Tipping my head back, I commanded my stomach to calm as I turned onto King Street and headed west. My gut responded by constricting with nausea and then finally relaxing. "Never say never."

Rachel rubbed the back of her neck with her hand. "I haven't gotten hammered since high school. After Mike died, there were many reasons to drink then, but I didn't. But I sure made up for lost time last night."

"Why?"

"If the girls had been at home I wouldn't have. But they were gone and the house was so quiet. And then I thought about Margaret leaving and her life taking such a great turn." A half smile tugged at the edge of her lips. "I felt sorry for myself."

"You are entitled." As I slowed for a yellow light, I offered her more ginger ale.

She accepted it. "When I popped the first champagne bottle last night, I said to myself, 'You deserve this.' After a glass, I was all warm and tingly. So I had another. Now I feel like an idiot. Life hasn't changed a bit and my head throbs as if a Mack truck flattened it."

I gripped the steering wheel, trying to minimize the movement of the car jostling my stomach. Gaze trained straight ahead, I took deep, even breaths. "Been there, done that. It will pass."

"From your lips to God's ears." She sipped slowly as if expecting her stomach to revolt. "So do you have the flu? You've been drinking these for a couple of weeks."

Though Rachel didn't often speak her mind, it was easy to forget she had keen powers of observation. "It hasn't been weeks."

"Yes, it has."

"I didn't realize." But as I ticked back through the days and weeks, I noticed a collection of queasy moments that normally would have caught my attention.

Rachel paused, can halfway to her mouth, and looked at me. Her gaze narrowed and then widened. "Daisy."

I lightened my hands on the wheel. "What?"

She cocked her head and her gaze roamed over my body, resting on my stomach. "Daisy."

Shit. "What?"

The light changed and a car behind us beeped when I delayed.

73

I shifted to first, but wasn't smooth with the clutch so we rabbit hopped a few feet before the gears clicked.

She gripped her door. "You're pregnant."

"What?" The word had a high-pitched quality.

"Daisy." Rachel, like our mom, had a way of saying my name with more underlying meaning than a five-page speech. Was this a talent reserved for mothers? Would the secret of injecting censure into a name be revealed to me when I became a mother?

Became. A. Mother. *Damn.*

A car beeped again and I drove through the intersection. I pulled into a fast food restaurant parking lot.

A lie would get me off the hook for a few days but what was the point? The secret would come out sooner or later. The clinic doctor had talked about options, but this baby was going to be born.

"Don't tell anyone yet," I said. "I've a lot of thinking to do."

She yanked off her sunglasses and studied me with bloodshot eyes. "You really are pregnant?"

"Yep." Tension rippled through my muscles as I braced for her reaction. I wasn't used to the idea of a baby.

Rachel pushed her sunglasses up on her head, grinned, and her wan face brightened as if she'd won a million dollars. She hugged me, and though I'm not a hugger by nature I hugged back, suddenly very grateful to feel as if I wasn't alone. Tears welled in my eyes and one spilled free.

"I thought your breasts were getting bigger," she said as she drew back. "I was a double D by the time the girls were born."

I glanced at my slightly fuller breasts. "I can't imagine these puppies making it past B. Boobs are definitely a McCrae trait."

"They are a pregnant woman's trait. And you've always wished for boobs."

"Yea, well, Mom always said be careful what you wish for."

"Have you told Gordon?"

"I received the confirmation this morning."

A brow arching, a conspirator's smile curled the edges of her lips. "The early morning appointment?"

"Yeah. I had a blood test yesterday and the results came in this morning."

"So you'll tell Gordon this afternoon when he gets back?"

"Yeah."

The smile faded and blue eyes darkened. "Where's the enthusiasm? Gordon seems like a nice guy."

"He is." My voice cracked a little.

Her head cocked, and I could imagine her radar beeping. "So he might be surprised, perhaps shocked, but he'll adapt."

"Maybe."

She frowned. "What do you mean, maybe?"

Why did life always have to be so complicated? I laid my head on the steering wheel, gripping it as if it were a life raft.

"What's wrong?" Rachel rubbed her hand over my shoulder muscles strung as tight as a bowstring. "Is the baby all right?"

"Yeah, sure. The baby seems fine." I eased my grip on the wheel. "I'm four months pregnant, Rachel. The baby is not Gordon's."

Her finger gripped my shoulder in a firm, gentle hold. "Are you sure?"

"We haven't done *it* since we got back together."

"It. By that, Miss McCrae who sounds like she's in the seventh grade, do you mean sex?" Without Simon staring at her as if he were starving, she could be adult about sex.

"Correct. In the past, *it* complicated things between us and blurred our good judgment. This time we wanted to take it slow. Be friends first. "

"Okay." She sat a little straighter, as if readying for trouble. "Then who?"

"You've never met him. His name is Roger Traymore. He worked at my D.C. firm. My last night in my apartment I had a party. He showed up after everyone left and stayed a little longer."

She raised a brow. "So have you told him?"

"He's in China. He landed a teaching job with a university in Beijing, I think. He left the day after the party. And even if he lived next door, he's not the daddy kind of guy."

"Doesn't matter what kind of guy he is, he's going to be a father." Resolve had pushed past the effects of her hangover. "Daisy, you need to tell him."

"Yeah, I know. Maybe one day soon. One tsunami at a time. I'm still trying to wrap my own brain around this, and I do have to talk to Gordon today."

She squeezed my shoulder a little tighter. "One way or another it's going to be okay, Daisy." Her grin wasn't exactly happy but more the stiff-upper-lip kind. "You are going to have a baby, and it's really scary now, but it's going to be a blessing."

Unshed tears clogged my throat. Oddly, the lion's share of my worries weren't for myself but for the kid. Was having me as a mom going to be good or bad? "Is it?"

"Of course, it is! Once you cradle your child all the worries will fade. This will work, and you will be a great mother."

Dark fears clawed and howled like a caged animal. "It didn't work out so well for my birth mother. She kept me for three years and then she bailed on me. What if I can't hack it as a mother?"

"You may look like Terry, but you are not Terry. She was seventeen when you were born and you are thirty-four. You have a deep sense of responsibility, and though she may now, she didn't when she was with you. You cannot make a comparison."

I thought back to our awkward meeting at the Alexandria hotel last month. We'd both been nervous at our reunion and neither of us knew how to negotiate the tempestuous waters. "When we met last month, she gave me a picture taken of us the day I was born. She held me close, my face touching hers. She was smiling and she looked tired but happy." Later, I'd studied her face, searching for clues hinting of my eventual abandonment. There'd been none. "Somewhere along the way it went wrong."

"She was a single, isolated teenager. She didn't have family. And she had a drug problem. The choices she made had no bearing on you. Don't allow yourself to think like a lost child. You are a strong woman."

I raised my chin. "I'm not thinking like a lost child. I'm thinking like an expectant mother who fears she's going to screw up her kid if she bolts."

"You won't bolt." Steely certainty underscored the words.

A sick feeling settled into the pit of my stomach. "Terry did a number on me when she left. I know Mom and Dad are the best parents, but no amount of love will ever totally fix Terry's damage. I don't want to screw up the kid."

Rachel shook her head. "You can be odd, demanding, and a little bitchy at times, but I never thought of you as damaged."

I arched a brow. "Really? Remember all the meltdowns I had as a kid. Hide and go seek? Fine when I was hiding but a mess when everyone hid from me. Or what about when we had to do the family tree in sixth grade? We had the same tree but the teacher put an asterisk by my name and wrote: *adopted*. I didn't take the notation well."

Rachel scrunched up her nose. "That old biddy deserved it. And as I remember Mom blew a fuse over that as well."

"I don't sweat my quirks and fears so much these days. Abandonment and rejection are kind of like my pals now. For the most part they don't bother me. But I'd sure hate them to burden the kid."

"You won't."

"I'm not off to the best start, Rachel. I got knocked up during twenty minutes of good-bye-feeling-sorry-for-myself sex to a guy now living in China and who is not my boyfriend. How messed up is that?"

Rachel smiled. "I don't care who the father is. All I care about is that *you* are going to have a baby, and I think you are going to be fine."

Nodding, I swallowed. "Keep saying that. One day I might halfway believe it."

"I can't tell you how many times I worried about screwing up my kids. Hell, I still worry about it."

"You do a great job with Ellie and Anna."

Genuine doubt radiated in her gaze. "I work crazy hours. I'm always tired, and now Mike's gone and it's just me. I really have the potential to mess up two people."

"So being a paranoid mess is normal?"

"Totally. If you weren't worried then you'd be in trouble."

"Really?"

"Really."

A bit of the stress knotting my back eased. "Thanks."

"You're welcome."

We sat silent for a minute, watching people stream in and out of the hamburger joint. "Hang on to those single-mother tips for me, because I'm going to need them."

She offered a bright, if not hungover, smile. "You don't know how Gordon will react. He might be okay with this."

"Would you have been cool if Mike announced he'd gotten another girl pregnant before he dated you?"

She frowned. "I might be okay with it. Nobody cheated on anybody."

I shook my head. "I've done a lot of emotional work for Gordon. I hurt him when I left him last year. Asking him to raise or accept another man's baby is asking too much."

My phone buzzed and Gordon's name flashed on the display. He texted, I'M BACK. CAN YOU COME OVER?

Rachel nibbled her lip. "You better go."

"I don't want to do this."

"Talk to him. It might not be so bad."

Laughing as tears pooled in my eyes, I shook my head. "Right."

"Hang tough."

"Let's get the paint and then you can drop me off at Gordon's."

"We can get the paint later."

"No, now is best."

"This is a delay tactic."

"You are very right."

And so I texted Gordon and told him I'd be by as soon as we got the paint. Rachel and I spent the next hour wandering through the paint section at the hardware store. In the end we'd settled on a buttercup yellow, which we both agreed was a happy color.

Rachel and I unloaded the paint, and I promised to return after my talk with Gordon. I made a joke about seeing her in minutes, suggesting Gordon would toss me out. Neither of us laughed.

The one-and-a-half-block walk to Gordon's bike shop might as well have been a thousand miles. It took effort and thought to put one foot in front of the other as I walked down the rough brick sidewalk. Ahead, Gordon's yellow bike shop looked so shiny and clean. He'd worked hard to rebuild his life after our breakup and then the demise of our company.

I twisted the handle and pushed open the door. As bells jingled over my head, Gordon glanced up. He held on to his smile for a couple of beats until he sensed trouble.

"Hey," I said.

"Hey." He set down a bike part, which I now recognized as a derailleur, and stopped within inches of me. He didn't touch or hug me because he knew me well enough to know when I bore bad news.

"You're breaking up with me, aren't you?" He shook his head. "I've been getting a bad vibe off you for at least a week."

"I've been sick."

His head cocked, asking. "It's more than that, Daisy. I know you well enough to know when you're hiding. And you've been sinking deeper and deeper inside of yourself for at least a week."

I'd not considered pregnancy until a couple of days ago, but on some level I must have known I carried a baby that was not Gordon's. "I don't want to hurt you. I love you."

His bitter, sad smile cut into me more than angry words. "You didn't the last time either. At least I should be grateful you didn't write a note and run this time."

When I'd left him last year, I'd scribbled a note. My hands had trembled, and I'd been crying when I'd been ready to tape it to the front door. He'd arrived home early and surprised me. He'd wanted to talk. But facing him had been too much. I'd simply run.

I took several steps toward him. "I'm not running away from you."

"You're not?"

"No. Not this time."

Blue eyes narrowed. "Then what is it, Daisy?"

And here it was, the moment I'd dreaded for days. *The* moment. I sucked in a deep breath and released it slowly. My skin prickled and pinched as if it shrunk two sizes. "I'm pregnant."

For a moment he simply stared. He didn't blink. He didn't breathe. "What?"

Suddenly another underlying ramification struck me. "It's not what you think."

His shock vanished as anger flashed. "Really?"

I tipped my head back wondering when my life would ever feel easy and natural. "I'm four months pregnant. I accomplished the deed while we were broken up. A day before I moved back to Alexandria. I didn't cheat on you."

His jaw worked.

"It was my last night in D.C. at my going-away party. I got drunk."

He rolled his eyes. "The classic excuse."

I lifted my chin. "No excuses. I screwed up."

He shoved balled fists into the pockets of his khakis. "Who's the father?"

"Roger Traymore." Roger had been one of the vice presidents at our company. Bad blood flowed between Gordon and Roger but he'd never told me why.

"Roger?"

An attempted smile fell flat. "When I screw up I go big."

My very lame attempt at humor went unnoticed. "You're sure?"

"Yeah, I'm sure."

Cursing, he shook his head. "Roger is an ass."

I agreed but had to defend my kid's biological father. "I didn't come here to debate. I came here to tell you honestly what is going on. I owed you the truth."

"Well, you've given it to me with both barrels." He shook his head and paced back and forth before he stopped to face me again. "I can always count on you for the unexpected left hook."

I could have marched off in a huff, but I had pulled the rug out from under Gordon and I owed him a moment to say his piece. "This one clipped me, too."

He shook his head. "When you didn't answer the first couple of texts I assumed you were busy. By the fourth I realized there was a problem, and I've spent the better part of the weekend trying to guess.

I catalogued all your moods for the last weeks searching for a clue. Moody. Distant. Quiet."

With no way to soften the moment, I relied on the truth. "Par for the course with me."

Blatant honesty didn't win me any points either. "Disconnected. That was the new piece of the puzzle. You were disconnected."

Shrugging my shoulders, I wrestled with tears. "I kept telling myself it was stress or the flu."

"When did you find out for certain?"

"This morning. The clinic doc gave me the results."

His face, a still, emotionless mask, mirrored the expression he'd worn after our breakup. He'd tracked me to my office and gently closed my door. He'd been quiet and logical as he'd asked me questions, but he'd not railed, begged, or ranted for my return. I remember wishing that he'd get mad. Yelling, screaming, or ranting would have been better than the wounded silence. I wished he'd get upset now. At least if he released his temper I could hide behind a little righteous indignation and not feel so much like I'd kicked a puppy.

"Have you told Roger?" His tone sharpened each word.

"No. Honestly that's the least of my worries right now."

Challenge darkened his eyes. "Shouldn't he have been your first call? Doesn't he have a right to know? I'd want to know."

"Roger isn't you. This is not the kind of info he'd like to read in a morning e-mail. Nor would he wish to receive it in any other form."

"Where is he these days?"

"China, last I heard."

All polite and all so controlled, and I wanted to scream. I wanted Gordon to get angry. I despised being shut out more than dealing with someone else's anger. Bad attention beat no attention every time.

Hell, what I really wanted was for him to pull me in his arms and tell me it was all going to be fine. Rachel had said as much, but I wanted to hear it from Gordon.

Instead, he turned and moved back behind his counter. "Thanks for the honesty."

His control kindled my anger and I was glad. Anger was an old friend and oddly gave me comfort. "That's all you have to say?"

He faced my frustration and sadness, deepening the lines at the corners of his eyes. "What do you want me to say, Daisy? Congratulations?"

"No, Gordon." My voice sounded louder than I'd intended. "You told me you loved me last week. I told you I loved you. And now we are *done*."

"You are pregnant, Daisy. Not with my baby. That is a problem we can't talk our way out of." He shook his head. "I thought you'd changed since the bakery. Thought you'd gotten a little more grounded, and if we reconciled this time the roller-coaster ride would be over. I can see with you the ups and downs will never be over."

I marched up to the counter and smacked my palms against the nicked wooden surface. "So what do you want from me? Some kind of flatline ride? Because, *Gordo,* the last time I checked flatlines equaled death."

He shook his head, and I caught the first spark of anger in his eyes. "Don't turn this on me, Daisy. This is all your doing."

Yeah, I was on shaky ground, but it wasn't like being in the right had ever stopped me before. "Hey, I didn't go looking for this."

He slammed both his hands on the counter just out of reach of mine and leaned toward me. "You never go looking for trouble, but it sure as hell has a way of finding you."

"Not fair!" I was upset, mad, and I wanted to yell if he wouldn't. Roger wasn't here, but Gordon was a handy target. Now seemed as good a time as any to go for a pound of flesh.

"What the hell do you want from me, Daisy? Want us to get married and raise this baby together? White picket fence. Two-car garage."

Tears welled in my eyes. "I didn't ask for this!"

"So what do you want?"

"I want . . . I wanted you to tell me it will be fine. That we will be fine."

He shook his head. "I can't tell you we'll be okay or I can handle this. We won't be fine because this is too much even for me. Too much."

I lifted my chin and swore I would not cry. Curling my fingers into fists, I dug my fingernails into my palms. "So we break up?"

"By anyone's standards I have good cause." He yelled the last words.

On a good day, I'd have come out swinging, but I didn't know if it was the hormones or the nausea but those damn tears spilled again. Embarrassed, I turned from Gordon. "Fine."

I moved toward the door but didn't hurry, half hoping his voice would soften, and he'd ask me to stay. But Gordon offered only stony silence.

Tears falling faster now, I left Gordon's shop, slamming the door behind me. I marched down Union Street toward the bakery, but with each step closer to it, my resentment bubbled. That damn place. It had been the source of so much pain and sadness for me.

Tempted as I was to keep walking and never look back, the bakery pulled me closer. A glance through the front window showed the paint cans and drop cloths waiting for me. The place beckoned as if it wanted to embrace me, but right now I could not bear it.

I walked around the bakery to the alley and cut through the back entrance. Grateful no one was on the main level, I climbed the back staircase to my room. By the time I pushed through my apartment door, I was still looking for a pound of flesh. I grabbed my laptop, plopped on my bed and clicked the computer on.

I opened my e-mail account. Under normal conditions I'd have worried and wondered over what I was about to type. I'd have scrutinized each word and triple-checked spelling.

But I was so upset, I didn't censor as I typed.

Terry,

It's been a month since we spoke. I know we both needed time to process, but I'm out of time. I found out I'm pregnant and I need more biological information.

    A. How did your pregnancy and deliveries go?

    B. Who is my birth father?

    I'm not looking for hearts and flowers or mother-daughter lunch dates, just answers.

Yours truly,

Daisy

Before I considered a word, I hit Send.

As I heard the message zoom off into cyberspace, I sat back on my bed and stared at the inbox as if somehow I half expected a quick response.

Daisy,

Pregnancies went fine. John Smith is your birth father.

I love you,

Terry

But the inbox remained empty. And the longer I stared at the empty box, the stronger my sense of rejection grew. When I couldn't stand it any longer, I shut off the computer and lay on my bed.

Rolling onto my side, I caught sight of the recipe box on my nightstand. I reached for it and held the small wooden box in my hands, tracing the embossed corner details.

If my life had been a book, pregnancy would have been the last plot twist I'd have written. The thought of another human so dependent on me always brought cold chills. I did not want to be so needed.

Years ago, I'd built an emotional life raft with room only for one. When I'd lost my job and the world had caved, I moved back to the bakery and discovered my entire family had pinned their hopes on me saving them. They'd scrambled onto my little raft. Despite fears we'd sink, somehow my vessel had expanded to include seats for Mom, Dad, Margaret, Rachel, and the girls. I didn't have any more oars, but my ability to row faster had grown. Somehow, I would save us all.

And now the boat needed to grow again. I sensed it would grow, but this time I wasn't so sure I had the strength or energy to row faster. What if I'd already reached my limit?

Had Terry harbored thoughts like these when she'd been carrying me? Had she thought she could build a boat for us only to discover she couldn't keep rowing? Had she looked at me that day in the Union Street Bakery as she ordered my favorite sugar cookies and decided she couldn't keep us both afloat anymore? What had finally pushed her to simply sail out of my life without a backward glance?

I opened the box and looked at the picture of Jenna. I traced her face. For some reason, Jenna's smile eased the tension banding my chest.

Fatigue seeped into my bones, draining my energy. My eyelids grew heavy and soon I simply let them drift closed. I hadn't napped since I was four, and I'd fought sleep as if my life depended on it. I needed to get up off this bed and prep the lobby for painting.

And I would. Soon. Right after I rested my eyes for a moment. Maybe for a minute to catch my breath.

The sounds of honking horns and the hum of car engines passing under my window grew more and more distant. The bed's warmth pulled me deeper and deeper, and instead of fighting, I leaned into its tug.

In one moment I was on my bed and in the next I sat alone in a white rocker by the river. An empty rocker set next to mine. How long I sat I couldn't say, but in the rocker I was content. A gentle breeze. A sun warming my face. Boats passing by on the river.

Finally, a woman approached. She looked worried, her curly blond hair framed an oval face, high cheekbones and a full mouth. A blue print dress flowed around her calves. Cupping her hand over her eyes, her gaze hungrily scanned the horizon.

"Can I help?" I said.

Her gaze still on the horizon, she shook her head. "My son. I am looking for my son."

I rose, ready to help. "What does he look like?"

"He is a baby. He has light hair like his father and peaches-and-cream skin like mine. He is a pretty baby. A good baby. Perfect."

"How did you lose a baby?"

Sadness tightened her button mouth. "He was in my arms, and then I closed my eyes for a moment. When I awoke, he was gone."

"Did someone take him?"

She shook her head, folding her arms over her flat belly. "I don't know. I don't know." She met my gaze, her blue eyes sharp and vivid. "Keep your baby close. Or someone might take it, too."

In that moment, the wind rushed and swept me from the riverbank toward the cold icy waters. I flew helpless, so out of control. I wrapped my hands around my belly and braced for impact.

I sat up in bed, heart racing, hands clutching my belly and sweat dampening my brow. "Don't worry, kid. I'll figure this out."

Chapter Seven

Monday, 6:00 P.M.
11 days, 11 hours until grand reopening
Income Lost: $500

Rachel sat in her apartment alone on the edge of her bed, wineglass teetering between her fingers. Hours ago she'd heard Daisy's panicked footsteps clicking past her apartment, but as much as Rachel had wanted to go to Daisy, she understood her sister needed time alone to process.

And so she'd spent the afternoon prepping the front of the store for painting. She'd removed pictures, caulked holes, sanded rough spots and wiped the dust from the walls.

It was after five when she'd finished and she'd gone to Daisy's room. To her surprise, her sister was sound asleep, looking more relaxed than she had in weeks. Rachel left Daisy sleeping and retreated to her apartment.

Alone in the quiet, she'd poured herself a glass of warm wine and then dropped in a couple of ice cubes. She had two bottles of wine left from that long-ago party with Mike, and despite a lingering head-ache, she believed a glass of wine wouldn't hurt.

This afternoon, when she'd taken a break she'd considered putting these last two bottles in the refrigerator, but then that would have meant she planned to drink again. There was something about intend-ing to drink that was far worse than just drinking. And so, she left the bottles on the counter beside the refrigerator.

She held the glass up to the light, swirled it, and studied the way the wine glided down the inside of the glass. Lord knows Mike would have frowned at the idea of her drinking on a weekday alone. He'd never been much of a drinker and grew annoyed if she had more than a glass of wine at a party.

Rebellion stirring, she drained the glass in a gulp and refilled it before moving into her bedroom and opening Mike's closest, packed full of T-shirts, jeans, and white chef's jackets. She could imagine Mike coming in the door and kissing her on the cheek.

He'd been gone a year and a half, and she'd still not cleaned out his closet. It seemed she should have tackled the task by now but then she wasn't sure how to time the grieving/mourning process. Should she have cleaned his clothes out within weeks of his death? Months? Eighteen months didn't seem excessive, but when did she cross the line between normal and weird widow lady at the bakery?

She gulped a mouthful of wine and set down her glass. Today was as good a day as any. She desperately needed more storage space as the girls grew. Saving Mike's clothes was a space luxury she could no lon-ger afford.

Intent on cleaning the closet out, she'd reached for the first shirt. Her hand skimmed the rough white cotton. And her fingers trembled.

Pulling back, she retreated to the edge of the bed and her wine-glass. Swigging again, she stared at the collection of dark trousers, white coats, and dozens and dozens of white tennis shoes. Mike had loved tennis shoes. And socks. In all the years she'd known the guy she'd only seen him barefooted when he was in the shower or in bed.

Mike didn't like his shoes to appear dirty or worn. Pristine white had been so important to him, his shoes lasted three months max before he replaced them.

When she'd gone to meet with the funeral director about his final outfit, she'd brought his newest pair of white sneakers. In fact, she doubted he'd ever even worn them, because she'd pulled them right out of the box. The funeral director had not raised an eyebrow as he'd taken the shoes, jeans, and white Union Street Bakery T-shirt. Mike had loved the bakery, lived and died at the bakery, and it had made sense he take a piece with him.

Rachel glanced at the empty bottom of her wineglass. She could fill up or clean out the closet.

She rose and grabbed a box of large green garbage bags from the kitchen. She jerked a bag free, snapped it open, and snatched her first handful of clothes from their hangers. The clothes weighed heavy in her hands as if they resisted her efforts. *Don't send me away, Rachel.*

Her chest tightened and she hesitated. Again she glanced at the wineglass. "No."

Fearing she'd stop to think, she shoved the first jacket in the trash bag and kept stuffing until it was full. Less than a half hour later, the closet was empty and five trash bags bulged with clothes and shoes.

She dropped to her knees and reached for the last remaining pairs of shoes. The clothes and newer shoes had been easy but the remaining collection of white sneakers . . . they were special and Mike had saved them despite their state of disrepair. They told the story of Mike. The chocolate cake stains on one pair spoke to the signature cake he loved to bake. Red and green dye on another pair reminded her of their last holiday rush. Yellow and green triggered memories of Easter and their last Mother's Day all-night bake-a-thon.

Gently, she skimmed her fingers over the shoes. The shoes, like the memories, had been valued treasures over the last year. But somewhere along the way they'd wrapped around her and had secured her in the past.

Carefully she collected the shoes and put them into a garbage bag, hoping the Goodwill would find some use for them. She moved at a steady pace until she reached the last pair. They caught her short, slicing through her like a knife. Stained with blood, they'd been the shoes he'd worn the day he had suffered his aneurism.

Hands shaking, she'd clutched the shoes to her heart. She'd been upstairs with the girls that day. Both had had colds, and she'd not been able to work in the bakery. Mike had been double-timing it to get the orders filled. They'd both had so little sleep the night before because the girls had been restless. She and Mike had been cross with each other their very last morning as a married couple. Neither had wished each other a good day. Neither had said, *I love you.* He'd grunted to her as he'd left, and she'd not bothered to respond because she'd thought if he'd *really* wanted to speak to her, he'd have turned around and made eye contact.

Fifty-six minutes later he was dead.

Tears filled her eyes and rushed down her cheeks. They'd had one last chance to talk and they tossed it away.

She'd carried the shoes along with his clothes home from the hospital after he'd been declared dead. She'd clutched them to her chest as her father had driven and her mother stared silently out her window.

Tears burning her eyes, Rachel dumped the shoes in a garbage bag and sealed it up.

As a strong pot of coffee brewed, she loaded all the bags in the Union Street Bakery van. She ate a chunk of bread, drank a coffee, and filled a travel mug with a second serving. Before she had time to second-guess she drove them to the Goodwill trailer six blocks away. The attendant, an old black man with a graying mustache, glanced up at her from a magazine as if surprised. "You made it in time. I'm closing my doors in a couple of minutes."

Rachel opened the back of the van. "Glad I made it."

He took the bags from her car, but she didn't accept the tax receipt he offered.

Instead she climbed back in the van. For several minutes she sat, letting the day's remaining heat seep into her chilled bones.

As the attendant loaded her bags onto the trailer, she thought about the shoes dripping with chocolate. The ones he'd worn the day she'd given birth.

Panicking, she climbed out of the car. "Mister, I need to look in one of those bags."

His gaze narrowed. "Why?"

"I think I packed shoes I should have kept."

He answered with the shrug and he unloaded the six bags from the truck. Rachel dug through the three bags and multiple layers of worn white shoes before she found the ones stained with chocolate.

Grateful, she clutched them to her chest and shoved out a sigh.

"That all you want?" he asked.

She studied the open garbage bags spilling over with shoes, shirts, and memories of Mike. She rose and carefully repacked the bags as the man watched. Quietly, he took the bags from her.

Salvaged shoes in hand, she took a step back. "Yeah, that's all I need. Thanks."

The old man reloaded the bags and locked the back of the trailer before walking to his old red Lincoln. He eased behind the wheel of his car and glanced in his rearview mirror at her. Finally, shaking his head, he started his car.

Anxiety tightened her throat as she watched him drive off. Carefully, she traced the shoe's silver-tipped laces. More doubt circled as she wondered if she were abandoning Mike along with his clothes.

Gripping the shoes, she entertained ideas of waiting here all night and in the morning when the attendant returned, begging for her bags back.

Tears dampening her cheeks, she didn't know how long she sat until finally she put the car in gear. Heart racing, she drove.

Ten minutes later, she parked in the alley spot behind the bakery's back entrance. As she got out of the van, a large green delivery truck pulled in behind her. Painted on the side of the truck was HOLDER BROTHERS WHOLESALERS. The driver set the brake and climbed out.

He was a short man, with a belly that overflowed a tight leather belt and stretched the limits of a dark blue Holder Brothers Wholesalers T-shirt. Jeans and worn boots finished the look.

Rachel knew the guy. Jeb. She didn't like him and had left the delivery side of the business to Mike and then Daisy.

"I got your delivery," he said.

"Jeb, Daisy sent you an e-mail. We are closed this week for renovations."

Jeb glanced at his clipboard. "It don't say closed on my clipboard."

Of course it didn't. "We are closed this week. We can't take deliveries."

"So what am I supposed to do with all this flour, eggs, and sugar? Where's Daisy?"

"She's not working today."

He sniffed and tugged at the waistband of his green pants. "Yeah, well, I want to talk to her. I don't believe she sent me the e-mail."

Was she invisible? Did he not understand? "She's not here."

"What about Margaret?"

"Just me."

"Great. The creative one."

She straightened, shoving aside feelings of blame, as if this was somehow her fault. "I'm sorry, Jeb. We can't take the order."

"Sorry don't cut it with me today. This is my last delivery and I'm tired."

If she'd had the money to pay for the order she'd have taken it just to end this. But she didn't have the money. Daisy had made it clear it was expenses-to-the-bone during the renovation.

She stood silent, hugging the shoes like a child.

Jeb stared at her. "Well?"

"I'm sorry, Jeb, for the miscommunication. But I can't take the delivery." Shit. Had she just apologized to him?

He muttered an oath under his breath. "This account has turned into a real pain in my ass. If I had half a mind, I'd drop you."

They needed the Holder Brothers and she'd lost too much in the last year to lose a steady supplier. "That's not really necessary. And it's just one order."

"And before this, it was like pulling teeth to get a payment. You've been trouble for a year."

Unwanted tears welled and her lip quivered. "I will have Daisy talk to you."

He glared at her tears before opening his door. "I don't need this shit. I don't need it."

She watched him back out of the alley. Anger and resentment bombarded her. Why hadn't she told him to back off? Why hadn't she fired him on the spot? He couldn't be the sole supplier in the region. The guy worked for her, and she'd let him walk all over her.

She'd apologized.

She'd f-ing cried!

Damn it!

God, how would she make it if Daisy quit the business? Running a bakery was a tough way to make a living without kids and damn near impossible with a baby. At least when the girls had been born she'd had Mike. Daisy didn't have anyone. When would her sister wise up and figure this job plus an infant equaled insanity?

As she climbed the stairs to her apartment, panic and fear crowded out the anger. She dumped her keys and purse on the table by the door and moved into her bedroom. The closet waited for her, wide, gaping, and empty. She should have taken time to close the closet before she'd left. Carefully, she set the single pair of sneakers in the center of Mike's side of the closet and shut the doors.

Overwhelmed by a sense of emptiness, she thought about the wine bottle in the kitchen. If she drank it all she'd be drunk, numb, and would fall into a heavy dreamless sleep like last night when the house had been far too quiet.

She moved to the refrigerator, opened the freezer and filled a glass with ice. She picked up the half-full wine bottle from the counter and filled her glass. She raised the glass to her lips and hesitated. The wine would get her through tonight, but what about tomorrow and the next day and the next?

Rachel poured the wine in the glass and open bottle down the sink and climbed the stairs to Daisy's door. She pounded on it. "Daisy!"

After a delay, footsteps sounded in the apartment and the door opened to a bleary-eyed Daisy. "What?"

Guilt deflated some of her steam. "You sleeping? It's eight fifteen."

"Resting my eyes." She sniffed. "Was that the Holder Brothers' truck I heard? Jeb can't shift gears without grinding them."

"Yeah. Jeb wanted to make a delivery."

"I sent an e-mail."

"He said you didn't."

Irritation widened her tired eyes. "I'll deal with him."

And Rachel knew she would. The problem was she should be able to deal with Jeb. Instead of digging into what she couldn't do she shifted to what she thought was safe. "I slept a lot when I was pregnant."

Daisy winced. "Don't say the P-word. I'm not there yet."

"Doesn't matter what you want. It's all about the . . ." She hesitated and found a smile. "It's all about the B now."

Daisy rubbed her eyes. "Why are you here?"

"I want to look at the recipe box."

Daisy yawned and rubbed her eyes. "You're kidding."

"I'd like to read through it. Maybe bake." She dealt with nervous energy by baking.

Daisy yawned again. "You have ten days off and you want to bake?"

"It's an addiction. What can I say?" She snapped her fingers. "The box."

Daisy raised a brow, surprised by Rachel's crisp tone. "Right."

Daisy vanished and reappeared seconds later. She handed the box to Rachel.

Rachel thumbed through the yellowed cards. "We should try and find Jenna. Dad's old bakery records are in his attic."

Daisy shook her head and rolled her head around as if working kinks from her neck. "My window of non-nausea doesn't open until later this evening."

She smiled. "I didn't have much nausea."

"Lucky you."

"Want to bake with me?"

Daisy's bloodshot gaze narrowed. "I'll drink a ginger ale, eat crackers, and talk to you while you do."

"Deal."

"She wrote lots of notes in the margins." Daisy nibbled a saltine and followed Rachel down the flight of stairs to her apartment. "You've scribbled notes on every cookbook you've owned."

While Daisy dug a soda from the back of the refrigerator, Rachel thumbed through the cards in the box. "There are times when the recipe comes out right and other times when it won't and doesn't gel no matter what. It's my way of keeping track. And then sometimes I try different flavor combinations." Rachel squinted as she studied one card. "This is a recipe for simple cake."

"Yum."

Rachel pulled bowls out of the cabinet and banged them hard on the stainless workspace. She grabbed ingredients, slamming all on the counter.

"So what's eating you?" Daisy said.

"I'm fine."

Daisy sipped her ginger ale. "It sounded like you were dragging dead bodies out of your apartment earlier. Thump. Thump. Thump. What was it?"

For a moment Rachel didn't answer as she unwrapped a pound square of butter. "I cleaned out Mike's closet."

Daisy sat silent, as if knowing there wasn't much she could say.

"I was fine until I saw his shoes." A half smile quirked the edge of her lips as sadness simmered like a pot of sugar water reaching the hard-ball stage.

"All those crazy tennis shoes?"

Doubt amplified her sadness. "I saved one pair." She frowned. "I chucked all his belongings into garbage bags."

Daisy offered no signs of judgment. "I love garbage bags. It's the suitcase for the girl on the go."

Her easy words softened the sadness. "I hauled them all downstairs and into the van. Made it as far as the Goodwill and watched the guy load them all on the truck."

Daisy winced. "And then . . ."

Worry drew her mouth tight. "I kind of freaked out. I made the guy pull all the bags off the truck."

Daisy winced. "You didn't bring all Mike's stuff back, did you?"

"No. Not that bad. But I dug through every bag."

"Looking for?"

"The shoes he wore when the girls were born."

"The ones stained with chocolate?"

She dumped the butter into the stainless bowl. "Yeah. I wanted to hold on to one memento."

"Reasonable."

She pulled a hand mixer from a drawer, popped two beaters into the sockets, plugged it in and switched it on low. The mixer strained against the hard butter, chewing at the edges of the brick. Rachel revved the speed of the beaters, shoving and pushing the butter until it lost its hard angles and dissolved into a creamy mixture. She shut off the mixer. "Mike never would have wished death so young. And he'd never have left us. I know."

Daisy glanced toward her can of ginger ale. "But you still feel abandoned."

Rachel nodded. "Yeah. In the days and weeks after he died I was so busy running around trying to keep it all together. I didn't have a lot of time to feel much. I mean I read about the stages of grief and kept thinking, 'Well, I'm at Acceptance. I must have skipped the Anger stage.'"

Daisy flicked her thumb against the can's tab. "Anger can be very tricky. It's good at hiding and lurking. But it always rears its head. In fact, I've seen it enough times that I think I can draw a picture of it."

Rachel smiled as she shoved a measuring cup into a white canister filled with sugar and scooped out two cups, which she dumped onto the creamed butter. "It was a complete stranger to me until the last couple of months."

"About time it arrived. Shows you are alive."

Rachel shrugged a shoulder. "When you came in the spring, I thought the cavalry had arrived. For the first time since Mike died the panic in my chest eased and I could breathe."

"Panic actually has its plusses. No time for much else when you are a little panicked. Definitely keeps you in the moment."

She frowned. "I thought I'd feel better without fear always chasing me, but the extra time gives me a chance to really miss Mike. And then in the last couple of weeks I've somehow stumbled from sadness to anger. I've been so pissed lately."

"Welcome to my world."

"I never could understand why you were always so angry. I thought, 'Yeah, her birth mother left, but she has Mom and Dad and we all love her. She should be fine.' Now I realize all the love in the world doesn't soften a terrible loss."

Daisy swallowed. "It's also easy to be angry, Rachel. It's easy to shake your fist and search for the next person to blame. But since I arrived here, I realized I'd gotten a little tired of being angry. It's kind of like carrying a big heavy rock. You're so focused on the rock you miss the scenery."

Rachel nodded. "It's all about the rock for me now."

"Sooner rather than later you need to put it down."

"And you have?"

"Most days. And then I send an e-mail to Terry and she doesn't respond right away and I find myself picking it up again. But at least now I know when I'm carrying it."

Rachel mixed a splash of vanilla into the batter and blended it in. "Have you talked to Gordon?"

"Oh, yeah."

"How did it go?"

Daisy shook her head. "Not well. I did a number on him."

"You didn't ask for this. If you could have chosen a different outcome you would have chosen it."

"Terry said the same to me when I asked her about leaving me. Woulda, shoulda, coulda doesn't really count." She sighed. "At least this time I was honest with Gordon. I didn't try to hide my feelings."

"He needs time to cool off."

"You didn't see the look in his eyes."

Rachel came around the counter and wrapped her arms around Daisy. "For the record, I'm excited about the baby."

Daisy's questioning gaze met Rachel's. "Really?"

"Yeah, really. And if it's a girl, she will be dressed to the nines. I've all the girls' clothes, in two sets."

She traced her finger around the rim of her soda can. "Given my luck, it'll be a boy."

"Dad will be thrilled with the first male McCrae in the house. I know he loves us, but he'd kill for another guy on the premises."

"Mom and Dad." Daisy groaned. "That's going to be an interesting conversation."

"They'll be a little surprised, but they'll adapt."

Daisy squeezed Rachel's arm. "Thanks."

Rachel returned to her mixing bowl. "We make a fine pair."

"Call us knocked up and hacked off."

Rachel laughed. Using the recipe card, Rachel finished mixing the cake. Soon she had the batter arranged in two parchment-lined cake pans. She popped them in the oven. The apartment filled with the sweet smells of vanilla and cinnamon.

As they inhaled scents of the baking cake, the room chilled, making them both shiver. Rachel rubbed her hands over her arms and moved toward the stove.

Daisy set her soda down. "I think I finally feel human."

Rachel held her chilled fingers toward the oven. "No nausea? Aren't you a little ahead of schedule today? Shouldn't it be two or three more hours before the non-nausea time?"

"I'm not looking a gift horse in the mouth. The kid is giving me a reprieve, and I'm taking it. When are those cakes going to be ready? I'm starving."

At that moment the buzzer dinged. "Ask, and you shall receive." Slipping a red oven mitt on her hand, she opened the oven door and pulled out the cakes.

"God, they smell great." Daisy inhaled deeply. "And they don't make me sick to my stomach."

Smiling, Rachel dumped a cake on a white plate. Steam rose and normally she would have waited for it to cool before she cut it. Tonight, she cut it immediately and plated a piece for Daisy. "Here ya go."

Daisy blew on the hot cake and then bit into it. She closed her eyes, chewing slowing. "I have died and gone to heaven."

Rachel picked up a hot cake wedge and bit into it. "Not bad."

"Looks like Jenna knew how to bake."

"I'll say. And no eggs. No small feat." She shuddered as a cool blast of air blew. "I think the AC kicked into overdrive."

"What do you mean?" Daisy finished the first piece of cake.

"I'm freezing."

"Really? I'm kinda warm. It must be ninety outside."

"It's twelve in here."

Daisy bit into the cake. "Maybe you're getting sick."

"I feel fine. But it turned cold in here."

Daisy shook her head. "This cake is amazing. It feels like I haven't eaten in weeks."

The chill settled deeper in her bones and suddenly all the loneliness of the last eighteen months rose up. Tears threatened, but she swallowed forcing them back. "Times like this I really miss Mike. He'd have loved discovering a new recipe like this."

Daisy reached for a second piece of cake and as if she hadn't heard Rachel, said, "I really hope I don't screw this kid up. I don't have a clue how I'm going to pull motherhood off."

Rachel swiped away a tear. "Mike's birthday is next week. He'd have been thirty-five. It's not fair he died."

"What if I'm like Terry, and I try but I fail?" As she nibbled the cake, her frown deepened. "I don't want to fail my child."

The two sisters, each lost in a web of fear and worry, stood in the kitchen for several minutes. And then outside a car backfired.

Both sisters blinked at the intrusion and then stared at each other as if they'd forgotten the other was there.

Rachel shoved a shaking hand through her hair and stepped away from the cake. She cleared her throat and shook her head. "My emotions were amped up one thousand percent."

"Me, too. And I do not like it."

Rachel glanced at the half-eaten cake and the counter now littered with crumbs. "It's like the cake cast a spell."

Daisy's gaze trailed hers. "It wasn't the cake."

"How do you know?"

"It was hormonal."

"You maybe, but I went through my cycle last week."

Daisy pushed her cake plate away. "It was the cake, Rachel. How could it make us feel so much?"

"I don't know. But we were fine until we bit into the first piece."

"It wasn't the cake." She reached for her ginger ale and sipped slowly. "We are both just on edge."

Rachel stretched her arms over her head. "Do you feel pretty good? Because I feel like a million bucks."

Daisy rose. "My feel-good window has passed. I think I might go rest. You okay here?"

Rachel nodded. "Yeah. I'm good. Real good. Thanks."

"Good," Daisy said. "I still feel like I've been hit by a truck."

"What can I do?"

"This time I don't think I'll be able to muscle my way through the problem. I'm not in charge anymore."

Chapter Eight

Tuesday, 7:00 A.M.
11 days until grand reopening
Income Lost: $600

From my attic desk, the sound of Jean Paul's drill grinding through wood rose up through the floors and snaked right up my spine. Normally noise and chaos didn't bother me, but lately it drove me mad. At my desk I buried my face in my hands wishing I could call Gordon. "I am going insane."

I'd worked with an older woman years ago. She'd been a secretary, and I'd been an analyst on the rise. When life got tough and I thought I'd go crazy, she'd always smile and say, "This too shall pass."

I'm not sure what had made me think of her. But I repeated the words, "This too shall pass."

I breathed in and out, hoping it passed before I grabbed the hammer from Jean Paul's toolbox and hit him with it.

Instead of using a hammer on Jean Paul, I picked up the phone and dialed the Holder Brothers. Three rings and I got their receptionist's perky, "Holder Brothers."

"Sandy, this is Daisy McCrae. How you doing today?" I'd start with nice.

"Ms. McCrae. How are the renovations going?"

"Well, thanks. Look, I've got a problem. Your man Jeb showed up here yesterday with a delivery. You and I agreed, no deliveries this week."

"We sure did."

"I don't mind the mistake as much as Jeb. He was rude to my sister."

A heavy silence followed. "I'll let the boss know. I'd put you through but he's in the warehouse now."

"No worries, Sandy. But if Jeb gives us trouble, especially Rachel, I'm firing Holder Brothers." The bakery wasn't a huge client but in this economy every penny counted.

"It won't happen again, Ms. McCrae."

"Thanks, Sandy."

I hung up and, sighing as I stood, my gaze settled on Jenna's recipe box. Hadn't I left that with Rachel? She must have brought it back up last night. Lately I slept like the dead, so I could easily have missed her.

Picking up the box, I thumbed through the cards. Rachel had mentioned Dad had old bakery records. As much as I didn't want to think about Jenna, she kept creeping back into my thoughts.

"So much work to be done, and I want to play history detective." But then what could it hurt to carve out a half hour. I'd take a peek at the records and return to work.

Downstairs, I checked in with Jean Paul, waved my cell as a signal I could be reached by phone. He held up his finger as he drove the drill deeper into a stud, halting when he'd punched through the wood.

He removed his finger from the trigger and the drill went silent. "My friend Gus has wine."

"Wine?"

Jean Paul pushed back a thick lock of dark hair with his typical must-I-explain-again glance. "Gus. He owns a restaurant that is not to be. He has lots of wine. We can buy it from him, and we can sell the wine at the bakery."

Right. Gus. "I don't have much cash."

"He will sell the wine to us for three dollars a bottle. We can sell it for fifteen dollars a bottle."

"Nice profit margin. How many bottles does he have?"

"One thousand."

"Three thousand dollars." A sum once insignificant was now a fortune.

"He will take half now and half in a month."

"He is that desperate?"

Jean Paul reached in his back pocket and removed a cigarette pack. "*Oui.*"

"And the basement could be a wine cellar?"

"*Oui.*"

"I'll need shelves." My mind played with the possibilities as it added and rearranged numbers.

He shrugged. "Of course. Wine must be stored on its side."

If I bought the shelves, I could do them on the cheap. And a wine cellar would set us apart. Bread, wine, and maybe cheese. It was a risk, but a risk with a high payout. "I'll do it. But it will have to be half now and half in sixty days. It will take me time to get a liquor license."

He nodded. "I will tell him."

"And he delivers?"

"I will ask."

"Okay." A little deeper in debt, I headed out the front door to my parents' house. "Have you seen Rachel?"

"She went for a walk."

"Where?"

"I am not in charge of her."

No doubt she needed a break, a day to breathe and regain her footing. Fair enough.

My folk's town house was next door to the bakery. Real estate in Old Town Alexandria had remained high despite the economy, but my folks had been in the neighborhood over forty years and thirty years in this house. When Dad pitched the idea of buying the house it had been cheap, but it had been a real reach for my folks. Dad had had to do some fast talking to get Mom to agree to the purchase. Because of his risk, they were sitting on some very pricey real estate.

Let's hope Gus's wine would do the same for me.

I climbed the front steps of their narrow brick townhome outfitted with wrought iron window baskets filled with red geraniums. The house had been built in the 1820s by a sea captain who'd made his money trading spices and slaves. The windows, original to the house, had a beveled wavy look that added a misty, watery quality. I dug my keys out of my pocket and opened the front door. Quickly, I moved to the alarm and punched in the year of Margaret's birth—my parents' universal security code. I'd tried to get them to vary the code, but the times we'd tried they'd forgotten the code and had to call me to help them reset it. I'd given up and reset them all back to Margaret's birthday.

The entryway was long and narrow and cut through the center of the house. Immediately in front of the door a slender, tall staircase climbed to the second and third floors. The walls, trimmed with waist-high wainscoting, were painted a creamy white and extended a good twelve feet. Pocket doors separated the hall from the first parlor. With an eye always on resale, Dad and Mom had chosen simple classic colors and finishes. However, when it came to furniture they chose what they liked. So the fireplace had been restored with a sleek marble and the floors were a light pine but the furniture was a couple of decades-old La-Z-Boys, end tables piled high with magazines, and a very wide-screened television.

I climbed the stairs to the second floor and glanced in my parents' room. Mom and Dad slept in a four-poster bed that had belonged to my dad's parents. Mom rarely made her bed, the exception being when they had company or she was on vacation. Mom had a fear of dying on the road, and the idea of everyone tromping through her house and seeing an unmade bed was too much for her. She wanted her last impression to be a good one.

I moved to the end of the hallway and opened the door leading to the attic. Thankfully it was a walk-up attic, so no pull-down rickety stairs. I switched on the light and climbed the roughly hewn stairs.

Dad had relocated the old bakery files to his attic about twenty years ago so that he had more room in his bakery office, which I was now having removed so we could add freezer space.

Halloween and Christmas decorations crowded the right side of the attic. My mother's favorite holiday adornments included a light-up snowman (with a bad right arm), a dozen careworn wreaths with red bows, assorted lights, and electric white candles for each of the town house's windows.

Dad had commandeered the left side of the attic, arranging his bakery files neatly in metal file cabinets. Dad had always been a good record keeper/historian of the Union Street Bakery, and as he'd gotten older the past drew him more and more. He'd talked about writing a book about the bakery's history but so far had not been able to sit still long enough to write the first page.

This early in the day, the attic temperatures were bearable, but by noon, the heat would be unmanageable. And if I'd waited until late July, heat plus the kid would have made this outing impossible.

Head bowed so I didn't bump into the rafters, I moved past the file cabinets designated for the 2000s, past the nineties, eighties, and then skipped quickly to the forties. The deeper I traveled back in time, the less space was dedicated to files. I knew if Dad had been alive one hundred years ago, he'd have saved every scrap of paper connected to the bakery. He grumbled often enough that his ancestors hadn't been the best archivists.

Like me, Dad favored organization because it gave him a sense of control. My birth mother had abandoned me at age three, and his father had died suddenly when he was fourteen. Both of us suffered a loss that ran so deep, we'd convinced ourselves if we were organized and orderly we could control the universe. Of course, neither of us had been widely successful. Dad had a heart that wouldn't tick much longer, and I was underemployed and pregnant.

I found the drawer marked *1940s* in the very back row. My grandfather would have kept these records. After this file cabinet there were only two more. The first one hundred years of the bakery garnered three cabinets, whereas the subsequent fifty had twelve. I glanced back toward the front to the five empty cabinets Dad had delivered weeks ago. These were going to be my cabinets. He'd anticipated I would be as dedicated a recorder as he. And honestly, he was right. I'd amassed more files in the last two months than Rachel and Mike did in their seven years of running the bakery.

With a hard tug, I pulled open the top file drawer. The marker read January–December 1940. I wasn't sure when Jenna came to work at the bakery, but her last recipe card was dated 1944.

These files, kept by my grandfather, were dusty and brittle. The handwriting on the tabs was bold, thick, and impatient. I understand impatient. Seems a baker is always stealing time. Time at the desk keeping records is time away from production, and no production means no money.

I pulled the first dozen files and moved back to the attic steps where the light was better and the air a touch cooler.

Smoothing my hand over the first file, I opened it. I was expecting to see the files and forms my dad used. Taxes, business license. But the first page contained a bill of sale for flour: forty pounds at twenty-five cents per five-pound bag. There were more receipts, and I marveled at the cost of butter, eggs, and sugar. There were ration books that my grandmother, like the wartime women, used to buy precious items such as sugar and butter. As a baker's wife, she'd have enjoyed extra rations through the business. By the end of file one all I'd gained was a lesson in inflation. Digging through the next three or four more files I found letters from my grandfather, a bank loan agreement to pay for the oven we used today, and information about local shopkeepers and merchants. But there was no mention of employees.

I neatly stacked and returned the files to the cabinet before grabbing more files to be searched page by page. As I went through the pages I imagined the grandfather I never knew. The bread, his customers, and the seasons ruled his life as they now directed mine. My father said his father had had a beautiful singing voice and customers marveled at his talent. Grandfather McCrae had dreamed of singing in New York on a grand stage. My father had a tin ear and his dreams were of joining the army and flying planes. Both had surrendered dreams for the bakery.

My dreams had changed over the years. First it had been college and then a master's. Then a top job. Then to make big bucks. And then, well . . . since my return to Alexandria, my dreams had ceased to matter. Maybe one day I'd make new ones.

Maybe.

Or was I going to be like my father and sacrifice the rest of my life for the bakery? And what about the kid? Was he going to grow up here with a mom frazzled by lack of sleep, shaky finances, and long hours behind the retail counter? I didn't exactly yearn for a return to finance. The money was good but lately the idea of getting on a plane in a suit didn't thrill me so much. But the bakery wasn't enough.

"Damn."

I opened the last set of files dated 1943 and discovered the first set of employee files. My grandfather notes he's advertising for new employees, a clerk to run the front counter: *Clean, reliable, good with people.*

There were no applications, only names with notes on a blank page. *Christopher is too brash. Rosa is too short. Willa—my wife doesn't like her. And finally Jenna. A pleasant girl, nice smile, can bake.* There is a check beside her name. This was my first bit of information on Jenna.

Pleasant, nice smile, and can bake.

I kept digging through the papers and found a black-and-white picture of six women and my grandfather. My grandfather's hair is dark and his body lean and fit. He's holding a plate of cookies and grinning at the camera. All smiling, young and slim, each girl wears a skirt dipping below the knees, a sweater, socks, and dark shoes. The girls have their arms linked together. A USO banner hangs in the Union Street Bakery window and snow on the ground suggests it's winter. I leaned in and studied the smiling faces. It wasn't hard to spot Jenna. She is the third from the left.

In this image her uniform hugs a narrow waist. Her face is slimmer than I remembered so I pulled the other picture of Jenna from my pocket. The first image, from the recipe box, appears to have been taken after this newly discovered image. The group photo of the girls taken in January and the picture of Jenna and the soldiers snapped later in spring. In the spring photo Jenna's face has definitely filled out.

"Working in a bakery is hard on your waistline."

For the first time I moved my hand to my belly, which now strained the snaps of my pants. Weeks of telling myself I'd put on weight because of the bakery seemed absurd. For a moment I kept my hand there, still wondering if I'd feel a flutter or a kick. But the kid was still. Definitely not going to move until he was good and ready. Stubborn. A chip off the old block, I thought with a bit of pride. Gordon had admired my stubborn streak.

Pushing aside a jolt of sadness, I focused on the photo's discovery. I returned to the cabinet, hoping to find some other scrap of the woman who'd hidden her recipes in the wall.

But a search of the entire decade reveals no more details. Jenna appeared twice. Once in the form of a scrawled note: *A pleasant girl, nice smile, can bake.* And in the photograph. Then she vanishes as if she'd never been at the bakery.

I fixated on the changes in her body from winter to spring. I didn't have hard and fast dates but I was guessing they were taken about four months apart. Four months. In my case a time of great, great change.

For reasons I cannot explain, as I looked at the spring image I got the whisper of an idea. At first I brushed it away as nonsensical. But the more I stared the deeper its roots grew.

Jenna was pregnant.

Or was she? Or am I looking for a kindred spirit?

The assumption of her pregnancy opened a host of questions for me. Was she married? Who was the baby's father? Was he one of the soldiers in the spring picture? What became of Jenna and the baby? The baby would be close to seventy now.

I wished Margaret were in town to do her historical-digging magic. She'd take a name and a photo and if given a couple of days would unearth all that had been written about the person.

What would Margaret do? *WWMD?* Assuming Jenna was pregnant and the baby was born at the end of 1944 and the baby was baptized, I could check the newspaper. Birth records. Church records. The 1950 Census records.

"All right, Jenna, let me see what I can find out about you."

"What do you mean there is a problem?" Five minutes back at the bakery, and I had trouble.

Jean Paul pulled a cigarette packet from his breast pocket, caught my irritated glare, and he tucked it back in his pocket. "The wiring in this place is ancient. I will need to do more to bring it up to standards. And I am worried about the floorboards and whether they can support the freezer."

Dollar signs danced in my head. After leaving Mom and Dad's I'd driven to IKEA and purchased shelves for the basement winery. The more I thought about the addition of wine and cheeses, the more I liked it. The profit margin on Gus's wine, if I could survive the cash outlay, would be tremendous and might enable us to come out of this renovation a bit ahead of the game. "How much and how long?"

He shrugged. "A thousand for the wiring and the floor."

"Can you be very specific? I'm counting pennies here."

He sniffed. Shrugged. "It is hard to tell now."

"Why? You said you've done this before."

"It's an old building. There are always surprises."

Dad had always said when you opened up an old building you never knew what you were going to find. I'd been hoping we'd catch a break.

"I need this bakery open and running in eleven days. If I am closed longer I will lose money I do not have. And I got a call from your pal Gus. He's headed this way with a thousand bottles of wine in two days."

Jean Paul ran the unlit cigarette under his nose, inhaling the tobacco. "It will all come together. Do not worry."

Easier said than done. This bakery supported Rachel and her girls, but it also had to feed the kid now. It had to make it.

"Jean Paul, you are going to get this job done. On time. And on budget. Figure out what must be cut from the budget to make this work."

"Of course."

"That's all you have to say?"

He rolled the unlit cigarette between his fingers. "What more is there?"

Clenching and unclenching my teeth, I held on to my temper as it struggled to break free. "Your answers are too quick and easy for me. I want more thought, more anguish."

He arched a brow. "Americans love their drama."

"The French have had their share."

He shrugged. "I do not have time for this. I have work."

"Right."

Jean Paul was a mystery to me. Not much riled him. He was even philosophical about my smoking ban as long as he could retreat to the alley for his smoke.

Jean Paul turned back to his wires threaded through the exposed studs. "Leave."

My skin bristled. "What?"

"There is no work for you here now and the stress is not good for you or the baby."

My heart pounded in my ears. "The what?"

He looked back at me, an eyebrow cocked. "Please."

A trio of arguments elbowed their way to the front of my brain, but logic quickly cast them aside. What am I going to say? "Is it that obvious?"

"To me, yes."

"Am I getting fat?"

He hesitated as if sensing he'd entered a minefield of fat questions. "There is a glow."

"A glow?" Artful dodge.

"Of course."

I'd never thought I'd had any kind of glow. Jaundiced or green around the gills, yes. It's nice to think I'm glowing around someone. "Yeah, well don't tell anyone. At least for now."

"Don't tell me. Tell your belly."

"I am getting fat!"

Again he weaved out of the loaded question's path. "No. Now go." He mumbled in French and waved me away.

"Fine."

Outside the bakery the warm afternoon air greeted me with a soft breeze. With a queasy stomach refusing to let me paint or assemble shelves, I cut across Union Street toward the meandering waters of the Potomac River. The waters were offset by the clear blue sky stippled with clouds.

The tourism season was in full swing and the bike and walking paths along the river were growing congested. As a kid I didn't like the summer season, hating to share my city with strangers. But now when I saw the buzzing streets I thought of income for the bakery. The more, the merrier. My regret was that the bakery wasn't open.

A young couple walked along the path, hands clasped and bodies close. As the woman spoke, the man listened with the eagerness of a new lover. Occasionally he smiled as she raised her other hand to punctuate her story.

My thoughts went immediately to Gordon. We had been that couple in the very beginning when we'd met two years ago. We'd barely been able to keep our hands off of each other and when one talked the other listened with rapt interest.

And then life happened. He'd become closed off and consumed by work, and I'd taken his disinterest as rejection.

We got caught in a riptide of emotions and unspoken words, and we'd been pulled apart. As much as we wanted to return to the other, neither of us had the strength to fight the current.

After the breakup both of us had gone on with our lives, never realizing the same tides that pulled us apart had brought us back together here in Alexandria. We both had new lives, new challenges, and it seemed a new chance with each other.

And then the wave I'd never seen coming crashed on me and separated us again.

Alone now, I worried how I would pull off motherhood. I could manage any business, but a baby? There were so many ways I could screw this kid up, and it scared me.

My mom had taught me how to be a mother. Mom never ran, and no matter how hard I pushed or tested, she'd stood steadfast. I prayed her training was enough to overcome the runaway genetics I'd inherited from Terry.

I walked for another half hour, and then suddenly my energy plummeted. This was my new pattern: nausea all day, feel human for an hour, and then the exhaustion.

All but dragging myself back to the bakery, I pushed through the front door, anxious to collapse on my bed. The place was eerily quiet. No hammers. No customers. No nieces or sisters. The emptiness should have unsettled me but I was too tired to care.

I climbed the stairs and made it to my apartment. A glance toward the clock told me it was minutes after seven. When had I turned into a woman craving bedtime at seven? And then, uncaring for the answer, I collapsed onto my bed, my body aching with fatigue.

Sunlight still burned bright outside and I could hear children giggling on the street below. People from my old life would have laughed at me if they'd spotted me pulling the blanket over my head. I'd regularly burned the candle late into the night and laughed at those who said they needed eight hours' sleep. I'd had the nerve to call them old. Jeez. My old life was less than six months gone, but it might as well have been a lifetime.

I worked harder than I ever had and made a tenth of what I had before. And to add a cherry on top of this bitter dessert, I was knocked up.

If I'd had more energy, I'd have been freaking out right now. Hell, I didn't have the energy to strip off my clothes and put on pajamas. The kid wasn't even here, and it was already sucking the life right out of me.

Tomorrow I really needed to call Rachel's obstetrician. Maybe those supercharged vitamins they gave pregnant women would help.

A gentle breeze blew into my room. We'd had to turn the air-conditioning off during the renovation, and I thought now how lucky we'd been with the weather. Not blistering hot as it could be during a Virginia summer. But moderate days. Cool nights. And then my eyes drifted shut.

As the day floated further and further away, the darkness surrounded me and slowly closed in like a storm cloud. Fear and panic rose up, and as much as I wanted to run, my feet felt stuck to the ground. Trapped. And then out of the darkness I saw a woman. She was petite, small-boned with a flat belly, and her shiny blond hair is coiled into a bun. Jenna. Even if I'd not seen two pictures of her, I'd have known it was Jenna. Of course not a logical thought but many truths don't always make sense.

She looked directly at me, and she smiled. "I think you're going to have a girl."

My hands slid to my gently rounded stomach. "How can you tell?"

"I just can."

Mom had raised me never ever to ask a woman if she were pregnant. *Unless the baby's head is crowning, do not ask.* But that didn't stop me from glancing at her belly.

She smiled. "His name is Walt."

"Who?"

"My son. His name is Walt. He looks like his father."

"Where is your son?"

The light in her eyes faded. "I don't know."

"Did you give him away for adoption?"

She shook her head. "They took him."

A terrible sadness welled as I thought of her child being taken. "Who took him?"

"I don't know. But I hear him crying all the time, and I know I need to find him."

"Why would they take him?"

She shook her head. "Don't let them take your baby."

Startling awake, my hand slid to my stomach. My breathing was hard and fast. My heart rammed against my chest. For an instant I feared the baby was gone. The baby I didn't plan or want was gone and my heart broke.

And then the very most delicate sensation fluttered below my fingers, below my skin. Tiny, tiny, flickers before it stopped. Holding my breath, I waited for the petite bit of movement.

"Come on, kid. Throw me a bone."

But the kid was mutinously silent. She wanted me to know she was there, but she wasn't taking requests.

The room was dark, the sun long since set. The streets were quiet and the moon full and bright. I laid back on my bed, my hands on my belly. In another life, Gordon would have loved this moment. He'd always wanted children and I'd been the one to shy away from children. He'd have coaxed the kid to move. He'd have nestled his head against my belly and spoken to her as if they'd been old friends.

Tears filled my eyes, and I was struck with a bone-deep loneliness. I wanted Gordon to wrap his arms around me and whisper words of love in my ear. I wanted him to tell me we were going to be fine.

But yesterday's memories of Gordon's stony features sent the fantasy skittering away. I had cut him so deep and inflicted so much pain he'd never forgive me.

Chapter Nine

Wednesday, 6:00 A.M.
10 days until grand reopening
Income Lost: $1,000

The next morning I rose early and settled into the office corner of my apartment. The small desk was overflowing with stacks of invoices and order forms and I realized working in my apartment wouldn't work. I needed to move the office to the basement. Granted, my commute would only be three flights of stairs, but it created some separation from the attic, and a little was better than none.

But for now, I'd suck it up and work in my room. Today, my plan was to dive into work and keep my mind busy until eight when I could call the OB's office and make an appointment. And then I really needed to paint or work on the basement. Sick or no, the clock was ticking, and I had no time left to waste.

When eight A.M. rolled around, I'd finished the last of the day's paperwork, and I dialed the doctor's office. The phone rang three times before I heard a brisk, "Westlake Obstetrics."

I cleared my throat and resisted the urge to hang up. "This is Daisy McCrae. My sister Rachel Evans is a client of Dr. Westlake's."

"Right. Preemie twins."

"She's the one. She suggested I give you a call. I had a . . ." Saying the P-word was not getting easier. "I had a pregnancy test, and it was positive. I think I'm sixteen weeks along, and I need to connect with a doctor."

"You're sure you're that far along?"

"Yes. I know to the day, hour, and second. It's been a crazy month or two, and I didn't notice all the changes."

"Okay, let me check the schedule." I heard the tap of computer keys in the background. "Can you come in today at five? She has a cancellation."

"Today?"

"If you're sixteen weeks, the sooner the better."

"No, I totally get it. I do." I combed agitated fingers through my hair. "I'll be there."

"You know where our offices are?"

"Still on King?"

"That's right." I spent the next few minutes giving her my basic info and then rang off.

I leaned back in the chair, nervous energy swirling through me. An appointment with an OB made all this a little too official for my tastes. I was going public with my pregnancy.

With no more paperwork to distract me, I made my bed and cleaned my room, which took all of about ten minutes, and then my thoughts turned to the front of the bakery. Rachel had cleaned and prepped it, and now it was time to paint. My stomach roiled.

Ten minutes later I was in the shop, glass of ginger ale close as I opened the first can of paint. It's a butter yellow, cheery without trying, and I was certain it was going to brighten up the place.

After filling the paint pan, I dug out the new brushes from the hardware store bag and then positioned the stepladder in the corner of the room. The plan was to cut in and then roll.

It felt good to have physical work. In the last couple of months I'd grown used to the manual labor demands of the bakery. I liked to keep busy and not think so much because I spent too much time in my head, worrying, which was why I loved finance. All the numbers kept my brain busy and distracted.

But bakery work required not just your head, but your back, arms, and pieces of your heart. At first the work had been painful and too demanding. I'd hated it. But somewhere along the way I'd grown used to and now I even liked it.

A rap on the front door had me turning. A regular bakery customer, Mrs. Ably, smiled and waved me over to the door. A bright blue dress accentuated gray, tight curls framing her round, well-lined face.

I never professed to be good with people, but I liked Mrs. Ably. She always had a nice word, and on Rachel's birthday she had brought her a cake. Rachel had been so touched she'd cried. That cake had won big points in my book.

Smiling, I crossed to the door and opened it. "Hey, Mrs. A. What's up?"

Petite, she favored loose-fitting dresses and very sensible brown shoes. "Daisy, why aren't you open?"

I pointed to the RENOVATION sign in the window. "We are moving a wall and adding a freezer and a wine room. We'll be closed for about another week."

She frowned as she studied the sign. "I don't ever remember this bakery being closed. In the snowstorm of '96 your dad was open."

"I know, and I hated closing. But the health department doesn't like construction and baking at the same time."

She waved a bent, heavily veined hand. "Oh, for heaven's sake. A little dust never killed anyone."

"Hey, I hear ya, but the Man says no so I gotta listen. You should love our new look."

She glanced beyond me at the lines of yellow trim clashing with the existing blue. "I like the old one."

"Give the new one a try." She lingered and I couldn't help but ask. "What were you looking for today?"

"Chocolate chip cookies. My grandkids are coming into town, and I'd like to have cookies for them."

"I don't have cookies made."

She frowned. "Oh."

"I do have frozen dough in the freezer. They are all mixed and scooped. All you have to do is bake them off."

Her gaze narrowed as her lips curled into a conspirator's smile. "And the house would smell like I'd been slaving all day."

I smiled leaning closer. "Exactly. Your grandkids will never know you and I had this little exchange."

She winked. "I like your thinking, Daisy."

I nodded. "Come on in and I'll fix you right up." She came into the shop, and I locked the door behind her.

As she took stock of the empty cases and the pictures off the wall, I moved toward the saloon doors. "How many cookies you need?"

She traced her finger over the cupcake clock resting on the display case. "A couple of dozen."

"Be right back." Through the doors, I nodded to Jean Paul, who was studying a wall joist. An unlit cigarette dangled from his mouth as he frowned and deliberated on the wood as if it held all the secrets of the world. I pushed the plastic off the freezer and pulled out a ziplock bag full of scooped cookies. There was more than enough to cover Mrs. Ably's needs. I scrounged a USB bag and dropped the frozen cookies inside.

When I came out she met my gaze but as I moved toward her, bag in hand, her smile faltered and turned questioning. She studied me like a hawk, and I found myself straightening my shoulders and holding the bag in front of my belly. The kid wasn't going to stay in hiding much longer. I dreaded the questions, but refused to worry. The kid and I would have to figure it out.

"Here ya go." I handed her the bag and resisted the urge to cover my belly.

Mrs. Ably glanced in the bag. "All I have to do is put it on a baking sheet."

"Heat your oven to three hundred and fifty degrees and then slide your pan of cookies in the oven. Be sure to leave a couple of inches between the cookies because they will spread a little. Bake ten to twelve minutes."

"I appreciate it, Daisy. How much do I owe you?"

"Not a dime. It's my gift to you."

"Honey, that is so sweet. But I can't take this."

"Sure you can. And I also expect you to take full credit for those cookies. In fact, splash a little flour on your sleeve. It'll add to the slaved-over-a-hot-stove look."

She grinned. "Very clever of you."

"I'm a wily one."

She studied my face and though she kept her gaze high, I sensed she'd already inventoried me from head to toe. "So how are you adjusting to work here at the bakery?"

"It's good. I'm getting the hang of it."

"I knew you'd jump in with both feet. You were high energy even as a kid."

Jump in with both feet. My mother had dragged me in kicking and screaming. "The place needed a bit of a boost."

"And you're feeling okay?"

"Right as rain." Mrs. Ably had her fingertips on the heartbeat of Alexandria. I wasn't ready to be grist for the mill.

"And what about Rachel?"

"The girls are on a vacation with my parents, and she's enjoying a bit of quiet time. And Margaret's working a temporary job on an archeology site."

Mrs. Ably shook her head. "The girl does love her bones and buried treasure."

There was a loud crash in the back room followed by a good bit of muttering in French. "Jean Paul."

She nodded and leaned forward to whisper. "He's French."

"Yes, ma'am."

"I hope he's more friendly than the other baker. He was always so touchy. And French."

Henri, Jean Paul's uncle, had been with the Union Street Bakery for nearly twenty years. He'd been as indispensable as he had been consistently crusty. And since I adored predictable, his demeanor had never bothered me. Jean Paul was not like Henri. I'd yet to get a read on him, and so I kept my distance.

"But Henri was a master baker. And his nephew is also talented."

"Well, then, honey, that's all that really counts."

"Enjoy those cookies."

"And what are you doing with all your free time?"

"After I paint this room from top to bottom, I'm going to tackle the basement. I'll need to get the old boxes and junk cleaned out and install shelves."

"I hope you're not going to work too hard. And if there is any heavy lifting you let the Frenchman do it. It's the *least* he can do."

Her conspirator's tone had me hesitating. Okay, she suspected I might be pregnant. Mothers had a way of spotting would-be moms at a glance. But did she also think Jean Paul was the father?

The Alexandria gristmill ground round and round in my head. "You know he and I are just coworkers, right?"

She studied me close. "Really?"

"Really."

This time she did let her gaze roam my body, and this time it sharpened when it met mine. It was killing her not to ask. I think in this moment she'd have given big money to ask, *Well, then, who did the deed?*

But Mrs. Ably was too much of a lady to ask and until I talked to Mom I couldn't say much more.

"Well, Daisy, I want to thank you for the cookie dough. And when your mom gets back in town I'd love to take her to lunch."

I'd been so worried about Gordon and my reactions to the kid I'd not thought about everyone else's. I suspected there'd be some fierce conjecturing. Alexandria was a big city in many ways but in this part of Old Town we were a small town.

This would be the third time I'd been the topic of conversation. The first had been when Terry abandoned me at the bakery all those years ago. There'd been a big search for her and any of my biological relatives. No one had stepped forward. Her abandonment had made local newspaper headlines, but our reunion last month had been painfully quiet.

The second time I made the gossip mill had been when I was seventeen. It was before my eighteenth birthday and a woman had come into the shop whom I was sure was my birth mother. She looked and sounded like me. And I'd been so taken by her I'd asked her point-blank if she was looking for me. Are you my birth mother? Long story short, the poor woman had come in for a cookie and had never expected to be lambasted by a crazed teen. When she'd left I'd been bawling right there in the middle of the shop. Mom was trying to comfort me. It had been a mess.

And now I'd returned to center stage once again. Pregnant.

Seconds after Mrs. Ably left, Rachel appeared. "I'm here to help."

I glanced toward the neatly applied blue tape hugging each seam in the room. "Looks like you've been on the job while I was MIA. Thanks."

"With the girls gone I'm a little at loose ends."

"No more clothes to toss?"

"None. But I spent yesterday cleaning. I feel caught up."

"How does that feel?"

"Good."

I picked up my tray of yellow paint and my paintbrush, ready to climb back up on the ladder and cut corners.

"Paint fumes aren't good for the baby," Rachel said.

I glanced around, half expecting to see Mrs. Ably. "Don't say the B-word."

She arched a brow. "Not talking about it doesn't mean the B isn't smelling fumes."

"We'll keep the windows and doors open, and, remember, we bought the nontoxic paint that doesn't smell."

She picked up a can and read the back label. "Seems like any smell would be bad for the baby."

"I'll get a fan. This is our only time to paint."

"So what do I do?"

I took the can, opened it, and poured it into the paint pan. "I cut corners and you roll."

Rachel shook her head and reached for the brush. "I'm a master at edging cakes. I'll cut in at the corners."

I handed her the brush. "Have at it."

And so she cut neat, precise lines while I rolled the long strokes that connected her edgings. We worked in silence for several hours. Painting was a simple, mindless task for the most part, and right now I craved simple. The smell was a little strong but with the door open and a breeze blowing I managed.

After a good four hours both of us were tired of the work and ready for a break. Rachel made us ham sandwiches, and I grabbed a couple of sodas from the refrigerator in her apartment. We sat picnic style on a blanket in the center of the newly painted room.

"It looks bigger without all the pictures on the walls," I said. "I like it less cluttered."

She pulled the crust off her bread. "It definitely looks different."

"You want the pictures back?"

"Not all of them. But it would be nice to have some. Our history is important."

"We'll sift through them later."

"Sure." As she said it, Rachel sounded broken and sad. I thought about the pictures of Mike that had been on the wall. One more reminder he was gone.

"I know it's different, Rachel. I wish I could give you your old life back."

"Thanks."

"But we're here now, and we've got to make the best of it."

"I know. And I'm trying."

"Me, too."

My cell rang and I glanced at it. "It's Dad."

She frowned. "Wonder why he's calling you?"

"Let's find out." I hit Send. "Dad, how goes it?"

"We're hanging tough." His voice sounded rough and tired.

Chuckling, I said, "Let me put you on speakerphone. I'm here with Rachel."

"Sure."

I hit the Speaker button and immediately could hear the girls hollering in the background. I glanced toward Rachel, but she didn't seem worried, as if she'd heard the sound a thousand times.

"Dad," she said. "Are they driving you insane?"

"They are little angels," he said. "But they are loud little angels."

"Where's Mom?" I said.

"She's making sandwiches in the kitchen."

"Can you put your phone on speaker, Dad?"

"What button do I push?"

"The green one on the top right." I'd gotten them new phones for Christmas. They had all the bells and whistles, but so far all they'd done was call in and out.

Dad sighed into the phone. "If I lose you then call me back."

"You won't cut me off."

I could hear him muttering oaths mixed in with "life was simpler when each house had one phone attached to a wall."

"Dad? Green button," I shouted.

"Hello, hello," he said. "Do I still have you?"

"We're here, Dad," Rachel said. "Mom, can you hear me?"

"Oh, I sure can, dear," she shouted. "How are you doing?"

"That's my question to you. Surviving the girls?"

At the sound of their mother's voice the girls stopped singing and squealed. "Mo-oom!!!"

Her eyes brightened. "Hey, girls. Are you being nice to Grandma and Grandpa?"

"Yessss."

Rachel shook her head. "Are you sure? Are you taking quiet time each day like we talked about?"

Silence.

Mom cleared her throat. "We've been on the go so much there hasn't been much time for sitting, Rachel."

Rachel leaned toward the phone. "Mom, my angels turn into devils when they are sleep deprived."

"They've been a delight."

This was not the woman who raised me. That woman had never sounded calm in the face of chaos.

"How's the bakery, Daisy?" Dad said. "The renovations coming along?"

"We're getting it done one brick at a time. Jean Paul is finishing up wiring today. And the new freezer will be here by Friday or Saturday." And with luck we wouldn't run into major wiring problems and the floor wouldn't collapse.

"You still painting the front of the store?"

I picked up Rachel's crust and nibbled on it. "As we speak."

"Same color?"

"Pretty much, Dad." I glanced at yellow walls needing a second coat to cover the blue. "So how's the weather?"

"Hot," Mom said. "We are going to putt-putt golf tonight. And then tomorrow we're going to the place where you mine for gemstones. It's in a nice air-conditioned building, they give you a pail of rocks, and you spend hours sitting and digging looking for gems."

"Will I find a diamond?" Anna said.

"I don't know," Mom said.

"Will I find a diamond?" Ellie said.

"Count on twenty minutes max, Mom," Rachel said.

"Send me your positive thoughts, Rachel," Mom said. "Think at least one hour."

Smiling, Rachel shook her head. "I will think as hard as I can."

"Hey, Mom," I chimed in. "Maybe if you click your heels three times the girls will spend the entire afternoon going through the rocks one by one."

"Funny, Daisy. Just you wait, dear. One day you will be a mother, and then I will sit back and laugh."

"My kid is going to be perfect." The conviction behind the statement surprised me. "She's going to be doing mathematical equations while I read my favorite novel."

Both my parents laughed.

Dad lowered his voice a notch. "Ten bucks says Daisy's kid is a ballbuster like her old mom."

"We can only hope," I said.

"Can I write those words down?" Mom shouted.

"Okay," I said. They were talking about the grandchild they thought would never be. I was talking about the baby scheduled to arrive by Christmas. Suddenly, all Mom and Dad's jokes took root. Was the kid going to be a ballbuster? Shit.

Rachel stared at me wide-eyed as if to warn me I played with fire. "We've got work to do. If you people of leisure will excuse us, we've got walls to paint."

"See you two lovebirds in a week." I turned the cell over to Rachel.

Mom and Dad said their good-byes while Rachel took the phone, retreating to a corner to speak to her girls.

As I tossed the remains of my sandwich away, my thoughts turned to the kid and then to Gordon. I moved to the window and glanced toward his yellow bike shop. We'd had our talk two days ago and I sorta hoped he'd cool off, see I was as thrown as he was, and return. He was always the peacemaker and the one who talked me off the proverbial ledge.

Down the street, he emerged from his shop, shepherding an electric blue bike outside. A teenager followed and watched as he tested the brakes. Frowning, Gordon pulled a screwdriver from his pocket and made adjustments before pronouncing the bike good to go. I'd learned over the last few months he took safety very seriously. I'd kidded him about it weeks ago, and his expression had grown serious. Screw up a company and send it out of business like I did, and you'd worry about the details, too.

Gordon glanced up, a smile on his tanned face. He pushed his long hair back with his fingers and watched the kid ride off. He turned and for an instant his gaze captured mine. I wanted to shrink from the window, but I stood steady, holding his gaze, raising my hand, hoping he'd smile back and saunter to the bakery. Instead, his expression hardened, and he turned and walked back into his shop.

A hard lump formed in my throat as tears burned my eyes. He had every right to be pissed but . . . I really wished he wasn't.

I pulled back my shoulders. I didn't handle rejection well at the best of times. And right now was not the best of times. "Rachel, I need to take a break."

"What?"

"I'm going for a walk." I didn't dare face her for fear I'd really cry. "Keep the phone and finish your call. I'll be back in a couple of hours."

"Okay?"

"Never better." My hand on the door, I jerked it open.

The door closed behind me, bells jingling madly over my head. I thrust unsteady hands in my pockets and headed down the street away from Gordon's shop. I didn't know where I was going, but I needed to move. To do. And not to think. I didn't want to dwell on the kid, the disaster renovation, or Gordon.

I ambled for several minutes before I remembered Jenna. *The Alexandria Gazette*. Stood to reason she might have been mentioned at some point. A wedding announcement. Birth announcement. Some details to tell me a little more about the woman who'd worked at the bakery. From many of Margaret's ramblings, I remembered the original papers were held in Richmond at the state library, but microfilm copies were available here. It could take hours and days to find a mention of Jenna, and that was time I did not have. Margaret, however, knew the shortcuts.

Realizing I didn't have my phone I went back to my apartment, taking the back staircase to the third floor. There were dozens of important tasks I should have been doing but right now all I cared about was Jenna.

I opened e-mail, knowing Margaret's went straight to her phone, and typed.

Margaret,

Hope your adventures with the dead are as thrilling as you hoped. All's well here. Mystery of recipe box is bugging me big time. Know anyone who has access to local papers who can track references to Jenna? E-mail or text.

I leaned back against the wall and scanned my inbox, which was fairly full of junk. No word from Terry and I couldn't say I was surprised. For her to suddenly open up in an e-mail seemed a stretch.

Still, her nonanswer hurt, not because I was looking for another mother. I had one. But I wanted a connection with the woman who'd given birth to me. And I also wanted information about my birth father's DNA.

I logged on to the Internet and typed on a whim: *Who is Daisy McCrae's birth father?* Bits and pieces of the search popped up. A Daisy in England. A woman searching for her birth father. A McCrae in Kansas. But of course the universe had no illuminating answers for me. It was about as helpful as Terry.

"Who the hell did you hook up with back in the day?"

From my desk drawer I pulled out the picture of Terry and me on the day of my birth. She'd been pretty with her long sleek black hair, and her smile was vivid. She looked happy when she'd been holding me. She'd looked like she was willing to give it her best shot.

Had she gone to my birth father? Had he been at the hospital when I was born or had he taken this picture? Had he rejected her and me? Had she told him, or worse, did she not know who he was?

As a kid I'd never given him much thought. All my musings had been for the woman who'd raised me for three years and then left me on the bakery steps. I'd developed long and complicated stories about her, but he'd barely registered. Once I'd imagined he'd been a brave prince killed in a war, but for the most part he remained faceless and unimportant.

Now, however, he was important. He was half my genetics. One quarter of the kid's DNA. And like it or not, he mattered. I wasn't looking for Father Knows Best or a daddy. I had Dad like I had Mom. But a 411 on my DNA would be good.

"Shit. He's probably a serial killer locked away in Leavenworth. Terry said she didn't have great taste in men, so it stands to reason she'd pick the worst of the worst."

Absently I smoothed my hand over my puffy belly, which still looked more fat than pregnant.

I wanted to tackle motherhood better than Terry, and part of doing that had to do with DNA. The kid's bio dad wasn't a *Father Knows Best* type. I held no illusions that I'd contact him and he'd rush to my side with an engagement ring in hand. Roger hated, with a capital *H*, kids. He didn't want any. And on some level I was relieved he wouldn't make a big fuss.

But the kid deserved to know him. The kid was going to look at me one day and ask me about Daddy. And I knew I'd have the answers. I would find out more about Roger than his taste in scotch and his favorite stock option. I would. Soon.

Just not right now and not today. One problem at a time. Bakery rehab. Freezer install. Prenatal checkup. And tell the parents they were not only parents to a ballbuster but would by Christmas be grandparents to one.

Christmas. The kid was due at Christmas. I'd yet to live through the holiday season as the manager of a bakery, but I'd lived through enough as a kid. It was all hands on deck. Dad often worked twenty hours a day. Mom worked every second she wasn't doing something for us, and we all helped after school.

By the time I was in high school I'd come to dread the holidays. Yeah, we were closed early on Christmas Eve and on Christmas Day, but we were so tired it was all we could do to heat up lasagna and open presents.

And this year I would be short a sister and birthing a babe in the midst of chaos. Dropping my head back against the desk, I closed my eyes. I did have a knack for choosing the worst time.

We were going to have to hire help. I'd not really thought it through when Margaret had said her good-bye, but I knew we'd have to hire a couple of teenagers to help in the back. I'd make a sign in the morning and put it in the window. We had enough interest from kids in the past, so filling the job shouldn't be but so bad. I hoped.

My computer pinged and an e-mail appeared in my box from Margaret.

I knew u couldn't resist. I've put out the word to the powers that be, and you should have answers soon. Keep checking e-mail. BTW, dead body in iron coffin and submerged in water. Coming up with plan to raise it. This is so f-ing cool.

Margaret

Smiling, I shook my head. Only Margaret would be knee-deep in water and mud with a two-thousand-pound iron coffin and talking about the coolness of her life.

A dozen smart-ass retorts danced in my head, but I couldn't seem to type a one. Instead, I typed, *You go, girl!*

I'd no sooner hit the Send button when another e-mail popped up in my inbox. I didn't recognize the e-mail address, but thinking it might have been one of Margaret's network, I opened it. It was from Terry.

Chapter Ten

Wednesday, 3:30 P.M.
9 days, 18.5 hours until grand reopening
Income Lost: $1,500

Traveling now. Will contact you soon. T.

Terry's brief, terse message lingered with me as I rolled the second coat of yellow paint on the bakery wall. I couldn't shake the simple message she'd most likely tossed out with little thought. I dissected the word choices, the sentence structure, and the way she'd signed with an initial instead of her name.

Traveling. Where was she? I knew she lived in New York. Was she headed back to Alexandria? I was, after all, going to make her a grandmother at fifty-one.

And why couldn't she have said when she was calling me? Would it have killed her to elaborate on *Soon*? A date and time weren't asking much. And how about signing her name? I didn't expect *Mom*, but how about spelling out *Terry*. And what was with her omitting my name in the e-mail?

The spin of senseless questions had me leaning into the paint roller as I applied the second coat. "Shit."

"What's with the *shit*?" Rachel cut another corner with paint. "Is the baby okay?"

I shoved out a breath. "The kid's fine. I'm actually feeling a little half human."

"A step in the right direction. Maybe you are through the worst of it."

"I'm thinking the worst of it arrives when I'm holding my screaming bundle."

Rachel grinned as she dabbed her brush in the paint can and wiped away all excess paint. "That's the best part. It's the part that makes you glad you went to all the trouble."

"From your lips to God's ears." I reloaded the roller. "The *shit* is for Terry."

Rachel's smile eased. "Did she answer your e-mail?"

"She did. She's traveling. She'll call me soon."

Cutting a straight neat line along the seam between the wall and ceiling, she shrugged. "That's a good e-mail, Daisy, for her. What are you moping about?"

"I don't know. Why can't she answer a simple question? Who is my birth father?"

"Maybe that's what she's going to do once she contacts you. Might not be an easy conversation or e-mail to send."

"Yeah, because I'm still her dirty little secret. She still hasn't told her husband and sons about me."

Rachel pursed her lips. "You don't know for sure."

"I know." Rushing to get paint on the wall, I overloaded the roller and a huge dollop fell on my shoe. "Damn it."

"Look, Daisy. Slow down. I know you've a lot on your plate right now. I know. Take it one step at a time."

Shoving out a breath, I grabbed a cloth rag and wiped the paint from my shoe. "I know. I know."

A knock on the front door had us both turning to find a slender thirtysomething man with short dark hair. He wore a white collared shirt and khakis and carried a clipboard.

I smiled but said without moving my lips, "Clipboards never bode well."

Rachel stood and also grinned. "Health inspector."

I laid my roller in the paint pan and wiped my hands. "Or building inspector."

"Place a bet?"

"Two million dollars."

"You are on." Rachel moved to the door and opened it. "Can I help you?"

He nodded glancing past her to me. "I'm with the building inspector's office. I'm here to check the progress of your electrical wiring."

"Our builder is on a break," I said.

He frowned.

I smiled. "Builders are a tough bunch to wrangle."

He nodded, no sign of humor. "Is there someone who can answer questions for him?"

"I can. I'm Daisy McCrae and this is my sister Rachel. We own the bakery."

"Grant Fraser. I'm with the city."

"Nice to meet you." I grinned, as if I were meeting a billion-dollar client at the investment firm, and shook his hand.

Mr. Fraser's hand was dry but his grip tentative. "I received a call to do the rough-in electrical inspection."

"Right."

His eyes narrowed. "Did you call me?"

My smile brightened. "My contractor called, Jean Paul Martin. Rachel, why don't you find Jean Paul and ask him to join us?"

Rachel gladly latched onto the reason to leave. "Will do. See you in a few."

She beat feet out of the place as if Mr. Fraser had announced he carried the Black Plague. We were going to have to work on her fear of confrontation. When the kid came, she'd have to take the reins for at least a little while.

"As you can see we are using the time to paint the front of the store."

He pulled a pen from his back pocket and clicked it. He glanced at the freshly painted walls and didn't appear impressed. "Where are you doing the construction?"

"In the back. The kitchen." I moved toward the saloon doors. "We are knocking out a wall, getting rid of what had been my office so we can make room for a new freezer."

"Why do you need the freezer?"

"So we can prep ahead of time. Make one batch of cookies and might as well bake twenty. With the new freezer we can make ahead more. Right now we have about a week's worth of freezer space."

"I thought bakeries baked fresh daily."

I pushed through the saloon doors. "We do bake fresh daily. But some batters and dough, like cookies, bake better if they've been in the refrigerator or freezer for at least twenty-four hours."

"Why's that?"

"You'll have to ask Rachel. She is our master baker. She can tell you why a cookie or cake does what it does. When it comes to the kitchen she is in charge. I do what she says."

I recapped Jean Paul's work on the floor. "And my job is finance, marketing, and long-term planning."

He nodded, as he knelt and studied the floor joists. He made notes on his clipboard.

"We're fixing that," I said. "That crew arrives tomorrow."

He nodded, but didn't speak.

I leaned over his shoulder, trying to read his handwriting but found it next to impossible.

Jean Paul and Rachel appeared at the back door. She looked hurried and harassed. He looked bored and a bit annoyed.

"Here is our builder," I said. "This is Jean Paul Martin. Jean Paul, this is Grant Fraser with the city building inspector's office."

Jean Paul nodded and shook his hand.

Mr. Fraser fired off several questions about the supplies Jean Paul was using. Jean Paul answered most but a couple of times seemed to struggle with the English words. I had no doubt he understood. This was a trick he'd used on me a couple of times when I asked him questions he did not want to answer.

Mr. Fraser, however, was not aware of this ploy and several times re-asked the question.

"Would you like to see our permits?" I offered. "We were told the only change we could not make was to the brick oven. And we have not altered the stove." For the most part.

Mr. Fraser shook his head, unwilling to keep asking questions. "No. Let me have a look at the electrical work."

"I have finished," Jean Paul said.

Mr. Fraser moved toward the wires, studying connections and pathways closely. His world was black and white. The wires were correct or they were not.

There'd been a time, with so many deadlines looming, I'd have rushed him through his inspection. But not today. I wanted to know the wires were right. Rachel's children lived in this building. The kid would live here. "How does it look?"

He didn't answer right away as he studied still exposed wires and junction boxes. I'd relied heavily on Jean Paul up until now, and I realized I'd gambled heavily.

Finally, Mr. Fraser sniffed and stepped back. "The work seems to be correct. I'll be back when you've installed the electrical boxes for the final inspection."

"When will that be?" I said.

Mr. Fraser fastened his pencil to his clipboard. "How soon can you have them installed?"

Jean Paul shrugged. "Soon."

Soon. Crap. Did the man ever speak a specific word in his life?

I willed the tension out of my voice. "Is it possible to have it done tomorrow?"

Jean Paul shrugged. "Of course."

Mr. Fraser nodded. "As soon as the work is done and I have your request for a new inspection, I'll put you on my schedule."

Another deadline, another line to stand in. "Do you have a rough idea when you could come back?"

"I can't make that determination until I have the request."

"I called you today," Jean Paul said. "And here you are within hours."

"Your timing was perfect. I had an opening so I came."

Of course. Jean Paul never, ever worried and the universe opened up for him. The universe, however, had a way of turning its back on me. I would put in the request as soon as I could, and Mr. Fraser's schedule would be overwhelmed and he'd not be able to return for weeks. "Thank you."

"Have a good evening."

After the inspector left, I looked at Jean Paul. "Tell me you can do that work by tomorrow."

"Of course."

"When should I put in the application for the next inspection?"

"I cannot predict problems. I cannot give you a time."

Realizing I was grinding my teeth, I relaxed my jaw. "What if I go by before closing today, put in the request and then hope you are done by the time he returns."

He sniffed. "Always a rush."

"I need to keep this reno moving forward. I am not making five hundred dollars a day right now. Which means you might be getting paid but Rachel and I are not. We need to get the final approval so you can finish the wall, fix the floor, and we can plug in our new freezer which arrives in two days."

"You worry too much. It will happen."

"I know it will. Or I'm going to kill you and stuff you in the new freezer waiting to be plugged in."

He arched a thick brow but overall seemed nonplussed by my somewhat empty threat. I marched back into the front of the store and picked up my roller. "Shit."

Rachel followed. "Daisy, we are going to get this worked out."

"It would have been worked out if I'd been more on top of the details. I've let my brain slide the last couple of weeks. This never would have happened to me a year ago. I'd have been a step ahead of Jean Paul with the applications. Now I am a step behind we cannot afford."

"Go ahead and submit the application. He'll get them done tonight. Mr. Fraser will return tomorrow for the final. It will work out."

"How do you know that?"

No smile or rousing cheer, only, "Because it has to." She picked up her brush. "Now we need to paint. It will happen. Sorta like wax on, wax off, grasshopper."

"You mixed *Karate Kid* and *Kung Fu*."

"Whatever, Daisy. Paint your damn wall." Her eyes blazed blue and an edgy irritation sharpened her words.

Surprised, I looked at her closely. "You okay?"

"Me okay?" She pretended to think. "Let's see. My husband is dead. My children are in another state with aging parents who will likely die from the exertion of babysitting. My bakery is inside out. The floor is rotting and the Frenchman doesn't seem to give a crap about anything. Other than that, I'm great."

Despite it all, I giggled. "You're spending too much time with me. I'm rubbing off."

"Maybe it's about time I grew a set."

Laughing, I pretended to dab a tear from the corner of my eye. "I think my little girl has grown up. Before I know it she will be giving the finger to a cab driver and swearing when she adds numbers."

Rachel raised a brow. "Really? Did I sound like a bitch?"

"Oh, yeah."

She pulled back her shoulders as she raised a brush to the wall. "Score."

Rachel and I stood back and studied the second coat of buttery yellow paint that had now completely covered the blue. The room looked bright, clean, and fresh.

"For the first time, I feel like I've made my mark on this place," I said.

Rachel wiped the yellow paint from her hands and arms. "What are you talking about? You blew in here like a steamroller and made the place your own within days."

Late-afternoon sunlight reflected off the walls. "I've balanced the books and the expenses are under control. Not exactly a lasting mark."

"If you hadn't made that mark we'd not be standing here now doing this. You are as much a part of the bakery now as I am, Daisy."

Instead of feeling fear or dread, pride welled. "I couldn't have imagined us having this conversation last year."

"Me either."

I pushed back a strand of hair. "I have to give credit to the bakery. It's not such a bad place."

"You give credit to the bakery?" Rachel raised her gaze heavenward and giggled. "Take me, Jesus, I've heard it all."

For all the years of bitching about this place, I deserved the jab. "Funny."

She sobered. "Finish your thought."

"No." Emotions, spoken almost without thinking, grew shy and silent.

"You are such a girl. Man up and say what you like about this place."

I lifted my chin, feeling a little vulnerable. "At the bakery I can see tangible results at the end of the day. So many cookies baked, loaves sold, cakes iced. Concrete returns. I like that."

"You didn't get satisfaction in Washington, D.C.?" Rachel rarely mentioned my job in Washington. I suspected she was afraid to invoke the past for fear it would steal me away.

"My old company offered great financial rewards. And sometimes I felt a glint of satisfaction. Quarterly earnings, a sales presentation won, a corner office. But those victories were few and far between the last years. For the most part the work didn't feel real. One electronic pile of numbers shuffled into another electronic pile."

"Do you still want to go back?" I knew it had been the question haunting her, and we'd done our best to avoid it.

"Sometimes. Like when Jean Paul doesn't tell me about electrical inspections. Or when the water heater blows. Or when I skip paying myself so we can buy supplies. At least at the last place I had the illusion of stability."

Rachel shrugged. "Dad told me once the bakery promised him hard work, and if he was lucky the sales and expenses broke even at the end of the year."

"Yeah. This place doesn't whisper sweet somethings in my ear. But

I'm okay with that. There is comfort in knowing this place won't lie to me. I might not like what I hear, but I know it is the truth." I glanced toward the wall, expecting the cupcake clock, and realized we'd removed it. "What time is it? I must light a fire under Jean Paul and get those plans to the city offices."

She glanced at her wristwatch. "A quarter to five."

"Let me see what Jean Paul is doing. If he's started on the electrical work, I'm going to put in our request."

"But he's not done."

"I'm going out on a limb here and hoping by the time he's done, Mr. Fraser's schedule will have an opening." I pushed through the saloon doors and saw no sign of Jean Paul. I found him in the alley, leaning against a brick, reaching for his pack of cigarettes. "Are you working on the electrical box?"

"What do you think?"

"I think time is precious, Jean Paul. And I hope if I submit the request for an inspection now you'll be finished with the work before the city inspector arrives."

"It is a risk, but what is life without a little risk."

"Are you telling me you will or won't be ready?"

He shrugged.

Tension crawled up my spine as I glanced around the alley.

"What are you looking for?" he said.

"I'm wondering who is around. I don't want anyone to hear you scream when I strangle you."

An amused grin quirked the edge of his lips as he lit the cigarette.

Flexing and uncurling my fingers, I tried to look menacing. "We've reached our quota of risk."

He inhaled deeply and blew the smoke downwind from me. "You live to worry."

"What?"

"Always finding problems. Do you ever have fun?"

Fun. "Jean Paul, I own this joint. My days of fun have ended."

He shook his head. "There will always be problems and there will also always be reasons to smile. Each day we choose the focus."

"Easy for you to say. You only have yourself to worry about. I don't have such luxury."

"We have the same luxuries. But you choose not to enjoy yours." He shook his head. "When the baby comes what will you teach him? Will you teach him to walk around sad and worried all the time?"

Baby. I opened my mouth to argue but the words didn't come. "I haven't thought that far ahead."

He shrugged. "Perhaps you should."

I didn't want to think of another way I could scar my kid with my personality quirks and hang-ups. For now I could only think about the application. "I'm submitting the application."

"A good idea."

Mumbling about insane Frenchmen, I hurried upstairs and grabbed my purse. Outside, the sun warmed my skin and the fresh air smelled sweet. A quick check of my watch told me if I hustled, I'd get to the inspector's office before closing.

I'd taken six steps away from the front door when I heard a young voice say, "Hey, do you work there?"

Summoning a smile before I turned, I found a girl who looked to be about sixteen. She had long brown hair, big blue eyes, and a pale complexion. Not stunning, but cute. Next to her stood a boy who seemed to be three or four years older. Same coloring. And he appeared to have Down's syndrome.

Impatience goaded me toward the city offices, but I kept my voice fairly steady. "What can I do for you?"

"Do you work there?" Her blue eyes turned keen.

Direct, careful. I liked that. "I do. I'm Daisy McCrae. I'm the owner/manager."

She took the boy's hand in hers and stepped forward. "My name is Meg Adams. I go to TJ High School. This is my brother, Tim. I heard you were looking to hire help."

I made a sign but hadn't put it up yet. "Who said?"

"My aunt owns the shop across the street."

"The gift shop?" I glanced toward the merriment shop and an image of a redhead with curly hair popped into my head. She sold souvenirs, cards, and novelty items.

"Yeah. She heard your sister moved away and thought you might need help. I thought we'd ask and see if that was true."

Initiative. Two points. "Where do you live?"

"In Alexandria near Seminary Road. We live in an apartment with our mom. She's a nurse at the hospital."

"Do you have any baking experience?"

Tim grinned. "I like to eat cookies."

Meg squeezed his hand in warning. "I bake at the apartment. I made Tim's birthday cake last week."

"Box or scratch?"

"Box."

Honest. Three points. "We are under renovation now but in about seven days we are going to put the place back together and prep for the Saturday grand reopening." There were so many hurdles standing between the reopening and me, but I decided to be more Jean Paul about the matter and not worry. "I'm not sure exactly what I need and will have to figure it out as we go."

Her eyes burned with eagerness. "I'm flexible."

"You have reliable transportation?"

She swept a lock of hair out of eyes. "The bus. We live on the bus line. It takes me about twenty minutes to get here."

Tim glanced at his sister for guidance. Clearly, she looked out for him. "Meg, tell her I want a job, too."

Meg met Tim's gaze. "She's hiring one person, Tim."

Tim's smile faded and he pouted as if he were a toddler. "But what will I do?"

Her voice was gentle and held no signs of irritation. "You are going to stay at home and watch cartoons, remember?"

Tim's face scrunched into a frown. "But I don't want to stay at home. I want to come with you."

Meg patted the boy on the arm. "I look out for him."

I folded my arms. "I can see that."

Meg's gaze was all business when she met mine. "If you hire me I will work this out with Tim."

Tim looked as if he'd argue but she took her brother's hand and squeezed it gently. He stayed silent but did not look any happier.

They were good, loyal kids. "Meg, what kind of grades do you make?"

"Bs, an A or two, and one C last semester."

"What did you get the C in?"

"Government."

"And the A?"

"English. I like to write."

I'd overthought so much lately, but this decision felt easy and right. "I think I'm going to need someone about twenty hours a week."

Her eyes brightened. "I can do that."

Tim stuck his lip out, his frown deepening. Meg squeezed his hand again but the gesture appeared more comforting.

"Tim, are you strong?" I said.

He glanced up at me and grinned. "I am very strong."

I thought about the time it took to scoop chilled dough and how much my hands ached. I thought about bags of flour I really shouldn't be lifting for the duration of my pregnancy. "Meg, I pay seven dollars an hour. I can pay Tim three dollars an hour."

Meg cocked her head. "You'd let him come here and work?"

"Is he a good worker?"

A frown furrowed her brow. "If you give him a specific job he will do it. He's good when directions are clear."

Tim grinned and nodded. "I work hard."

More weight and more responsibility settled on my shoulders, but I was getting used to the load. "Fair enough. I will need you to bring a copy of your last report card. And I want to meet or at least talk to your mom on the phone." I fished a card out of my purse and handed it to her. "Have her call me."

Meg accepted it, holding the card close to her heart. "I can so do that."

"You are going into your senior year?"

"Yes."

"You will need to keep your grades up while you work here." In high school my English grade had dropped from an A plus to a C, and Mom had to cut my hours. Though I'd initially been glad to be out of the bakery, I hated not getting a paycheck. My English grade was up in a matter of weeks.

Meg's hair swished around her shoulders as she nodded. "I will."

I eyed the boy. "Tim, are you going to listen to your sister and me?"

He jabbed an excited fist in the air. "Yes, and double yes!"

The enthusiasm coaxed a smile. "We'll put the place back together this coming week. I'll call with more details as long as this works for your mom. We'll give it a two-week trial."

Meg beamed. "You won't be sorry, Mrs. McCrae."

Mrs. McCrae made me cringe on multiple levels. "Call me Daisy."

Her eyes widened and again her head bobbed like a bobblehead doll. "Will do, Daisy."

"Come on inside. Let me introduce you to my sister Rachel."
I backtracked to the front door and found Rachel gathering up the
painting supplies. "Rachel, I'd like you to meet Meg and her brother
Tim. They applied for the job. I'm giving them a two-week trial."

Meg stepped forward and offered her hand.

Rachel pushed back a lock of blond hair with the back of her hand
and accepted Meg's as she surveyed the two and grinned. We'd not
discussed the hire but I knew Rachel would welcome help.

When Mike had run the bakery he'd had trouble delegating. He'd
done most of the baking, and she'd done the selling. It wasn't until the
girls arrived that he'd hired help, but they'd had to let those employees
go when Mike died. "It's gonna be a crazy couple of weeks getting this
place ready and back on line."

Meg's grip was firm. "We will do a good job for you. You'll see."

Tim elbowed his sister aside and offered his hand to Rachel. "We
like this place. It's yellow like a lemon."

Meg stepped aside as if accustomed to Tim's ham-fisted methods.
"My aunt comes here sometimes for the carrot cake."

"Who is your aunt?" Rachel said.

"Caroline Henley. She owns Caroline's Gifts."

"Red hair?"

Meg nodded. "Yes."

"I know her. Nice lady."

"Rachel, would you mind giving these two the ten-cent tour. I'm
on my way to city hall before it closes."

"Don't you also have a doctor's appointment?"

I'd already forgotten. Jeez. "Yes. Thanks."

A quick check of my watch told me if I hustled I still had a prayer
of making it.

Chapter Eleven

Wednesday, 4:49 P.M.
9 days, 19 hours until grand reopening
Income Lost: $1,500

I left as Rachel, Tim, and Meg pushed through the saloon doors. Outside, I hurried up King Street and found my way to the city offices. In the municipal building, sign after sign led me finally to the permit office where I ended up standing in front of a glass window staring at a woman with graying hair and half glasses. She glanced up at me. She clearly was not happy I'd skated in at closing. "May I help you?"

"I'm here to file a request for an electrical inspection. Grant Fraser was at my shop today doing a rough-in inspection."

She glanced at the clock and frowned. "You can file online."

I leaned a little closer to the glass. "I kinda like that personal touch."

"Right." She pushed papers toward me. "Fill these out and return them with the appropriate fee."

I scrambled for a pen in my purse. "I can fill them out now."

"We are closing in thirty seconds." The last two words carried extra weight.

I stopped digging. "Right. But I can drop them off in the morning."

She offered a curt nod as she reached for her purse. "We open at eight. Or you can file them online."

"Right. Thank you." I did everything else online. Why not this?

A whisper of a smile tugged at the edges of her mouth as she glanced at my Union Street Bakery T-shirt. "I like that bakery. Really good chocolate chip cookies."

"You should come by next Saturday. We're having our grand reopening and a two-for-one sale. And we're having a drawing. Winner gets a free birthday cake."

"I love cake." She winked. "As soon as that application comes in I'll send it through."

Ah, the allure of fat and sugar. It worked wonders. "You are wonderful." On a high note, I knew the time had come to make my retreat while she remembered me in a good way.

I hustled up King and toward the doctor's office. I arrived after five and signed in. The room was filled with a half-dozen women who appeared to be in varying degrees of pregnancy. The ones with the roundest bellies shifted in their seats as if no angle was comfortable. Several had swollen ankles and one had brown blotches on her face. Pregnancy mask. Rachel had had the mask with the twins.

The receptionist took my insurance card and gave me a clipboard full of forms to fill out. I retreated to a corner seat away from the pregnant women and filled out the medical forms. I'd grown accustomed to not being able to fill out the entire form. My own medical history I could fill in but *family* history had always been a big question mark.

I did have some information from Terry, allowing me to fill in a little more than I ever had before. History of cancer: *yes*. Heart disease: *no*. Hypertension: *no*. However, father's side remained a blank.

Annoyance poked me in the back. Why couldn't Terry give me the basics of the man who'd help make me? I wasn't looking for Father Knows Best. Another key piece to my puzzle.

After turning in the forms, I sat and searched the magazines on the coffee table. They all had to do with babies and parenting. Not even a *Newsweek*. I longed for any distraction. Flexing my fingers, I drummed them on the chair's arm before settling them in my lap. If Gordon and I were in this together, he would have seen I was nervous and made some quip to make me feel better. But we weren't in this together.

"Daisy McCrae," called a nurse from a side door.

I put down the unread magazine and grabbed my purse. Smiling, I tried to move as if I were cool with all this, but in reality I was scared stiff. How the hell did I land in this alternative world?

In an exam room the nurse, a tall thick woman with blond hair, took my blood pressure and pricked my finger for a blood test. "My records tell me you are sixteen weeks pregnant."

"Correct."

She arched a dark brow as she collected the blood. "And you've not seen a doctor yet?"

Feeling a little judged, I sat straighter. "I put the pieces together days ago."

The nurse glanced up at me. She didn't have to say a word to put me on the defensive.

"Yeah, I know. I'm old enough to know better, but I've had so many life changes recently this detail slipped past me."

"Periods?"

"A light one a couple of months ago."

"Light erratic periods usual for you?"

"Yes. And you toss in stress of a job change and a move and it gets worse."

"Okay. Go ahead and change into the paper gown and Dr. Westlake will be right in."

"Thanks."

Dumping my purse in a chair, I stripped and put on the gown. Seconds later there was a knock on the door, and I said, "Come in."

A woman in a white lab coat appeared, smiling. Her name tag read *Dr. Westlake*. In her fifties, she wore her graying hair pulled back in a ponytail. The salt and pepper might have aged her some, but it contrasted well with olive skin and set off her dark brown eyes. Silver star earrings dangled from her ears.

"Daisy McCrae?" she said, extending her hand.

Clutching the front of my gown, I leaned forward and extended. "Thanks for making time for me, Dr. Westlake."

"I like your sister Rachel. She and those girls of hers gave us a run for our money. How are they?"

"Five years old and at the beach with my parents. I'm betting the girls wear my folks out by tomorrow."

Chuckling, the doctor shook her head. "I don't think I could chase a couple of five-year-olds. God bless them for attempting the vacation." She glanced at my chart. "So you had a positive pregnancy test at the clinic?"

"I did."

"How many weeks?"

"Sixteen. I know the day and about the hour."

A smile tugged at the edge of her mouth. "Well, that will make picking a due date easy. Let me get my nurse, and I'll examine you."

The doctor vanished. I glanced at a picture on the wall taken of Dr. Westlake somewhere in a far-off mountainous country. A decade younger, she stood with two men who looked like guides. I'd never been much for exotic travel. I'd always been about work, which now was a good thing because work was what faced me for the next two decades.

The doctor reappeared with the blond nurse, who stood, chart in hand, by the door.

Dr. Westlake tugged on rubber gloves. "Why don't you lie back and let me examine you?"

I lay back, slipped my feet into the stirrups, and stared at the tiled ceiling. A small part of me hoped the doctor would tell me it was all a huge mistake and another growing part trusted she would tell me the kid was fine and doing well.

Dr. Westlake's exam was brief. She pulled her gloves off before helping me sit up. She thanked the nurse, who quietly left. "Yes, you are very pregnant. Sixteen weeks is right on the money."

"So it is really, really official."

"Yes."

For a second my thoughts went out of focus. I had the sense of falling while someone from below screamed the net had broken. "I'm guessing a Christmas bundle."

A smile didn't dilute a direct and searching gaze as she helped me sit up. "That's right. How are you feeling?"

"Sick to my stomach. Isn't the sickness part supposed to come earlier in the pregnancy?"

"It can come at any time."

"That's not how it happens in the movies. And aren't I supposed to be glowing? And what's with my butt getting bigger? The baby's in my stomach."

Laughing, she pulled a prescription pad from her coat pocket. "Pregnancy is different for everyone. I had not one problem during my first pregnancy and I had gestational diabetes with my second.

It changes our bodies in many unique ways. And each pregnancy is different."

"I'm not a fan of unique. I like to plan. I like my old body, which was nine pounds lighter and could fit into pencil skirts."

She raised a brow. "Is this baby planned?"

Hysterical laughter bubbled. "Not even close."

"Do we need to talk?"

"About options?" A cold chill slithered along my spine. "There's that nice word again. The doctor at the clinic mentioned it. No. The kid stays." The strength behind my words had me sighing. "What's next?"

She scribbled on the pad. "You are to get these prenatal vitamins filled, and I want you back here in four weeks for your next checkup."

I took the paper, not bothering to glance at it as I folded it. Shit. My head spun. My body numbed. What was I going to do? "Super."

Her expression softened. "It's going to be okay, Daisy. Rachel's a great mom, and she'll show you the ropes."

"I know. Rachel is great. I know. This is such a game changer."

"My game changer was my second child, the one that gave me the diabetes. She came when I was forty-three. Threw me for one hell of a loop. She's seven now. And I can't imagine life without her."

"I don't have a clue about mothering." I felt as if I were sharing a deep dark secret. "Not. A. Clue. I never dreamed about this when I was younger. I didn't carry around baby dolls or make up names for my one-day kids."

"I never did either and somehow I'm managing to raise a seventeen-year-old and a seven-year-old." She grinned. "And so far they are doing pretty well." As she studied me, her head cocked. "What's bothering you?"

"I know the kid will be fine. Healthy, I mean. My birth mother raised me until I was three. And from all accounts I was healthy as a horse."

"But."

This part still stung to say out loud. "She bailed on me."

Frowning, she nodded. "I remember the stories in the newspapers."

"Abandoned Bakeshop Baby." Might as well cut to the chase so she could stop fumbling through her memory.

Nodding, she touched her finger to the side of her nose. "There was a big search for your birth mother."

The details churned up my worries. "I don't want to bail on my kid."

Her brows drew together. "You won't."

I held my breath tight in my chest. "How do you know for certain?"

"Maybe because you are so worried about it and because Rachel told me when you returned home it was akin to the cavalry arriving."

"I don't feel like the cavalry."

"You are going to be fine. I'm not saying this is going to be easy, but you'll figure it out. And Rachel will help you." She lowered her voice, but there was no censure in her tone when she asked, "Does the baby's father know?"

"Not yet. He's overseas."

"Are you going to tell him?"

"Like it or not, yes. The kid deserves to at least know the biological father's identity."

"Sounds like experience talking. Do you know your birth parents?"

"No, Terry, my birth mother, hasn't told me about my bio dad. I'm not sure why it's such a secret. I've asked her a couple of times but so far no answer."

She clicked her pen closed and tucked it in her pocket. "Keep pressing. It's good information for you, and the baby."

"I hear ya, Doc. I do." I extended my hand. "Thanks. And I'll see you in a month."

Her handshake was firm and comforting. "I look forward to it."

She left and for a moment I sat in the quiet room listening to the ticktock of a clock on the wall. My phone buzzed in my pants. I dug it out of my pocket and read the text. MARGARET SAID YOU WERE LOOKING FOR INFO ON JENNA, CIRCA 1943-1944. FOUND THREE ARTICLES. WILL E-MAIL TO YOUR COMPUTER. GIGI.

I'd never met Gigi but at this point in my life it was the least of my problems. I texted back. THANKS.

Happy to have another project to think about, I dressed and headed back to the shop. The sound of a hammer pounding greeted me, and I glanced in the kitchen to find Jean Paul closing in the exposed wiring. An unlit cigarette dangled from his mouth.

"I haven't submitted the application for the second inspection yet. I'm doing it tonight. What if Mr. Fraser wants to see those exposed wires again?"

"My work was good. He only needs to see the fuse boxes."

"Don't you think that's a little risky? I mean what if they don't say yes?"

He shrugged. "I suppose I'd have to rip out the wall."

A fist of tension pounded behind my right eye. "And you don't worry you've made a mistake?"

He grinned. "Mistakes or no, the wall must be built, and we must install the freezer soon. You are the one in such a rush."

"Yeah but . . ."

He held up his hand, silencing me. "No buts. You are arguing about a problem that is not a problem."

Potential problems danced around my brain singing doom and gloom. I was pregnant and ready to quibble over a wall. Time to prioritize the disasters. "Fine. Whatever."

Upstairs in my bedroom, I dropped my purse on my bed and went to the computer. I opened e-mail. No message from Terry. But there was a message from Historydude6. I stared at the name and wondered what had happened to Historydudes 1-5. Margaret and her pals.

I clicked open the e-mail, which contained three links to three different articles.

The first, dated May 2, 1944, featured a photograph of the Union Street Bakery. I leaned forward and studied the picture of my grandfather and grandmother holding my dad, who couldn't have been more than eighteen months. My grandparents looked stoic while my dad grinned broadly and clapped his hands. To the right of my grandparents stood three young ladies dressed in white dresses and aprons and very sensible brown shoes. I spotted Jenna instantly. She was on the end, the farthest from my grandparents. Her smile was tentative. Like the other girls, she wore her hair back in a fishnet. She looked young, not more than twenty. The caption below the picture read, "Union Street Bakery Joins War Effort."

The next link was a small article, no picture, and dated June 1, 1944. "Union Street Bakery baker wins contest. Union Street Bakery counter girl won the prize in the Arlington County fair for the best cookies. Jenna Davis, formerly of Frederick County, Virginia, entered her Maple Brown Sugar cookies and took the top spot. Second place . . ."

I didn't care about second place. I cared about Jenna, who now had a last name and a place of birth. I had more clues.

The last link connected me to an obituary dated December 31, 1944. "Jenna Susan Davis, 21, formerly of Frederick County, Virginia, and an employee of the Union Street Bakery, died Monday at Alexandria Hospital due to complications from delivery. An infant son, reported to be ailing, survives her."

I sat back and stared at the article. An infant son. I'd been right when I'd looked at the other picture and imagined she was pregnant.

This picture taken in May 1944 didn't show signs of pregnancy but her solemn expression suggested to me more than a heavy mood. It was the face I now saw in the mirror. It was the face of morning sickness. If the baby were term, she'd have been newly pregnant in the May image. She'd also have been pregnant in the other picture taken of her and the two servicemen.

The obituary gave no mention of a husband. Surely if she'd been married there'd have been mention of her husband. So had she been alone with a baby on the way like me?

I dug out the picture of Jenna and the two Marines. All three were grinning. "Which dude is the daddy?"

Soldiers and out-of-wedlock babies weren't a novelty, but in 1944 the stigma would have been huge.

My hands slid to my stomach. A tremendous sense of loss and sadness washed over me, and I found myself mourning for a girl who had died seventy years ago.

Chapter Twelve

Wednesday, 6:45 P.M.
9 days, 17 hours until grand reopening
Income Lost: $1,500

When I came downstairs in search of a snack, I found Rachel gripping the phone in her hand. Her face was pale and her lips a little blue.

"What is it?" I braced for the next disaster. "Are the girls okay? Mom and Dad?"

Carefully she hung up the phone. "They are all fine."

"Then what is it? Margaret?"

Rachel shook her head. "No, Margaret is fine."

Fingers fisted at my side. "If you don't tell me what is going on in a second I will scream."

"It's Simon."

"He canceled his order. Damn. Too bad I'd counted on the profits. Could have offset some of the losses."

"No, he did not cancel." Panicked blue eyes met mine.

"Okay, tell me or I might faint."

She moistened her lips. "He asked me if I'd like to go to a food and wine demo this evening. Said he thought it was the kind of show I might like to see."

I shoved out a breath, shutting off the Red Alert buzzer in my brain. "And this is bad because . . ."

Rachel shook her head as if the words refused to be spoken.

"You've talked about this show before," I coaxed. "You said you always wanted to go."

"I know. Funny he would remember a trivial detail."

"So did you say yes?"

"I didn't know what to say at first. I was stunned. And then I said yes, but now . . ." She shook her head. "My God, Daisy, it sounds like a date. A date!"

"That's good," I ventured.

She shook her head. "I should call him back and pull out."

"Why?"

"Because, Daisy. It feels *weird*!"

Folding my arms over my chest, I tried not to smile. "How do you mean weird?

"I don't know! Weird." Her voice had reached a high-pitched, panicked note.

Amusement jostled aside worry. "You mean you're nervous like you used to get before a date?"

Rachel pressed her fingers to her flushed cheeks. "Is this a date?"

"Could be."

"He never said a *date*. He suggested the food and wine show."

"What's he supposed to say, Rachel? Alert, Rachel, this is a date!"

"No. Yes. I mean that might have been helpful. If you haven't noticed, I'm out of practice."

"So he asked you out. Go. It will be fun." I'd remembered how

Simon had looked at Rachel at the bar Sunday night. He'd definitely been into her. "And it's to a place you've always wanted to attend."

She nodded. "I mentioned it to Mike once or twice, but at the end of the day he was always so tired."

"Well, now you have the chance to go."

She wrung her hands. "But it feels weird. I always thought when I went it would be with Mike."

I laid my hand on her shoulder. "When is this outing supposed to take place?"

"One hour."

"One hour?"

She paced back and forth. "He said it was casual, and he could come right after work."

"Casual is good, Rachel. Just two friends going to enjoy food and wine."

She thrust her arms up in the air. "But what does casual mean, Daisy? I have no idea what people wear in the outside world."

"Outside world?"

She pointed toward the door. "Out there where people wear more than mom jeans, T-shirts, and aprons. I don't speak that language anymore." She shook her head. "Do you realize, I've not been on a date in seventeen years."

"Weird, but not terrible. Besides it's not like he's going to jump your bones or ask you to marry him."

Her eyes rose with relief. "Really?"

Now I did laugh. "Really. This is a few hours of fun with a nice guy. And if he doesn't act like a gentleman, I will act as Dad's surrogate and show up in a wife-beater T-shirt, toting a shotgun."

She laughed. "You're not bald enough to pull off a Dad imperson-ation."

"Maybe not, but I've the potbelly."

Rachel glanced at my hand on my round belly. Her eyes widened. "I can't believe I forgot to ask. How did it go at the doctor's?"

"All's good. The kid is fine and set to arrive at Christmas."

Rachel shook her head. "Your kid would show up at the busiest season."

"Stirring the pot from day one. Chip off the old block."

Rachel sighed and her eyes grew a little misty. "Has she moved yet?"

I rubbed circles on my belly. "Once, a little. She's laying low. But the doc says soon."

"The girls really moved around fifteen or sixteen weeks."

"Then it's any day now. But enough about the kid and me. You have a date, I mean, an evening out with a guy you casually know. We have clothes to pick out for you."

Rachel shook her head. "I hate this feeling."

"What feeling?"

Her cheeks flushed a bright red. "Dizzy, out of control, not sure what is next."

"Ah, my three favorite emotions. Don't worry, you'll get used to it."

"I don't want to get used to it. I want predictable back."

Directing her toward her apartment, I gave her a gentle push. "Tell it to the judge. Now let's get to your apartment."

I followed her up the stairs and into her room. She opened her closet, now noticeably half-empty, and stood and stared. "So this is going to be business dress casual."

Her gaze on a collection of jeans, she said, "In English, please."

"Dark slacks, a nice blouse and maybe heels."

"Okay." Settling a fraction she moved to the closet with purpose, dug into the racks and pulled out a pair of black slacks and a white top.

I touched the material. "The pants are wool. You will die of the heat. Do you have a lighter-weight material?"

Horror flickered before she turned and dug into the closet again and this time removed a pair of blue lightweight capri pants and a white silk top. "I have scarves for color somewhere."

"With a pair of wedges it might be cute. Try the pants on real quick and let's see."

She slid off her jeans and pulled on the dress pants. She wriggled into them with some effort but she had to suck in her breath to barely zip up the zipper. It took three tries to fasten the top button. "I can't breathe."

"Pre-baby pants?"

"Yes," she whispered as she struggled not to pass out.

"Breathing always makes a date more fun. Got any other pants?"

She unfastened the pants, and let them fall to the floor.

"No. I had a winter pair and a summer pair. But I've not been out during the summer since the girls were born. Damn. I'm getting fat."

"Join the club."

She pulled out a dress she'd worn to a funeral months ago. "This is nice."

"Church lady, funeral dress. What about skirts?"

"Skirt. Makes sense." She stepped out of the pants pooling at her ankles and found an A-line dark skirt with an elastic waist. "I wore this after the girls were born. We had some meeting with the bankers." She slid on the skirt and then tried on the white silk top. I dug a brown belt from the closet and a pair of brown sandals. I shook my head. "The look is causal but nicely pulled together. It says I care, but I'm not so obsessed I spend hours in front of the mirror."

"Like Dragon Lady?"

"Exactly."

"Does it say low maintenance?"

"It says fun."

Rachel shook her head. "I don't want it to say I'm too low maintenance. I mean I know I'm happy with a cracker and a juice box, but I'd like to be a little more difficult."

"A shower and makeup will help with the image. Go ahead and clean up. I'll help you with your hair."

"Right. Clean is good."

She hurried to the bathroom, pulling her bra off as she went. Soon the hot spray of the shower swooshed from the bathroom.

I laid out the clothes on the bed and went to her jewelry box and dug out a couple of long chains of costume gold jewelry and hoop earrings.

Before I'd dated Gordon, he had been the man to catch in the office, which meant I'd gone out of my way to hide my interest. When he'd finally asked me out I'd refused. I didn't want to be a quick yes. I suggested he try again. I had always been standoffish with men and gave them a reason not to come back. Many didn't come back, but Gordon had. Two weeks after his first offering he'd countered with a second. A concert. Despite all my defenses I'd been charmed and the date really had been lovely. We'd ended up in bed within hours.

Rachel emerged from the steamy bathroom, her body and hair wrapped in towels. She sat in front of her makeup stand and met my gaze in the mirror. "What am I going to talk about with him?"

I removed the towel and brushed out her hair. "Whatever you want to talk about. The renovations are a good start. Tell him about the recipe box and Jenna Davis."

She met my gaze in the mirror. "Davis. When did you get her last name?"

"Margaret knows someone who sent me links."

"I swear, Margaret and her connections. Frightening."

"I know." I gave Rachel the latest on Jenna, wishing it had been a happy ending.

She reached for moisturizer and dabbed it on her face. "What do you think happened to the baby?"

"I don't know."

"He survived her?"

"The obit said he was ailing."

"And what about the dad?"

"Not mentioned."

A rush of sudden strong emotions welled up. I wanted to cry. What the hell? Crying was not me. And yet unshed tears burned my throat.

I grabbed the hair dryer and switched it on. While I dried her hair she applied her makeup. Within fifteen minutes her hair and makeup were done, and she was slipping into her skirt. Ten minutes later she was nibbling her lip as she stepped over the threshold of her apartment. "In high school only the geeks stood by the corner and waited for their dates."

My hands on her shoulders, I gave her a push. "Yeah. But you're not in high school, and it doesn't hurt to pretend to care."

She dug in her heels. "Would you come with me to meet him?"

"Why?"

"We can be pretending to talk about inventory or the renovation. I'm not really waiting downstairs for him, but I am working with you. What do you think we should be talking about when he pulls up?"

I laughed, tugging her down the stairs. "It's not like we need an elaborate backstory, Rachel. We can just be around." She nibbled her bottom lip more. At the rate she was going she'd not have a lip when Simon pulled up. "But I guess we could be figuring out where we're going to rehang pictures."

"Or maybe we could talk about our new wine cellar. Fits perfectly with the evening."

"And it will give you the flawless jumping-off spot for the evening. Our new wine cellar."

She frowned. "It will be a fun evening."

"Don't make it sound so forced. It will be fun."

"Right." She picked up a clipboard, which I suppose was a prop in our little play.

On the main floor we waited in the front part of the store. The fumes of the yellow paint had eased and the color had softened a fraction. The room had a bright, sunny feel and I imagined our grand re-opening, the cases uncovered, sparkling clean and filled with pastries.

Outside, a long sleek black car pulled up in front of the bakery. Simon got out of the car and moved toward the front door.

Rachel handed me a clipboard. "He's here."

I glanced at the clipboard and pretended to read. "He's coming to the door. What a nice young man."

"Daisy, he's older than you are."

I pointed to an imaginary notation and grinned. "Manners always count."

"Jesus, you sound like Mom." Pretending to look at the clipboard, she shook her head. "The change is starting."

I kept my gaze on the board. "What change?"

"You're turning into a Mom."

"Oh, I so am not!"

Rachel chuckled. "Wait, you'll see. Before you know it you'll be wearing jackets with big pockets crammed with kid crackers and bottles."

I wrapped my knuckle on the clipboard. "Never. I am not going to be nerd mom. I'll be a supercool mom."

"Wait until you are so tired you can't see straight. Then you won't care if you are covered in spit-up or if your socks match."

After the twins were born Rachel had looked like she'd been hit by a truck. Baby spit-up had been her new accessory and sweats and T-shirts her daytime look. I remembered thinking then I definitely didn't want to be a mother. Babies, it seemed, sucked the life out of you. "I'll care."

Her grin broadened. "Yeah, sure."

The sound of Simon's knuckles rapping on the front door erased

Rachel's smile. She took a step back, and I wasn't sure if she'd go to the door or run back upstairs.

To be sure, I blocked her retreat. "It's a quasi date, Rachel. You are not being fed to the lions."

Her grin broadened. "I'm not so sure."

"I am. Go. Have fun. And know I'll be waiting up polishing Dad's shotgun."

Nervous laughter bubbled. "Great."

Simon wore a blue sport jacket, white shirt, and khakis. All looked sharp and expensive. Good. Anyone dating my sister needed to bring his A game. "Want me to come out and have a word with your young man?"

"Yes. I mean, no." She straightened her shoulders. "No. I got this."

I waved to Simon and smiled.

He smiled back.

"Of course you do," I said. "It will be fun."

She released a breath, plastered on a bigger smile, and moved toward the door. "See you in a few hours."

"Take your time. The kid and I are going to hang. Maybe bake a Jenna cookie."

"Good." The far-off quality of her voice told me she'd barely heard.

As I watched Simon escort her to the car, open her door and wait until she was settled before sliding behind the wheel, I realized we were both entering new phases of our lives. Motherhood was my next destination and the single girl's life was Rachel's. We'd flipped roles. Two years ago we'd have laughed at such a notion as we held on tight to the lives we had. But the universe didn't so much care about what we wanted. It did what it did.

As much as I wanted to wish back my old life, to do that meant wishing away the kid, and I was growing fond of the little gal.

In the kitchen I could see Jean Paul had roughed in the area where the new freezer would go. Soon we'd be painting in here. A good thing. The new freezer came in days, and if we missed our delivery window the warehouse couldn't guarantee when they could deliver next. Gus's wine came in three days. Time enough for me to build the shelves in the basement.

So many pieces had to fall together to make this place happen.

I startled awake, expecting darkness. Since returning to the Union Street Bakery, I'd grown accustomed to waking up in the inky black of night. When I'd made a comment about this last week, Dad had laughed and welcomed me to the Baker's Club.

So as I looked around, I saw the dimming summer light seeping in my window and my laptop resting at the foot of the bed. I struggled to collect my bearings. The clock on the nightstand read 8:59 P.M. Shoving a hand through my hair, I realized I'd not slept through the night but had dozed off right after filling out the electrical inspection application.

I moved to rise but a heavy weight pressed me into the mattress. It pushed the air from my lungs. I tried to rise again and failed. Instead of panic, my annoyance flared.

No one touched me, but I sensed someone was in the room. I searched the shadowy corners just out of reach of the fading sun.

Someone was close. Watching. Judging. The air around me shifted, thickened and brushed my skin like a spiderweb.

Whenever I'm scared, I don't cower. I come out swinging. A survival mechanism developed at the ripe old age of three when Terry sauntered out of my life. Fight first. Worry second.

And now with a kid on board, I had more to lose and much more to protect.

In a clipped and angry voice, I said, "What do you want?"

The air around me grew heavier and colder. However, instead of sensing demanding energy, I detected a desperate and pleading quality.

Come at me with both barrels, and I'll go out of my way to nail you. But if you give me a hurt-puppy vibe, I melt. This very chink in my armor explained my current position at the bakery. If Mom had demanded my return, I'd have refused. If she'd shouted, I'd have yelled right back. If she'd insisted, I'd have said no.

But she hadn't pushed at all.

Instead, she'd plied me with daiquiris and asked nicely. *Your sister needs your help.* Mom knew me. Knew I caved to kindness. And she'd used it.

I yearned to pull the covers over my head and ignore this new desperate energy pulsing around me. But the piteous urgency strengthened, and so did my resolve to dismiss it.

"What do you want?" My voice lost its edge.

Find him.

It wasn't like I heard the words. No creepy far-off whisper to be mistaken for the wind. No chill cut through me. Just a *knowing*.

Find him.

"Find who? Who am I looking for?"

My heart thumped in my chest as I waited and listened, but no answer came. *Find him.*

"Specifics please."

Find him.

The pressure weighing me lifted. Frustrated, I sat up and searched the darkness. Silence radiated in the room. Waited. Listened. Nothing.

Leaning forward to click on a light, my fingers reached for the switch, when my stomach tumbled, turned and tumbled again. My breath caught in my throat. The voice forgotten, my attention shifted to the kid.

Had it moved?

Carefully I slid my hands under my T-shirt and laid them on my naked belly. Heart beating, I closed my eyes, turning all my energy inward as I waited, barely breathing. And then when I thought it had all been imagination or worse, gas, my stomach fluttered again. The movement was soft but distinct. The kid had moved.

My throat clogged with emotion and tears filled my eyes. I was dumbstruck. The other day when it had moved the sensation had been featherlight and could have been dismissed. Not now. There was definitely a person living inside of me and she was now moving.

I rubbed my belly in a soothing way. I thought about Gordon and what he would have said if the kid had been our kid and it had moved under his tanned, calloused palm. He'd have been thrilled. Tears would have welled in his eyes because Gordon had always been a softer touch than me. He liked all these mushy moments, and when we'd been together I often teased him about it. But not now. Now I wished with all I had he was here, and we'd shared this moment with the kid.

A tear rolled down the side of my cheek and for the first time since I found out about the kid I let the chained emotions free. Rolling on my side, I cried, not caring this time if it meant I was strong or weak. I didn't care. All I knew was I'd experienced a most miraculous moment, and there was no one to share it with. I was all by myself. Again. And for the first time in a long time I couldn't convince myself being alone was okay. I ached for Gordon.

I'm not sure how long I lay there letting the tears flow. I didn't bother to censor myself. I allowed the feelings to tumble freely.

My hands curled on my belly. "I promise you, kid, we'll figure this out. You are going to have a good life. I won't ever leave you."

Terry might have said the same words to me. But somehow I doubted it. We looked alike in so many ways, but I was stronger than Terry.

With renewed confidence, I swung my feet over the side of the twin bed. The floor warmed my feet.

Rising, I moved to my computer and opened e-mail. There wasn't any correspondence from Terry. Not surprised, I typed,

> I don't think it's asking a lot to have my genetic background.
> I want to know who my birth father is. I've tried to play nice, but
> I've run out of patience. Either tell me who he is/was, or I'll be on
> your doorstep asking the question in front of your family.

I signed the message "Daisy, your daughter." *Your daughter* might have been a little snippy and over the top, but I didn't care. I wanted information for the sake of the kid and I wasn't messing around. I hit Send.

I leaned back in the chair and for the first time since I'd met Terry, I didn't let guilt or worry overtake me. Maybe I'd grown more accepting of my birth-mother reunion. Maybe it was the late hour. Or maybe the kid deserved to know as much as I did.

Chapter Thirteen

Wednesday, 11:00 P.M.
9 days, 8 hours until grand reopening
Income Lost: $1,500

Rachel arrived back at the bakery after eleven. She was so grateful to be on home turf, she almost wept. Too nervous to eat all night, her stomach now growled as she moved into the kitchen to snag frozen cookie dough or day-old bread.

Unable to face the silence of her apartment, she tossed her purse and keys on the counter and pushed through the saloon doors. Switching on the light, she cringed at the chaos. A week ago she could locate any pot, pan, or spoon in this room. The kitchen had been her friend and her companion. Demanding and difficult at times, it was always here waiting for her. Now the place was as much a stranger to her as she was to herself.

She stepped around boxes and a circular saw and opened the stainless steel fridge to see bottles of wine and exotic cheeses. Jean Paul. The invader. The one that didn't belong.

Unable to find the cookie dough, she grabbed the wine and cheese, scrounged a Union Street Bakery mug and sat on a stool by the saw-horse worktable.

She filled the mug full of wine, and as she raised it to her lips she heard footsteps. Turning, she saw Jean Paul, unlit cigarette dangling from his mouth, staring at her. He wore a worn, brown leather jacket, jeans, and a black T-shirt, and in his hand he held a mesh sack filled with fruit and vegetables.

"What are you doing here?" She drank from the mug, enjoying the wine all the more because she'd taken it from him. In her mind, he'd taken her kitchen so turnabout was fair play.

Jean Paul came and went as he pleased much like a stray cat. Whether it was eleven o'clock at night or two in the morning on his day off, if he needed something, he appeared.

"You are up late." He glanced at his bottle, which she'd left on the counter, and set his bags beside it before grabbing a second mug. He filled his to the halfway point. "You like my wine?"

She smiled. "It's very nice."

Grunting, he took a sip and nodded his approval. "Life is too short to drink bad wine."

She stared into the depths of her cup. "Life is too short. But yet there are times when it drags on endlessly."

He arched a brow. "It slows when you allow it to dictate. If you are in charge, it does not dawdle."

She lifted the mug to her lips and paused. "Is it that way for you? Are you always in charge?"

"I do not worry about fast or slow. In charge or not. I enjoy." He sipped his wine and then from the sack pulled out a square of cheese wrapped in wax paper. He unwrapped it and then broke off a piece, which he offered to her.

Rachel took the cheese and bit into it. Creamy and buttery, it all but melted in her mouth. "Life is also too short for bad cheese."

He held up his glass to her. "Of course."

A smile teased her lips. "So what are you doing here?"

"I came to work. I'm used to working at this time of night. Each night I arrive before my shift and enjoy a café or a wine and a bit of cheese. I think about the dough, and then when it's time to cook I am ready."

Jean Paul had been working at the Union Street Bakery for over a month. His Uncle Henri had been a family friend and bakery employee for over twenty years, and when Henri recently retired he'd sent Jean Paul. That had been enough for Daisy, who'd been in desperate need of a baker. No resume necessary. Rachel had been grateful for his hire and resentful. He was yet another change in a life with too many changes.

The wine eased the tension in her muscles and wiped away some of the awkwardness. Her curiosity about him grew. "Have you heard from Henri recently?"

Jean Paul shrugged. "From what my mother says he is well. Visits the local bakeries in Nice and complains about the quality of the baking. Says bakers today don't understand tradition."

Rachel missed the old Frenchman. He'd been silent and stoic while he'd been here, but there'd been a steadiness about him that she'd not really appreciated until Mike died. "Sounds like Henri. Has he asked about us?"

"We have not spoken. I would have to ask my mother. They talk weekly."

"Please tell your mother I miss Henri."

He studied her with dark eyes filled with interest. "You and Henri were good friends?"

"I can't say I knew him all that well. My dad hired him, and he barely spoke to any of us. But Dad always said Henri was a master in the kitchen. No one baked better than Henri."

He tore off a piece of cheese for himself and took a measured bite as if he were analyzing it. "So, what are you doing here? There is no work for you this time of night."

The question had Rachel wondering who owned this kitchen. Perhaps at this time of night it was Jean Paul's and the space shifted back to her control at four in the morning. "Can't sleep. Thought I'd eat and maybe bake. But I forgot the kitchen had been pulled apart."

"You bake to relax?"

"You'd think I wouldn't, but it soothes me."

He shrugged as if the idea made perfect sense. "And why do you need soothing?"

"A long story."

He swept his hand before him as if reminding her they were two cooks in a nonworking kitchen. "I believe we have time."

The wine warmed her and allowed a smile. "I'd rather talk about you."

He arched a brow. He didn't tell her no, nor did he invite a question. So Jean Paul. So French.

Rachel sipped more wine, feeling bolder and more relaxed. "So what are you going to do tonight? There is no bread to mix."

"Fixing the cracks in the wall. Making it smooth before we paint."

Rachel glanced in his direction toward the drywall. "You are sanding."

"Yes."

"Ah." There'd be no cooking here tonight and she knew nothing of carpentry. It made sense for her to leave and go to her apartment. Tomorrow would be a long day, and she'd need all her sleep. But a restless energy churned her gut, and she sensed if she laid her head on her pillow her mind would swirl with all the what-ifs birthed tonight with Simon.

"I think I will clean out the spices. No sense restocking what is old."

He studied her as he sipped his wine. "It is a job that can wait, don't you think? Not so good to have spices mixing with drywall dust."

Rachel frowned. He made sense, of course, but she didn't want to go to her apartment. She could find Daisy but her sister had looked exhausted and no doubt had fallen asleep. Without the kitchen, without Mike, and without the girls, what would she do with her time?

"I could help you sand."

His gaze slid over her. "You are dressed for the evening. Not work."

"I could put on an apron."

Again a sly smile quirked. "Are you so desperate to be with me you will sand walls in the middle of the night?"

Heat rushed to her cheeks. "I am not desperate to be with you."

He set down his cup and shrugged off his jacket. Lean muscles rippled under a snug T-shirt as he walked toward the door and with great care hung his jacket on a hook. He moved like a cat that liked to be admired and petted.

Rachel stared at his butt and broad shoulders built by years of manual labor. Even as she imagined touching those shoulders, her mind scurried to a safe topic. "Will the wall be ready to paint soon?" Her voice cracked. She cleared her throat. "The freezer arrives day after tomorrow."

He turned as if sensing her gaze on him. For a moment, dark eyes held hers. In the mocha depths she saw raw sexual energy. "It will be dry by tomorrow, and I will paint tomorrow night and then your new freezer will have its place."

Her mouth grew as dry as stale flour. "Ah."

"Why are you so dressed up? Is it for me?"

Rachel straightened, embarrassed because she couldn't stop ogling. She reached for her wine, lifted it to her lips and then thought better of having more. "I had a date tonight."

He arched a brow, curious now. "Ah. A date. What man took you out?"

His proprietary tone thrilled and intrigued her. "Simon Davenport."

He folded those lean muscled arms over his chest as if posturing. "He is a client, no?"

"A very good client."

He did not seem impressed. "So where did this Simon take you?"

She traced the rim of her cup. "The wine festival."

He studied her. "And the date was not to your liking?"

A small shrug lifted her shoulders. "It wasn't bad." A sudden memory flashed in her mind. "No, it was bad. So very bad."

Dark brows rose. "Why? Was he terrible to you?"

"Oh, no. God, no. He was the perfect gentleman. I, however, was a mess. I couldn't stop talking about the girls and Mike." She closed her eyes as if trying to will away a memory. "I could hear myself talking about my dead husband and the little voice in my head told me to shut up, but I couldn't."

He leaned a fraction closer, his gaze settling on her mouth. "And what did this Simon say?"

"He barely spoke. He listened because I couldn't stop talking. I know I bored him to tears. I know he was so grateful to drop me off and run as far away from me as he could."

He studied her a beat. "Did he kiss you?"

"What?" Heat burned her cheeks. "No."

Jean Paul grunted.

Rachel leaned toward him. "What does that mean? Is that bad or good?"

He shrugged. "I would have kissed you."

A laugh startled from her. "You'd have kissed me knowing I was a blathering idiot much like I am now."

He unfolded his arms and picked up her hand. Slowly he traced her palm. "You are a very beautiful idiot."

She frowned, not sure if she should be mad or pleased. But as he continued to trace her palm with his calloused fingertip, her thoughts scattered and ran like frightened rabbits, leaving her alone with a forgotten sensation in the pit of her belly.

It had been so long since Rachel had been kissed or been held by a man. So long since she'd lost herself in an embrace and given in to pure sensation.

Simon had been utterly polite when all she'd wanted him to do was take charge of the conversation as Mike would have. But he hadn't. He'd simply listened as she'd dithered.

Jean Paul raised her hand to his lips and he kissed her palm.

As much as logic told her to pull away, she didn't. She liked being touched, liked the sexual need growing and the fact that in that moment she could melt into the floor from wanting.

Jean Paul kissed her palm again and then he kissed her wrist and the crease at her elbow.

She kept her gaze on him, not sure if she fully trusted herself or him. Of herself, she feared she'd lose her nerve and hide. Of him, she feared he'd stop.

He shifted, tugged her arm until she stepped toward him and they were less than an inch apart. Their lips did not touch, but barely a whisper separated them.

"Kiss me," he said.

She wasn't expecting words and had to shift her brain back to conscious thought so she could speak. "What?"

"Kiss me."

If he'd ordered her to alter a recipe or change her menu she'd have argued with great passion. But he wasn't asking about ingredients or baked goods. He wanted her to kiss him.

Her heart thundered so hard in her chest, she feared it would burst free. She was so scared. So unsure. And so wanting this moment. And he was Jean Paul—confident, patient, and waiting.

Finally, she moistened her lips, leaned in, and touched her lips to his. It was a feather-soft touch. Maybe not an official kiss. But skin did touch skin.

He put his hand at the base of her neck and pressed her close until her lips flattened against his. As they did so, he opened his mouth and teased the underside of her top lip with his tongue.

She opened her mouth, awkward and unsure, as if she'd been transported back to high school—the last time she'd known such unexplained and terrifying wonder.

Rachel leaned into the kiss, moved to deepen. She wrapped her arms around his neck. She didn't know where this was going and she did not care.

And that's when she heard the kitchen door open and Daisy say, "Really? *Really?* What are you doing?"

Rachel froze. Stiffened. She was mortified.

Jean Paul, relaxed as if he did not have a care in the world, looked at Daisy. "Isn't it clear? I am kissing your sister."

From Rachel's apartment refrigerator, I grabbed eggs and butter and set them on the counter.

"They really need to be room temperature," Rachel said as she sipped her mug of wine.

"I've never been good at waiting. I can cheat the butter a bit in the microwave and the eggs will have to find a way to blend cold."

"Patience is a must."

Mise en place—everything in its place. It's a lesson Dad grilled into me since I could stand on a stool beside him in the kitchen. No matter how reckless or rushed, I took the time to line up the sugar, vanilla, salt, baking powder, and nuts.

When I came down the stairs to ask Rachel about Simon, I'd have bet a paycheck I'd never have found her in an embrace with Jean Paul. Their kiss was so not *mise en place*. "You didn't look so patient when you were kissing the baker. What was that about?"

She stared into the depths of her mug. "I'm not really sure."

I unwrapped a pound of butter, dropped in it a ceramic dish and popped it in the microwave. I pressed the thirty-second button. This cheat required I pay attention. Too many times I'd walked away thinking the butter would simply soften and when I returned it was a pure liquid. Still delicious, but unusable for cookies. And so I stood close, watching the butter turn in circles and soften. At twenty-three seconds I pulled it out. Seven seconds separated usable butter from liquid. Seven seconds standing between success and failure.

But then bakers lived their lives on the margin. Profits were slim, hard-won, the difference found in scraps of dough or slivers of bread.

"Want to tell me about it?"

Her cheeks still glowed a light pink. "Not much to tell. It just happened."

I measured brown sugar and dumped it into the butter. "How did the date with Simon go?"

"Terrible."

I paused as I reached for a wooden spoon. "Was he rude?"

"No. He was sweet. I kept rambling about Mike and the kids. I could hear the words coming out of my mouth but I couldn't stop them."

With the spoon, I mixed my cookie dough as Jenna might have. It didn't take long, mixing the dough by hand, before my arm started to ache. I'd grown strong since I'd returned to the bakery, but like everyone I relied on the machines to do the heavy mixing and blending.

"So are you going to see him again?" I said.

"Simon?"

I arched a brow. "One man at a time."

That coaxed a grin. "I doubt *Simon's* interested."

I creamed the batter faster. "How can you be sure?"

"I called him Mike. Twice."

I winced. "Okay, well you did break the ice. You wondered what it would be like to date and now you know. Sometimes good. Sometimes very awkward. That's good." Glancing at Jenna's careful handwriting, I measured out vanilla and cinnamon. After mixing more, I measured the dry ingredients and sifted them together into a separate bowl before spooning one-third into the wet ingredients. "So about Jean Paul?"

"I have no idea where that came from. He came up to me, asked me if Simon had kissed me and the next thing I know I'm kissing him." She shook her head. "It was a onetime event. Never again. Feeling sorry for myself after my date."

"It's okay if it happens more than once, Rachel. You are a big girl."

Her eyes widened. "He's our baker."

"So was Mike."

"And you don't see the parallel? I think this is a little too close to the past to be right." Panic turned her normally calm voice shrill.

"Mike and Jean Paul are night and day."

"I don't know Jean Paul well enough to know. But he is a baker, and he works here." Rachel buried her face in her hands. "Dating is so damn much work."

Grinning, I nudged her arm. "But you must admit, this day was pretty memorable."

She shook her head. "Many more days like today, and I'll have a nervous breakdown."

The bakery's front door bell buzzed. I glanced at the clock. "It's midnight."

Rachel's eyes widened. "Do you think its Simon?"

"Could be."

Groaning, she held up her hands. "I am not here. I have moved to Africa."

Chuckling, I wiped my hands. "I'll check it out. Should I say you are in Kenya or the Sudan?"

"Funny." She peered toward the window in her living room that overlooked Union Street. "Who comes to the bakery at this hour?"

"Jean Paul is working in the kitchen. Someone must have seen the light."

"Still," she said as she rose. "People do not visit the bakery at midnight."

I tossed my rag on the counter. "Suppliers? A customer? A neighbor? Could be an emergency. I'll go see."

"Not alone. I'll come with."

"What if it's Simon?"

"Then I'll run."

As we moved toward the first floor, I heard Jean Paul speaking to another man. The voice was too clipped and deep to be Simon. As I rounded the corner and saw our visitor, my mouth dropped and my belly tightened. "Gordon."

When I didn't move, Rachel laid her hand on my shoulder. "He is not here for me."

Now it was my turn to worry and entertain thoughts of running. "He might be."

"No, this drama is all yours. I'm happy to sit this one out." She pushed gently. "Go talk to him."

I descended the remaining stairs into the kitchen and pushed through the saloon doors. Jean Paul had flipped on the lights, softening the buttery yellow on the walls. The soothing glow did little for my uneasy nerves.

Jean Paul glanced at Rachel, his gaze lingering just a split second, and then he turned and disappeared back into his kitchen. Rachel scurried back up the stairs, leaving me alone with Gordon. Coward.

The exterior light above the entrance shined on Gordon as he stood by the front door. His hands shoved in his jeans pockets, he wore a gray short-sleeved T-shirt and sneakers. Despite a downcast gaze, I could see he looked exhausted. Why hadn't it ever been easy for us?

I moistened my lips and pushed my hands through my hair. "Hey."

He looked up and I got a good look at the dark circles hanging under his eyes. Once again I'd upended his life. "I saw your light on and took a chance you were in the kitchen."

"Jean Paul is working late."

He frowned. "Did I wake you?"

"No. Rachel and I were trying out a recipe upstairs. We found a recipe box in one of the walls. Weird. It's turning out to be a very interesting story." I was blathering just as Rachel had done with Simon.

His gaze sharpened. "I didn't come here to talk about recipes, Daisy."

Smoothing hands over my pants, I shrugged. "No. I suppose not."

"Can I come in?"

"Sure." I stepped aside and let him into the shop and then locked the door behind him.

He glanced around the shop. "I like the color."

A quip came to mind. *So you came to talk about paint colors?* But I forced myself to stay silent. "Thanks. The place needed a little brightening. The construction in the back is nearly done, too. Soon as our electrical inspection gets done, we'll be installing the freezer. And the wine arrives early next week. No doubt we'll be stocking shelves and baking all week to be ready for the opening next Saturday."

"Is all that work good for . . ." He stopped, flattening his lips into a grim line.

"The baby. Is it good for the baby? So far so good with the kid. The doc says she's fine, and I'm on target for a Christmas due date." Might as well get the difficult details out of the way.

The frown lines in his forehead deepened. For a moment he didn't speak. "So you know it's a girl."

"Girl? No, I don't know for sure one way or the other, but I've been saying *her* for the last few days. Makes sense, I guess."

"Christmas isn't the best time for a baker to have a baby."

"No, it is not. But first I have to get the renovation finished before I freak out about that. I did hire a couple of kids to help in the afternoons."

"Good."

More heavy silence settled between us. Each of us had so much emotion needing a voice but neither of us could find the words. "I don't know what you want me to say, Gordon. 'I'm sorry' doesn't come close. This kid is so unexpected, but she's here to stay. I know that sucks for you. I do. If you'd knocked up another woman during our breakup, I'm not so sure how charitable I'd be."

He swallowed. "I get you didn't intend this. I understand you didn't cheat."

"But it still hurts."

"Yeah. It hurts." His gaze lowered to my belly hidden under the oversized T-shirt and then back up to my face.

"I'm sorry. You deserve a much less complicated woman than me. You really do."

He pulled his shoulders back. "I expect complications from you. I might not like them, but I know they are part of the package."

"This complication is a whopper."

"It is."

"I care a lot about you, Gordon. I've even used the L-word." A sigh shuddered through me. "I understand we won't survive this as a couple but I'd like us to at least be friends."

He swept back his bangs with his hand. "Have you told the baby's father about your pregnancy?"

"No. One can of worms at a time."

He rattled change in his pocket. "Are you going to tell him?"

I nodded. "I have to, Gordon. It wouldn't be fair to the kid not to."

"Roger isn't father material, Daisy."

"I know. But the kid has his DNA. And DNA is kinda important, especially when you don't have access to it."

"DNA doesn't make a parent."

"I know. But DNA is an important piece of the puzzle. I should know." How could I make him understand? He could trace his family back to the Revolutionary War. "Terry has yet to return my e-mails or phone messages about my birth father."

"Whoever the guy is who got Terry pregnant, he is not your dad."

"I know. I have a great dad. The best. And a great mom. But this guy is a piece of my puzzle. I'd thought I could live with pieces missing but since the kid, I want to know what's lurking in the genetic family tree. Whoever this dude is, he's part of the kid."

"So what are you going to do if Roger wants in your life?"

Jealousy had crept in between the words, and it pleased me. I wanted Gordon to want me. I wanted him to say the L-word back. I wanted him to hold me and tell me it would all work out. That we would work out. "Roger will not want back in my life."

"What if he does?" I glimpsed the tenacity that had allowed him to rise in the financial world.

"It's irrelevant. I don't want Roger back in my life. Period. End of story. He was an unfortunate waste of time that wouldn't have happened if I'd been remotely sober."

He nodded. "Okay."

I pressed fingertips to my head. I'd been so full of energy a half hour ago and now fatigue taxed heavily on my shoulders.

The kid chose that moment to do a full summersault in my gut. The sudden move had my eyes widening and my hand slipping to my stomach.

Concern widened his eyes. "You all right?"

"The kid moved." I'm not sure what made me reach for his hand, but I did. I unfurled his fisted fingers and laid his palm flat against my rounding belly. His touch warmed my skin and sent my heartbeat racing. For a moment we just stood there, both of us shocked to be so close and touching in such an intimate way.

The kid had been touchy about moving on command, and I didn't expect her to jump to action now. She was difficult like her old lady. But every so often I stepped up to the plate and helped out when no one expected it. I hoped the kid would take pity and do the same for me now.

And she did.

She kicked hard against my belly and the palm of his hand as if she wanted him to know she was also a part of this conversation.

"Did you feel that?" he said. No missing the amazement in his voice.

"Oh, yeah. The kick caught me right in the ribs."

His hand remained on my stomach. "Has she been moving much?"

"Just started today." I liked the feel of his warm hand on my belly. It felt right and so natural, like this is what a million other couples had done millions of times before. I wanted to kiss him. To celebrate the child. But I didn't dare. This sweet moment rested on a shaky foundation of surprise and politeness, not of a shared child or a bright future.

As if reading my thoughts, Gordon pulled his hand back, curled his fingers into a fist at his side and straightened. "I'm glad she's all right."

"Thanks."

Silence settled between us and for a moment the awkwardness rose up again. Gordon cleared his voice. "So you are going to call Roger?"

"More like e-mail. And honestly I'd rather deliver the news via the Internet, give him a chance to scream and rant, and then talk to him over the phone."

He drew in a breath. "You don't have to tell him, Daisy. I know Roger. He's a dick."

That jostled free a laugh. "You don't have to tell me. I know. But I need to tell him."

"Why?"

"Like I said before, it's all about DNA. The kid has a right to know."

He shook his head. "The child has a right to a family. Parents who love her."

My hackles rose. "I intend to give her a family."

"How? You're barely making it now. A baker works long damn hours. Where's a kid going to fit into the mix?"

Raising my chin, I swallowed my doubts. "There will be a space for her. Rachel said she'd help."

"Have you told your mom and dad?"

"Not yet. They are out of town with the twins. I'm going to tell them when they get back."

"I'm surprised your mom didn't pick up on this."

"I've been living in large T-shirts and wearing aprons all the time. And she's been busy with Dad. He's been back and forth to the heart doctor."

"He doing all right?"

"Yeah. He says he feels great. It takes more work to keep him on track healthwise."

"The baby is going to be a shock."

"Hey, you don't have to tell me. I can list all the ways I've f-ed up because I didn't control my reproductive system. But the problem is not going anywhere."

He studied my face as if trying to peel back layers. "You couldn't have done this two years ago. You'd have taken a different route. An easier solution."

"I'd like to think I'd have gone through with the pregnancy even then, but you're right. I don't know if I could have done it."

"As much as it pains me to know Roger was the man to get you pregnant, I know you'll be a good mother, Daisy."

Before I could think, tears welled and I was swiping away tears. "Thanks, Gordon. That really is sweet."

He paled. "I didn't mean to make you cry."

My laugh sounded sloppy. "I'm a bit emotional these days. Moody."

He arched an amused brow. "You, moody? I can't believe that."

Laughter made me cry more. "Would you give me a hug? I know it's messed up between us, but I could use a hug."

He hesitated a moment and then opened his arms wide. I stepped into his embrace and hugged my arms tight around his body. Carefully, as if I were made of china, he held me close. I inhaled his scent, savoring the subtle blend of soap and the faint aroma of bike oil. I'd not realized how deep my loneliness had burrowed. Having him hold me now tempted to make my knees to buckle.

"God, I've missed you," he whispered.

"I've missed you." The words all but rushed past my lips as if refusing to be stopped or censored.

"On the bike trip when you didn't call, I could feel trouble. And then when you told me about the baby I was so angry."

I nestled my face close to his chest. "I'm sorry."

"I'm not angry at you. I'm angry the baby's not mine. When we were together you weren't ready for us to have a baby, but I was."

I sniffed back tears. "Our timing has been one disaster after another."

He pulled back, cupped my face in his hands, and kissed me on the lips. He tasted sweet and salty and better than he'd tasted before. I wrapped my arms around his neck and kissed him hard on the lips. I can be ham-fisted with words and have a talent for messing up the right line. But I could pour all my unspoken feelings into a kiss. I hoped I could *show* him how I wanted him and not Roger. I pressed my body against his, knowing if he gave me the slightest hint he wanted me now we'd end up in bed.

Instead of pulling me deeper into his arms, he broke the embrace and looked me directly in the eye. "Don't tell him, Daisy."

For a moment I blinked, my lips left swollen and parted. A moment passed before my brain clicked back online. "Don't tell Roger?"

His hands slid to my shoulders and his fingers tightened as if he held on for courage. "Don't tell Roger. I'll help you with the baby. I'll be the father. We'll pretend Roger never happened."

I didn't pull free also knowing I didn't have the courage in this moment to stand alone. What he was saying . . . the solution he offered . . . would fix all my problems. I'd have a partner. The kid would have a real dad. I'd have a safety net. The cost for this very perfect life would be to deny the kid its DNA. Sweep Roger and all his chromosomes under the rug and forget.

Forget him.

Tears welled in my eyes. "I want to give you what you want right now. God, how I want to give this to you."

He frowned. "But you won't."

Emotion clogged my throat. Why was love so hard? "It's not about what I want. I need to think about the kid."

Frustration deepened the frown lines on his forehead. "That's who I'm thinking about."

"I know. But information like this doesn't stay buried forever. We might think we'd be fooling the kid but it would come out. Somehow."

"Who else knows about Roger?"

"Rachel knows the story."

"She'll keep the secret."

"Secret." Such a little secret now. Barely consequential. But it would grow with each passing year. The baby would notice she didn't look like Gordon. She might realize they didn't have the same sense of humor or their ears were shaped differently or her hair was too curly like Roger's. She'd eventually ask, *Who do I look like?* And then I'd have to look her in the eye and lie.

"That's no way to parent. I know your heart is in the right place, but one day the kid is going to put two and two together. She's mine after all and curiosity is buried deep in her DNA. I have to be honest with her about how she was made."

"Why?"

"To lie about where she comes from is as good as saying she's not good enough."

"Daisy, that's bullshit. You are reading far more into this."

"I was the adopted kid. I know how it feels to be out of step."

"You were abandoned at age three. You suffered trauma. From day one this kid will have real parents who love her."

I traced his jawline with my thumb. "I really believe you'd love her like she were flesh and blood."

"I would."

"I can't lie to her. I have to tell Roger. I can't keep secrets because they come home to roost. One day the kid would put the pieces together and resent the hell out of me and you."

He stepped back and rubbed a tense hand against the back of his neck. "So you are saying no to me."

"I'm saying yes to being honest with my kid."

"Your kid."

"She could be ours."

"With pencil-dick Roger in the mix." His eyes narrowed. "You know why the son of a bitch went to China? Yeah, he took the job over there because he's running from a hell of a lawsuit. The guy lied more times than I can count."

"I didn't know."

"Shit, Daisy, if your goal was to pick the biggest piece of slime to go down on, then you found him. Great job."

His verbal sting had me racing past hurt, and annoyance, and straight to really pissed off. "Why don't you stop while you are behind and leave?"

Sad eyes darkened with anger. "That's always your solution, isn't it, Daisy, to kick someone out or run. You never stay and fight."

"Fight for what? More insults?" My voice reverberated off sunny yellow walls.

"Stand your ground and don't be such a coward. People do get mad at each other without running."

"You aren't mad," I said my voice rising. "You are being an ass. You insulted me, and yet it's my fault I want you to leave?"

He jabbed tense fingers through his hair. "Look, I was over the line, but I have a right to be angry."

"You don't have a right to speak to me the way you did!"

The saloon doors slammed open and Jean Paul appeared in the doorway, casually holding a hammer in his hand. He looked at Gordon, his gaze fairly menacing. "Is there a problem?"

I stepped back from Gordon, my hands trembling as I held them up. "I'm fine. We were having a fight."

"Yes, I could hear," Jean Paul said. "I imagine you also upset your sister."

Gordon shoved out a breath. "Go back to your kitchen and let us finish."

Jean Paul didn't move. "I think not."

"Daisy," Gordon ground out.

I understood Gordon was hurt and upset. He'd offered what he saw as one hell of an olive branch, and I'd all but slapped it out of his hand. But I didn't take rejection well on a good, nonpregnant day, and his reckless words still rattled painfully in my head. "Go, Gordon. This is not the time to have this kind of conversation."

"When is the best time?"

"I don't know if there is a best time. But I can't stand here and be insulted."

"Look, I am sorry." His brusque tone didn't help his case.

"So am I. We are two well-meaning people who can't seem to get it right."

"So you are giving up?"

"Right now, yes. My life is eggshells, Gordon. I don't have the reserves to look after your emotions, the baby's, and mine. I barely have enough for the kid and me."

His lips flattened. "Fine. Have it your way." And he turned, fists clenched, and stalked out of the shop.

Chapter Fourteen

Friday, 8:00 A.M.
8 days until grand reopening
Income Lost: $1,700

Rachel and I had retreated to the basement, putting together the shelves that would stock our new wine collection. Jean Paul had finished prepping the walls and was painting upstairs. The inspector, Mr. Fraser, had come early and inspected Jean Paul's electrical work and given it the official thumbs-up. The movers had yet to come and haul the baking equipment to the main floor, but Jean Paul had assured me we'd have the basement cleared before the wine arrived. We were inching forward.

I'm a linear thinker, and I like to tackle one task at a time. Multitasking had never been my strong suit. But I was learning if I didn't multitask the bakery would close. It required someone who could keep juggling lots of balls.

The shelves were black and sleek and had been on sale, but

deciphering the instructions threatened to drive me to drink, swear, or scream. "These don't make sense to me."

"I can see why these shelves were such a deal," Rachel muttered. She looked panicked as she stared at the collection of screws laid out on the white sheet. I'd insisted on the sheet knowing I'd crack if we lost a screw or a bolt.

"I choose to believe if we follow the steps correctly, we'll have shelves."

"Too bad life doesn't work that way."

Smiling, I reread the third section. "So I think I have it. You hold boards A and B, and I will connect with bolt one."

"Which ones are boards A and B?"

"The farthest board on the right is A. We read from left to right so I arranged from left to right."

Rachel nodded and picked up the boards. "If you ever really want to punish me, put me in a room with one of these to assemble."

"I'll remember that."

She held the boards together so they formed a long L.

"Board B is backward," I said.

Frowning, she studied the setup. "How can you tell?"

"Because the sign facing me says *Back* not *Front*."

She studied the instructions, shook her head and flipped the board around. "Right."

This went on for another hour. For the most part it went smoothly. Once I attached a board backward and Rachel caught it. Muttering words, I unscrewed the fastener and reattached it. When we finished the first set of shelves both of us stood back to admire the work. The shelf was seven feet tall, black, and had vertical slots that held the wine. Against the basement's brick wall it looked kind of cool, and for the first time in a couple of days I thought maybe all of this might really come together.

"Three to go," I said.

Rachel groaned. "Kill me."

"It should get easier."

She brushed back a stray curl. "From your lips to God's ears."

And so we tackled the second set of shelves, which took half the time to assemble. More progress. At least this one small part of my life was under control.

"We've got this."

Rachel offered a tentative smile. "You have jinxed us."

"We'll be fine." I needed to master these shelves. I needed something to go really right. *A little control, please.*

The third set of shelves was missing three screws, which I had to steal from the fourth set. When the third set was complete, I studied the fourth incomplete box. "We know we're missing screws from the top section. So we know we can at least build two-thirds of the shelf."

"And then what?"

"If Jean Paul can't rig a fix I'll have to make a run for the hardware store."

"Great."

Rachel held boards A and B in an L shape. "So how was your meeting with Gordon last night?"

She'd not asked so I'd pretended it had never happened. "Not too well."

I screwed in the first fastener. Maybe if I could make the pieces of the shelves fit I could reassemble my life without having to borrow pieces or rig joints.

"I didn't exactly listen at the door," she said. "But I heard the tension in his voice and yours." She held up the next set of boards while I repeated with fasteners.

Gaze on the screws, I maintained a steady tone of voice. "I'm fairly sure I blew my life out of the water."

"Why?"

I focused on twisting the screw into place. My voice was barely a whisper. "He said he'd be the baby's father. He said we didn't need to tell Roger, the bio dad, and we could raise the baby ourselves."

Rachel paused. "Daisy. Do you realize what he was saying to you?"

Emotion choked my throat. "Yes."

She studied my face. "So why did he sound mad?"

A sigh shuddered from my chest. "I said I had to tell Roger about the baby. I couldn't keep a secret like that."

She nodded slowly. We'd been together since we were three and though we didn't always agree we knew each other very well. "He was pretty mad."

"He doesn't understand why I need to tell Roger." A bemused bark of a laugh escaped. "I can't say I understand. Maybe if I knew who my biological father was I could let this go. But I can't deny the kid what has been denied me."

"You've not heard from Terry."

I arched a brow.

"She's playing games again."

I shook my head. "I don't think she means to be cruel. I think dealing with me and her past is hard." The admission stung deeper than I thought and for a moment I stared at the screwdriver in my hand.

Rachel put her arm around my shoulders and hugged me close. I shrugged off her embrace, pretty sure I'd cry if she hugged me. And this she understood, too. It wasn't the first time I'd run from comfort.

We finished assembling the first section, bringing the last set of shelves up to my hips.

"Do we still have that order with Simon?"

She arched a brow. "He hasn't canceled it. And canceling would not be his style. He is a gentleman."

"So, you're going to have to see him when we make the delivery."

"No, you're making the delivery. I will bake, but I will not go see him. Not yet."

"Rachel, you cannot be a baby about this. You are going to have to go do the delivery. I can't do it alone."

She pouted a little. "I don't want to."

"I could give you a list of all the things I don't want to do, but I won't bore you. Running a bakery isn't for sissies."

Her frown deepened. "If Mike weren't dead I think I'd kill him right now. He said we'd be together forever and he lied."

"He didn't mean it, Rachel."

Her blue eyes blazed with anger. "I don't give a shit! He left. Period. End of story."

In the last eighteen months Rachel had kept a stiff upper lip. But that lip had quivered a lot lately and frankly I was glad. No way you could take a hit like she did and not feel gutted.

"You are supposed to be angry," I said.

"Why the hell do I have to be angry? I don't like being angry!" she shouted.

"Because you've got to get pissed to move forward."

"You've been angry all your life, Daisy. Where has it gotten you?"

I sat back, stunned. I wasn't sure if I should be hurt, amused or . . . angry.

Rachel's eyes widened. "I'm sorry, Daisy. I didn't mean it."

I shook my head, deciding on amused. "You are right. I've been angry for a long time." I sighed. "I don't want you to end up like me, which is why venting emotion is good. Bottle it up like me, and the anger will burrow bone deep."

She blinked. "Are you that angry?"

"Some days, yes. Some days, no. You aren't wired like I am. Happy is your style."

"Happy. I'm not sure what happy feels like anymore."

"It will return."

"When?"

No cute wisecrack came to mind. "I don't know."

We finished the shelves, a heavy silence hanging between us as we each brooded over our own worries. Despite all the trouble, the black shelving looked very sharp against the ancient stone wall. Clear out the debris, add wine bottles to the shelves, we'd have our own wine room.

"Damn," I said. "This is coming together, Rachel."

She folded her arms over her chest, studied the arrangement, and shrugged. "It looks pretty good."

I nudged her with my elbow. "And it's going to look great when the wine arrives. We will turn a nice profit on those wines. We are making this work."

She stuck out her bottom lip. "Maybe."

"Maybe, my ass. This is happening, Rachel."

The squeal of little voices and the thunder of excited feet had us both looking toward the stairs.

"Sounds like the girls," Rachel said.

"Yeah." I'd bet Mom and Dad would last three days. Rachel had bet two. They surprised us both by making it five. "Hopefully they haven't killed Mom and Dad."

"I better go check." She bounded up the stairs, the spring returning to her step. She'd missed her girls.

I rose and followed. We found Jean Paul showing Mom, Dad, and the girls our progress. Mom and Dad both looked a little pale. Mom didn't wear any makeup and her blue T-shirt was stained with something purple. Dad hadn't shaved in a couple of days and his shirt was inside out. They both looked like a truck had hit them.

But the girls were dressed in rumpled blue shorts and matching yellow T-shirts that read, *Outer Banks Rocks!*, which were no doubt a souvenir from their gemstone rock adventure. Their ponytails were askew but they were giggling and jumping with energy.

"Hey!" Rachel said.

"Mom!" The girls squealed as they ran to Rachel. She hugged them close, kissing one as they talked excitedly about their trip.

Dad nodded in my direction as he scanned the new buttery yellow. "Looking good, Daisy. Coming together. I like the yellow."

His approval made me smile. "We're getting there, Dad."

Rachel removed Ellie's crooked ponytail, smoothed her hair with her fingers and then refastened it with the hair tie. "Wait until you see the kitchen."

Jean Paul's gaze flickered briefly to Rachel but he gave no hint of what had happened last night. Rachel blushed ever so slightly. However, I sensed awareness between the two that made the air crackle.

"I will give you a tour, Monsieur McCrae," Jean Paul said. "Please follow me."

Dad nodded, his gaze now alight with interest. He glanced toward me and I nodded for them to continue. "Lead the way."

As Dad and Jean Paul left for the kitchen, Mom crossed and gave me a tight hug. She pulled me close and then for a split second her body stiffened. She pulled back and her gaze dropped to my belly. "Daisy Sheila McCrae."

I smiled, sheepish.

She frowned. Her hand slid to my stomach as if she needed to confirm her thought.

"Surprise?"

She closed her eyes for a moment. "Why don't we have a chat in your room?"

No avoiding this conversation. I'd not really worried about telling Mom about the baby, but now that crunch time had arrived I wasn't so sure of myself. "Sure."

"Frank, Daisy and I are going to catch up. Rachel has the girls."

No missing the relief in Dad's gaze as he nodded and headed into the kitchen. "See you in a bit."

Rachel glanced over the head of the girls at me. She raised a brow as if to offer help, but I waved her away as I followed Mom up to the third floor.

When I closed my door her gaze narrowed. "You are pregnant."

I shoved out a breath. "Yeah."

She rubbed her temple with the tips of her fingers. "How did you manage this?"

"Would you like a play-by-play?"

"Don't be smart, Daisy Sheila. I know how you managed it. Start with when and then maybe who."

"The night before I returned to the bakery. Call it a memento of my going-away party."

"Daisy, you are thirty-four years old, and I taught all you girls about the birds and the bees."

Having this kind of lecture from my mom rankled, but I deserved it. "Stuff happens. I didn't plan it. And believe me, I've been in a state of shock."

She glanced at my belly. "How long have you known?"

"About a week. I didn't catch on right away and chalked the difference up to stress."

She sighed, clearly frustrated she'd missed it as well. Mom prided herself on keeping her finger on the pulse of the family. "So that flu you had the last couple of weeks . . ."

"Delayed morning sickness. Seems morning sickness can come at any time in the pregnancy, and I'm here to say it doesn't occur only in the morning but can linger all day long."

Mom shook her head, a hint of sympathy softening her features. "It was that way when I carried Margaret. She made me sick as a dog."

"Well, my kid is doing the same to me." I rubbed the back of my neck. "How'd you get through it?"

"I look back and wonder how I did do it all. Your dad and I had only been married months, I was still adjusting to working in the bakery, and your grandmother wasn't crazy about me. And then I found out I was pregnant."

It didn't occur to me my pregnancy experience could mirror Mom's. "So what did you do?"

"A lot of ginger ale and crackers behind the counter and I just kept putting one foot in front of the other."

"What did Dad say?"

"I think he was terrified and excited. We were barely making it, and soon we'd have another mouth to feed."

I groaned. "I'm feeling the same way. Scared, sick, and worried."

"You are Dad and me rolled into one." She patted me on the shoulder. "But you are the strongest of us all, Daisy. And you are not alone. You've the McCrae clan, as imperfect as we are, behind you."

Love and gratitude tightened my chest. "The kid and I are going to need you."

"The kid." Her eyes softened. "I didn't think you wanted children."

"I didn't. But I'm growing fond of this kid."

Mom placed her hand on my belly. Round and hard, there was no missing the fact it was a baby bump. "When are you due?"

"Christmas."

She laughed. "Oh, dear. That'll make for a hectic season."

Unable to read her tone, I was suddenly unsure. "I'm sorry about all this. I thought I had a handle on my life."

She shook her head, an amused look in her eyes. "Sometimes good luck comes disguised as disaster, Daisy." And then a smile brightened her eyes. "I've missed having a baby in the house. It'll be nice."

Tears filled my eyes. I'd not realized how much I needed to hear her say she was happy about the kid. "You're not mad?"

"Honey, I've been in your shoes. Granted I was married, but I didn't plan on getting pregnant with Margaret so soon. But after Dad and I got over the shock we felt more and more protective of her. After a week of knowing I was pregnant, I'd have been devastated if I lost her."

"That's how I feel."

Mom grinned. "Oh, you wait. She's going to take over your heart. You won't know what hit you when this child arrives."

I swiped away a tear. "Thanks."

Mom frowned as she stared at my belly. "Gordon is not the father." When my gaze turned from weepy to surprised, she arched a brow. "I wasn't born yesterday, Daisy. I get you were having sex when you were in Washington. And from what you've told me you and Gordon weren't seeing each other at all then."

"No, we were not."

"Have you told him?"

"Gordon or the birth father?"

"Both."

"Yes to Gordon."

She smoothed a stray lock of hair out of my eyes. "How did it go?"

I shook my head, feeling the weight of Gordon's disappointment. "About as badly as you can imagine. He told me to get out."

Mom frowned. "That doesn't sound like Gordon."

"If the shoe were on the other foot I'd have thrown sharp metal objects at him."

She patted my hand. "That I would expect from you."

A faltering smile faded quickly. "He came by last night. He said he'd be the baby's father if I didn't contact the birth father."

She didn't speak. Mom had navigated the emotional minefield of my adoption for over thirty years. Her gut reaction would have been to agree with Gordon. But, like Rachel, she knew me. Knew my old, lingering frustrations about heritage. "Judging by your red eyes I'd say you said no."

"I understand his offer was made out of a generous love. I do. But I couldn't make that kind of promise. I couldn't lie to my kid for the rest of her life."

Mom's eyes widened. "Her?"

"I keep saying *her* but I don't know for sure."

She smiled. "I like the idea of another girl."

"Another me?"

A laugh burst from Mom. "I'd never wish you away. I'm glad you are in my life."

"But I gave you a few gray hairs."

"One or two. And I think I now stutter sometimes," she teased.

"And now you're about to meet Daisy Part Two." The lightness in my voice did not match the tension in my gut.

She squeezed my hands. "We survived Daisy Part One and seeing as I'm the grandmother of Daisy Two I get to do the fun stuff. You get to do all the heavy lifting."

The weight of that comment settled squarely on my shoulders. "Mom, I don't want to fuck this up."

"Language, Daisy." Her gaze softened. "And you aren't going to mess up. You are going to be a good mother."

All my insecurities rushed up and tightened my throat. "Are you sure, Mom? I don't have a strong genetic history where motherhood is concerned. Terry abandoned me."

Mom's lips flattened. I knew she didn't like Terry but had kept her thoughts to herself for my benefit. "Terry was seventeen when you were born. She had a drug problem and no family. You can't compare yourself to her." Mom cleared her throat. "And from what you've said she's parenting her two younger children well enough."

The comment had been meant to soothe but it fueled my anxiety. "Why wasn't I good enough to keep?"

Mom wrapped her arms around me. "You were good enough. She just had too many problems. I've tried to hold my tongue where Terry is concerned, but you need to understand the flaw was in her, not you."

Dark fears lurking in the back of my mind elbowed their way to the front. "What if it's in me? What if I inherited it?"

Mom shook her head, frustrated I'd ask such a question. To her the answer seemed obvious but not to me. "When Daddy got sick ten years ago, which of you three girls did the vigil at the hospital?"

"We were all there."

Mom shook her head. "One of my girls barely left his side. Which one was that?"

"Me."

"And when the bakery ran into trouble four years ago, who gave Daddy the money to give to Mike?"

I'd written one hell of a large check, which had about wiped out my savings. "But it had been easy because I was making a lot of money and had thought the good times would go forever."

Mom shook her head. "A lot of kids would have shrugged and said not my problem. You didn't, Daisy."

"And when I asked you to come back to the bakery, what happened?"

"Was this when you got me drunk?"

Mom shrugged, no hint of apology. "What happened?"

"I came back with a terrible hangover."

"And when you sobered up, you could have backed out." She squeezed my hands. "My point is, Daisy, you are not a runner or a quitter. You stay and fight. You have for this family and you will for this baby."

"How can you be sure?"

She shoved out an exasperated breath. "Daisy, your biggest weakness is your lack of confidence. I've done all I can to instill it in you, but there is a deep fear in you that I can't reach. You need to get to the root of it so you can find some peace."

"Yeah, I guess."

"Damn it, kid. You are going to drive me to drink. Have you called Terry? What has she said about you being pregnant?"

"She hasn't said. I've sent her e-mails but no response. I was mad the last time I sent mine and got a little bitchy."

"Good. She owes you answers, Daisy."

"I want to know who my birth father is, Mom."

"That's fair. Whoever he is, he is part of the equation." She sat back. "And speaking of fathers, we need to tell your father."

Butterflies gnawed at my gut. I worried about Mom's reaction, but Dad's really troubled me. He and I were wired alike. We thought alike. Got along well when we weren't clashing heads. And the thought of seeing the disappointment on his face upset me. I didn't want Dad to be disappointed in me.

"Why don't you tell him? You are really good at smoothing over the rough spots with Dad."

Mom shook her head. "Oh, no. This little gem is yours to share. But if you want me to be with you I can sit by your side while you tell him."

Crap. When was this pregnancy going to get easy? "No, I can tell Dad by myself."

Footsteps sounded and we heard Dad say, "Tell Dad what?"

Chapter Fifteen

Friday, 9:00 A.M.
8 days until grand reopening
Income Lost: $1,750

Dad's gaze held no hint of worry as it moved between Mom and me.

Mom rose. "Frank, give Daisy a minute."

Dad frowned as he studied me. "What's wrong?"

I smiled but didn't rise, feeling the need to camouflage my belly before I told him the news. "Dad, meet me in the basement in fifteen minutes."

He studied my face. "This about the teenagers you hired? Rachel told me they start in a couple of days."

"I've got an item or two I want to run past you."

He shook his head. "Is this about the wine? Jean Paul told me. Is there a problem with the renovation?"

I balanced my tone between perky and serious, knowing too much in either direction would arouse more suspicion. "Actually, it's going pretty well."

He arched a brow. "What's wrong? City inspector problems?"

"No. We got our electrical inspections, and I've applied for a liquor license. We are good. I can show you the numbers."

He studied me a beat longer and then looked at my mother. She nodded her head toward the door. "See you in fifteen minutes."

I tossed him a thumbs-up. "Great."

Mom and Dad left me alone and I rose, tugging the T-shirt over my belly. I washed my face, brushed my hair, and headed down the stairs.

As I passed Rachel's apartment, I heard the girls giggling and Rachel talking to them with her calm, patient voice. I envied how soft and kind she sounded with them. All her words were wrapped in fur and cotton. No hard edges. Ellie was like her mother. She was the gentle one. Anna was more like me. Always questioning, pushing.

Anna's clear voice rose above her mother's and sister's. "But I don't like blue icing. I like pink icing. Nobody eats blue icing."

"I eat blue icing," Ellie said.

"You are dumb," Anna shot back.

Rachel's rebuff was quick but so gently spoken I couldn't make it out. My sister had said more than once she wasn't perfect, but when it came to mothering she was pretty darn flawless. I hoped I did as well.

Heading to the first floor I passed Jean Paul, who had begun to paint the new wall a stark white. After my quick wave went unacknowledged by him, I moved down the stairs. In the basement I took a moment to admire the shelves that had nearly driven me insane. Assembled and in place it was hard to believe they'd been such a job.

I smoothed my hand over a sleek black shelf, and in that moment the kid kicked me in the ribs. Smiling, I lowered my hand to my belly.

An odd energy whooshed around me. My head swirled and my heart beat a little faster. Uneasy excitement hummed over my skin, and the world upstairs faded away.

"Can you go home?"

"No. Not like this. They wouldn't understand."

"And the baby's father. Can he help?"

"I've written him." Soft weeping echoed. *"He wants to help but he can't right now."*

And as quick as the energy came, it vanished, and I stood in the basement alone with the sounds of the ceiling above creaking as Jean Paul moved around the kitchen.

I glanced around the stone walls, half expecting to hear or feel a message. But as the seconds ticked by, I heard nothing.

This bakery was old and had a vibe all its own. I'd grown up with its creaks and whispers and for the most part had ignored them. But since my return months ago, the place all but pulsated with energy. I wondered if the bakery had changed or if pregnancy had changed my frequency and made me more susceptible.

Find him.

Was this some kind of haunting? I'd always thought a haunting came with a bit more fanfare. I figured chains rattled or curtains rustled, but all I was getting were whispers just as easily imagined as heard.

Find him.

"Find who?"

And then without skipping a beat, Jenna's name came to mind. Again, was it my imagination or a real answer? I couldn't say.

And yet I knew.

Find him.

Jenna wanted my attention.

She wanted me to find *him*. But who was *him*?

I heard a creak on the stairs and straightened, thinking it was Dad. But as the seconds passed and Dad didn't show, I shoved out a tense breath. Dad wasn't stupid. He'd lived with Mom during two pregnancies. He'd figured it out, but didn't know how to talk to me.

I could sit here and wait for him to gather his nerve or I could go to him. "If Mohammed won't come to the mountain then the mountain would go to him."

I found Dad in his workshop in the basement of his house. The dark room was crammed full of every kind of broken appliance you could imagine. Since his retirement Dad had fancied himself a handyman who could fix any appliance. Why buy it new when the old one worked well enough after a few tweaks? So far the jury was still out on his newly acquired skills.

He leaned over a toaster looking as if it had been gutted of its wires and circuits. He picked up a screw but it slipped out of his hand and fell between the ruts of his workbench. "Damn it to hell."

"So this is not a good time," I said.

He glanced sharply up at me. "Daisy Sheila McCrae."

He rarely used my entire name. This wasn't going to go well. "Hey, Daddy."

"Don't you Daddy me. You say 'Daddy' when you're in trouble."

A tentative grin curled the edges of my lips. "Well, that's about where I am right now."

He looked at me, his expression a mixture of anger and frustration. "How the heck did you manage it?"

"We don't need a lesson in mechanics now."

"Not what I mean." He tossed his screwdriver on the bench. "You are my smart one. You are the one who thinks through every move."

"I missed a couple of key details."

"You sure did, young lady." He glanced at my rounding belly, flushed, and looked back at his gutted toaster. "What am I gonna do with you?"

His tone triggered faint memories of when I'd been sixteen and dented the fender of the delivery van. Now, like then, I needed him not to be angry but to tell me he loved me. "Baby's due at Christmas."

Dad shook his head. "Your mother told me." He sniffed and planted his hand on his hip. "She says you think it's a girl."

"I do."

"Your mother was like that when she was pregnant with your sisters. Knew she had girls both times."

Moving a step closer I sighed. "She told you about Gordon."

"Yeah."

I shoved my hands through my hair. "You must admit when I make a mistake I don't do it halfway."

He shook his head. "Not funny, Daisy."

"If I'm not laughing, Dad, I'd be crying. This is so huge I don't know how to wrap my brain around it. Shit. A baby."

His scowl softened and for a moment he stared at his toaster. Finally, he laid down his screwdriver, faced me, and held out his arms. I went quickly into his embrace and cried. All the emotions and fears swirling inside of me rose to the surface and wouldn't be ignored. "I'm sorry, Dad."

"Don't be sorry, monkey. We'll figure this out. One way or another."

I lingered another beat before I pushed away. "I'll make this work."

"We all will." He handed me a tissue box he kept on the shelf. "So what about the father?"

"In China. Not father material. Don't hold out hope. Even if lightning struck him and he had a sudden personality shift and offered to marry me, I wouldn't. Not much of a man."

"Man enough to get you into this mess."

I coughed. "Right. Well, beyond that he's not worth much."

He shook his head. "You sure it's a girl?"

"I don't have evidence. Just a feeling."

"So it could be a boy?" Hope clung to each word. The lone man in a house of women held out hope for another male.

"Yeah. I suppose."

"I'm holding out for a boy. Could use a little more testosterone around this house."

"Well, we'll see what Mother Nature comes up with." I studied his well-lined face. "So we are good?"

"Yeah. We're good." He shook his head. "I guess I'd best get up in the attic soon and find that old cradle that belonged to your grandmother."

"I don't remember a cradle."

"Margaret and Rachel slept in it. You were too big by the time you came along, and I didn't pull it out when the twins were born. Now I'll dust it off and fix it up for my grandson."

"Dad, I really think it's a girl."

He waved me away. "Let an old man dream."

Leaving his house, my step was lighter. My clan was behind me, meaning the baby and I would be fine.

When I arrived back at the bakery, Rachel met me at the front door.

"The deliveryman is here with the wine."

"Gus's wine?"

She wiped her hands on her apron. "One and the same. By the looks there is a lot of it."

"Yeah, I bought them out. Is he parked in the alley?"

"In the process of parking and wants to know where you want the boxes."

I glanced at the shelves, slid in the last piece still in my hands. "Have him bring them. We'll put them on the shelves. Then we can clear out the boxes."

Her eyes brightened and I knew having the girls back had calmed her. "Daisy, it's more progress."

I smiled. "I think you are right. By the way, I thought you were spending time with the girls."

She held up a baby monitor. "They fell asleep on the couch watching their Barbie Princess video."

"Barbie is watching the girls."

Rachel shrugged. "She's done it before." She winked. "Actually, I highly recommend her if you're ever in a pinch. She's reasonable and the girls love her."

Knowing Rachel needed Barbie every so often lifted my spirits. Even perfect moms had their tricks of the trade. "Yeah, but she's so pretty. And her hip-to-waist ratio. Doesn't seem right."

"I'm hearing laughter and good humor in your voice." She cocked a brow. "The parents gave you a stay of execution?"

I blew out a breath. "They did."

Her gaze bored into me. "They take it okay?"

Nodding, I ran my fingers through my hair. "Yeah. Very cool."

She grinned, wide and bright. "See, it's all going to be fine."

I held up my hands. "Don't jinx me."

The deliveryman arrived minutes later and studied the low ceiling, the bakery equipment pushed close to the brick oven. It would be a tight fit until we moved the equipment upstairs. Shaking his head, the deliveryman turned and headed back up the stairs to get the boxes.

Rachel and I broke into the first box. We quickly fell into a system where she pulled wine bottles out of the crate, handed them to me, and I loaded them on the shelves. Slow and deliberate progress, but we were making our way fast enough that when the deliveryman returned we gave him the empties to take upstairs on his return.

"Hey, I'm not here to take out the trash," he complained.

I could have argued, but I didn't have the time or energy. Instead I played the girl card and smoothed my hand over my rounding belly. "Look, dude, I'm pregnant. Can you help me out?"

His frown softened. "Yeah, sure."

As he headed back up the stairs I glanced at Rachel and whispered, "Do pregnant bellies have a magic power?"

She giggled. "Wait until you are really showing. People will be nice to you even when you act like, well, you."

I laughed, not able to deny I could be one hell of a hard case when

I was on a roll. Upstairs, Anna's giggles drifted through the floorboards. Rachel paused, held up a finger, and then a second later Ellie screamed, "Stop it!"

"Barbie is falling down on the job," I said.

Rachel headed toward the stairs. "She promised me forty-seven minutes of quiet."

"Better get your money back."

"No!" Jean Paul voice was quick and sharp. "In my kitchen we act like grown-ups or you will go to the basement with the women."

Rachel glanced over her shoulder at me. "I'm not sure I like the way he linked *basement* and *women*."

"Yeah, like our fate is not one to be envied."

A second later there was silence.

Rachel went upstairs to check on the three and came back within seconds. "Jean Paul has the girls polishing dishes with rags."

"And they are doing it?"

"With smiles on their faces."

"Looks like Barbie has competition."

We continued with the wine bottles. I nestled several bottles in an alcove. "I thought I'd dig up info about Jenna."

Rachel ripped open a new box, paused, and handed more boxes to the deliveryman. She smiled at him. He smiled back, his gaze openly appreciative.

When he was gone, I said, "Really? Don't you have enough going on with Jean Paul and Simon?"

Rachel laughed as she pulled out two wine bottles and handed them to me. "I hope this tastes good."

"Jean Paul says it does."

"And you trust him?"

"I trust him not to drink bad wine."

Nodding, she handed me the bottles. "So any luck with Jenna?"

"Not so many answers as questions. I've been thinking about the newspaper article I read. 'Survived by her infant son.'"

"What do you want to know about Jenna?"

"For starters, where is she buried? And what happened to her infant son, and who was the baby's father."

"Text Margaret."

"You'd think I could do this on my own without running to her each time."

Rachel shrugged. "Yeah, you could do it on your own or you could beat your head against a wall. Might be more fun."

I stuck my tongue out at her. "Hilarious."

"Besides, if Margaret's on the job we can bake those cookies for Simon's party, which is Monday."

"Do you think we'll have the oven to the first floor by tomorrow?"

"The electrical is done." She nodded toward the stove, now shoved in the basement corner. "Jean Paul says he's called his friends, but no answer if they'll be here or when."

"They can't give a time?"

"Daisy, it's free help. Beggars can't be choosers." She glanced toward the ceiling. "Besides, he's done right by us so far."

"I'm sorry, did I hear you correctly?"

"I know I didn't like him when I first met him but he's growing on me. He's good with the girls, and he's kinda made this place his own."

"He kinda kissed you like he was a man starved for a woman's touch."

She offered a goofy grin. "Yeah. He did."

"Let me remind you, you've shared one kiss with him."

"I know."

"Remember how Mike slipped into the family without anyone really noticing?"

A frown furrowed her brow. "He's not Mike."

"No, he is not."

"I'm not looking for a replacement for Mike," Rachel said.

"You sure? I mean old Jean Paul up there is kinda cute, can bake like a god, and he likes the girls. And you did kiss him like you were just as starved. It would be easy to fall for him."

A wistful smile touched her face. "I'm not falling for anyone."

"Not even Simon?"

"Simon's from a different world, Daisy. He and I barely speak the same language. I doubt he remembers my name after the date from hell."

"I don't know. He could be worth a second chance."

"I'd be willing but I'm not so sure about him."

"You'll never know if you don't ask."

Instead of a quick no, Rachel nodded as if she'd considered the idea herself.

As we continued to work and Rachel chattered about the girls, my mind wandered to finding Jenna. Before I'd been vaguely curious, but now I had the sense time was running out. *Tick tock*. Find Jenna. Find him. Whoever he was.

Irritated, I pulled my cell from my back pocket and texted Margaret the request.

"Asking Margaret?" Rachel asked.

"Yes."

"Have you told her you're pregnant?" Rachel said.

"Not yet."

"Why not?"

"I don't want her to come back here. She needs to do her iron coffin adventure and find dead bodies."

"You mean she escaped the bakery, and you don't want to pull her back."

"This place has a way of pulling us all back."

"I never minded."

"It's different with Margaret."

"What about you?"

"It sure was different with me at one time. Still could be again, I guess. But for now this is where I belong."

She smiled. "Tell Margaret. You'll find a way to keep her away, and she hates being out of the loop, Daisy."

I reached for my phone, and I texted.

"What did you say?"

"I finished with, 'BTW, I'm four months pregnant and you are still fired.'"

Amusement danced in her gaze. "That's it?"

"I don't want her getting any warm fuzzy feelings for me. She needs to stay where she is."

Rachel giggled. "Ah, Daisy, you do love Margaret."

"If you ever tell her I was looking out for her own good, I will bake you into a pie."

"I'd love to see her face when she reads the text."

The rain started minutes after six. The wine bottles had been loaded and stocked and the first level prepped and ready for the ovens and mixer, which would be moved upstairs tomorrow. Though it seemed we were at a stopping place, I knew I should be doing more. There was always more to be done at the bakery, but a weary fatigue had settled in my bones. My lower back hurt, my legs ached, and an exhaustion I'd never experienced had taken over. Six months ago I could have done the work I'd accomplished today and been ready to go out partying. But the thought of going out and being around people made me shudder. The kid had drained me of all my reserves.

As I moved toward the steps leading to my room, the front door of the bakery opened. My first thought was Rachel or someone had for-gotten to lock the door and a customer had tried the door. Ready to give the "We will be open soon" speech, I turned to find Margaret standing there, rain glistening from her hair and tan jacket.

She studied me from head to toe and shook her head. "I thought no f-ing way are you having a kid, but now that I look at you . . . Damn, how come I didn't see it last week?"

I couldn't help but grin. It was good to see her. To know she'd come back from her dig to see me because of the baby. "I thought I was getting fat or had the flu or both. I never figured baby."

She closed the door behind her and locked it. "Holy crap, Daisy."

"Yeah. That and more."

"I'm guessing unless Gordon has super sperm the kid isn't his."

"Nope."

"You told him?"

"Yup."

She grimaced as if sensing I didn't want to talk about it. "Can I shack with you for a couple of days?"

"What's with your place?"

"Friend of a friend renting it for five weeks. Thought I wouldn't be back and could make some cash."

"Yeah. Come on upstairs. But I'll warn you, I'm beat."

She glanced around the bakery as if seeing it for the first time. "Like the yellow. How goes the other renovation?"

"Going well. Jean Paul's making it happen."

Margaret chuckled. "Good to know. He's a lot more laid-back than Henri, and I was afraid it might not go as well. But you saw something in him, and you are a good judge of people."

"Is that a compliment?"

"Maybe."

As I climbed the steps I gave her the short version.

"So you are gonna pull this off?"

"You mean the reno?"

"The baby."

I pushed open the door to my apartment. "Good question." I pushed open my bedroom door and eased into a chair and kicked off my shoes. My feet had swollen at least 50 percent and I feared by the end of the pregnancy I would not be recognizable.

"Want a cup of tea?" Margaret offered.

"Oh God, yes."

She shrugged off her jacket, hung it up, and dumped her purse on the floor as she kicked off her shoes. Moving to the microwave, she snagged a couple of mugs and tea bags, and filled both mugs with water. She placed them in the microwave and hit four minutes.

I wiggled my toes. "So you came all this way to see me?"

"Partly. We knew we were gonna get some big rain the next few days and couldn't work the site. I thought about going to New York but then your explosive text arrived. Figured it best to touch base."

"I'm touched."

She shrugged. "The iron coffin isn't budging, and we're trying to figure out how to get him out. Might as well come home."

As the tea brewed, Margaret dug milk out from the small fridge and sugar from a ceramic apple holder. When the timer dinged she prepared the cups, handed me one, and then sat cross-legged on my bed with hers cradled in her hands.

The last person to make me tea had been Gordon. It had been a month ago, and I wasn't feeling great. Again I'd thought it was a bug, but it had been the kid all the time. Gordon really would have been a great dad. He loved kids, and he had a knack for taking care of people. Thinking about the kid and how its life would have been so different if it had shared Gordon's DNA triggered a pool of tears in my eyes.

"It's a cup of tea, Daisy," Margaret said. "It's not like I gave you a kidney."

I sipped the hot brew. Normally, I took my tea black, but since the baby, I gravitated toward the sweeter tastes. "I was thinking about Gordon."

She raised a brow, clearly surprised by my lack of sarcasm and honesty. "He must be upset."

"Think how'd you feel if your boyfriend found out an ex was having his kid."

She arched a brow, cradling her cup in her hands. "Actually, that did happen. With Mark."

I flipped through my memories of Margaret's ex-boyfriends. "Mark?"

"I met him in grad school. He was working on his thesis in ancient societies, and I was still working on my master's. Majorly hot and heavy and I thought we had a shot at marriage. Then he gets a call from the ex. She's pregnant. At first I was cool about it. It's not like he cheated on me. But then they spent more and more time together. Doctor's appointments, ultrasounds, baby furniture. I felt left out and realized I wasn't as cool as I thought."

Dropping my gaze to the cup, I thought about Gordon's offer to make this work. "Gordon said we could make a go of it if I didn't tell the baby's father."

"And?"

I glanced into the milky depths of the tea. "Can't lie to the kid, Margaret. I'm so grateful Mom and Dad were always honest with me, but it still was an issue not knowing everything. Shit, I still don't know who my birth father is."

"And Terry?"

"Traveling and will get back to me."

She sipped her tea. "I could offer my opinion, but I'd hate to scar the baby. I hear they absorb a lot. So tell me about Jenna. Did Gigi send you the articles?"

"Yeah. They were helpful." I relayed what I knew. "I've been thinking about her a lot the last couple of days. And I really want to find out what happened to the baby and his father."

"Any clues on the dad?"

"The dog tags and the picture I found in the recipe box, but I don't know if they belong to him."

"They are a good place to start."

"You think you could find out more?"

She arched a brow, her gaze now amused. "Child's play."

"How?"

"There's a dude in California I know. He's retired army, and he'll find service records for a low price." She dug her phone out of her back pocket, typed quickly for a few seconds, and then set it on the bed beside her.

"He texts?"

"No, he thinks e-mail is pretty space-age. I sent him an e-mail." She glanced at her watch. "It's still early out west so we might hear from him tonight at least to let us know he's got the ball rolling."

"Margaret, I am humbled by your mastery of history."

She took the compliment as a matter of course. "In some circles they call me the Seeker."

That brought a smile. "Really?"

"Absolutely. I can find people. I mean dead people from the past. The living I'm not so good with but I'm A-1 with the dead."

We chatted about her project, the cute dude who was working the dig, and the time frame of the project. They'd secured more funding and it looked like the project would be extended another six months.

"Of course, I'll bail at the end of the summer," she said.

"Why?"

"The kid, of course."

I sat up straight. "No. You are not allowed to come back. I said in my text you are still fired."

A smile quirked the edge of her lips. "Really? You are still canning me?"

"Yep. No coming back."

"In case you can't add, Daisy Junior arrives at the holidays."

"I know. We'll be fine."

"Really?"

Shoving aside a jolt of panic, I struggled to look relaxed. "I have hired a couple of teens. They seem capable and should help fill in the afternoon gaps."

Margaret studied me, searching. "My shoes are too big to fill."

"Literally or figuratively?"

"Hilarious." Her gaze narrowed. "You look dead on your feet."

"I am."

"Then get into bed. I'll take the spare and make myself at home."

Too tired to argue, I set my tea carefully on the small end table and rose. Groaning, I pushed my hand into my lower back. "It's like this kid came out of nowhere."

She helped me to the bed. "Yeah, Daisy, I still can't figure how you missed the pregnancy."

"She's a sneaky kid."

She grinned. "She. So, it's a girl?"

"Don't know. Just a guess."

Margaret nodded. "I like the idea of another girl toddling around the joint. The girls were a hoot when they were babies. If it's a girl you should name her Margaret. Of course, we can't call her Margaret. That would get confusing. Big Margaret and Little Margaret is awkward. But we could call her Maggie."

All the muscles in my back groaned as I lay back against the pillow.

Margaret covered me up with a blue and white quilt Mom had bought at a yard sale years ago. "I've always wanted to call you Big Margaret."

"I'm not going to let you offend me. Baby Maggie needs her mom calm and cool."

I laughed. "Baby Maggie. Does have a ring."

"Of course it does. Now close your little eyes and go to sleep."

"And dream weird dreams. Yeah."

"Weird dreams?"

"About Jenna. Guess the old subconscious is working overtime."

She sat on the edge of the bed. "I remember Rachel having weird dreams when she was pregnant."

"Really?"

"Yeah. She could never pin 'em, but they bothered her. Drove Mike nuts."

I rose up on my elbows. "I never heard that."

"Six years ago you were living in D.C. You'd started at that financial company and were busy."

"Yeah." That had been a hectic and exciting time. I'd been dazzled by the offer to be a vice president and thrilled by the salary. The work had been all consuming but I'd been happy with the full, hectic days.

However, as I looked back, I couldn't figure why I worried and fussed over my new job so much. Company deadlines and corporate meetings had seemed so important.

The times I'd seen Rachel pregnant she'd been radiant but she'd also reminded me of Terry and what she'd looked like when she was pregnant with me. I didn't picture Terry glowing. I imagined her afraid and angry. So, I used deadlines and meetings to avoid Rachel's rounding belly.

Sorry now that I'd missed Rachel's pregnancy, it would have been nice to rub her belly and buy her ice cream and pickles instead of ordering baby items online and having them shipped to her with a computer-generated card.

I was back in the thick of the family and I was . . . glad.

The kid needed to grow up around her cousins and her aunts and grandparents. I wanted her to live in this building and feel the sense of peace I could never manage. And maybe if I were lucky she could show me how to live here without always feeling like I had baggage to lug around.

"I'm not making the same mistake you did," Margaret said.

"What?"

Margaret rested her hand on my shoulder. "I'm going be here when you are pregnant."

Warmth spread through me, and tears, which were appearing with an annoying frequency, formed. "Margaret, it would break my heart to see you give up the job. Really. Feel free to come home on the weekends, but I don't want you to leave a job you love."

She shook her head. "It's going to be insane here this fall."

"I hope we are busy. We need to make money and grow, which I believe we will do. I'm good at growing business, Margaret. This is my wheelhouse. If I need more people I'll hire them. So dig up your bones and let me run with the bakery."

Margaret shook her head. "When the archeology site closes in December, I'll be back to the bakery to get us through the holiday rush."

Us. Sounded good. "Won't you be cataloguing artifacts during the winter?"

"My grant doesn't pay me that far. And my sublease will be finished by then."

"I will accept you back on one condition."

Margaret folded her arms. "What are your terms, boss?"

"That if they extend your contract you go back. Don't give up your dream. I know this job is everything."

"It's not everything to me."

"Please. I bet you are at the job site an hour before everyone else each morning."

"A half hour."

"You love it."

"I do."

"Then promise me you will talk to me before you toss it away to sell cookies."

She crossed her finger over her heart. "I promise."

I lay back. "I'm going to hold you to that."

"Go to sleep before you pass out." She shut off the light.

"Where are you going?"

"To Rachel's to see if I can score wine. I can't be nice for long stretches unless I'm buzzed."

I chuckled. "Right."

The door closed behind her and instantly, my eyes closed.

Seconds or maybe hours might have passed. I didn't know, but the dream did come. Again it was Jenna, and she was looking at me as if I'd disappointed her. She cradled her full belly with her hands and shook her head.

"You need to find them."

"Them. I thought it was him."

"Find my son and his father. Time is running out and they need each other."

Chapter Sixteen

Saturday, 8:00 A.M.
7 days until grand reopening
Income Lost: $2,000

When I woke the next morning, I braced as I sat up waiting to feel the wave of nausea. Holding my breath, I pressed my hand to my stomach, trying to gauge whether I should run to the bathroom or not.

My stomach was calm. I drew in a deep breath and waited. Nothing. Still calm. You'd think I'd be thrilled at the passing of the sickness, but immediately I worried. What if baby was in trouble? My hands slid to my belly, still round and hard, and I waited for the kid to kick. I needed feedback from her and again she was being coy.

"Come on," I whispered. "A kick or a tap would be greatly appreciated."

Nothing.

"Damn."

"Why are you cussing?" Margaret's groggy voice rolled out from under the blue sheet on her bed.

"I'm not sick," I whispered.

"Why are you whispering?"

"Because what if not being sick is a bad sign?"

Margaret peeked her head out from under the sheet. A riot of red curls framed a face lined from a pillow's crease. "Are you cramping or bleeding?"

I glanced under the sheet. "No. All clear."

She sat up and yawned. "Is the baby moving?"

"No, but she goes dark for long stretches. She's a mind of her own."

She reached for her thick dark glasses on the nightstand and looked at me with now-magnified green eyes. "Imagine that."

"This could be serious."

"Drink a soda or eat a cookie. The sugar will juice her little ass into action."

"Really?"

"I've known my share of pregnant women." She rose, her bare feet curling as they hit the bare wood floor. "Are there any cookies in this place right now?"

"I've cookie dough in the freezer."

"Better be cooked. Salmonella."

"Right. There's a ginger ale in the back of my refrigerator."

"There was. I cut it with bourbon last night."

"You took my baby's ginger ale and mixed it with booze?"

"Hey, I remember you taking a bottle of Rachel's breast milk and putting it in your coffee."

I shrugged. "It had been a late night."

"Exactly."

"Fine." I rose. "I need to hook up with some sugar so I can make the kid move."

Margaret sat up. "When did you become such a girl, Daisy?"

"I'm not sure when I crossed that dark line, but I'm there." I grabbed shorts from the edge of the bed and pulled them on. I reached to fasten the button, but discovered I couldn't. "Crap."

"Ah, the tall and slim Daisy has joined the ranks of the mortals."

"I wasn't always slim."

"You have been for at least fifteen years, and that's a lifetime in my book."

I tried to suck in my belly, but it wouldn't budge. "I thought you weren't supposed to show for like five months."

"And you would be about at the four-and-a-half-month mark?"

"Yeah. Five months is technically two weeks away."

"Tell it to the kid." Margaret laughed. "Time to get some fat-girl pants. Wonder if Rachel has any?"

"If she does, they'll be too short." I dragged a hand through my hair. "My life is out of control. Totally out of control."

"Chill, Diva Daisy. I'll get some clothes on and we'll hit the box store for some maternity clothes and some sugar."

"Maternity clothes." A groan rumbled in my throat. "You might as well be talking about space aliens or alternate universes."

As she chuckled she dug a safety pin from her satchel and handed it to me. "This will hold the drawers up until we can get supplies."

"I need to be back by nine. The new workers are showing and Jean Paul's movers are coming."

"It shouldn't take long. Not like we're looking for fancy clothes."

A half hour later I stood by the maternity sign in the Walmart. We'd stopped at Starbucks, and I'd bought a coffee and a couple of sugar cookies. The cookie had tasted so good. It seemed as if it had been years since I'd eaten food that wasn't a saltine. When the kid did not move after the first sugar cookie I ate a second. This was an emergency, after all.

Finally, as I sipped my coffee, the kid kicked. My hand slid to my belly. *Do it again*, I thought. One more time.

And miracle of miracles, she kicked.

Margaret stared at me over the rim of her coffee cup. "She moving?"

"Yes." I took her hand and placed it on my belly. Baby Maggie kicked again.

Margaret grinned. "Well, imagine that."

The stress seeped from my body. "Okay, now that I know the baby is fine I can think."

"Then let's hit the maternity section."

Minutes later, staring at the shapeless clothes, a full-blown panic attack threatened. In my regular clothes, I could fool myself into believing the kid was abstract. Yeah, she'd moved, but I was still me. But in these clothes, I wasn't myself.

Margaret handed me several pairs of black shorts with elastic waistbands and a pair of jeans with a full elastic front panel.

"The shorts will get you to mid-October, maybe early November. But the jeans will take you through the duration."

I accepted the hangers. "Right."

Margaret pointed toward the changing rooms. "Now you have to go into the nice dressing room and try them on."

"Does it matter? It's all elastic."

Margaret sipped her coffee. "Try the damn clothes on, Daisy."

"Fine. Come back with me."

"Are you two years old?"

"My maturity level has diminished in the last weeks. So yeah, two about sums it up."

We chose the handicap changing room for the extra space. Margaret sat, and I handed her the garments before I unfastened my safety pin. The pants dropped to the floor, and I couldn't resist scratching my belly.

"That's sexy."

"I gave up on sexy when the nausea hit. It's all about what feels good now."

Margaret rifled through my choices. "They're all black."

I accepted the first from her. "Black is my favorite color."

"Yeah, but don't you think you should go for the lighter shades of tops or pants now that you are dressing for two?"

"I'll do whatever I have to do keep this kid safe but I will not walk around in light-colored pants that make my ass look bigger. That's asking too much." I slid on the pants, which comfortably hugged my belly. My pants had been tightening for weeks, and I ignored it. "Nice to have pants that don't squeeze the life out of me."

I turned sideways in the mirror, inspected the pants and my growing belly and then glanced at Margaret.

She shrugged. "Not a fashion statement, but it gets the job done."

"I've seen women who breeze through pregnancy and look so trendy."

"Rachel always looked cute and pulled together," Margaret said.

"I never thought much about it, but now I wonder how she did it. She is a goddess in my book."

Margaret studied my Union Street Bakery T-shirt draping over the pants. "Make peace with the fact you won't see fashionable for a while."

"How can you say that?"

"You work in a bakery, which is manual labor in anybody's book. Not many knocked-up, sexy bakers in the world. Rachel was the exception."

I studied my image in the mirror. I'd not taken the time to remove my mascara last night, which left darkened smudges below my eyes. My hair was pulled into a wild ponytail but wisps of hair had escaped to frame my face and make me look a little crazed. My boobs also spilled over the edges of my bra. "This baby is gonna tear me a new one."

Margaret laughed. "If it's any consolation, Rachel looked pretty wretched toward the very end. Fat ankles, puffy face, and her ass was big, too."

"That's supposed to make me feel better? I'm only at the halfway mark."

Margaret shrugged. "Cut yourself some slack. Your plate is full. And Rachel did get back her figure months after the girls arrived."

"Months after the delivery." I groaned. "That means I'll look like hell for another seven or eight months."

Her gaze softened. "This isn't forever, Daisy, and it will be worth it in the end when Baby Maggie arrives. Now try on the rest of the pants and the jeans. There's work to be done at the bakery."

Twenty minutes later I was one hundred and fifty dollars lighter, wearing a new pair of black shorts, a maternity bra under my T-shirt, and carrying a bag filled with more pants, bras, and panties.

I was officially for-the-world-to-know pregnant.

My stomach settled, my appetite returned with a vengeance so Margaret stopped at a chain restaurant for a couple of egg bagels. The food tasted so good, and I gobbled the bagels. I toyed with going back for a third bagel but Margaret reminded me Baby Maggie was the size of my thumb and did not need the calories.

When we arrived at the bakery, Jean Paul was talking to three very burly-looking men who looked as if they'd tripped out of prison. Long hair, tattoos, stained T-shirts, faded jeans, and boots. As tempted as I was to ask where he found these guys, I didn't. I'd learned with Jean Paul that knowing all the details wasn't always the best course of action.

Margaret and I introduced ourselves, and I showed the men the equipment in the basement in need of being moved to the main floor.

I couldn't imagine anyone being able to move any of the equipment, but the men didn't appear worried over the task.

"You must go upstairs," Jean Paul said. "It's not safe for the baby."

A couple of the men glanced at me and then to my belly. One craggy-faced guy actually beamed. I'd heard tales of men giving up seats for pregnant women, opening doors, and acting generally silly. The power of the bump.

And so Margaret and I moved back to the first floor to stand and direct the placement of the equipment. The first large standing mixer made it up the stairs in the arms of two men who barely appeared to be straining. Encouraged this might not be so bad and might actually go quickly, I made the mistake of mentally revising the schedule that had been set aside for moving.

The second mixer, a good 50 percent larger, didn't cooperate as well as its smaller cousin. I heard a couple of bangs and crashes and curse words rise up from the basement. While the first mixer had taken fifteen minutes the second took an hour of maneuvering. And when it arrived the movers were red-faced and breathless.

Jean Paul appeared and went straight to his toolbox. "I must take out the back door for the ovens," he said. "They must be moved to the alley around the corner and through the front door."

"But what about the front door?"

"It will also have to be removed. But do not worry. It will all be fine."

Margaret shrugged. "It will be fine."

"Of course."

And so we spent the rest of the day listening to Jean Paul hammer away door frames, listening to the grunts of the workmen as they struggled to get the oversized stove out of the basement, into the back of a truck, and then through the newly dismantled front door.

All I could think about as I watched them push the monster

machine through the front door was my new paint job, which Jean Paul had already chipped when he removed the frame. Progress was slow. Very slow at times. But finally the last piece of equipment was brought up to the first floor and positioned in the new main-floor bakery.

I shook my head. "Think, Margaret, no more traveling endless flights of stairs."

"Granted it was a pain, but it kept the size of my butt in check. This place, if you haven't noticed, is full of very delicious foods."

I placed my hand on my expanding hip. "At least I can chalk my fat rear up to the kid and not the cookies."

"Lucky you. Here's hoping when you deliver it goes away."

My cell rang and I glanced at the number, which I did not recognize. "Daisy McCrae."

"This is Irene Adams, I'm Meg and Tim's mom. Meg said for me to call you."

"Yes." I moved away from the noise so I could hear better. "Did Meg tell you I offered them a job?"

"Yes. You're right across the street from my sister's place."

"That's right."

"I'm sorry I haven't called you sooner. I've been working double shifts this week."

"That's fine. Since Meg is under eighteen I wanted to talk to you before she started work. She's the first teenager I've ever hired."

"Meg's a real good girl." Irene sounded tired. "I couldn't manage Tim without her."

"And it won't be a problem with Tim."

"He's a good boy, and he listens to Meg. Just give him specific instructions, and he'll be fine."

"And it's okay they work here?"

"I think it's great, a blessing even. Meg could use spending money, and I don't have it to spare."

"I'm not paying her a fortune."

"She's a hard worker." She released a shuddering sigh. "It's hard raising them alone. I can't give them what they deserve. This job means a lot to her."

Emotion tightened my throat. "I'm looking forward to it."

"If there is ever a problem, you can call me." She rushed to say, "But they are good kids and there won't be a problem."

"I'd love you to come by so I can meet you, Irene."

"I'll be by soon. Lots of crazy hours at the hospital, and I've got to take the work when they offer it. But I'll be by soon. Thank you again."

"Sure." We exchanged a few more pleasantries and I rang off. Would I end up like Irene, the single mom working long, crazed hours and grateful for a stranger's help?

Jean Paul announced the move was done and I was grateful to push Irene out of my thoughts. I doled out cash payments to the movers along with batches of cookies Rachel had baked in her apartment last night for Simon's party and bottles of wine, and said good-bye to all of them before one.

Rachel, Margaret, and I stared at the newly configured kitchen.

Rachel scrunched her face. "I'm not sure if I like it."

Laughter bubbled in me. "Really? Well, then let's put it all back."

Margaret rolled her eyes. "Sarcasm does not become pregnant women, Daisy."

Rachel shook her head as she moved to a stainless steel table and trailed her finger along its smooth surface. "It's not like I don't think it won't work. It's, well, I don't *know* this kitchen."

"You've used every piece of equipment in the joint, Rachel," Margaret said.

"Yeah but not in this configuration. What if the flow is off?"

"We'll find a way to love the flow." I pictured the strained red faces of the movers. "Because this ain't changing."

Rachel opened the oven and peered inside as if making sure all the pieces and parts were intact. "I'll make it work."

"Great."

My cell phone buzzed and I glanced at the number. "Speak of the devil. It's the delivery guy with the new freezer." I picked up and instructed the guy to come through the front door. "Won't be long before we are up and running."

Rachel grinned. "Thank God, not baking has been like going through detox. I'm surprised I don't have the shakes."

Laughing, Margaret shook her head. "Really, Rachel, you need to get laid."

Rachel's eyes widened as a ruby blush rose up her cheeks. Talk of sex always sent Rachel skittering but instead of retreating she nodded. "Send up a message to those pagan gods you talk about so much and tell them Rachel could use a little love."

I laughed. "Rachel, you naughty girl."

She shook her head. Her cheeks remained red as cherries. "It's been over a year and a half." She glanced at my stomach. "You two have at least gotten some love in the last year."

The new freezer arrived an hour later and slid right into the place Jean Paul had created. It was massive, and I caught Rachel opening and closing it several times as she marveled at the empty white interior.

My office was officially gone, the kitchen had been moved, and the wine cellar was at least partly in place. Now, just a couple of days of finishing work and we'd be back in business.

Rachel had to clean her kitchen. The doors had to be rehung. The wine cellar needed a clean and final reorganization and then there was the minor detail of baking enough goods to fill the front case. Any one of those items could have filled a couple of days each, and we had seven to tackle all of them along with refilling our inventory.

"Rachel, your sex life is going to have to wait," I said.

She laughed as she shook her head. "It's been on hold for eighteen months so a few more days won't make a difference."

Margaret shook her head. "Eighteen months. No sex. Damn."

Rachel nodded. "It has had its challenges."

Sex with Roger had been very uneventful. The last time I'd had great sex had been with Gordon. Up until my stomach had started acting up recently, I'd been dreaming about more sex with Gordon. I missed how good he could make me feel.

Margaret rested her hands on her hips. "The definition of hell is no sex and working in the bakery."

I shrugged. "I could certainly do with more sex, but as far as the bakery is concerned, the place is growing on me."

"It's official," Rachel said. "I have heard it all."

Chapter Seventeen

Saturday, 1:00 P.M.
6 days, 12 hours until grand reopening
Income Lost: $3,700

I was working in the kitchen, cleaning equipment with Rachel, when the overnight packet of papers arrived. I signed for the thick envelope made out to me. The sender was a Billy J. Hoyt from Fresno, California. His handwriting in blue ballpoint pen was precise and indented as if the man put weight behind each letter.

"Margaret!"

"What?" she shouted from the basement.

I hefted the envelope, and judging by the weight it was a heavy stack of papers. "Know a Mr. Hoyt?"

Next came the thumping of her feet up the basement stairs. "Is that from Billy?"

I held out the package to her. "That would be correct. He one of your pals?"

"He's the one we wrote to about the dog tags."

"But you e-mailed him last night."

"He must have really hustled the request through. He's got so many connections." She took the package from me and ripped open the back flap. "Billy is retired army. He spends his golden years locating information on the men and women who served. It's amazing what he can find."

I glanced over her shoulder as she scanned a typed note from Billy. The concise letter detailed what he'd found and ended with a *don't worry about the cost, tell Maggie hi* and *I'll keep digging*. Again the signature was bold, clear, and direct. I pictured a man with a gray high-and-tight haircut, white collared shirt, and khakis.

"So, Maggie, does Billy have a crush on you?"

She waggled her eyebrows. "I think he does. If I were thirty years older, I'd definitely date him. He is such a sweetie. He served three tours in Vietnam and has more medals than I can count. A real stud in my book."

I laughed. "Margaret."

"What? I can admire his service." She shuffled through the papers and the first sheet was a military form looking as if it had been copied from microfilm. "At the top of the form it read, AUTOPSY REPORT. It's for Walter Jacob."

That was the name on the dog tags. I braced. "How did he die?"

Margaret's frown deepened as she read the form. "He was hit by artillery fire. His legs were blown off in the initial explosion. He also lost a hand and sustained head trauma."

Blowing breath from my lungs, I shoved the image out of my mind and prayed Jenna never received such details. "What's the other paper?" As she shuffled I saw the heading at the top of the next form. It read, BURIAL INFORMATION.

The clear, simple words came with a one-two punch sobering all my humor. Margaret read, her gaze as sharp and serious as when she catalogued artifacts. "The form is also for a Walter F. Jacob. He was a sergeant in the Marines. Date of Birth: 12 June 1920. Date of Death: 15 July 1944."

"He lived to be twenty-four. So young."

A silence settled around us and the weight bore heavy on me. I pressed my hand to my belly, not able to wonder what it would be like to lose a child over twenty.

"It says, 'The remains of USMC Walter Jacob were first buried on the Island of Saipan, Plot T, Grave 1040.'"

"Saipan?"

"The invasion of the island was called the D-day of the Pacific. Very strategic bloody battle that lasted several weeks. We won but the price was very high."

"So is Walter still on Saipan?" So far from home.

Margaret flipped through more papers, her frown deepening. "There is a Joey Ludenburg listed as next of kin and . . ." She paused for effect. "There is a letter here to Mrs. Jenna Davis Jacob, Union Street, Alexandria, Virginia."

Our Jenna. "What does it say?"

She tossed me a look as if to say *slow*. She read:

As requested, the United States Marine Corps is forwarding to you the following personal property, belonging to Sergeant Walter F. Jacob Jr.

    1 carton and contents

    1 Bureau check for $89.12—enclosed

    1 medal (by registered mail)

    When delivery has been made, I shall appreciate your acknowledging receipt by signing one copy of this letter in the spaces provided below, and returning it to this Bureau. For your convenience, there is enclosed an addressed envelope which needs no postage.

    I regret the circumstances prompting this letter, and I extend my deepest sympathies on the loss of your husband.

The form letter had all the pertinent information, and had been typed correctly, but it was the misalignment of the last word, *husband*, robbing all the heartfelt emotion from the letter. Walter Jacob had become a number. As had Jenna. Inserting *husband* had been simply another detail to be handled by a clerk in a nameless office.

Sadness burrowed deep. "The letter sounds so cold and uncaring."

"But think of how many thousands of remains that office handled, Daisy. So many men died, and keeping track of their remains, their belongings, and their loved ones was no easy task."

"The effects were sent to Jenna Jacob but according to the article in the paper her last name was Davis." I glanced at the dates and did a quick calculation. "He died about five months before the baby was born and this letter would have been received about a week before she gave birth."

"Maybe he listed her as his wife. Maybe he knew about the baby and had every intention of coming back and marrying her."

"It does say here that his body was interred in the Alexandria Cemetery, Plot A222."

That was the first bit of good news. "Really? So we could go see it?"

"Sure."

I glanced at unfinished work at the bakery yet to be done and didn't feel like I could leave.

"An hour won't make a huge difference," Margaret said, reading my expression. "This will always be here."

"You're right."

The heat of midafternoon had passed and the air had cooled to a nice temperature. I wanted to get out of the bakery and breathe a little fresh air and walk on the cemetery's green grass.

We left Rachel scrubbing and grumbling about bad *flow* and how every pot and pan was in the wrong place. When she said, "Not to worry. I'll figure it out," we knew she was headed to martyr-ville, and it probably was best we did leave.

The walk to the cemetery was a little over a mile but given I'd been on my feet all day it made sense to drive. It was after six when we arrived and most of the offices had cleared out for the day, so we could find street parking. The grassy lands of the Alexandria Cemetery rolled like a park shading the granite and limestone grave markers.

"How do we begin to search?" I said. "There must be thousands of markers."

Margaret and I went to the main office, arriving shortly before closing. The woman looked up at me, clearly annoyed by my late arrival.

She had dark hair tied back in a bun and wore wire-rimmed glasses. She wore a white shirt and a United States flag pin on her lapel. "Can I help you?"

Margaret sauntered up as if she were expecting to be recognized. "My sister and I are looking for a grave."

She glanced at the clock. "A grave."

"That's right. Walter F. Jacob Jr. He was interred here in 1945. The plot is listed as A222."

Some of the strain vanished from her face. It appeared Margaret had asked an easy question. She pulled out a map and spread it out on her desk. "This is where we are and this is the section where you need to search. I don't know the exact location on the map but this will put you in the neighborhood."

"Thanks."

It took us a half hour to find the stone located at the base of a small rolling hill. The thin granite marker tilted thirty degrees to the left. The deeply etched letters read WALTER F. JACOB JR. US MARINES, JUNE 12, 1920–JULY 15, 1944.

I knelt by the marker and carefully traced the letters of his name with my fingertips. "Twenty-four years old. So young."

I touched the granite, wondering if this was the *him* I was supposed to find. *Find him. Jenna, am I on the right track?* I waited a beat, hoping for an answer, but not a whisper or even a feeling.

"Hey, look," Margaret said.

I rose and looked at the marker. It read, JENNA DAVIS JACOB, JUNE 3, 1926–DECEMBER 31, 1944. She'd been eighteen years old. They'd died within months of each other.

"They were babies," Margaret said.

"Is there another marker around here? According to the paper she was survived by an infant son, but it also said he was ailing."

Margaret and I spent the next minutes moving around the spot, looking for a child that might have died close to his birth.

But we didn't find a marker. "If he died he wasn't buried here."

"So where is he?"

Find him.

"I don't know."

Rachel offered the next link in the growing chain to find *him*. She suggested we talk to Sara. At ninety-five she was one of the oldest customers of the bakery. She'd come once a week for the last seventy years, but had broken her hip two years ago and now lived in a nursing home. Rachel didn't know if she'd remember Jenna, but suggested if anyone did it would be her. Armed with maple cookies, which Rachel had made, I drove to the nursing home located ten miles away in Arlington.

It took a U-turn and two missed tries before I spotted the low-lying building off Glebe Road. Shady Acres Retirement home was nondescript, outfitted with tinted windows that didn't open, an entrance covered with a wide awning, and scattered flower planters next to benches.

Inside, the place looked clean and well run but the antiseptic smell turned my still-delicate stomach. I found reception and introduced myself. After showing an ID and explaining whom I was here to see, the receptionist directed me to a visitor's lounge.

The tiled floor sparkled with polish, and on the walls hung pictures of what appeared to be smiling older residents. In the corner stood a card table with cards and poker chips still scattered on it as if the players would soon return. A large flat screen televised the news.

I studied the pictures on the wall and did my best to look relaxed. However, the more I stood there the sillier my quest seemed. I was going to ask Sara Morgan if she remembered a woman who worked a bakery counter in 1943 and 1944. What were the chances?

Finally, an older woman, leaning heavily on a cane, came to sit in the room. Judging by her appearance, I guessed her age to be mid to late seventies.

Squinting, the older woman openly assessed me. "Who are you here for? Getting a little late for visitors."

"I'm here for Sara," I said.

The woman's gaze brightened as if all conversation was welcome. "Sara doesn't get many visitors."

"Really?"

"It's hard to hold on to family when you've reached your nineties. I think her last son passed last year. Heart attack."

"I'm sorry."

"He was sixty-nine." She smiled. "My name is Edith. Sara and I are friends."

"Oh." I shifted in my seat, knowing I had a narrow window of opportunity before I had to return to the shop and finish the day's work. The kids would be arriving on Monday and we were going to begin our first day of employee training.

"So are you Sara's family?"

I tapped my index finger on the white USB box. "No. She's been a customer of our bakery for a long time. I wanted to drop off cookies." And pump her for information about the 1940s.

"That's so sweet. What did you bring her?"

"Cookies. Maple. My dad tells me that's her favorite."

"I love sugar cookies."

Glancing at the Union Street Bakery box, I hesitated before asking, "Would you like a cookie?"

She beamed. "I'd love one."

I broke the seal on the box and held it out to her.

"These are lovely. When I was expecting I craved sugar all the time." She smiled at me as she nibbled the edge of her cookie. "When is your baby due?"

I stared at the bump. "December."

"A Christmas baby. I was a Christmas baby. My only word of advice is not to wrap the baby's birthday presents in Christmas paper. I hated that."

"I'll try to remember."

"And don't take the birthday picture around the tree. The mingling of dates leaves a kid feeling cheated."

"Got it." Great, I'd not only made a kid by mistake but I was further traumatizing it with a Christmas birthday clearly loaded with disappointments. "I will remember."

Before Edith could comment more on my baby's birthday, Sara arrived in a wheelchair. Though Sara slumped over in her chair, her eyes were clear and bright. "Those Union Street Bakery cookies?"

"Yes, ma'am." I lifted the lid and held it close to her as she peered inside like a child. Dad had always said that cookies were magical. Always made people happy.

She bit into the cookie. "So who are you?"

"I'm Daisy McCrae. You know my dad."

"Frank?"

"That's right."

Her eyes narrowed. "You worked in the bakery as a kid."

"I did."

"Moved to Washington, D.C., from what I remember. Big shot finance person."

Here I'd thought I'd been invisible behind that counter, but the way this woman talked you'd have thought we were part of the same family.

"I'm not in finance anymore. I manage the bakery now."

Frowning, she nibbled her cookie. "Why?"

"Do you want the long version or the short?" I quipped.

She chuckled. "At my age the short might be best."

"The company I worked for went out of business. Mom and Dad needed help. It was a perfect match from the get-go."

She stared me as if she didn't believe me but let it go. "You didn't come here to talk to me about why you moved back or to give me cookies."

Edith leaned over. "She's pregnant. Her baby is due at Christmas."

Sara raised a brow. "This isn't your conversation, Edith. It's mine. You get lots of visitors, and I don't."

Edith's brows rose. "I don't see why I can't talk."

Sara glared at the cookie clutched in Edith's hands. "Looks like you already had one of my cookies. Now go over there and wait for your son. He's never late."

Edith took a big bite out of her cookie and moved several seats over.

Sara grunted, smiling behind her cookie. "She always is trying to horn in. She gets visitors all the time and I don't, and still she wants a piece of what I have."

"Sorry to hear that."

"Don't worry about it. I bet she was a pesky kid on the playground. People don't change."

I was looking at a couple of old ladies and to my shame I'd not thought much about priorities. I saw old. Sitting here with Sara I could now see I'd underestimated her.

"So why are you here? I know my memory is bad but I'm pretty sure we've never formally met."

"No, ma'am, we've not met." I scooted to the edge of my seat. "My sister sent me here to see you."

"Rachel or Margaret?"

"Rachel."

"I always liked Rachel. Good woman." Her gaze narrowed as she stared at me. "You're the adopted sister."

The adopted sister. There was no malice behind the description, but it always needled, made me feel a little less. "That's right."

"So, Daisy, the adopted one, what can I do for you?"

"We're renovating the bakery. Knocking out walls. We found a recipe box dating back to the 1940s."

"Good years. I was in my late twenties and I was between my first and second husbands. I was full of piss and vinegar during the war."

"I don't doubt it."

She met my gaze, searching for any trace of sarcasm. "That's right. Don't you doubt it for one minute. I was a catch back in the day."

I could have plowed on with my questions but sensed she wanted to talk. She'd already said she didn't get many visitors. The clock ticking to return to the bakery, I relaxed back in my chair.

"So what were you doing between husbands one and two?"

Her gaze twinkled. "Other than getting into a bit of trouble I was working at the torpedo factory. Making bombs. There were a lot of dames like me working in the factory then. The boys were all off to war."

"The town was different then."

"Not the hustle and bustle it is now, but we thought it was mighty fine. The music and the dancing. I was a USO dancer. And I was good. Cut a swing better than anyone."

"You lived in Old Town."

"Rented a room near your bakery on Union Street. Old lady had a boardinghouse." She paused. "Old lady. I think Miss Carol wasn't more than fifty or fifty-five. Here I am forty years past that age."

"My sister Rachel said you were a regular at the bakery."

"Every morning I bought a croissant." She scrunched her face in a smile. "So good."

The sharpness of her memory gave me hope. "I was actually trying to find a gal who worked in the bakery about then. Her name was Jenna." I reached in my pocket and pulled out the picture I'd found and handed it to Sara.

She studied the picture through her thick glasses. "Brings back memories, this picture does."

"What do you remember about the bakery?"

"Well, your daddy wasn't more than one. He was a scrappy little kid who liked cookies."

Dad's round belly came to mind. "He still eats cookies."

"And lord what a crier he was. If someone wasn't carrying him around he was fussing." Her eyes glinted. "I didn't like him then. He made me swear off kids. Of course that promise lasted less than a year. Met my second husband, and our son was born in forty-five."

I laughed. "Dad said my sisters and I were enough to break a man."

"Don't take any of his bellyaching. He was the worst."

I tucked the nugget aside knowing one day I'd use it. "Do you remember any of the women who worked in the bakery?"

She glanced at the picture, the wrinkles in her face deepening. For a moment she didn't speak, and then she tapped her gnarled finger on Jenna's face. "I do remember her. She was a firecracker."

I studied Jenna's smiling face and thought about the obituary in the paper. What had happened? "She met a serviceman, I think."

Slowly Sara nodded. "She did. A fine-looking boy. Not much more than twenty-one or -two. He was Marine Infantry. Was all full of himself."

"You remember him?"

"I remember the three of them at a USO dance. That's how they met."

"Three of them?"

"He always traveled with his buddy. They came up on the train from Quantico whenever they could get leave. Memory serves they were training officers. Joey and Walter."

Joey. Joey Ludenburg had signed for Walter's belongings after he'd died. I pulled out the picture of Jenna and the two men. "Which one was Walter?"

She studied the picture but after a moment shook her head. "I couldn't tell you. So many GIs then. They ran together."

"But you remember Jenna at the dance with Joey and Walter?"

"Sure. One of them took her out for a dance and had a devil of a time letting her go to dance with the next solider. He stared at her all night. Made me realize why I divorced my first husband. He never stared at me with so much lust."

I studied the smiling faces of the men in the photo. Both looked so happy, and I could have sworn both were in love with her. "So he loved her."

"Well, he sure did lust after her." She cackled. "But he did like her. Saw both those solider boys a couple of times at the bakery."

"I read about Jenna in the paper. She died giving birth."

For a long moment, Sara was silent as if some details escaped her. And finally she said, "There were customers who wouldn't speak to her when she was expecting. Called her bad news."

Overwhelming sadness washed over me as if it weren't Jenna who had been hurt but me. I thought about my kid being diminished because I wasn't married to her father. Homicide came to mind when I thought about anyone hurting my kid.

"Must have been hard on her."

"I think it was."

"Did she have family in the area?"

"She came from the western part of the state. I don't remember where exactly but I know Alexandria wasn't her home."

"Why did she come to Alexandria?"

"Said she wanted to see a real city. Wanted more than the country." She broke off a piece of cookie and ate it. "And then her man died in the war and she didn't want no more parts of the city. She hated it all."

"But she didn't go home."

Sara folded gnarled, thickly veined hands in her lap. "Not unmarried with a baby in her belly. She told me they'd not take her."

"She and Walter didn't get married."

"She talked about it. I know she loved him. But if they got married, I never knew it."

Single motherhood scared me. I didn't have Gordon, but I had family. I wasn't alone and I would make it. "Jenna had no one."

Sara nodded. "I didn't hear about her dying right away. I was working and newly married. But a couple of weeks after the fact I came by the bakery. Mr. McCrae told me what had happened. They were all torn up."

"What happened to the baby?"

"I suppose he went home with her kin."

"In the western part of the state."

"That's what I hear."

Frustration had me scooting to the edge of my seat. "You've no idea where?"

"Well west."

"I heard she was from Frederick County."

"Maybe, I don't know. Honey, it's been seventy years. I think I'm doing pretty well considering."

"You are doing great." I shuffled through the towns in the western part of the state near Frederick County. I wished I'd paid closer attention in fifth-grade geography.

Sara nibbled her cookie, frowning as she dug through her memory. "Her daddy owned an apple farm."

"My sister Rachel buys fresh apples from an orchard out in that area."

"Jenna came from apple country. Said she eaten enough apples to last her a lifetime."

"Did she ever talk about her family?"

Sara frowned. "Not much. She was too sweet a gal to say a bad word." She cocked her head. "She did get a letter from home once. Made her cry. Explains why home might be the last place to go with a baby."

Chapter Eighteen

Monday, 8:00 A.M.
5 days until grand reopening
Income Lost: $3,700

Finding Jenna's baby and her lover had to take a backseat as we really rolled into high gear with reassembling the kitchen and finalizing the wine cellar room. I followed up on my liquor license and found it might be weeks before we could sell wine but at least it was in the pipeline.

Margaret's dig was delayed a day or two so she'd remained at the bakery, and my new workers, Meg and Tim, showed up right on time. Tim was grinning and though Meg had a smile on her face I sensed worry as they came into the shop and inspected the setup.

"Hi, Meg," I said.

Rachel grinned. "The cavalry has arrived."

The welcome seemed to allay Meg's tension. Her smile widened. She'd been worried the job might not come through. The kid was used to disappointment, which made me all the more determined to make all this work so we could afford to keep them.

While Rachel schooled Meg on the finer points of mixing dough, Tim sat on a stool and watched. He seemed content to wait until a job was handed to him. When Jean Paul asked if he could help move a piece of equipment, I'd had my doubts. But Tim stood right up, grin broadening, and hurried to help Jean Paul. The kid was strong as an ox and quickly proved to be a real help. Several times he helped Jean Paul move equipment impossible otherwise.

By the end of Meg and Tim's first day, the kitchen had been fully restored, the basement was cleaned, and Jean Paul had begun to frame off a corner of the basement for another office for me. Though I didn't love the idea of working in a basement, I really didn't like the idea of working in my apartment.

That night when I crawled upstairs to my room, exhausted, Jenna was not far behind me, dogging me up the stairs, tapping me on my shoulder and reminding me that I'd said I'd find her baby and lover.

Find him. Find him.

I flopped on my bed and lay back against the pillow. "I know what I said, Jenna. And I'll find your men. But right now I can barely see straight."

The energy in the room shifted and some of the tension melted way. I wasn't sure if Jenna was chilling or I was too tired to care.

My eyes closed as soon as my head hit the pillow, and I was swept up into darkness. Sleep came so hard and fast I didn't dream. Blissful blackness washed over me like a wave, which I gladly rode. A year ago I'd have fought the wave but now understood the kid needed it as much as I did. Somewhere along the way I'd stopped being number one in my life. The kid had nudged to the front of the line. How many times had I seen Rachel put herself second to the girls? I'd thought she was nuts. Now, not so much.

When I woke, the room was dark save for the slash of moonlight cutting the room in half. Drool trickled from my mouth, which I swiped away as embarrassment had me glancing around the darkness. I half expected to see Margaret staring at me, laughing. But she was nowhere in sight. I was alone.

Gordon had once said he liked watching me sleep. He liked that I looked so relaxed and didn't have a white-knuckle grip on life twenty-four seven.

"Shit, I don't have a tight grip on life right now, Gordo. I am an out-of-control mess."

I swiped my hand over my mouth one more time and swung my legs over the side of the bed. I stared at the rumpled sheets of Margaret's bed and couldn't tell if she'd come and gone or if she'd not spent the night here. I'd been so out of it when my head hit the pillow that I had no way of knowing.

Never had I slept so hard. Mom said as a kid I'd never been a good sleeper. She said she'd had to sneak upstairs on her belly because she knew I'd be in my room, hanging over the baby gate barricading me in my door, searching for her.

But last night I'd slept like the dead.

I rose and moved to the bathroom, filled a tumblerful of water and drank.

Find him.

Jenna might have allowed me to sleep but she'd not forgotten her request.

"You're a pushy broad, Jenna," I said. "I've feelers out. What more do you want?"

I refilled the glass and moved to my computer to see if there was any bit of news that might have popped up. I scanned e-mails from suppliers and spotted one from a friend of mine I'd worked with in D.C.

Brenda. She and I had been in tough competition at the company. We both were ambitious, and we both wanted the corner office. Plenty of times we'd gone head to head and she'd made me so mad I could scream. But knowing she was chasing me in the corporate world had made me better and sharper at what I'd done.

Big D.

How goes the new Betty Crocker life? Last I heard you couldn't use an Easy-Bake oven and now you are churning out cookies and pies. Thought I'd let you know I've finally landed on my feet after six months of unemployment. As much as I loved sleeping until ten, eating too much, and building a tight relationship with Jerry Springer (we have a date everyday at five), I've been called back to the corporate world. I'll be moving to Seattle to take a job with a financial company. I think I'm the last of our core group to get back into the real world. Bill has a gig in San Francisco, Gwen is working in D.C., and Mike moved to Dallas. And of course old Roger is in China. (From what I hear he's still a douche.)

Call me. We'll grab a drink before I load up the wagon train and move west.

Bigger B.

I sat back in my chair, absently smoothing my hand over my belly. Six months since I'd been in the real world but it might as well have been a lifetime. Each day took me further and further away.

And of course old Roger is in China.

Roger. I'd been avoiding thoughts of him like the plague. I was half hoping he'd vanish from my mind, and I'd never think about him again. "Gordon, why couldn't the baby be yours?"

As much as I wanted to ignore Roger, I couldn't. Roger was my kid's biological father. And he needed to know. He'd always been a jerk, and I didn't like him but none of that mattered.

Dear Roger

I thought for a moment as I looked at the line and then deleted *Dear*.

Roger,

Been a while but I needed to touch base with you. Remember our last night before I left D.C.? Yeah, well, I don't remember much, but I do remember the basics. And the basics seem to have been enough to make a baby. I'm pregnant and the kid is yours. Baby is due at Christmas.

I'm not looking for money, but I have an obligation to tell you. If you want to contact me and find out more details I'm here.

Daisy

For long, tense seconds my index finger hovered poised over the Send key. The note had to be sent but I did not want to open this can of worms. I didn't like Roger and the idea of a lifetime of co-parenting with him made me sick to my stomach. But we had done the deed. And this was not about me but my kid. She deserved her biological history.

"Damn it." Closing my eyes I pressed Send, watched as the bar on the send log filled, and listened to the whooshing e-mail sound as it was whisked away into cyberspace. No going back now.

I smoothed my hand over my belly and imagined Gordon wrapping his arms around me. My heart ached as I thought about losing him. "No matter what, you have me, kid. I'm not pulling a Terry. I'm not. We are in this together."

I scanned the rest of my e-mails and almost missed the last, which was from a Teresa Miller. Teresa. Terry.

Daisy,

I apologize for the delay but work and the kids have kept me very busy.

The kids. The ones she'd kept and loved. Tension built in my chest and for a moment I had to turn away. I reminded myself she hadn't injected a hidden meaning behind the comment. There was no veiled truth. She was stating the facts of her life.

My pregnancies have all been easy. I was never sick except with my second son and the morning sickness didn't arrive until about the fourth month. It lasted about six weeks and then it was gone. My deliveries were all textbook, and my recovery was quick. You look so much like me I can't help but think you will have the same luck with your pregnancy as I had with mine.

I know you want more information about your birth father, and I wish I could give it to you. But the truth is I was sixteen when I got pregnant with you and I made a lot of bad choices during that time, including excessive drinking.

I'm not proud to admit this but I don't know your birth father's name. I wish I could give you answers, but I can't.

You've a tough road ahead of you, Daisy, but you are a tough gal. You've been a fighter since day one. Here's hoping your baby is a better napper than you were. I've found more pictures that I thought you might like, and I've sent them to you Priority Mail. Knowing your curious nature I know they will be of interest to you. I wish you the best.

Terry

I sat back in my chair feeling as if the wind had been knocked from my lungs. Tears stung, pooled, and trickled like an endlessly leaky water faucet. I didn't bother to stop them.

I wish you the best.

She was sorry for failing me but there was no mention of a future or a relationship with her grandchild or me. The kid and I were part of her past.

By late afternoon, Jean Paul had finished the drywall and spackling of my new albeit tiny office. As I stood in the rectangular room that measured ten by five, I knew I'd have to be efficient with furnishings. No sprawling or tossing stuff in piles on the floor.

The space did not have a window, but it did have a door and if I pushed my desk against the far wall, I could glance over my shoulder and see the winery and the brick oven with ease. I could also hear what was happening in the kitchen. For some reason the sound traveled right through the ceiling of my office. That was going to be good and bad.

Despite the office's shortcomings, it was done, and after I applied a coat of paint, construction could be classified as officially over.

I'd considered several colors, but in the end chose the yellow paint left over from the front of the shop. It was enough to cover my walls in two coats and best of all it was already paid for. Watching the money going out in the last week and a half had been stressful, and I was looking forward to seeing it come back into the bakery.

And so I finished the paint job and tossed out the empty paint can and paint brushes in the Dumpster. I headed up to the front of the store to hang what had been on the walls before. In the end I settled on rehanging the cupcake clock. I didn't want to rehang the posters

Mike had liked, and decided to dig through the old bakery pictures and put together a collage. Another project, one I didn't need, but it made sense to celebrate the bakery's history.

I pushed through the saloon doors so I could offer my help to Rachel.

My sister stood over the large mixer and was dropping in chunks of butter while Meg watched. Meg had tied back her brown hair and wore a frown on her face as she listened to Rachel's explanations about mixing. The girl wanted to learn and as far as I was concerned that was more than half the battle.

"Did Margaret go back to her dig?" I said.

Rachel unwrapped another pound of butter and dropped it into the mixer. "No, she had an errand to run."

Annoyance snapped. "She says she's here to work and now she's running an errand?"

Rachel shrugged. "She took the girls with her, which gives me time. That makes her a goddess in my mind."

"Margaret and the girls. What could those three be up to?"

"My guess is it has to do with chocolate ice cream. I'm fully expecting the girls to come back covered in dirt and hyped on sugar, but at this point, I don't care as long as it it buys me an extra hour to get this dough mixed so Tim can scoop it and we can have cookies baked for Simon's party tonight."

She met my gaze, her cheeks flushed. A lock of her hair stuck up and her mascara looked a bit smudged as if she'd been rubbing her eyes.

"Take a deep breath, Rachel," I said.

"A deep breath?"

"We will get it all done."

Rachel shook her head and then glanced at Meg. "Have you heard curse words before?"

Meg giggled. "Yes."

"Well, you still might want to cover your ears because I'm about to say one."

Meg unwrapped the next pound square of butter. "My mom says bad words. A lot. She said she used to be a nice person before she had kids."

Rachel nodded. "And it's not that she doesn't love you. It's not that I don't love my girls. But I'm about to lose my, well, you-know-what mind."

Meg giggled.

I saw the signs of my sister's impending breakdown. "Rachel, what can I do?" I said. "Put me to work."

She turned on the mixer and the large paddles creamed the butter. "Meg, when it's creamy, then drop in another chunk of butter. One at a time."

She nodded. "Okay."

Rachel wiped her hands on her apron and motioned me toward a rack filled with trays of cookies. "These need to be iced and these need to be dunked in the chocolate. And they all need to be set back on the tray to dry."

"I can do that."

"You must be precise. Sloppy does not work."

I grinned. "I will be careful. I promise."

"When it comes to the numbers you are on track, Daisy. But your mind can wander when you ice. I can't have that."

I patted her on the shoulder. "You are such a bossy little girl. I'm so proud."

A half smile tugged the edge of her lips. "Let's get to work."

Margaret arrived back at the shop three hours later with the girls just as we were putting the last of the cookies on the trays. The girls were covered in dirt. Chocolate ice cream strained their clean T-shirts. Their shoes were untied and Annie was missing a sock. Margaret looked as she always did, a bit disheveled but unworried as she slurped the last of a milkshake from a paper cup.

"*Hola,*" she said.

The girls ran up to their mom, their dirty faces beaming. They talked so fast and quick, no one could understand them.

Rachel absently plucked a leaf from Anna's hair and smoothed out Ellie's bangs. A year ago if the girls had marched in here this unkempt, Rachel would have scurried them to the showers and cleaned them right up. Now, she seemed in no rush to reestablish perfection.

Ellie's eyes widened. "And then we went to the park, and Aunt Margaret bought us ice cream."

"And then," Anna said, "we ate cotton candy and took our shoes off in the park."

Ellie smirked and in a stage whisper said, "And then Aunt Margaret told a guy to go to hell."

"And she showed him her finger." Anna held up her index finger.

"No," Ellie said. "It was this finger." She held up her middle finger.

Margaret's eyes widened and she moved to explain when Rachel said, "My goodness, it sounds like you had a great day." Rachel slowly lowered Anna's index and Ellie's middle fingers.

"Can we go with Aunt Margaret again?" Ellie said.

"She said she'd take us swimming," Anna hurried to add.

Rachel nodded. "Sure, sounds good. Maybe you could hang out with Aunt Margaret a little longer today. Maybe she could give you dinner while Aunt Daisy and I deliver these cookies."

Margaret shrugged. "Sure. I can feed the munchkins, and I can hose them off if you like and toss them into bed."

Rachel brushed a lock of hair from her eyes. "Sounds like a plan."

Margaret glanced at me. "She's not freaking out about the girls being such a mess."

I shrugged. "I think we broke her."

Rachel lifted a tray of cookies. "I'll freak out later. Right now, we need to move it."

I glanced at the clock. We had a half hour. Just enough time.

Fifteen minutes later the bakery van sputtered and stopped in the loading dock of Simon's sleek office building on Duke Street. I snagged a delivery cart from the loading dock and pushed it down the ramp to the van, and we carefully loaded the cookies onto the cart.

Rachel glanced up at me. "This is a hell of a way to earn a living."

Laughter bubbled in me as I hefted a tray. "You are telling me."

Rachel's eyes didn't reflect humor. "No really, there must to be an easier way."

Fatigue added brittleness to her tone. "If I knew it, I'd do it."

We pushed the cookie cart up the ramp to the elevators, and I pressed the button.

"Seriously," Rachel said. "My kids look like vagrants, and I don't have time to clean them up. We've been busting our asses the last ten days, and we're how many thousands behind?"

"I don't know." I did, but Rachel didn't need a blow-by-blow of our finances. "And the girls are happy, Rachel. That's all that matters."

Tears pooled in her eyes. "But they weren't having fun with me. In the last two weeks they've had more fun than they've had in their entire lives, and I wasn't there for any of it. I was working."

"The last two weeks have been a little crazy. And the exception to the rule." The doors dinged open, and we pushed the cart into the elevator.

"I'm really afraid it's always going to be this way. I was back to work when they were three weeks old. We had a big order and Mike needed me. When they turned two, I had to get up early to decorate a wedding cake. I didn't have time to ice their birthday cake. They start first grade in six weeks, and I honestly can't tell you where the time has gone."

I wanted to assure her there'd be no more missed special days, but

I couldn't. "You've said it yourself. The bakery takes a chunk out of your life."

Anger brightened her blue eyes. "Yeah, well, what if I don't want to do it anymore?"

Shit. Rachel was talking about abandoning the ship. Where she'd go, I didn't know, and I doubted she did either. But I did know if she bailed I couldn't hold it together. And if the bakery went under, where would the kid and me go? And what if I did manage to keep her on board. Did I want her life? Did I want to leave a three-week-old infant to return to work?

I glanced in the mirror doors of the elevator and studied my reflection. My hair stuck up and the buttons on my chef jacket were fastened one loop off. I quickly refastened the jacket and smoothed down my hair.

I did my best to keep the panic out of my voice. "Let's get through tonight, and then we'll talk. I'll figure it out."

She nodded and for a moment we were both silent. Elevator music hummed above our heads.

"I had two more orders for frozen dough yesterday," she said as an afterthought.

"Really?"

"For chocolate chip cookie dough. Seems Mrs. Ably has been talking about us."

"How much did you charge them?"

"Twenty-five dollars for three dozen."

"And if we'd baked them we'd have made thirty-two dollars."

"But half the labor and electricity."

I did quick calculations. "The profit is slightly higher when we sell the dough."

"That's what I thought but didn't have time to crunch numbers. Have you thought about being more of a mail-order business?" Rachel said. "We could actually be open for business Friday and Saturday and the rest of the week we make and sell dough?"

The idea was different. Our business model would change radically. But the idea had merit. "I'm surprised I didn't think of it."

Rachel straightened her shoulders as if a little bit of the weight lifted. "You've been distracted."

"I'm going to have to really run the numbers, Rachel. It's not a change we can make overnight."

She brushed a lock of hair from her eyes. "I don't need overnight as long as I know there might be a light at the end of the tunnel."

"Understood."

"We need to think differently, Daisy."

"Oh, I'm totally hearing you. I am." And I was. My mind was already spinning in a dozen different directions.

The doors opened to Davenport Developers and a very thin and sleek receptionist watched as we pushed the cart into the reception area.

I grinned. "The Union Street Bakery order has arrived."

The receptionist's plucked eyebrows raised. "In the conference room."

We'd delivered here before and knew the drill. As we made our way over the carpeted hallway past the slick development pictures on the walls, an odd sense of disconnect settled on my shoulders. Six months ago I'd have sold my soul to be readmitted to this sterile corporate world. I liked the air-conditioned air, the windows that did not open and offered a distant view of the Potomac, and the distance from life.

But as we unloaded the vibrant, rich cookies onto the polished mahogany conference table, I wasn't so sure this was for me anymore. I liked the idea of my kid stumbling into the bakery with Aunt Margaret covered in dirt and ice cream. I liked calling the shots and knowing the risk I took with the business was on me, and not some guy at corporate. I liked having my family close.

Odd that Rachel would pull away from the business as I moved closer to it. But maybe I could figure a solution workable for us both.

Simon appeared in the doorway as he did before every corporate event we'd catered to inspect what had been delivered. He wore a neatly tailored charcoal gray suit, white shirt, and gold cuff links. Rachel kept her gaze on the cookies but I could see her hands now trembled a little and a faint blush colored her cheeks.

Smiling, I turned to Simon ready to run interference. "Simon, thank you again for using Union Street Bakery."

His gaze shifted from Rachel's bent head to me and he smiled. "Your work is always a big hit with our employees."

"We aim to please."

Rachel straightened, turned and faced Simon. She held out her hand and moved to shake his. "Thank you for your business."

He took her hand. Instead of speaking he simply stared at her.

I'd been around enough to know when a man craved a woman. Not merely liked but *craved* a woman. Blushing myself, I quickly rearranged already perfect cookies.

"Simon," Rachel said. "We got off on a bad foot the last time."

I stiffened. Was Rachel taking the bull by the horns? She wasn't scurrying for cover? Crap. I'd seen it all.

He didn't smile, but his eyes softened. Instead of answering he remained quiet. A good negotiator didn't tip his hand, especially when the stakes were high.

"I'm so far out of practice when it comes to life outside of work or motherhood. I was out of my depth and I wasn't very entertaining." She drew in a breath. "If you're interested, I'd like to take you out to dinner."

His head cocked a fraction. I'd done my share of negotiations and I knew a win when I saw it. Rachel had Simon.

Slowly he nodded. "What do you propose?"

He was going to make her work for it, which told me he really liked my sister. He was a guy who didn't like sweets and yet had placed six orders with the bakery in the last six months. His employees lost work time and complained about getting fat and still he ordered baked goods from the Union Street Bakery—from Rachel.

Rachel moistened her lips. "We've our grand opening on Saturday so I am booked solid until then. But maybe Saturday after next. There's an art show in town and we close at noon."

Silent, he seemed to consider her offer and then slowly he nodded. "Sounds intriguing."

"I'll pick you up?" she offered.

I pictured Rachel pulling up in front of Simon's sleek building in the Union Street Bakery van, or worse, in her old Toyota. That was a scene I'd pay money to see.

"I'll pick you up," he countered as if the image skittered through his mind.

"I don't mind driving. Really," Rachel said.

A smile tugged at the edge of his lips as if he seemed to like this assertive version of Rachel. "I can manage the drive."

She nodded as if she finally remembered to breathe. "Good. Would two o'clock work?"

"It does."

I felt like the fairy godmother in Cinderella. Forgetting she was plump and gray, I focused on her sparkly blue dress, which I'd always envied as a kid.

When the awkward silence settled between the two, I said, "Rachel, we've a bakery to fill."

"Right." She smiled at Simon. "See you next week."

"I look forward to it."

Neither one of us said a word as we left the offices and rode the elevators to the first floor. It wasn't until we were in the van and I fired up the engine that I grinned and said, "Who's the brazen hussy now?"

Her eyes widened with shock. "Was I?"

I laughed as we pulled onto Duke Street. "No. You were not. I'm teasing."

"Really?"

"Really."

Shaking my head, I checked the rearview mirror for traffic. "I think old Simon is shier than you are."

She pressed her palms to her rosy cheeks. "I don't think so. He is so in control."

"It doesn't take a lot to stay in control. It takes balls to put yourself in the game when there are a million of reasons not to."

She flopped back against the seat. "I can't believe I asked him out. I mean I've been thinking about it, but I never thought the words would come out of my mouth. And then I was asking him out."

"You did it."

She rolled her head to me. "What am I going to wear?"

"We are not going to spend the week obsessing over this date, Rachel. We are not."

"Yeah, I know." She was silent for a moment. "Should I wear the blue dress or the green one with the flippy skirt?"

Grinning, I shifted gears as we moved through a light and then turned the corner that took us to Union Street. "So are you also dating Jean Paul?"

Her eyes widened. "No. At least I don't think so."

Shaking my head, I laughed. "There is no law that says you can't date two men."

"Then maybe I will."

"You are a wanton woman, Rachel."

She smiled, satisfied.

When we arrived at the bakery, Margaret was waiting for us in the kitchen. Her duffel bag packed and at her feet, she nibbled on a sugar cookie. Jean Paul was mixing a batch of dough. He glanced up at us as if annoyed by the interruption and then went back to his dough.

"Is something wrong with the girls?" Rachel said, searching for the kids.

"What?"

"The girls. Where are they?" She articulated each word.

"Oh, with Mom. Zonked out. I ran them ragged." She sounded very pleased with herself.

"What's up?" I nodded to the bag.

Bracelets jangled as she swept her hand through her curly, wild hair. "Just got a call from the site. I have dead guys waiting for me. The rain has cleared and the dig resumes tomorrow."

As sorry as I was to see her go, I recognized the excitement humming in her body. "That is great."

She lifted her bag, her bracelets jangling as she hefted the strap on her shoulder. "By the way, I found him."

"Found who?" I asked.

"Joey Ludenburg."

At first the name did not register. "And he is one of your dead guys?"

"No. He's one of *your* guys. Joey was mentioned on the burial form as Walter's next of kin. He was in Walter's platoon. He served with him."

Excitement buzzed. "Is he dead?"

"No, Joey is very much alive."

I couldn't believe this bit of news. "And he knew Walter?"

She nodded. "He did. And I'll bet you a dollar he knew Jenna."

Energy rushed through my body. "Where does he live?"

Satisfaction warmed her gaze. "Would you believe about twenty minutes from here?"

"When can we see him?"

She dug a crumpled piece of paper from her pocket and handed it to me. "It will have to be you. I'm back to St. Mary's. Here's the address. I called and told him he could expect you. Good luck."

"You called?"

"Sure. This is a lead and the sooner you see him the better. He is in his nineties."

I had the sense of invisible hands pushing me forward. "Okay."

"You're going?" Rachel said.

"It's not very practical," I said. "The work's going to be insane this week."

Rachel shrugged. "We'll live."

I searched her face. "I won't be gone more than a couple of hours."

"I know. Just go." She glanced at Margaret. "And happy digging to you."

Margaret all but shivered with excitement. "I'm hearing there are all kinds of goodies waiting for us."

I glanced at the scrawled address and name. "Do I call this guy?"

"He's expecting you. I spoke to the nursing home and they said you could visit anytime tomorrow afternoon."

I barely had time to breathe, and now I had to slip away to chase the mist. "Thanks, Margaret. You've worked a miracle."

"I know. And you're welcome." She hugged Rachel and then me. "Good luck."

Joey Ludenburg. Was this guy *him*? "Do you think he'll remember?"

"Your guess is as good as mine. But he'll have more answers than you have now."

Chapter Nineteen

Friday, 1:00 P.M.
1 day until grand reopening
Income Lost: $6,000 (including $1,500 for the wine)

The bakery buzzed with activity by lunch. Rachel was icing cupcakes, the kids were mixing and scooping cookies, and Jean Paul was baking his bread. We were all moving at a breakneck pace, and we were going to make our deadline of tomorrow morning. But I worried how long we could maintain this pace. Dad had kept it all going for forty years. His father had worked for thirty years. Owning this place was a way of life. And Rachel had said she wasn't sure if this was the life she wanted anymore. I'd promised I'd find another way for us to earn a living and I would. I just didn't have the answers yet.

I'd been trying all week to find time to see Joey but no time had opened up. And each night when I lay my head on the pillow exhausted I felt Jenna standing close, prodding me.

So, today when a small opening of time had presented itself, I'd grabbed it. Now as I cut through city traffic toward the beltway, my mind was not on the bakery but on the old man who'd served with Walter during WWII. He'd been one of the last people on the planet to see Walter alive, and he very well had heard firsthand information about Jenna.

I hurried along the beltway, the speedometer pushing well past the speed limit. I'd been in charge of cleaning the display cases. Though they were perfect and ready for Rachel's baked goods, the task had taken longer than I'd expected, and I'd been late pushing away from the bakery.

Now I was trying to make up time.

I took the exit for I-95 south and followed the interstate to the Woodbridge exit. Glancing at Margaret's handwritten notes, I struggled with her scrawl. "Damn it, Margaret, did you write these out with your toes?"

Hoping the last abbreviation really meant *left*, I took a left at the third stoplight off Route 1. Three miles later, several U-turns to correct overshooting, and a handful of curses aimed at Margaret's directions, I found the entrance to Sandy Hill Estates.

It was a retirement community that honestly wasn't my idea of a dream destination. The sign was missing a brick on the top and the *S* in Sandy had snapped at the bottom tip. However, the grass was cut very short in a military-utilitarian way suggesting efficiency more than curb appeal.

I found the main registration sign and parked by a blue awning in the visitor spot. As I grabbed Jenna's trinkets and headed toward the main double doors, I really had to question my sanity. My bakery staff was working like crazy, and I was here chasing the destiny of a man who'd died over a half century ago. This quest made no sense. And yet it didn't occur to me to turn back.

Inside, my nose wrinkled at the thick scent of antiseptic and metal. It smelled of old people. Not dirty or foul, but stale, as if life had been sucked out of the air.

Mere feet inside the front door, I followed welcome signs and found the receptionist. She was as simple and unassuming as the desk she sat behind. Dirty blond hair tied at the nape of her neck accentuated a round face and wide-set eyes. No makeup and a pale yellow shirt robbed her of any features.

She glanced up over half glasses at me. "May I help you?"

Thankfully, her voice wasn't as bland as her face. "I'm Daisy Mc-Crae. I have an appointment with Joey Ludenburg at two. I was told that was a good time to see him. He's apparently finished his nap and had lunch by now."

The woman rose. A pale yellow smock hugged full curves. "You called Monday?"

"Yes." Well, Margaret called but I didn't want to get into the whole story. "And then this morning."

Her gaze skimmed over my face, my Union Street Bakery T-shirt, and my rounded belly. "Are you family?"

"No. But I knew someone that knew him years ago, and I thought we could talk." To get into an explanation of why I needed to see Joey would surely have sunk my chances with this woman.

"He's in his room. He was a little surprised when someone called asking for him."

My fingernail scraped at the bakery box in my hands. "Two weeks ago, I'd never have pictured myself here either."

She squared her shoulders and pursed her lips. "No one ever pictures themselves here, dear. Not a dream location."

The bite under her tone had me reassessing her. I sensed steel under the soft exterior. Vivid blue eyes glanced at the box in my hands. "What's that?"

"Cookies. I own the Union Street Bakery. I thought Mr. Ludenburg would like a cookie."

She arched a brow. "I'll have to ask our resident dietitian if he can have a cookie. Many of our guests are on strict diets."

I lifted the lid to the Union Street Bakery box, knowing Rachel's cookies could soften the hardest of souls. "Would you like a cookie or two?"

As if pulled by an invisible string, her gaze dropped to the box. The harshness softened and the hint of a smile tugged at the edge of her mouth. "Maybe one or two."

I wasn't above using cookies to get what I wanted. "Our chocolate chip is made with real chocolate we hand chop, and our sugar cookies are made with the best butter. The maple is our newest cookie. We use real maple syrup."

She moistened her lips. "Hard to decide."

"Take one of each." The Devil would have been proud of my ability to tempt.

She plucked two cookies from the box and bit into the chocolate chip. "My god."

A conspirator's smile curled the edges of my lips. "I know. Heaven. Have one more."

She took a maple. "Mr. Ludenburg is this way."

As I followed her along the very industrial hallway I wondered why anyone would want to be on a strict diet here. So sugar and fat killed you a little early. There were worse ways to go than death by cupcake.

The sunroom was located at the end of the hall and thankfully really was sunny. It appeared to have been a recent addition, made of glass walls with a sliding glass door leading out onto a patio. The back yard of the home was small and rimmed by a privacy fence separating the property from a housing development butting up to the property line. However, a collection of lush green potted plants softened the hard edges of the fence.

The room's soft wall colors created a cheery look and eased the hum of emptiness I'd sensed when I'd first arrived. If I lived in this facility, I think I'd spend as much time as I could in the sunniest spots of this room.

"Where is everyone?" I said. "Seems it would be full with folks enjoying the sunshine."

"It's a little hot for many this time of day. We have a lot out here in the morning and evening but not so much about this time. Joey is our exception. He's not fond of crowds."

I liked Joey already.

"I'll go get him." She held up the cookies. "And thanks for these."

"My pleasure." She left me standing alone in the sunroom and I stared at the marigolds, begonias, and pansies contained in the pots. Beyond the fence I could see the rooftops of several houses and through an open window heard the laughter of young children.

"I can push myself." The old man's voice was hoarse and raspy but he had fired each word like a bullet.

I turned to see the receptionist wheel in a man who sat hunched in a chair. His white hair was all but gone and what remained was cut in a signature Marine's high and tight. Gnarled hands curled inward with arthritis, but he wore a white dress shirt, creased khaki pants, and tennis shoes secured with crisp bows.

She leaned closer to his ear. "Chief, this is your visitor. Her name is Daisy McCrae."

He lifted a watery gaze to me. He studied me a beat before his eyes narrowed. "I don't know a Daisy McCrae. She's not one of those damn social workers, is she?"

"No, Chief, she's not a social worker. She's here to talk to you about someone you know."

"All the people I know are dead."

My admiration for this crusty old guy grew with each salty glance he tossed my way. He wasn't taking old age lying down. I hoped I barreled into old age kicking and screaming until I skidded into the grave.

"Mr. Ludenburg," I said. "I'm trying to find out about a man who served with you during World War II. You both fought in the battle of Saipan in June of 1944. He died in July of the same year."

Joey's eyes narrowed and he seemed to turn inward as if recalling the faces of too many men he'd lost during the battle. "That was seventy years ago. There were a lot of good boys that died, and I'm sorry to say I don't remember all the names."

I'd been lucky with Sara Morgan's sharp memory. The chances of me hitting pay dirt twice appeared slim. "Yes, sir, I understand. But I hoped if I told you a name it might jog your memory." I moved closer to him and pulled out my paltry collection of pictures.

"You smell like cinnamon." He lifted his gaze and really met mine for the first time. I was struck by how clear and bright his eyes were.

Smiling, I took a seat beside him. "I own a bakery."

He arched a brow. "Did you bring me a cookie?" He nodded to the receptionist. "She had cookies in her hand."

"I brought cookies. But the receptionist said you were on a special diet."

"I'm ninety-five years old and she cares about me eating sweets?" Humor underscored the words. "Sooner rather than later I'm gonna die. Rather it be a cookie that kills me."

Grinning, I opened the box. "Chocolate chip, sugar, or maple. Pick your poison."

He sniffed. "Grab me a sugar cookie."

I chose the most perfect one and handed it to him.

He took a bite and then a second before nodding. "What did you say your name was?"

"Daisy McCrae."

"McCrae?"

The name teased a memory. "I own the Union Street Bakery."

He cocked his head. "Union Street. In Alexandria?"

"That's right."

He waved a gnarled finger at my pictures. "What you got there?"

"Pictures of three people taken in front of the Union Street Bakery in 1944. I know the woman's name is Jenna. And one of the men is Walter."

His brow furrowed and his head cocked a little as if he didn't trust his hearing. "You got a picture of Jenna?"

"Yes, sir. We were knocking out a wall at the bakery, and I found Jenna's recipe box. I found her in the bakery records. This picture was in her file."

I handed it over to him and with a trembling hand he accepted it. For a long moment he didn't look. Finally he lowered his gaze, and through thick glasses he studied the picture. His hands trembled a little as he traced a bent finger over Jenna's face. He'd been transported back to another place long ago.

"Do you remember them?" I said gently.

"Yeah." His voice thick with emotion sounded like rough gravel. He cleared his throat. "I met Jenna at the USO dances. She was a peach. And I was half in love with her after that first dance we shared."

When I headed out here today I'd truly believed I was on a fool's errand. I'd never expected him to remember. But I'd underestimated Sara as well.

"You said you met her at a USO dance?"

"Yeah. A local church sponsored it the first and third Fridays of the month. She was one of the local girls who came to dance with us guys and serve us cookies and punch. Jenna and me, we danced to Glenn Miller's 'Old Black Magic.' I must have stepped on her feet a dozen times but she didn't seem to mind none." He pointed at the picture. "The man on the right is Walter. The man on the left is me."

"You?" I studied the picture and then him. Seventy years had erased most of the resemblances. The only remaining likeness lingered in his eyes. Mr. Ludenburg's eyes were the same as the man's in the picture.

"Walter and I took the train up from Quantico a couple of times to Alexandria for USO dances. We were both artillery. We both knew we were headed to the Pacific and decided the few weeks we had left Stateside we'd have us a little fun. At the first USO dance, we met Jenna." He traced her face with his finger. "I got the first dance but then Walter cut in. He'd been watching us dance. I think he also loved her from the first time he laid eyes on her. Once he had her in his arms I never had a chance with her."

He closed his eyes and again silence slipped around him, cocooning him from the present-day world. Did he hear the big band music playing from that long-ago USO party? Did he smell the scent of cinnamon lingering on Jenna's skin or the scratch of his uniform against his skin?

I shifted. "She worked for the Union Street Bakery, and I hear she was from western Virginia."

He cocked his head, and I knew he was riffling through old memories to find the answer. Such a small nugget of information. It would be so easy for it to get lost in time and a failing memory. "Winchester."

"Winchester?"

"She talked to me about her hometown when we danced but I didn't pay much attention to what she'd said. She felt good in my arms, and I liked holding her. That's all I noticed. Later, I'd think back on the dance and scrounge whatever details I could." A smile twitched the edge of his lips, and I had a very brief glimpse into the man he'd been.

"Mr. Ludenburg, you were a player, a man about town," I said.

His grin widened. "I was one of the best. I treated the ladies right, and they treated me good."

"Was Walter a ladies' man?"

He chuckled. "No. He was a Regular Joe. Like I said, it took him all night to get the courage to dance with Jenna. But when he did, she had him hook, line, and sinker. He never stopped talking about her.

That's how I remember so much about her. He spent the next couple of weeks talking about her."

"When did you meet?"

"First dance was in January 1944. Cold as hell and snowy. Fact, the weather was so bad a lot of the girls didn't come to the dance."

"Jenna dated Walter after the dance?" I knew Jenna was dating someone about that time. She gave birth eleven months later in December.

"They was like two peas in a pod. Every second he wasn't drilling he was with her. After a couple of weeks he talked about marrying her."

"They never did marry, did they?"

"Was planning to. But we got shipped out faster than we thought. He couldn't get up to Alexandria for a proper good-bye, but had to call her on the phone. He kept telling her he loved her, and he'd be back for her and marry her proper in a church."

"He wrote to Jenna often."

"He was always writing that gal. So in love it was enough to curdle your stomach. I kidded him about it a lot. But he didn't care. No. He was gonna write his girl."

"Did she write him back?"

"She surely did. As faithful as he was. When the war turned rough for us her letters kept him going. Hell, they kept me going. See, he'd read them out loud." Another smile appeared. "Her letters smelled like cinnamon. Like you."

"Can't get away from it when you work in a bakery."

"It's nice. Wholesome."

He dropped his gaze to the picture and again I sensed I'd lost him. He closed his eyes and I wasn't sure if he nodded off or was giving himself over to the memories. Finally, he sucked in a breath and opened his eyes. Stared at me as if I'd intruded into a world where I didn't belong.

"You were on the invasion team at Saipan."

He cleared his throat. "We were. We knew it was gonna be a meat grinder. We weren't the first off the boats but close to it. Fighting got bad. Real bad. But we made it that first day. And then as we moved inland the fighting got worse, I lost Walter in the chaos. When the fighting settled, I went looking for him. Found him, shot up bad. A miracle he was alive."

Joey didn't supply the details of Walter's injuries but I'd remembered the autopsy report.

"Almost sorry he wasn't killed right off. Would have been kinder. Death took a while, but he never regained consciousness."

I couldn't imagine what it must have been like to find him so badly mutilated. "I'm sorry."

Tears welled in the old man's eyes, and he didn't seem to notice or care that they streamed over his face. I suppose at his age, seeing all he'd seen, tears didn't matter.

"What happened to you after he was injured?"

"I kept on going. Kept on fighting. I wanted to go visit him and sit at his bedside but I couldn't. And when he died I wanted to give up. Walter was like a brother to me. But there were other kids, Marines, who needed me. And I kept fighting until mid-July when the Japs surrendered."

His jaw stiffened as he raised it a fraction. "The worst days of my life. There were so many other guys who died like Walter. So many of them didn't deserve to be blown to bits or torn in two by mortars. Every time I lost one it felt like Walter all over again."

"I'm so sorry, Chief."

He shrugged. "A job had to be done."

"Were you injured?"

"Shot in the arm."

"Did they pull you out of the fighting?"

"Hell no. They tried but I wouldn't let them. My buddies had died on that ground, and I wasn't gonna pussy out and go home. Stayed until the final surrender." No missing the deep pride simmering below the words.

"Did you ever hear from Jenna?"

"I wrote to her first chance I could. I wanted her to have Walter's dog tags. I sent those along. The Marines held his personal belongings for family. There'd have been lots of red tape getting his property sent to a woman not his kin or wife, but I knew a guy, who knew a guy. We got it put on the forms she was his wife so his body was shipped back to Alexandria. She wrote me back. Thanked me for sending him home. She said she'd buried him proper in the Alexandria Cemetery."

"When was that?"

"I got her letter in late December."

She'd have been ready to deliver by then. Silent, I let him talk.

He shook his head. "I went back to Alexandria after the war to find her. I wanted to return the letters she'd written to Walter. I went by the bakery but they wouldn't tell me about her. Said she was gone. It took me a good two days to find Walter's spot at the cemetery. When I was leaving, I saw another new headstone. It was hers. I bawled like a baby."

Sadness burned sharp in his gaze as if this had happened to him yesterday and not seventy years ago. "What happened to her? No one would tell me."

"She died on December 31, 1944, giving birth."

He blinked and shook his head as if the news struck like a fresh blow. He stared at the cookie, looking at it as if he imagined Jenna had given it to him. "There was a time when I feared dying. Figured it was the worst thing. But it's not the worst thing."

He'd been a warrior, a man who loved women, and now here he sat alone in an old-folks' home with a controlling receptionist telling him he couldn't eat cookies.

I'd never feared death or worried about it. That might have been because I'm young. Might have been because deep in my soul I didn't think I had much to lose. Terry had left me, and I didn't think I mattered.

But now with the kid on the way, I had an anchor in this world. For my child, I'd move mountains. I feared losing her more than dying.

"So what happened to Walter's kid?" Joey asked.

"I don't know. The newspaper said he'd been sick when he was born. But I never found a grave near Jenna's."

"She was from Winchester. Her kin owned an apple farm. I remember she told Walter she'd moved to Alexandria because the apple crop had gone bad that year . . . killed by a frost and she needed to make money. She and her father also got into some kind of fight but she never said over what."

"An apple farm in Winchester. Last name Davis. That'll narrow the search."

"Why you looking into this? She ain't your kin."

I struggled to put into words what I didn't really understand myself. "Maybe I feel for a woman alone with a baby on the way. She had to have been scared."

He straightened his shoulders. "Wheel me back to my room."

"What?"

"Wheel me back. I got something to give you."

I glanced around for the nurse, and seeing no one who said I couldn't, I moved behind his chair. "The old lady gonna give us a hard time?"

"I bet she might. But I ain't worried about it." He cackled. "What the hell could she do to me? I got two feet in the grave."

I unlocked the brake on his wheelchair and turned him around. He sat a little straighter, holding Jenna's picture in his hand as if he were on a mission.

I pushed him out of the sunporch and along the long cream-colored hallway smelling of bleach and flowers, to a room at the very end. As I tried to turn him into the room, I bumped the edge of the wheelchair on the wall.

"Women can't drive worth a damn," he grumbled.

"Hey, don't blame me. I've never driven one of these contraptions before."

He waggled his finger over his shoulder. "Back up and try again."

A glance behind and I pulled the wheelchair back. "I'm doing it."

"Well, you are taking forever."

"I'll get you there."

"When? I'm damn old if you haven't noticed. I could be dead by the time you figure out this door."

"Shut your yap."

He grunted and went silent, but I didn't sense any annoyance. This was an adventure for him, and I treated him like a man and not a potted plant to be shuffled around.

Finally, I got the angle right and pushed him into his room. It was a very simple room with a hospital bed, dark curtains kept drawn, and a chewed-up La-Z-Boy. No books on a small nightstand by the bed. No extra sundries on the bureau. No pictures on the wall. I had the sense he hated this place so much he wasn't giving it the satisfaction of any kind of decoration.

He pointed toward the nightstand. "Push me over there."

I wheeled him the remaining feet and he pulled open the drawer. He removed a well-worn Bible from the nightstand and then closed the drawer.

"This was Walter's Bible. It never made it into his effects because I'd borrowed it the day before we landed on Saipan. I'd put it in my footlocker. My hope was always to give the Bible to Jenna. That's one of the reasons I went back to Alexandria. To give it to her. And when she was gone I didn't know what to do with it. So I kept it."

Of all the death, sadness, and glory he'd witnessed in his life. His had been a rich, full life and he'd saved scant few items including a change of clothes, which hung in the closet, and the Bible.

I didn't speak, because he really had so little time and I sensed he'd had a lot to say.

He lifted his chin a fraction. "I wanted to be buried with it. That was the only request I had. But now it don't seem right."

I studied the cracked, worn leather and the embossed gold cross. "You should keep it. You've guarded it all these years. Seems right you'd keep it."

His shook his head as his jaw tightened with determination. "No. I don't want it with me no more. I want you to have it."

Leaning back, I held up my hands. "Chief, I cannot take your Bible."

He pushed it toward me. "You can take it. And you will. Seeing as you might find Jenna and Walter's baby, you need to have it so you can give it to him."

Worry prickled my skin. "What if I don't find him?"

Chief cocked his head, eyeing me as if I were a new recruit. "You don't strike me as a quitter. If that kid is out there, you'll find him."

"That kid will be in his late sixties now. What if he's also passed from old age?"

"I don't believe you'd be here if he were. Jenna wouldn't have sent you. She wants you to find him. Wants him to know about his father."

"How do you know Jenna sent me?"

"Can't believe death would get in that gal's way. She went after what she wanted."

What if he didn't know he'd been adopted? That happened back in the day more often than people realized. Babies were taken in and folded into families without a word ever spoken again about their pasts.

"Take the Bible and find that kid. Do my heart glad to know I kept Walter's Bible safe for his kid all these years. Do my heart glad."

When I returned to the bakery, Rachel was standing behind the display case with Meg and Tim. I checked my watch and realized it was after six. "So how did it go?"

Rachel nodded. "I think we are going to make it. I think we will open tomorrow. Though we won't have a full menu, we won't shame ourselves."

"It's not the end of the world. Less might be more in our case."

Rachel rested her hands on her hips. "I know we only have the six basic cookies, but I think you're right. Chocolate chip, sugar, peanut butter, pecan, elephant ears, and maple are our best sellers, and I didn't have the energy to bake the rest."

"I think the basics are fine. Right now we really should stick to what we know."

"I also got a call from Mrs. Cranston. She heard about the cookie dough and wants to buy enough to make five dozen. She also mentioned her daughter's school is having a fund-raiser and they sell dough to raise money for the school. She thought our dough would be a big draw."

"Really?"

"I told her we could talk to her on Monday. We needed to get through tomorrow and the reopening. That'll also give you time to crunch the numbers."

I grinned. "Rachel, you sound like a grown-up businesswoman."

She nodded. "Maybe not completely grown up but I'm getting there."

I looked at Meg. "So how was your first real day of baking?"

"Sweet. Tim and I loved it."

"Where is Tim?"

"He's in the back scooping the last of the cookie dough to go into the oven."

Meg untied her apron. "What time do you want me back in the morning?"

"Eight o'clock," Rachel said.

She nodded. "I'll grab Tim, and we'll head out. If we hurry, we can catch the bus."

"Thanks, Meg," I said.

"No, thank you. This is totally cool."

She vanished into the back, and I was left shaking my head. "She thinks this is totally cool."

"That used to be me," Rachel said.

"It will be again."

Rachel shook her head. "I'm pretty sure that ship has sailed."

"Never say never." I pressed my hands into the small of my back and stretched out the kinks. "So they did well?" Better to shift to what seemed like a happier topic.

"The kid is strong. He can operate the scooper for hours and not miss a beat." She smiled. "Though I learned very quickly not to leave him alone too long. I left him for an hour and came back to fifteen pans full of perfectly scooped cookies. I'd forgotten to tell him to stop at five."

I winced, dollar signs dancing in my head, as I calculated the waste. "You cover them with foil?"

"Yeah, yeah. No real problem. No loss. Only a word to the wise."

Nodding, I couldn't stifle a grin. "Meg and his mom said to be specific with him."

"Oh, I will be very specific going forward." She whisked a stray curl from her face. "So how did your trip go?"

I filled her in and told her about the Chief. "This is Walter's Bible. He's been holding it all these years."

Rachel smoothed her hand over the book. "That is amazing. We never would have found him if not for Jenna's recipe box."

"Yeah. She seems to be our little guiding light."

Rachel cocked her head. "You look tired."

My back ached and my feet throbbed as if they'd grown five sizes. "I tell you this kid is kicking my ass."

Rachel smiled. "Wait until she's born. She's only just getting started."

I grimaced. "Thanks."

She held up her hands in mock surrender. "Just keeping it real."

I yawned. "What can I do for tomorrow?"

"Your winery awaits its liquor license, but the front of the shop will be stocked and ready to go."

"I'm going to take a nap and then I'll finish up the wine shop."

"You really don't have to," Rachel said. "It's a bit of a soft opening, and we can't push the wines until we get our license in a couple of weeks."

"We'll have good traffic tomorrow, and I don't want to miss an opportunity to at least show off our wine room if someone is curious."

"You think we'll sell that wine?"

"I do. Fat and sugar pair well with wine. You'll see."

Chapter Twenty

Saturday, 7:00 A.M.
Opening day
Income Lost: $6000

Red, white, and blue balloons wafted in a gentle wind as I tied them
to a white sandwich board that read GRAND REOPENING, which
we'd borrowed from a shoe store up the street. Nervous energy humming, I flipped the sign on the front door to Open and waited for the
parade of customers. A half-dozen patrons showed up the first hour, not
a grand start by anyone's standards. And so armed with a plate of cookies, I headed out into the street to stir up business. A glance toward Gordon's shop told me he was open, and wanting to stay positive, I turned
the other way to greet potential customers. Several times the temptation
to turn and look in his direction was so strong but I held fast. Though
several times the hair on the back of my neck rose and I imagined his
gaze on me. Instead of turning, I kept smiling and walking away, unable
to endure the sadness vibrating from every muscle in his body.

By ten the trickle of customers had grown stronger and by eleven we actually had a line in front of the display case. Word had also spread about the frozen dough, and we'd sold four orders. As the cash register dinged with each new purchase, I imagined the debt on our books shrinking. Life was looking up . . . a little.

Finally at two, I locked the front door and flipped the Open sign to Closed. Our first day back open had been a hit. We might survive.

Rachel grinned. "We survived the renovation and the reopening."

"I told you we would."

She laughed. "Yeah, you did."

"I'm smarter than I look."

Meg and Tim carried the remaining cookies back behind the swinging doors. They'd been great. Tim had stayed in the back, carefully restocking trays, and Meg had been on the register smiling brightly at customers while Rachel and I took orders. We'd been a good team today.

As Meg reached for an empty tray of sugar cookies, I thought about Joey. On and off all day and most of last night, I'd worried about him alone in his room. I suspected he'd been on his own for a long time but that didn't make it right. The young man in the picture had been so full of promise. And he'd ended up alone in a corner room with no pictures and a crappy view of a privacy fence.

After we cleaned the cases and swept the floors, Meg and Tim said their good-byes, Rachel vanished upstairs, and I boxed up a healthy dose of sugar cookies and headed to see Joey.

Saturday traffic on the beltway was heavy, so it was past three when I parked in front of the retirement home. The receptionist was at her post but I was ready for her this time. I handed her a box of assorted cookies for her, she beamed and sent me to Joey's room.

I found Joey sitting in his room in his well-worn chair, a box resting in his lap. His eyes brightened when he saw me, and he sat a little straighter.

I closed the door, reaching in my backpack as I crossed the room to him. I sat on the edge of the bed and pulled out a pink Union Street Bakery box.

"You brought cookies," he said.

"Not cookies but Jenna's cookies. I told you we found her recipe box."

He took the box and inspected it as if it were a great treasure. "I used to love her cookies." He bit into one and closed his eyes, savoring more than the flavors but the memories they evoked. I could see him traveling back in time to Old Town Alexandria. He would have been wearing his Marine uniform, sporting his cap and walking with a spring in his step.

"It's delicious."

"I made you a couple of dozen and wrapped them in small packages in case you have to hide them from the gatekeeper."

His grin turned devilish. "She's never admitted to it but I know she searches my room. She never takes nothing. She just moves my things a little. I'm old but I know when my stuff has been touched."

He'd been a warrior, and he couldn't count on privacy in his own room. "We'll hide these all over the room before I leave."

"It's a date, doll." He offered me a cookie and I took it. One bite and I relaxed.

"Not bad."

"You couldn't miss one of Jenna's recipes. She had an angel's touch when it came to baking."

I glanced at the box in his lap, wanting to ask but deciding this was his to share and he would explain when ready. "We reopened the bakery today. It was crazy but busy, and busy is good."

"You're a smart gal. I can see that. And I bet no one can resist you."

I laughed. "Oh, you'd be surprised."

"So did you make good money?"

"Not bad. Made about a thousand dollars today, which will put a dent in the debt we racked up while we were closed." I'd not spoken about the debt to anyone. Candid talk about the bakery business stressed out Rachel and Dad, so more and more I kept details to myself. It was good to speak openly.

"You'll make it work."

"I hope."

"Hope ain't part of the equation. It's hard work, elbow grease, and know-how that gets the job done. You're a go-getter and you don't shy from work, I can tell. You'll make it happen."

His confidence bolstered my spirits and nervous laughter bubbled inside of me. "I sure hope you are right. There's a lot riding on the bakery."

He smoothed his hand over the box. "You haven't asked about the box."

My gaze flickered quickly over it. "I've been waiting for you to tell me."

"I almost gave it to you yesterday but then decided to think on it. Parting with the Bible was hard enough."

"It's in a safe place. And my sister is working to find Jenna's child. She can find anyone. She found you."

Through thick glasses his eyes twinkled. "Did she?"

"She's like a ninja historian. She'll find Jenna's family." I nodded. "What's in the box, Joey?"

With a trembling hand he removed the top. "These are Jenna's letters to Walter."

A rush of cool air brushed up my spine. "What?"

"They was in his effects. They'd meant so much to Walter, and I couldn't let them go. Made me feel like I had them both with me. I figured I'd give them to her in person like the Bible but, well, you know the rest."

"Did you read them?"

"I wasn't going to at first but in the days after Walter's death I was pretty low. Didn't see much reason to go on. And so I read the first letter. Didn't sit right at first but then the more I read the closer they was to me, and the easier it was to pretend she was writing to me. She had a way of speaking that made me feel at home. I read them all except the last. Came after Walter was killed, and it didn't seem right to read what he couldn't."

"What was she like?"

"The nicest girl. But strong. She worked hard and said one day she wanted to own her own business." His gaze seemed to go out of focus as he seemed to fall back in time. "She had a wicked sense of humor, and she loved to dance."

He held a yellowed envelope in his hand. Jenna's handwriting, reminiscent of the recipe cards, was bold and clear, and her lines were straight as if she'd put great care into addressing it. "Did she tell Walter about the baby in her letters?"

"Not in the ones I read. But she was always telling him not to worry about her. The folks at the bakery were good to her, and she'd wait for him as long as it took." A half smile tugged his lips. "She was smart not to tell him. He'd have worried. He'd have wanted his baby to have his name but with thousands of miles between him and Jenna there was no fixing the problem. She knew that and that's why she kept quiet. Every time he wrote her he asked her to marry him."

"And then he died."

He nodded. "Walter was like a brother to me. I know he went to his grave kicking and screaming. He wasn't so worried about himself but Jenna." He shook his head. "She was like him. She'd have fought for her life even after losing Walter, for the baby's sake. Would have taken a force of nature to drag her away from this world."

I thought of my own baby and the anguish I would feel if I were forced to leave her behind. I sat straighter, not wanting to travel that dark path. "I don't know why she put the recipe box, picture, and his dog tags in the wall."

"Maybe she had a sense something was gonna happen. If she left a piece of her and Walter behind then she figured they'd never be forgotten." He smiled at me. "And she was right."

"How could she have known?"

"Walter said he thought she might have had the Sight. She seemed to know when events was gonna happen."

That could explain the odd energy in the bakery. Jenna hadn't really left. She'd stuck around. Waiting.

Joey glanced at the letters and then nodded. "Seeing as she sent you to me, I think you should have these letters."

Rachel had had odd sensations in the bakery while she'd been pregnant. And now I was pregnant, seeing and feeling things always closed to me before. "You really think Jenna sent me to you?"

"I know she did. You didn't find me on your own. She sent you."

My skin tingled. "How can you say that?"

"When you get close to death the line between the living and the dead thins. You see things."

"Like Jenna?"

He grunted and met my gaze direct. "It ain't like she strolls in here and we have conversations."

"No. No, of course not." I smoothed my hand over the letters. "Kinda like a whisper. A feeling."

He nodded. "Yeah. And I feel her presence. Began weeks ago. I wasn't sure why I thought so much about Jenna and Walter. But they've been on my mind."

"I keep sensing I need to *find him.* Do you suppose you are that him?"

"No. She liked me well enough but she loved Walter and she'd have loved their baby. Knowing Jenna she'd want you to find her kid."

I glanced back toward the door, hoping no one was close to hear me. "What about Walter? Have you, well, heard a word from him?" I could not believe I was having this conversation.

He chuckled. "That poor slob wasn't much of a talker when he was alive. Great solid guy, always a good soldier, could follow and give orders. But when it came to conversation he wasn't the best. More of a listener. Jenna was the go-getter. The one that took risks. Knew no strangers. She went her own way otherwise she'd have lived her life on that apple farm. If we're hearing from anybody, it's gonna be her."

The only person alive now to tell the story of Jenna and Walter was Joey, and his days on this earth were very numbered. If I was going to find Jenna's child, I had to hurry.

"Have you read her letters recently?"

"Not since she died. When I saw her grave I put them away. Didn't seem right to read them no more."

"Do you mind if I read them? They might help me find her boy."

He nodded. "She sent you here to get them. She wants you to find her baby. So you go on and read all you want."

I took the box, feeling as if I'd been given a great treasure. "I'll take extra good care of these, Joey." A frown furrowed my brow. "And if I don't find him I'll bring the letters back to you."

"No. Keep them for good. With you at least there'll be someone alive to remember them. To remember Walter and Jenna and me."

He settled back in his easy chair as if a great weight had been lifted from his shoulders. He appeared lighter as he nibbled his cookie.

"So can I come see you again? I want to come back."

"I wouldn't mind a visit. Wouldn't mind it one bit. But I can't promise I'll be here."

"Where would you go?"

He winked. "Kid, I'm ninety-seven. I ain't gonna be anywhere for much longer."

I laughed. "Yeah, but it's not like you're gonna die real soon."

"It's gonna be like that, kid. I can go any minute."

A deep sadness rose up in me, and I had the sense that I was losing an old friend. "I'll be back real soon."

"You got your bakery to run, and if I ain't lost my touch you got a kid on the way. You got a full life."

"And you are a part of it now."

His chin trembled a little. "That's nice. Real nice. But don't get too attached."

I thumbed through the letters, anxious to find a quiet place to read. "Too late."

He grunted. "Now I'm tired, and you got to go."

He didn't sound tired. He sounded energized. "But I thought I could stay and visit. Thought we could talk about Jenna and Walter."

"Naw. I'm not much of a talker. Hell, we covered seventy years' worth of my stored-up thoughts in two conversations. It'll take me another ten years at least to come up with more conversation."

More laughter bubbled. "My dad is like you. Doesn't talk much."

"Looks like you didn't inherit silence from him. Bet you could talk a man's ears off if you got rolling."

"Actually, I'm adopted. So I didn't inherit anything from him." Dad and I were wired much the same but I'd always likened that to luck or chance.

He cocked his head. "I wasn't adopted. But I was an orphan. Spent my first sixteen years in a home."

Behind the faint smile, I saw sadness. "What happened to your parents?"

"Died, from what I was told. Both caught the fever. Died when I was one or so."

"I'm sorry."

"No need to be sorry. The home wasn't so bad. And I got along fine. Then when I had enough, I lied about my age and joined the Marines. I'm guessing that's why Walter and I got on so well. We had each other and the Marines."

He'd not been protecting the cherished items of old friends but of his family. "They were lucky to have you in their lives."

For a moment he pursed his lips as if he struggled with emotion. He cleared his throat. "Naw. I was the lucky one."

Fresh tears welled in my eyes.

He cleared his throat. "And don't you cry, because I don't like a woman's tears. Upsets my day."

I sniffed. "Sorry. It's the baby's doing. I'm not much of a crier."

He looked at me with such tenderness I almost cried. "Now, you really do have to beat it."

I rose, leaned forward, and kissed him on the cheek. "I'll see you soon."

He patted my shoulder with his bent hand. "Sooner's always better than later with me."

The bakery was quiet when I returned. The front end of the shop was clean and ready to receive guests, and the front display case sparkled waiting for Rachel and Jean Paul to fill it again. I pushed through the saloon doors and dropped my purse on the counter. As I crossed to go upstairs there was a fresh loaf of bread. The handwritten note on it read, *Daisy, this is for the baby. Eat. JP.*

I smiled as I tore a piece of bread and bit into it. The crust was crunchy and the interior soft. A touch of salt brought out the qualities of the wheat, creating a magical blend.

The box of letters tucked under my arm, I headed to my new

basement office and flipped on the lights. I wouldn't miss running up and down these stairs every day with baked goods. Carrying up bottles of wine was far more preferable than lugging one-hundred-pound sacks of flour and sugar or heavy trays of baked goods. No, I would not miss the old arrangement.

In my new basement office, I stared at the receipts piled on my desk. Good to have the paperwork—it meant the bakery was coming back to life. I glanced at the clock on the wall. It was already after eight, but I could squeeze out a little time working.

Sitting at the desk, I reviewed receipts that showed we'd had a good day. A good day. Laying the slips of paper down, I leaned back in my chair. Was today good enough?

I thought about my earlier conversation with Rachel. She had said she needed a change. That she could no longer keep the pace she'd maintained for the last couple of years. And I also feared with a baby on the way I might not be able to balance the life this place required.

When I'd first come back to the bakery, I'd been thinking in temporary terms. I thought I'd have this place shipshape by now and be on my way to the next high-powered job. And then the bakery had wormed its way under my skin, proving it was indeed a jealous and selfish master. But I'd expected I could handle the bakery's demands as I had handled so many difficult clients in the financial world. And then Gordon had come waltzing into the bakery, and I'd thought maybe, just maybe, this wouldn't be such a bad life. No huge paychecks but satisfaction.

Now with no Gordon and a baby on the way I wasn't so sure a handful of receipts and satisfaction were going to cut it. I needed more time and money.

Suddenly, too tired to work on the accounts, I shut off the lights, leaving the paperwork until tomorrow. Holding the letters close, I climbed the stairs to my room, where I flounced back on my bed and kicked off my shoes and lay very still. My body pulsed with fatigue. Glancing at my feet, I could have sworn they'd grown two sizes since yesterday and my belly, no longer a letting-yourself-go pouch, was now a full-fledged baby bump.

"Jenna, how did you do it?" I muttered. "How did you bury the man you loved and find the strength to bring your baby into the world?"

By all rights I should have fallen asleep, but thoughts of Jenna's letters to Walter had unwanted energy surging. I didn't need to read letters. I needed to sleep. I needed to block out the world and the worries so I could recharge and find a way to set my sights on tomorrow.

But as I glanced at the letters, overwhelming curiosity struck. I swung my legs over the side of the bed and reached for the box of letters. "Just one. I'll read just one."

I thumbed through them and realized Joey had kept them in chronological order, leaving me with the decision of where to begin.

I'm one of those people who reads the last page of a book before I buy it. Annoying, I know. Blame it on abandonment and adoption but I like to know where the path trails before I take it.

And so I reached for the last letter. The envelope was yellowed and the paper brittle. Unlike the other envelopes, this one was sealed and had never been opened. I studied the postmark over the stamp. It was dated July 2, 1944. July. When his letter had been stamped by the post office, Walter lay critically injured, his body badly mangled. Jenna's pregnancy would have been evident, and she'd have been so afraid.

Carefully, I ran my thumbnail under the flap that hadn't been opened in seventy years and pushed it back. The faint scent of cinnamon rose up and greeted me as I peeled back the flap. Joey had said Jenna had always smelled of cinnamon.

Removing the letter, the deeply lined folds cracked as I opened the one-page letter to find Jenna's neat script. Without reading a word, I knew she'd taken great care when she'd written this letter.

Dearest Walter,

It's after two in the morning, and I can't sleep a wink. I've been dreaming about you—about us—that last night you were in town. Remember how we'd walked along the banks of the Potomac, hand in hand, and you'd told me that when you came home we'd marry? I cherish that moment and I hang on to it. I live for the day you return.

I've a beautiful secret to share with you. I'd hoped you'd return in time but now realize I must take this moment to tell you that I am pregnant with our child. Now, please do not worry because I know how you worry. We are fine. Mr. and Mrs. McCrae have been so kind to me and tell me the baby and I will always have a place here.

The baby grows and kicks often. The doctor says the child will arrive in late December or early January. That's a mere six months away but I confess I cannot wait. I ache to hold my child, our son.

Yes, I said son. I am now certain I'm going to have a boy. Perhaps I simply want a little version of you for I've often imagined lately you as a little boy. I dare say you were cute.

Despite the kindness of Mr. and Mrs. McCrae, I've written to my sister Kate and told her about the baby. This is a time for family. She's already promised to smooth the waters between my father and me. She tells me not to worry, and I will take her advice and keep good thoughts.

I'm hoping you'll be home by spring so you and I and our child can enjoy the apple blossoms. There is no lovelier place than the Shenandoah Valley in the spring.

Do not worry about us. We will be fine. When you write again, don't send your letter care of the bakery but to my sister's farm. Kate Davis, Rural Route 10, Winchester, Virginia.

I send you all my love and wish you a speedy, safe return,

With all my love,
Jenna

I sat back on the bed, staring at her neat, clear handwriting. Had she felt his life seeping away on that far-off island as she'd written a letter no one opened?

Two o'clock in the morning would have been nine o'clock Pacific time. The fighting remained constant in July on Saipan, and Walter, wherever he lay, would have heard it.

I traced Jenna's name with my fingertip.

Find him.

The feeling rose up in me and I sensed this wasn't a trick of my mind. It was Jenna. She wanted me to find her son. And now I had an address for her sister Kate.

I opened my laptop and typed in Kate Davis, Winchester, and hit Enter. The chance of Kate being in the same location after all these years was slim but not out of the question. Farms, like bakeries, could stay in families for generations.

Several hits popped up.

Mrs. Kate Davis Simmons of the First Presbyterian Church of Winchester was honored for her service to the church.

Mrs. Kate Simmons pays tribute to veterans on Memorial Day.

Mrs. Kate Simmons and her oldest son, Walt.

Walter . . . Walt.

Chapter Twenty-one

Sunday, 8:00 A.M.
One day after grand reopening
Income Lost: $5,000

When I pushed out of bed, the sun shone bright in the room. The baby rested heavily on my bladder and despite the bed's comfort and warmth, I quickly made my way to the bathroom, took care of business, and then jumped into the shower.

As I stood under the hot spray, savoring the water beating against my skin, I realized I still wasn't sick to my stomach. I'd become so accustomed to feeling bad, a day or two of feeling good hadn't been enough for me to fully trust I'd turned a corner. The fact that I might really be rejoining the ranks of the living had me feeling hopeful. Opening my eyes, I smoothed my hand over my stomach. It seemed as quickly as the nausea had come it left.

Score one for the home team.

Feeling freshened and actually hungry, I toweled off and dressed in my maternity fat pants and a larger size bakery T-shirt. A side profile in the mirror had me wincing. I wouldn't be making the best-dressed list anywhere today.

In the kitchen I found a coffeepot gurgling and it smelled surprisingly good. I poured a cup as Rachel pushed through the doors.

"Morning," she said. Her face glowed with a pink hue, and her smile looked bright and natural.

"You look chipper." I pulled out the flour, sugar, and maple syrup and lined them up on the counter.

"The girls and I are headed to the park. It's an all-girl day of fun. Want to join us?"

"No, you enjoy your girls all by yourself. You three deserve a fun day."

She beamed. "I can't wait."

I poured a cup for her and I sweetened it with sugar and milk. When I'd lived in Washington I'd given up sugar and milk in my coffee in lieu of counting calories, but seeing I was officially in fat pants I decided to treat myself with milk and sugar. The coffee tasted smooth, and after weeks of not being able to stomach it, it tasted really, really good.

"So what are you going to do today? And please don't say work," she said. "Baking?"

"Jenna's maple cookies."

"Why?"

"I'm taking them as a treat."

"I've several dozen wrapped up in a bin from yesterday."

"I know. I wanted to bake these."

"Why do you need the cookies?"

"Joey gave me the letters Jenna had written to Walter."

Her eyebrows rose. "Letters?"

"Love letters."

"Have you read them?"

"Only the last."

She smiled. "You always did like knowing the ending."

I went to the refrigerator and loaded up on butter. "What can I say?"

She picked up her cup, cradled it close, and then took a sip. "So give me the punch line."

"She told Walter about the baby and said she was going to stay with her sister until the baby was born."

"And do we have sister's name?"

"We do. Kate Davis of Winchester. I searched her on the Internet. I found a Kate Davis Simmons of Winchester. She has a son named Walt. The reference is two years old."

Rachel's brows rose. "If this Walt is Walter's son then he'd be about sixty-nine now."

"I know."

"That's assuming they are still alive."

"I've thought about that." But I wasn't worried. Jenna wouldn't have gone to the trouble if he were gone. "I need to try."

A knock at the front door startled me. With a shrug I moved through the saloon doors and glanced toward the front door. It was Gordon. He wore jeans, a dark shirt skimming his flat belly, and his blond hair brushed back and still damp from a shower. He looked so fine I could have melted.

Very aware of my fat pants and an oversized T-shirt, hair pulled back tight, the sight of him tugged at locks around my heart as caged feelings struggled to break free.

I unlocked the door. "Gordon."

His slid a hand in his pocket. He met my gaze and for the first time since we'd talked about the baby, I saw no hint of anger. "Daisy."

I wondered if we could hold the armistice or if we'd end up fighting within minutes. Rachel pushed through the saloon doors and stood inches behind me. "Hey, Gordon."

Gordon shifted his attention from me to Rachel and grinned. "How's it going, Rachel? Grand reopening go well?"

"Went great. The new kids Daisy hired saved the day."

His grin was warm. "She's always had a knack for finding talent."

Rachel nodded. "I'd say so."

"Rachel," I said. "You and the girls have an outing today."

She laid her steady hands on my shoulders. "It's no rush."

I appreciated her acting as my wingman, but Gordon was my issue. I patted her hand. "It is. Go and have fun."

"Sure?" Rachel straightened in her mama-bear mode.

"Yes. Very sure."

Gordon smiled at Rachel as if to assure her he'd behave. "I just want a word with Daisy."

Her hands slid from my shoulders but she hovered close. "Everybody be nice."

I smiled. "I'll do the best I can."

Gordon shrugged as if to say trouble wouldn't start on his end.

"Fine. But I'll be close." After Rachel vanished upstairs, I tried to pretend the air didn't snap and crackle between us. "Why don't you come through the kitchen?"

"Great." He followed me to the new kitchen, taking a moment to survey the newly relocated and designed layout. "You've been busy."

"It's been pretty crazy the last week and a half. But we made it. Even installed the wine shop in the basement."

"I'd heard you'd bought out Gus's wines."

Alexandria was a big small town. "Seemed a good way to grow the business." I shoved open the back door to the alley, knowing out there we'd have real privacy. I waited until Gordon followed before letting the door close.

The day's growing heat warmed the sudden chill in my bones. Not sure what to do, I folded my arms and then unfolded them, thinking

I should look casual and not tense. I was tense, but it didn't hurt to hide it or the fact I had no idea what to say to Gordon. None. I'd apologized. Explained my position. And still my stomach fluttered as if I weren't much older than a teenager.

His gaze darted over my body, taking in my growing belly that could no longer be hidden. "I bet you haven't eaten."

"I did manage coffee this morning. A milestone. No morning, or rather, all-day sickness for me right now."

His face tensed a little but he seemed to recover. "Good. That's good. So you and the baby are doing well?"

The baby. Not our baby. One day, I supposed, it wouldn't be awkward when we talked about this child. "We are hanging tough. Little McCrae is as hardy as her old lady."

An awkward silence settled between us. We were both trying to be adult and mature. We were trying. But it still felt so weird between us. To fill the silence, I said, "I e-mailed Terry and she did get back to me. She said she had morning sickness midway through her pregnancy, not with me but with her last boy. Stands to reason, I guess. She would have been about my age when her last child was born."

His gaze bore into me. "She got back to you. That's good."

"Yeah, not a gushing motherly note, but I've the sense she was trying to help. And I appreciated that."

He shoved his hands in his pockets. "Good. I know you've wanted a connection with her."

"I thought I was fine without it but her e-mail really meant a lot. I've read it. She's not Mom, but she is my birth mother and we should be friends, don't you think?"

"Yeah."

More silence. The elephant in the alley lumbered around us and finally, I drew in a ragged breath. "I also e-mailed Roger. Haven't heard back yet."

Gordon's lips flattened into a grim line. "That guy is an ass."

"I *know*. But there's no changing the past no matter how much I want to. I really wish I could but I can't. I wished with all my heart that this baby was yours. But it's not."

He glanced at his hands and then tucked them in his pocket. "I'm sorry."

I cocked my head. "For what? You haven't done anything wrong, Gordon. You are a saint for putting up with me for this long. I get that I'm not easy."

The lines in his forehead furrowed deeper. "I've not been very helpful. All the changes you made to the bakery, being sick and the news of the baby, you really didn't need me heaping onto the pile."

"I'm a tough bird, Gordon. And I get that I hurt you. I know if I could turn back the clock I would." I reached out and took his hand, wondering if he'd flinch and pull away. When he didn't I rubbed my calloused fingers against his. "It's okay. I can do this alone. I will figure it out."

He tightened his fingers around mine. "That's what's digging at me, Daisy. I hate the idea of you having to do it all alone."

"I'm not the first woman to raise a baby alone, and I won't be the last. It's okay." And I meant it. I loved Gordon enough not to saddle him with guilt because he couldn't accept my mistake.

He tipped his head back as if weighing words he might later regret. "I miss you."

"I miss you, too." I cleared my throat. "None of this changes my feelings for you. I do love you, Gordon. I do."

He met my gaze. "I love you, too. You drive me crazy, but I love you."

The words sounded so sweet. Stepping away from the loneliness that had dogged me, I leaned and kissed him gently on the lips. He tasted so good and it took all my energy not to lean into the kiss.

He closed his eyes and he leaned into me. He rubbed my palm with his thumb. Shots of desire pinged around in me.

Sexual desire was a welcome feeling. Couple that with the love I had for Gordon and this could be very beautiful and explosive. But as much as I dearly wanted to give in to these feelings, I resisted. It wasn't about me anymore.

With a great effort I pulled back. "It's not the two of us anymore, Gordon. There is the kid, and we are officially a package deal."

He didn't pull back as he met my gaze. His voice sounded rough when he spoke. "I know. And I'm still struggling. I'm sorry."

"Don't be. This is one of those problems that doesn't have an easy fix."

He raised his hand as if to touch me and then hesitated. "How about we spend the day together? If you can break away from this place."

Smiling, I nodded. "I'd like that. But I need to visit this person in Winchester."

"Winchester? Is he a supplier?"

"Not exactly. He would be in his late sixties."

The first hints of amusement danced in his gaze.

I explained about Jenna's recipe box and my visit with Joey. "So I'm trying to locate this kid."

"Who is now in his late sixties."

"Exactly."

He shrugged. "I've bikes to fix this morning but I'm free after eleven."

He was offering an olive branch. He wasn't saying we'd be together forever, but he was trying to be my friend. I wanted his friendship and his love but to expect both right now was greedy. "I can pick you up."

Now amusement did spark. "In the bakery van?"

"It works. For the most part."

"I'll pick you up, Daisy."

There'd been a time when I would have challenged his need to take the lead. I always had to be first. Always had to drive. But I liked this. For the first time in my life, I liked not feeling as if I had to control every detail.

"Sounds good. See you at eleven."

He leaned forward, hesitated a split second as if he'd kiss me. Instead he smiled and promised to return.

The rest of the morning was spent baking Jenna's maple cookies. I knew Rachel had leftovers but I'd wanted these cookies to be fresh and to be made by me. Rachel always believed we put our energy into the food we made, and though I'd often scoffed and teased her, I had to agree. If Jenna's son ate these cookies today, I wanted him to feel his mother's love.

After I'd boxed up the cookies and tied a yellow ribbon around it, I saw I had minutes before Gordon arrived. I dashed up to my room, ran a brush through my hair, and put on lipstick. I practiced smiling in front of the mirror because I wanted to have fun with Gordon today. No sour faces.

Hurrying to the main floor, I grabbed my cookie box and stood by the front window. I thought about playing it cool and making Gordon knock for me, but then laughed at the thought. "Jeez, Daisy, aren't you a little past making the poor man work?"

When Gordon and I dated the first time around in Washington our relationship had its share of problems. He worked long, long hours and often left me waiting, annoyed, and feeling very alone. I didn't handle his lack of attention well, and instead of talking to him about it like an adult, I'd sulked and eventually left him because I'd so convinced myself he didn't love me.

But he had loved me. He was a crappy communicator like me.

And so when he pulled up in front of the bakery one minute before eleven, a surge of well-being and love filled me. Since our move to Alexandria we were both trying. It hadn't been all smooth waters, but for a time we'd been doing really well.

If not for the teeny, weeny problem of me carrying another man's baby we'd have been perfect.

The devil is in the details, which is a misquote. The actual line has to do with God being in the details. It didn't really matter because the little detail in question wasn't so little.

Tossing him a wave, I hurried outside, opened the front door of his truck, and slid into the seat. Weeks ago it would have been natural to lean over and kiss him. I wanted to kiss him but wasn't sure if I should . . .

Was I overthinking this? Should I go ahead and kiss him?

"Good morning again," I said.

He studied me a beat. "So what conversation are you having in your head?"

I laughed. "How do you know I was having a conversation in my head?"

"You've that panicked, far-off look. You get that look when you're thinking."

"What does that look like?"

He made a face, which I was sure did not look like my expression.

I laughed. "I was thinking I would have kissed you if it were a couple of weeks ago. That I'd be totally comfortable and not tense."

His hand rested casually on the steering wheel, but his eyes bored into me. "You could kiss me."

The rough timbre of his voice had my toes tingling. "I could?"

"Sure."

"But . . ."

A brow arched. "Has the baby somehow damaged your lips?"

God bless him, he was trying. I moistened my lips and pretended to inspect them. "No. I don't think so."

He sat still as a stone, not moving toward me. If I wanted this I would have to make the big move. Moistening my lips again, I scooted across the seat, glanced into his steady gaze for any sign of doubt and when I saw none, I leaned into him and kissed him softly on the lips. The touch was gentle and tentative like a couple of middle school kids. But sweet quickly warmed to hot when Gordon slid his hand to my waist. My pulse throbbed under his fingertips as I leaned into the kiss hoping to deepen it, and the baby kicked. Hard. So hard we both felt it.

He straightened but didn't remove his hand. "She kicked the last time I touched you."

I glanced at his tanned, lean fingers lying over my full belly. "She seems to be trying to figure you out."

He nodded, staring at my belly. "Looks like she and I are in the same boat. We both love Mommy but aren't sure if we can love each other."

He was being honest and I appreciated that. But it stung to think the two people I now loved most in the world might not ever like each other. "I'm hoping when you two meet you'll find a way to like each other."

He nodded. "Me, too."

His honesty stinging, I patted him on the hand and then slid to my seat, clicking the seat belt in place. "Ready?"

Frowning, he studied me. "I hurt your feelings."

"Yeah, a little." I'd vowed my days of pretending problems didn't exist had ended. The phrase "Put your money where your mouth is" resonated. "But I appreciate the effort you're making today. You could have dumped me and run for the hills."

His arm rested on the back of the seat, his fingertips brushing my shoulder. "I want to figure this out, Daisy. I don't know how I'm going to do it, but I want to try."

"For today let's not worry about the baby or what's next. Let's go to Winchester and see if we can solve a mystery."

He nodded, a smile teasing the edge of his lips. "You sound like Nancy Drew."

A laugh bubbled. "If Nancy was as curious about her cases as I am about Jenna, then maybe I finally get ol' Nancy. As a kid, I read a couple of her books, but she annoyed the hell out of me."

Laughing, he pulled into traffic. "Why is that?"

"Perfect hair, perfect grades, always had the right answer while I was schlepping around with twenty extra pounds, always angry and without a clue of who I was."

"You've come a long way."

"Let's hope."

The drive around the beltway and then out I-66 west was uneventful though not particularly scenic. But I was grateful there was no traffic, and the day was pretty. It took under an hour before Gordon pulled into the city limits of Winchester.

I dug my phone out of my purse. "I entered her address on my phone before I left the bakery, so here's hoping GPS can find her."

Gordon's wrist rested casually over the steering wheel. Dark shades covered his eyes. Blond hair brushed his collar. And he looked as if he had no care in the world. "This is your show, Daisy. I'm the driver."

He looked so sexy and cool. It would be easy to forget about Jenna, Walter, and Joey and focus on us. But as much as I wanted to toss every bit of my life aside but him, I couldn't.

And so I gave him not-so-perfect directions leading us around the outskirts of the town of Winchester past the rows of strip malls and box stores and farm chemical suppliers. Finally, we looped around and headed out toward a rural route cutting through rolling green hills dotted with apple trees.

Gordon seemed content to drive and enjoy the views and the nice weather. I, as always, grew restless without the buzz of conversation and needed to fill the silence.

Searching for a neutral topic, I rejected talk of the weather, choosing an equally banal subject. "Did you know Winchester is noted for its apples?"

He kept his gaze ahead but his lips quirked as if he'd expected I couldn't take the silence for long. "I did not know."

"Lots of apples. Rachel buys apples from a guy out this way. She makes apple pies at Thanksgiving. Margaret says after last Thanksgiving she never wants to see another apple again. Said her left hand could have passed for Captain Hook's claw by the time she was done last year."

His head cocked like it did when he was thinking big picture. "So you gonna make the pies this year?"

"I suppose so. It's all hands on deck when the holiday season starts. And now that we have our fancy new freezer in place we can make the pies ahead and freeze them."

"That doesn't mess with the taste?" He had a knack for sounding interested no matter what I babbled about.

"I don't think so but I know we will be taste testing in the fall. Rachel and I will figure it out. And did I mention we also had a couple of e-mail orders today for the frozen cookie dough?"

"I didn't realize you sold frozen dough."

"We don't, or didn't. Kinda fell into that one last week but it seems to be catching on." I shook my head. "People like the idea of bringing the bakery home and baking without the work."

"Bring our bakery home. Sounds like a slogan."

"Maybe." His offhand comment had me thinking. "What if we not only baked and froze the pies ahead, but cookies and maybe some bread dough? Maybe cakes. What if we packaged holiday desserts in a box and sold them before Christmas? I've been worried about what we're going to do this Christmas, in case I'm out of commission earlier than I expected."

Tension rippled through him but he kept his tone light. "It's good to be thinking ahead."

Sorry I'd taken a wrong turn in the conversation, I glanced at my phone and then at the road ahead. "According to the phone we should be turning up ahead."

His gaze followed the direction of my finger, which had zeroed in on a rusted mailbox leaning slightly to the left. By the looks there'd been a name painted on it but the lettering had long ago faded and chipped.

He slowed and we both peered up the long, graveled driveway snaking up the hill. By the driveway was a large sign that read *Posted*. Beside it another read *No Trespassing*.

Gordon slid his sunglasses on top of his head and glanced at me. "Doesn't look very welcoming."

"I don't think those signs are for us."

"Really? What kind of strangers do you think they might be referring to?"

"Bad strangers. We are good strangers."

He chuckled. "Right. Good strangers from Alexandria bring obscure questions about a woman who may or may not have lived here seventy plus years ago."

"Well, if it were me living up on that hill and seventy years had passed and someone had information about my long-dead sister, I sure would want to know. Wouldn't you?"

"Maybe."

"Gordon. You wouldn't want to know?"

"Not necessarily."

I was so starved for information about my biological family that his viewpoint was foreign to me. "I couldn't imagine anyone not wanting to gather every morsel of information."

"Not all information adds value."

I straightened the yellow bow on the box of cookies. "How do you know?"

He shook his head. "You think more than I do."

"You can trace your line back to the *Mayflower*. You have all the pieces."

"True." Again, he tossed me that heart-stopping smile. "Let's find out what they say."

I relaxed back into the seat. "Thank you."

"You're welcome."

He shifted into first and drove up the hill. Gravel crunched under the tires, and I stared out at the fields covered with tall grass and willowy dandelions reaching toward the hot sun.

As the truck rounded a corner I spotted a dilapidated barn to the right. Ravaged by time, the main support beam had collapsed long ago, pulling the building in on itself. Weeds grew up through the sun-baked beams covered with faded patches of red paint. But set against the crystal-blue sky it had its own kind of beauty. Old and broken, the barn still had a presence that telegraphed it belonged.

Gordon didn't say a word as we climbed the gravel driveway. He played along, keeping his good humor, but I knew he thought I'd lost my mind. The Daisy he'd known in Washington, D.C., would never have put herself out like this. Sure that Daisy was a ballbuster professionally and would go toe-to-toe with the toughest brokers or bankers, but when it came to personal issues, Daisy never stuck her neck out.

That Daisy bristled at the first sign of emotional turmoil. In so many ways, she was so fragile.

And here I was six months out of D.C. with my neck stuck out so far metaphorically with Gordon and Jenna's family a slight chop would sever my head from my body. And I was oddly okay with the risk. These last months, meeting Terry, connecting with my family, had made me stronger.

Gordon rounded a second corner and this time we came upon a white farmhouse. Clay planters filled with tall, full marigolds stood silent and welcoming at the foot of three steps leading up to a deep, tongue-and-groove porch that wrapped around the front of the house. Twin rockers swayed ever so slightly in the breeze on the porch by floor-to-ceiling windows flanking a large black front door. A simple brass knocker hung on the door.

Faced with the reality of speaking to perfect strangers about a dead woman had my stomach rolling. "The flowers look welcoming."

Gordon parked the car. "Yeah. And the house looks nice and there isn't a sign that says *Warning*."

I smiled. "So basically the house is saying it wants us here."

"As long as Freddy Krueger doesn't answer the front door we should be good."

"Right." I slid out of the front seat, box in hand, and met Gordon in front of the truck. Together the two of us walked up to the front door. I searched for a bell but when I didn't see one, I opened the screened door and rapped the knocker against the door a couple of times. I slowly closed the screened door, and we both took a step back. With Freddy Krueger still in mind I wondered how fast I could make it to the truck in a full-on sprint.

Gordon smiled as if he'd read my mind. "I'd beat you to the truck. But don't worry, I wouldn't drive off until you have at least one foot in the front seat."

The tension knotting my back eased. "Thanks. But I'd beat you."

"You're pregnant and a girl."

The pregnant reference came easier and easier to both of us. "My survival instinct is so honed right now it's as sharp as a razor. You wouldn't stand a chance."

He grinned when we both heard footsteps in the entryway. Seconds later we saw the rustle of curtains to the right of the door and then heard a lock click open. Slowly the door opened and instead of finding ourselves face-to-face with a fictional killer, we were greeted by an elderly woman.

She barely stood over five feet. Thinning white hair was tied back in a bun and wrinkles deepened the lines around her eyes and mouth. Laugh lines, I thought as I stared into her clear green eyes.

"I don't entertain solicitors," the woman said in a crisp voice.

"We aren't solicitors, ma'am. We're from Alexandria. My name is Daisy McCrae. I manage the Union Street Bakery. And this is Gordon Singletary, a . . ." Who was this man standing next to me? ". . . a good friend of mine. We came to ask you about a recipe box."

A slight cock of the woman's head conveyed annoyance more than curiosity. "I don't know about a recipe box."

She didn't make a move to open the screen door, and I didn't ask her to. This had to be so weird. I dug in my satchel purse and held it up. "We were renovating the bakery and taking out walls last week. We found this box in the wall. It belonged to a woman who used to work at the bakery. Her name was Jenna Davis."

The old woman's gaze sharpened as she dropped it from my face to the box. "How do you know the box belonged to Jenna?"

Yes, she looked at me like I was crazy, but I also knew in an instant she recognized Jenna's name. Excitement rushed through me. "You knew Jenna?"

The older woman pursed her lips, but her gaze remained on the box. "I didn't say that."

A cloud of impatience swirled around and I could hear the chant, *Find him, find him, find him.*

Annoyed, I swiped a lock of hair away from my eyes as if I could also brush away the restlessness. "Her first name was written inside the box and then I searched bakery records from 1940 onward. I found the name Jenna Davis. From there I traced a picture I found of her and two soldiers. And then I was given a letter Jenna had written that gave this address. I took a chance she still had family living here."

The woman stood silent for a long moment. Her hands trembled slightly and she nibbled her bottom lip.

"Did you know Jenna?" I asked.

The woman looked at me, her sharp eyes now watery. "Yes, I knew Jenna." She unlatched the screened door and pushed it open. "My name is Kate Simmons."

"You're Jenna's sister."

She swallowed, as if struggling with emotions. "Why don't you come in, and I'll fix you a lemonade."

I smiled and glanced back at Gordon, very grateful he was there. I wasn't sure why, but I was suddenly unsure of this entire trip. I clearly had dug into a deep and painful wound this woman harbored. Understanding what it was like to carry such a wound, I took pity on her.

We followed her into the house, lighted by the sunlight streaming in through the large windows. Instead of being dark or dreary, the room had a bright, cheery feel. White lace curtains hung from clean windows and fresh daisies filled several mason jars and vases in the room. A soft beige color gave the walls a fresh look and there were dozens of framed black-and-white photos. A rose floral fabric covered a couple of wing chairs and an overstuffed couch. All old and well-worn but well cared for.

Along the hallway Gordon and I followed Kate, drawn deeper into the house by the soft, sweet smell of goodies baking in the oven. It reminded me of the maple cookies I'd baked this morning. Jenna's cookies.

Kate nodded toward a chrome kitchen table surrounded by six chairs, seats covered in red leather. In the center of the table sat a ceramic bowl filled with oranges and apples. "Have a seat."

I hovered close to a chair but stood, too nervous to sit.

Kate opened a refrigerator that dated to the 1970s and reached for a pitcherful of lemonade. She glanced at my belly. "Go on, have a seat. You shouldn't be standing too much."

I took a seat at the table but couldn't relax back into it. Carefully, I let my purse fall to the floor as I set the recipe box on the table. "Thanks."

"Can I help you with that?" Gordon said.

She glanced toward him, surprised, as if she wasn't accustomed to help. I expected her to refuse but she said, "Thanks. That would be real nice."

Gordon took the pitcher and carried it to the table. I glanced up at him, and he looked at me as if to say, *Speak.*

"The lemonade looks great," I said.

Gordon cocked an eyebrow. *Really? That's the best you've got?*

I shrugged.

Kate retrieved three glasses from a whitewashed cabinet. Gordon took the glasses from her and filled them before replacing the lemonade in the refrigerator.

Kate carried a platter of cookies to the table. "Have a seat."

Gordon pulled out a chair for her and when she sat, he took the chair beside me. I shouldn't have been nervous. I offered information to Kate. This wasn't like searching for my birth mother. The moments and seconds shouldn't have been loaded with emotion but every ticking second was charged with a nervous energy I didn't understand.

I held up my bakery box wrapped in yellow ribbon. "I baked cookies today, too. Maple cookies."

Kate stared at the box but didn't reach for it. "I haven't baked them in years."

I sipped, needing a task more than I needed refreshment. The lemonade blended sweet and tart. "I'm sorry to drop in on you like this."

Instead of reaching for one of my cookies she opened the recipe box. Her thickly veined, bent fingers trembled a little when she fingered the first card.

I traced the rim of my glass as I watched her thumb through the cards. Carefully, I picked up one of her warm cookies. "When we found the recipe box we couldn't resist baking some of Jenna's recipes. These cookies are Jenna's maple cookies."

"Jenna always had a knack for baking." Her head cocked as she removed a card and studied it. "I haven't seen her handwriting in so long."

"We had a mini–grand reopening yesterday and sold cookies like this. We sold out in an hour."

Kate nodded. "That would have made Jenna happy. She liked to watch people eat what she baked."

I searched the old woman's face for similarities to the pictures I had of Jenna. There seemed little resemblance except for the eyes. They were Jenna's eyes.

"The cookie recipe was our mother's. We grew up making these cookies every Saturday to have with Sunday dinner. Like I said, I've not baked them in years, but today I had a hankering for the sweet taste. I made them by memory and wasn't sure if I'd get them right."

I took a bite. "They are perfect."

She smiled and nodded. "How did you say you found this?"

"We were taking out a wall in the bakery and I found this wedged between the beams."

I reached in my purse and pulled out the photos I had found. Gently, I slid them toward her. "I found these pictures of Jenna."

Kate picked up the picture of Jenna, Walter, and Joey standing arm in arm smiling in front of the bakery. "She was so full of energy and life. She was two years older than me, and I followed her around everywhere. I cried fiercely when she left for the city."

"Why did she leave?"

"She wanted to see the city. It was the fall of 1943. Daddy wanted her to get married but she'd have none of it. They fought something fierce. But he couldn't sway her. She was supposed to be gone six months. Daddy wouldn't speak her name after she left but I know he missed her. We all figured she'd come back within the year."

By the fall of 1944 Jenna would have been noticeably pregnant. "She didn't come home, did she?"

"No. I wrote her in October of 1944 and told her I was getting married at Christmas. She wrote me back right away and told me about her young man."

After seventy years, Kate still protected Jenna. "Did she tell you about the baby?"

Tears welled in Kate's eyes. "She did. Said she'd met Walter, and she'd received word he'd died in the Pacific. He wanted to marry her but never got the chance. She was afraid and alone." She traced the line of Jenna's young and smiling face with gnarled fingers. I had the sense she'd cut through the years and had landed in the past. "I told Mama. She shook her head as if she'd known all along Jenna was in trouble. She told me not to tell Daddy. Said Jenna needed time to find a husband or a home for a baby he'd not want."

A baby he didn't want. My throat tightened and for a moment I couldn't speak.

Gordon cleared his throat. "What did your mother do?"

Kate swiped a tear from her lined cheek. "I told Mama she had to tell him, and finally she did. He was furious. Said he didn't want to talk about Jenna ever again because she'd disgraced her family. Mama wasn't one to argue with Daddy, but she did that night. Said she'd send him to the barn to live before she turned her back on her girl." A faint smile tugged at the edge of Kate's mouth. "I told my Billy what was happening and that I wanted to take the baby. No one needed to know where it came from. We could make up a story that hid the truth. And he agreed." Tears again filled her eyes. "Lord, but I loved that man."

The image of Jenna's headstone darkened my thoughts. "Did you and your mother go to Alexandria?"

"No. It was my Billy that went with me. We arrived after the New Year in January. Went to the bakery and they sent us to the hospital. Jenna had died the day before. And there was the baby lying in his crib, crying and sucking on his hand so hungry for his mama. Billy and I buried Jenna there in Alexandria. She'd told me she'd never leave the city until her Walter came back from the war, and seeing as he never came back, it seemed she should stay. We wrapped the baby in blankets and left the day she was buried."

"There was a small mention of Jenna on the Death Notices page. The piece described Jenna's baby as ailing."

Kate nodded. "He was sickly. Could barely stomach any milk. Billy and I didn't have any idea what we were supposed to do. We were so young and didn't know the first thing about being married, let alone being parents. Baby cried all the way home. We was at his parents' place spinning our tale of how we'd come to find the baby, the orphan of a married couple who'd passed. Billy's parents and grandmother were listening. Grandmother was old and bent and gray-haired. Like me now. I thought she was ancient, and I didn't think she could help that baby. But she sent my father-in-law out to the barn and told him to fetch some goat's milk. He did and she put it right in our one baby bottle. The boy suckled hard because he was so hungry. Minute he took his first taste, he settled right into Grandma Simmons's arms and ate his fill. After that day, he got stronger and stronger."

"So the baby survived?"

"That he did. Grew into a fine man. A fine son. Turned out he was the only child the Lord gave Billy and me, but we couldn't have asked for better."

"Where is he now?"

"Out in the fields. Walt oversees the orchards."

"Walt. Walter. Who chose that name?"

"Jenna. She named him in the hospital before she died. It didn't seem right to change it."

"She named him after his father, Walter."

"Yes."

From my purse, I pulled out the Bible Joey had given me as well as the letters. "These belonged to Walter. He had a friend who kept his Bible all these years."

Kate's hand hovered over the Bible but she didn't touch it. "I always knew I'd never carried Walter inside me, but it wasn't more than a minute or two he was in my care that he was mine. Seeing all this now reminds me that I wasn't his mother."

"Sounds like what you did for him is what any real mother would do. Don't ever doubt that." Terry had brought me into the world, but Sheila McCrae was my mother.

Tears glistened. "Thank you for saying that."

For a moment we sat in silence as she opened the Bible and studied the family tree scribbled on the first page.

I scooted to the edge of my seat. "You said Walt's in the fields?"

She didn't look up and her voice sounded faraway. "Won't be home until dinner. I inherited my family land, and Billy got his family's land. Our son Walt manages both lands."

Our son. She said it with such pride and love. A part of me envied her. Her husband had taken in her sister's child and loved him as his own. It was a wish I had for my child and Gordon. But then Kate and Billy had both been Walt's adoptive parents. They'd been on equal footing. Gordon and I weren't on a level playing field when it came to my baby.

"I'd like to meet him," I said. "Would that be possible?"

Kate shook her head and glanced away from the Bible. "I'd like to have a word with my boy alone first. There's a lot Billy and I didn't tell him over the years. A lot."

Secrets. Did Walt know about Jenna? A shot of anger rose up in me as I sat there. I nodded toward the oven. "The cookies still in the oven smell done."

"I suppose they do." Kate rose, her hands trembling a bit more. She grabbed a dishtowel, opened the oven and pulled out the cookies that had been on the verge of burning. "I'll see you to the door."

I wanted to meet Walt. I wanted to personally give him the Bible and tell him about all I'd found. I wanted to push. But I didn't. This was their family matter. And no matter what I wanted or what Jenna wanted, this was between Kate and her son.

I rose and laid my business card on the table. "He can find me here if he wants to know more."

She didn't look at the card as she tucked it in her apron. "I'll tell him."

Gordon placed his hand on the small of my back as if to say, *Let's go.* And so we left. I settled in the front seat of his truck, my chilled bones soaking in the warmth from the leather seats.

Out of the house and away from Kate and the Bible, a rush of doubts chased after me. I shook my head. "What if she doesn't tell him?"

He started the engine and put on his sunglasses. "I think she will."

Fear niggled at me. Trust would never come easy to me. "She doesn't want to share him."

"Daisy, she will tell him."

"How do you know?"

"I just do."

"I have an image of her throwing all of Walter's belongings in the trash."

He shook his head. "It's clear she loves her son. She wouldn't hurt him like that."

"She wouldn't be the first adoptive parent to lie to her child."

"Your parents never lied to you."

"I know." But that didn't calm the fears. "What if he doesn't know he's adopted? What if the family kept his truth from him?"

He dropped his voice a notch. "You are borrowing trouble, Daisy."

My head dropped back against the warm leather seat. "That's because I don't have enough trouble in my own life."

He grinned as the truck rumbled along the driveway, a cloud of dust kicking up behind the back tires. "Give her time, Daisy. She's old. This was one hell of a shock."

I closed my eyes. "I feel like I've failed Jenna."

Chapter Twenty-two

Thursday
5 days after grand reopening
Income Lost: $1,000

T he bakery was finding a new rhythm, Rachel thought, as she opened the back of the display cabinet and transferred freshly baked bread from a tray into the case. Jean Paul had baked his bread early this morning before he'd selected a loaf for himself, winked at her as she'd iced a cake, and left until his shift began again at midnight. The bakery had been officially open for five days and so far business was brisk and profits were on the rise. Daisy talked more and more about changing their business model, and the girls spent most of their days with their grandmother. Rachel could concede that life was on the upswing.

The bakery phone rang and she wiped icing from her hands as she snapped up the receiver and said, "Union Street Bakery."

"Rachel. It's Simon."

Warm energy flowed up her spine and she nestled closer to the phone. "Hi."

"Just checking in. We're still on for Saturday at two P.M.?"

"Yes." She'd been too busy to think about the date, but the sound of his voice churned nervous energy in her belly. "I'm looking forward to it."

"Great."

She cleared her throat. "If the weather is nice, I can make us a picnic lunch."

"Sounds good."

A silence settled and she scrambled for a question or statement that didn't pertain to the time, weather, or food. The words wouldn't gel and her panic grew as the saloon doors swooshed open. Daisy, carrying a tray of freshly iced cupcakes, moved to the display case, opened the glass, and began to line up the cupcakes in single file.

Rachel turned from Daisy back to the phone and said, "I've got to get back to work but I'll see you on Saturday."

"Sure," he said. "See you then."

Rachel hung up the phone, relieved but disappointed she'd been so tongue-tied.

"You are frowning." Daisy closed the display case and set the tray on the counter.

Rachel imagined Simon in his office blushing as he sat back in his executive chair. She glanced up at Daisy. "Simon was making arrangements for our date. He likes me."

"So why the frown?"

"I'm not good with conversation, especially with him. All I know are kids and baking and I just can't imagine those topics interest him."

"Conversation will come in time. And all the talking doesn't rest with you." Daisy's knowing grin sent a fresh wave of nervous energy racing through Rachel's body. "How do you feel about him?"

Rachel moistened her lips and wondered how different his kisses would be from Jean Paul's. "I like him. But beyond that it's hard to say." She frowned. "I could read every one of Mike's moods and expressions. With Simon I'm starting from scratch."

"And Jean Paul?"

Color warmed her face. "We have reached an accord. I leave his breads alone and he leaves my baked goods alone."

"I'm not talking about the working relationship. I'm talking about whatever it is that snaps and crackles when you two are close."

She nibbled her lip, remembering the kiss. "He's very exciting."

"Which means?"

She laughed. "It means I don't know where I stand with either one of them. Who's to say I'm not just a passing amusement for both."

"I wouldn't say that."

"I'm not so sure."

Daisy waved away her concern. "If you were trapped on a desert island with one or the other, which would it be? And don't think or analyze. Just give me your gut reaction."

"Jean Paul." She blurted the name out before she could censor her thoughts. She lowered her voice a notch. "The sex and food would be amazing and I could talk shop with him when the conversation lagged."

"Is it is because Jean Paul reminds you of Mike?"

She glanced at her ring finger and the groove where the gold band had rested for thirteen years. "He's not like Mike. Not at all. He's a free spirit. Simon is stability. He plans like me. Between the two of them I have the best of Mike." Excitement and fear collided. "I don't know where I'll end up or with whom, but I can accept that I'm not married any more. I'm single. And I'm not as afraid as I was a year ago."

"That's a good thing."

"It's very good."

Daisy pressed her hand into her back. "You can date both men, because we aren't on a desert island and you do have choices."

A sly smile curved the edges of Rachel's lips. Images of Simon and Jean Paul marched in and out of her thoughts. For the first time in her life, she had the chance to explore, to take the unknown road, and just the thought made her heart beat faster.

Listening to Rachel talk about her budding love life had made me very aware that my love life had fallen apart.

I'd not seen Gordon since Sunday and that bothered me. I understood I couldn't rightfully claim him and the baby. I'd had to choose. And I had. My kid came first. But that didn't stop me from missing Gordon. Missing his touch. His smell. During the renovation the crazy pace had been enough to push him from my mind. But now that we'd returned to our normal dull roar there was too much time in the day to let my mind go to him.

The front bells rang and I glanced up hoping it was Gordon, all the while admonishing myself for wanting to see him. And, of course, it was not Gordon. It was an older gentleman, nicely dressed in khakis and a polo shirt. His white hair brushed back accentuated a deeply tanned and lined face.

"Welcome to the Union Street Bakery."

He nodded. "Thanks." He glanced at the display case, a bit lost like most new customers who were trying to scan the array of goodies.

"So what do you have a taste for?"

A frown furrowed his head. "In all honesty, I didn't come to buy baked goods." He lifted his eyes and a curious, doleful gaze met mine. "I'm here to see Daisy."

When people came looking for me by name my suspicions tend to rise. Surprises. Never good. "You found her."

He studied my face as if trying to read my thoughts. Just then the doors jingled and a young woman entered the shop.

Blond hair framed an oval face and large, expressive eyes. Her bobbed hair grazed a strong jaw and she wore jeans and a purple T-shirt. But as I stared at her I could have easily imagined her in a calf-length skirt, bobby socks, or saddle oxfords. There was no mistaking her connection to this place. She was Jenna.

"Granddad," she said. "I found a parking spot, two spaces from here."

"Great, Del. Great."

The man looked at me. "My name is Walter. Walter Simmons. This is my granddaughter Del Johnson. My mom told me you visited."

Realization dawning, I studied his face for traces of Jenna's eyes and smile. "Kate is your mother."

"That's right. And Del's great-grandmother."

I wasn't sure Kate would tell Walter about my visit. "How's she doing? I'm afraid I might have upset her the other day."

"You did," Del said.

I thought about the sweet old woman who'd baked Jenna's cookies. "I'm sorry. That was not my intention."

Walter drew in a deep breath and glanced around the bakery. "Mom told me her sister lived in Alexandria but she never said what she did while she lived here."

"You mean Jenna?" I chose my words carefully, not sure what Kate had told her son or great-granddaughter. I didn't want to trip over any family secrets.

"Yes." He pulled an envelope from his breast pocket and from that removed photos. My photos. The ones that I'd given Kate. "I found this on her kitchen table. I'd never seen them before."

"We only found them. I thought it should be returned to her family." Wiping my hands, I came around the counter. "According to her employee file she worked here between 1943 and 1944. She made a name for herself while she was here."

Del grinned. "There's no missing the resemblance. I look like her."

"Yes, you do," I said.

"The family doesn't talk about her much," Walt said.

Sadness coated each of the words. "I'm sorry to hear that. I heard she was a vibrant woman."

"You heard?" Del said.

"There's a man in a nursing home not far from here. His name is Joey. He knew Jenna."

Walt's gaze sharpened. "He knew my aunt."

"He also knew her fiancé, Walter. Joey and Walter served together during World War Two. Joey was one of the last people to see Walter alive."

"How did you find Joey?" Walt said.

I hated dancing around a truth that was so much a part of this man's history. I wanted to say clearly and directly, "We are talking about you birth parents." But I didn't. I'd dropped enough grenades for the week.

For the next fifteen minutes I talked about how we'd found Jenna's recipe box during our renovation and detailed my winding route to Winchester. "I could introduce you to Joey if you'd like."

Walter listened, his face stoic and stern. I wasn't sure how much of this he wanted to hear and half expected him to thank me for my time and leave. But he surprised me when he said, "I'd like to meet Joey."

My heart skipped a beat. "I would suggest sooner than later. He's ninety-seven."

Walt cleared his throat. "Today would work for me."

"Sure. Does now work?"

"Yes," he said.

"Let me grab a box of maple cookies for him." I moved around the counter, my growing belly leading the way. "The recipe was Jenna's, and it's a hit with our customers."

"I thought I recognized them. My mother used to bake them when I was a kid. They are my favorite."

I wrapped one in paper and handed it to him. "Compliments of the Union Street Bakery."

He took a bite and for a moment I sensed he was transported somewhere. "Why did you do this?"

"Do what?"

"Find me."

I edged closer to the facts. "I'm adopted. I found my birth mother this spring, and I've had no luck finding my birth father. If someone had information about him it would have been nice if they'd tried to find me and tell me about him."

Walt glanced at the cookie. "Mom and Dad never told me I was adopted." For a long moment a heavy silence hung between us. "I found out from a relative at a family reunion when I was fifteen. It slipped out. I pretended not to hear, but it made so much sense. My parents loved me and I loved them, but there was a missing piece."

"A critical piece to a puzzle."

"Maybe. I never said a word to my folks, but I did do a little digging. I learned of her older sister, Jenna. Mom didn't talk about her much, but when I learned she died the day after I was born, it wasn't hard to wonder. You know she's buried here in Alexandria."

"I do. I've been to the grave. They wrote about her in the local paper when she passed. You know Walter Jacob is also buried near her."

"I did not."

"I'd be happy to show you his place."

He stared at the cookie and then took another bite as if he needed another second or two to process. "I also saw the article you left with Mom."

"Your mom told you all this?" In Kate, I sensed a woman who'd guarded a secret for nearly seventy years and to think she'd release it so easily didn't jive.

"No. Not a word. But I guess you could say she told me in her own way. She left your package out on the kitchen table. It was there when Del and I came in from the orchards. She's my farm manager."

Del grinned. "The apple heir."

It would have been easy enough for Kate to hide the recipe box and the photos or destroy them, but she left them out.

"She wanted you to find it."

"Maybe. She won't go as far as to talk, but I give her credit for trying."

So much emotion. Love, sadness, loss, and more love. Adoption brought with it a complicated blend of feelings. "Let's go see Joey."

"I'd like that."

And so I made excuses to Rachel, grabbed my purse, and drove to Woodbridge, Jenna's cookies on the seat beside me. Del and Walt followed in their car.

It was after three when we arrived and I greeted the receptionist with a smile and a box of cookies. She accepted them and nodded for me to go back.

When Walt hesitated, Del nudged him forward. "We've got to do this, Granddad."

He cleared his throat. "Right."

I knocked on Joey's door and when I heard a gruff *what* I pushed it open. "Joey, it's Daisy."

He sat up a little straighter and actually smiled. "What are you doing back? Afraid I might die on you?"

I grinned. "I actually have a couple of visitors for you."

His eyes narrowed. "I ain't one for visitors."

His gruffness had grown endearing and didn't deter me in the least. "Well, you might like these two visitors."

"Two!" He scrunched his face as if he'd eaten a sour apple.

I laid his box of cookies on his bedside table. "Buck up, Joey. And stop whining."

He grunted and fussed with the cuff of his long-sleeved shirt. "I'm not whining."

I patted him gently on his shoulder. "You sound like a little girl."

He glared up at me but didn't complain. I motioned for Walt and Del to come into the room. Walt hesitated by the door but a firm shove from Del had him moving into the room.

Joey stared at Walt with annoyance and a mild hint of curiosity. I half hoped he'd look at Walt and see hints of his old friend. But I got nothing. And then Del stepped into the room.

Joey sat up straighter as his gaze settled on her face. His sour expression softened and he blinked hard behind his thick glasses. "Jenna?"

"No, Joey this is Del Johnson. She's a relative of Jenna's." I'd let Walt and Del define the relationship as I looked at them. "Joey was good friends with Jenna and her fiancé, Walter. Walter and he served in the Marines together in Quantico and later in the South Pacific. They met Jenna at a USO dance in Alexandria."

Walt looked stunned, as if a hundred-pound sack of flour had fallen on his head. I knew the look and the sense of being hit by an emotional tsunami. I'd been there. Been hit by the same rush of thoughts and feelings. "Joey, why don't you tell Walt about the first time you met Jenna? I think he is very curious about her."

Joey tore his gaze from Del and zeroed in on Walt. "How did you know Jenna?"

"I never knew her. She died when I was a day old." He hesitated. "She was my mother."

Walt's voice broke under the weight of words he must have thought a million times but had never been able to say out loud.

Del smiled and laid a hand on his shoulder. "My great-grandmother."

Walt laid his hand over hers. And so Del and Walt sat on chairs by Joey's wheelchair as I quietly backed out of the room to the sound of Joey saying, "Walter and Jenna would have loved you so much."

By the time I returned to the bakery, I felt pretty good about myself. Jenna had to be pleased with me. She and Walt could rest in peace knowing the loop between past and present had been closed. Their son knew he'd been loved and wanted even before he'd been born.

Karma should have been grinning like a circus clown over the good deed I'd done. Karma should have been tossing a break my way. But, as my mom often said, karma could be a bitch.

When I entered the bakery, I saw a man talking to Rachel. His dark hair brushed the collar of a worn leather jacket and his worn jeans hugged well-muscled legs. However, Italian loafers gave him away as a man of means.

Rachel's smile strained with tension as she glanced over his shoulder at me. "Do you ever read your texts?"

No missing the frustration sharpening her words. "I was busy."

"This gentleman is asking for you but he won't tell me why."

The man turned and I recognized his angled, lean face and gray-blue eyes immediately. My appearance may have downgraded over the last five months but his had improved.

"Roger."

His gaze wandered from my face to my belly. "So, it is true."

The sense of goodwill I enjoyed seconds ago vanished. Outrage chainsawed into my composure. "Do you think I send random e-mails out telling men they are the father of my baby for giggles?"

Rachel's mouth dropped open and her eyes widened. Her gaze

shifted to Roger as if seeing him for the first time and then back to me. She cocked her head and mouthed, "Really?"

I shrugged. One matter to talk about mistakes, it was another to have one walk around.

Unaware of Rachel, Roger shoved a hand in his pocket and rattled change. "I'll expect a DNA test before I fork over a dime."

I rubbed the tension banding the muscles at the base of my skull. "Why aren't you in China?"

"I've been back in New York for a couple of weeks. When I received your e-mail I thought I should see you myself so we could deal with this."

"Deal with this?" Anger, sharp and hot, surged in my chest. "How do you propose we deal with this?"

The steel reinforcing my words tugged Rachel out from behind the counter. "If you attack from the front, I'll take the rear."

Roger's head whipped around as if he'd forgotten Rachel. "I came here in good faith."

"Good faith?" I said. "Sounds like you're worried."

Roger stiffened. "That won't be necessary."

The thought of Roger having my baby on alternate weekends sent a chill through my veins, and I realized if I didn't get a handle on my temper Roger would demand visitation out of spite.

I shook my head. "I told you about the baby because I thought you had a right to know. Beyond that I don't want anything from you. Consider yourself off the hook."

"You don't want anything?" Suspicion coupled with hope.

"Not a damn thing," I said, jaw clenched.

Roger's stance relaxed and he glanced toward the door.

"Unless of course the baby asks questions one day," Rachel added. "Let's face it, Daisy, the baby is going to ask questions if she's like you."

I'd been ready to toss Roger out of our lives forever, but Rachel was right. I could eject him out of my life, but I didn't have the right to make that decision for the baby. One day she might have questions and she deserved answers.

Roger shook his head. "Once I have DNA confirmation I will provide the genetic information you need so the child can answer whatever medical forms come its way. But I don't want a relationship with the child."

I shook my head. "I wasn't thinking you'd have a relationship with her. But one day she might like to set eyes on you for her own peace of mind."

He tugged at a monogrammed white cuff that peeked out from the leather jacket. "I don't want any surprise visits. That could be unpleasant for all of us." He reached in the breast pocket of his jacket and pulled out neatly folded papers, extending them as if wielding a knife.

My fingers curled into fists. "What's this?"

"I've had papers drawn up. I've agreed to terminate parental rights in exchange for a cash payout."

Outrage curdled in my belly. "You said you wanted DNA testing."

He hesitated. He was a jerk but he knew me well enough that I didn't cry wolf. "I want this over and done with."

"I don't want your money."

He jabbed the papers toward me. "Don't you want to see how much I'm offering?"

"No."

He arched a brow. "Money is your driving force, Daisy."

That might have been true for the Daisy he'd known. Now it was the kid and the bakery that drove me. "I sign the papers and you go away."

"Like I never happened."

So tempting to wash away an old mistake that still made me cringe when I remembered.

His lips curled, a conspirator's smirk. "Sign them, Daisy. It's what you want."

Signing would clear the way for Gordon. Without Roger in the picture we could forge our own lives with the baby. Oh, but that vision tempted. However, as much as I wanted Roger to vanish, I didn't have the right to rewrite the kid's history.

Rachel huffed in a breath. "I can kill him now if you want me to, Daisy. We can cut him up and bake him in a pie."

Her protective fire jostled loose a smile. "Not necessary, Rachel. I'm used to Roger. I understand his tactics." I snatched the papers from him, moved to the counter and grabbed a pen. A scan of the document revealed a cut-and-dry, bloodless agreement. So Roger.

I crossed out the cash settlement paragraph and wrote in a paragraph that demanded he supply *all family medical history* and *meet with the child at a meeting to be determined by the child*. I signed my name and handed him the duplicate copies.

He glanced at my changes.

"Initial and we are done," I said.

He removed a Montblanc pen from his jacket pocket, initialed the changes and handed me back my copy. "We are done."

"*We* are done. But I can't and won't make promises for the future kid. If he or she wants a meet and greet, you will honor it."

He frowned. "I don't want any nasty surprises."

"It won't be up to me. It's up to the kid." I clutched the pen in my fingers and resisted the urge to throw it after him.

His jaw ticked as it did when he was angry but he didn't say another word. He realized he was off the hook for a couple of decades and opted to leave. Italian loafers clicked against the floor as he crossed the room, jerked open the door, and left.

"What an ass!" Rachel said, coming around the counter. "How could you ever have slept with that?"

I smoothed a trembling hand over my head. "We're all capable of stupid behavior if you dial up the right combination. In my case the perfect combination included too many glasses of wine, job loss, and thoughts of moving back here."

Rachel's brow furrowed. "I don't think the last bit really made you have sex with that? It was the wine."

I wished I could have blamed it all on the wine. "Coming back here felt like the ultimate failure, Rachel. I was back at ground zero. And it scared the hell out of me."

She cocked her head, her eyes sharp with worry. "It's not such a scary place anymore."

A sigh shuddered past my lips. "No. Not so scary."

She leaned a little closer to me and nudged me with her elbow. "And you must admit the bakery has its moments."

A smile tugged at the corner of my lips. "There were one, two, okay maybe three good moments."

Laughing, she punched me in the shoulder. "You love us. Admit it. You would be lost without us."

Six months ago I could have denied the claim easily, honestly. Now, I couldn't. "Maybe."

"Maybe, my ass."

"Rachel," I said, laughing. "You said a bad word."

"Yeah, well, get used to it. The nice Rachel is on vacation."

"What happened to her?"

"I sent her away."

"Not forever."

"Don't be looking for her anymore." She glanced past me through the window toward Gordon's shop. "Trouble."

"What?"

We hurried to the window in time to see Gordon throwing Roger out of his bike shop. Roger stumbled and fell to the curb. We hustled outside, the front door bells jangling like an early warning system.

"Why would Roger go to Gordon's shop?" Rachel said.

"There was a time when they were best pals. They had a falling-out about two years ago. I never found out why but knew they shared bad blood. He must have heard about the bike shop and stopped by to gloat."

As I saw Gordon advance on Roger, his fists clenched, I hurried toward the bike shop. "Gordon! What are you doing?"

Gordon glanced up at me, his face flushed with rage. "Throwing out the trash."

Roger scrambled to his feet, scuffing his Italian loafers. "What the hell is wrong with you, Gordon?"

Gordon glared at Roger, his teeth baring a smile reminiscent of a lion right before he pounced. "Remember what I said, Roger. Remember."

Roger paled as he hustled to his feet. "Shit, I don't know why you are defending her. I thought you finished with her months ago."

Gordon advanced another step toward Roger, who quickly hustled back several steps.

"Stay away, Gordon. I don't want trouble."

"Of course you do," Gordon said. "If you didn't you'd have handled this long distance."

"I'm trying to be civil," Roger shouted.

"I'm trying not to rip your damn head off, Roger."

Roger cursed and then, digging keys from his pocket, turned and jogged toward a black BMW. The engine fired and seconds later the car zoomed off.

Roger's wheels squealed as he rounded a corner, and I went to Gordon. "What did you say to him?"

Gordon, a bit breathless, puffed out his chest like a lion defending his territory. "It doesn't matter."

Looking at Gordon, so angry and huffy at this moment, made me weak in the knees with love. Unshed tears burned in my throat and it took all my self-control not to hug him close.

He glared at me. "Damn, Daisy, what did you see in that guy?"

"That's what I said," Rachel offered. I'd been so distracted by Roger and Gordon, she'd slipped from my mind.

"It was a very, very bad call!" I shouted, throwing my arms up in the air. "I get Roger is an ass. I get that! But my kid has his DNA so I'm stuck with his biological history."

A few folks on the street stopped to stare. I glared back at them knowing full well it made me look all the more crazed. When they turned and kept walking, I shifted all my attention back to Gordon. "I'm sorry."

"He's not going to throw any trouble your way," Gordon said.

"He signed away parental rights," I said.

Gordon frowned. "Just like that?"

"He came with the papers in hand." I explained about my contract revisions.

Gordon shook his head. "If he falls short on the biological history crap, I want to know about it. Understood?"

I didn't know what kind of threat Gordon had made to Roger but suspected it was a whopper. Roger didn't scare easily. And it was kind of Neanderthal for Gordon to insinuate himself into my mess but . . . it was also so sweet and hot.

I'd hardly seen Gordon in the last week and barely touched him in the last couple of weeks, but I couldn't resist anymore. I closed the distance between us and without a thought to right or wrong, good or bad or appropriate or inappropriate, I cupped his face in my hands and kissed him on the lips.

His hand went to my waist and he kissed me back.

"That was hot," I said.

He grinned. "I like to think I still have the moves."

"Oh, you do." I kissed him again. "Thanks."

He drew in a breath. For a long moment he stared into my eyes. He traced my jawline with a calloused finger. "Daisy, will you marry me?"

My heart stopped, somersaulted, before resuming a racing pace. "What?"

"Will you marry me?" he said.

I'd always been careful never to want too much. I understood the danger of hope. "I come with baggage."

He squeezed my hand. "Don't we all. Don't we all."

His energy pulled me toward a breathless *yes* but still I resisted. "What about the baby?"

"I'll legally adopt her so all she'll ever need from Cheese-Dick is DNA information."

"Are you sure, Gordon?" I still didn't understand the ramifications of parenthood, which meant Gordon sure did not. "This is a game changer."

"I know." No hesitation blinked warnings from his gaze. He had the determination of a cyclist barreling down a hill at thirty miles an hour, excitement thrumming in his veins. "But it's a change I want."

Warmth spread up through me, and I couldn't stem the tide of emotions rushing. "Yes, Gordon Singletary. I will marry you."

Rachel clapped her hands. "This is so cool!"

Epilogue

December 20
Last day before end-of-the-year closing
Income Profit: $19,243

"Jingle Bells" chimed on the radio, but I wasn't feeling very festive. The kid rested heavy and low in my belly, and Rachel and I had at least a couple more hours of packaging frozen cookie dough and pie orders that had come in from our website last night. The frozen dough had become more popular than we'd ever expected. The pies were a sensation. A good problem to have, as my mother said over and over.

And yes, it was a good problem. The bakery had been running in the black for two months straight and we'd set up a rainy day fund. All good.

And it would be perfect if the kid would get off my bladder. She'd been doing somersaults on it for the last hour and I spent half my days now in the bathroom. My back also ached as if a herd of mules had kicked it.

"Daisy." Rachel called out as she loaded another mail package in the bin that Dad would take to the post office in thirty minutes. "You need to get off your feet. That kid is practically waving at me."

I pressed my fist into my back. "If we could finish this load we will be done for the holidays." Years ago Dad had closed the bakery between Christmas and New Year's, using the time to regroup with the family and for him to clean the bakery from top to bottom. If I could hold on another hour, I'd have reached the finish line, and I could deliver this kid in peace.

The front door bells jingled and I glanced over my shoulder. "We are closed. I locked the door," I grumbled.

"It's Gordon," Rachel said.

I glared at Rachel as I placed a USB sticker on a frozen dough order and loaded it into a box. "You called him."

On cue, Gordon pushed through the swinging saloon door. "I told her to call me if you stayed on your feet."

Before I could grumble he kissed me on the lips.

"We are almost done," I said. He smelled of soap and bike oil and being close to him soothed my seething blood pressure.

"No, you are now done." He blocked me from reaching for the next bag of dough and roll of stickers.

Gordon and I had married in mid-October on a sunny afternoon under a tree by the Potomac River. My sisters had been there, Mom and Dad and the girls. Gordon's parents had also been present as well as his brother Scott. I'd worn a simple white dress with an empire waist and carried a bouquet of red roses.

Rachel had made a stunning wedding cake we'd cut back at the bakery and enjoyed with a toast of ginger ale. I'd moved into the small apartment above Gordon's bike shop, trading one attic apartment for a second-floor loft apartment.

As I'd cut back in the last week, Rachel had really stepped up.

She'd done preliminary site visits to several locations where we'd considered moving our dough-making operation. We'd had several good offers to rent but she'd insisted we hold out for better prices. She'd turned into one tough negotiator.

As I opened my mouth to argue, my stomach cramped and water trickled down my legs. My first thought wasn't for the kid but the health department. Spilling amniotic fluid had to be a code violation.

Gordon froze and blinked. Like most men, he realized he had tripped into the dark and scary world of the feminine and the unknown.

Rachel, however, knew exactly what to do. "Gordon, where is your car?"

He hesitated for a moment, as we looked at each other stunned and unsure. "In the alley, right were you told me to keep it."

"Good. Daisy, where is your bag?" She tugged off her apron and reached for the cell clipped to her waistband.

My gaze darted to the puddle at my feet and back up to Gordon's face. Damn. "Oh, my God."

"Daisy!" Rachel snapped as she opened the phone. "Bag."

"In the car," I muttered.

Rachel snapped her fingers and pointed to the back door. "Gordon, put Daisy in the car. Go to the hospital."

She treated us like errant puppies. Go. Stop. Sit. But we were grateful for the direction. In this area, Rachel was the expert.

"Mom," Rachel said into the phone. "Baby's coming. Is Margaret headed back to town? Good. Tell her to go straight to the hospital."

Gordon and I remained rooted in our spots when Rachel glared at us.

"Go. Now."

And so Gordon and I stumbled out of the back door of the bakery kitchen and into his waiting truck. I didn't remember the drive to the hospital. I did remember the back labor, which grew in intensity with each passing moment. I remembered how the car bumped on the city's ancient cobblestone roads. We arrived at the emergency room in the late afternoon, and I was put in a room where I changed out of my apron, jeans, and T-shirt and into a gown. The nurse gave Gordon a green scrub that read DAD on the back.

When I read the letters, tears welled in my eyes. Gordon had already officially adopted the baby and as far as I was concerned we were a family. We would one day explain to our child about genetics and bloodlines and what makes a parent.

Terry had sent me an e-mail two weeks ago. It had been brief and to the point. *Thinking of you and your baby.* I'd taken them as gushing words of love from Terry, who was offering what she could. She was trying. And that was enough.

As my parents, nieces, and sisters gathered in the lobby, a nurse did a quick exam and determined that the baby was breech. Stuck. Ass first. My kid.

A C-section was ordered and within an hour I lay on a table, my belly curtained off, with Gordon sitting by my head. He stroked my hair as he clutched the video camera ready to stand and film the birth.

"You don't like blood," I said.

He smiled and turned on his camera. "It shouldn't be too bad."

I was about to launch into a description of a YouTube video I'd seen on C-sections, when the doctor entered the room and moved to the table gowned, gloved, and masked. "I hear baby Singletary is being difficult."

"Just like her mother," I said.

Walter Gordon Singletary arrived into the world twenty-one minutes later, wailing and highly insulted we disturbed his routine.

He was perfect.

UNION STREET BAKERY RECIPES

Jenna's Maple Cookies

*Jenna's maple cookies have become a staple at the Union Street Bakery.
Each time I smell them baking I think of the young woman who loved
her son so much she was willing to reach across time and space to give
him the answers he needed.*

MAPLE COOKIES

½ cup butter, softened

1 cup packed brown sugar

1 egg

⅓ cup maple syrup

½ teaspoon rum extract

1-½ cups all-purpose flour

2 teaspoons baking powder

½ teaspoon salt

½ teaspoon cinnamon

1 cup chopped toasted walnuts (optional)

Cream together butter and brown sugar and then blend in one egg. Mix in maple syrup and the rum extract. In another bowl sift together flour, baking powder, salt, and cinnamon. Mix flour mixture into the butter and sugar. Mix walnuts into batter. Chill for 30 minutes. Bake at 350 degrees for 10 to 12 minutes.

Jenna's Pumpkin Bread

This became a fall holiday favorite at the Union Street Bakery and became a staple of our mail-order business. It's easy to make and one of the moistest breads you'll ever eat. Once it's baked you can leave plain, dust with powdered sugar, or ice with your favorite icing to give it a cakelike quality. My favorite is pairing it with a cream cheese icing.

2 cups all-purpose flour

½ teaspoon salt

2 teaspoons baking soda

2 teaspoons baking powder

2 teaspoons cinnamon

2 cups sugar

1 cup corn oil

4 eggs

2 cups canned pumpkin

Sift together flour, salt, baking soda, baking powder, and cinnamon. In a separate bowl blend sugar and oil and then mix in eggs one at a time. Add pumpkin to oil/sugar mixture. Add dry ingredients and beat until smooth. Bake at 350 degrees for 40 to 50 minutes in a 8.5 x 4.5 x 2.75 greased pan lined with parchment paper. Makes 2 loaves.

Cream Cheese Icing

8 ounces cream cheese at room temperature
1 stick butter, softened
1 teaspoon vanilla
1 box 10x powdered sugar

Cream together cream cheese, butter, and vanilla until well blended. Mix in powered sugar until smooth.